JACK JUNK;
OR, THE
TAR FOR ALL WEATHERS.

A ROMANCE OF THE DEEP BLUE SEA.

BY THE AUTHOR OF "RICHARD PARKER; OR, THE MUTINY AT THE NORE."

CHAPTER I.

"The wind that blows, the ship that goes,
   And the lass that loves a sailor."

THE FIRST OF MAY.— THE OLD TAR'S TALE.— THE SHIP ON FIRE — THE LOVERS.— JACK AND HIS RIVAL.— THE FETE.— THE INTERRUPTION.

IT was the first of May, and a more bright and lovely first of May never gladdened the children of the earth, imparting health and happiness to all. The sky was brilliantly clear, the atmosphere was light and refreshing, and a delightful breeze springing up, counteracted the scorching heat of the sun's rays. Nature's carpet displayed its richest green, and the trees were clothed in their most luxuriant foliage, while numerous birds carolled forth their most mellifluous notes from every bough. The scene at which our tale commences was in the vicinity of a sea-port town, and although it was very early, everything gave token of some approaching festivity. The church-bells

No. 1

were ringing forth their merriest peals, and from the mast-heads of the different vessels lying at anchor, the gay streamers waved playfully in the wind. In the centre of a green lawn, and immediately before a quaint old tavern, whose walls were thickly mantled with ivy, the Maypole reared its gay head, and gave cheerful omen of the happy sports to which the day was dedicated, and the landlord of the house, as quaint and venerable, and comfortable in appearance as the aspect of his hostelrie, might, as soon as it was daylight, have been seen with his servants bustling about, and making all the necessary preparations for the accommodation and enjoyment of the numerous guests whom he expected to do honour to him on that day with their company. The whole of the establishment at "The Ship" were pressed into active service, and Kit Breezely, the landlord, as he thus busied himself, and urged his servants on to increased industry, whistled, and sang, and laughed by turns, in a state of the highest glee and expectation. While Kit and his servants were still thus occupied, they were interrupted by a loud shout of "Ship a-hoy!" uttered in the voice of a Stentor.

"That's old Joe Trennant for a wager," said Kit, leaving off his work for a moment, and looking around him. "I could tell his voice from a thousand."

"Ship a-hoy!—Kit Breezely a-hoy!" again shouted the same distinct voice. "Damme! where's the skipper? Is there no one aboard? Have ye all deserted the ship?

'My name it is Tom Tough,
I have seen a little service,
Where the mighty billows——'

Ah! Kit, my old sea-gull, give us your fin, and then we'll splice the main brace together; and mind it is not three water grog, or shiver my timbers I'll toss you overboard in less time than you could cry 'peccavi.'"

"Ah! Joe, my old friend, welcome—welcome to the old Ship on this glorious bright May morning," said Kit. "I thought that you would be my first guest this morning, as you are usually my last at night."

"Ay, Master Breezely," replied Joe, "I wouldn't give the value of a biscuit for a fellow who thinks of sneaking to his hammock till he is quite seas over. My old dad—God rest his soul, 'tis thirty years since he was summoned up aloft—used always to say that there was a dry humour about me; and I think he was right, for I feel something within me that constantly wants wetting."

"Ha!—ha!—ha!" laughed Kit: "very good, Joe."

"And you just be so good as to belay your palaver, and bring the grog I ordered, you son of an old shark."

"You shall have it in a moment, Joe," said Kit "for I never like to keep any of my customers waiting."

With these words Kit Breezely departed, and left old Joe Trennant singing the burthen of a sea song in tones far more powerful than musical. Joe Trennant was a fine sample of one of old England's naval veterans, with thin silvery hair, a rubicund visage, and features profusely decorated with grog blossoms. The loss of one eye, one leg, and one arm, an iron hook being substituted for his hand, showed that he had suffered much in the service of his country, and bore ample evidence of the authenticity of the numerous tough yarns he was accustomed to spin when surrounded by his old companions. A merrier fellow than Joe Trennant did not exist, or one that was more respected for the generosity, benevolence, and honesty of his character. Kit soon returned with the grog, and him and Joe having seated themselves on a

bench outside the tavern, pledged each other in bumpers with hearty good will.

"We shall have a merry day of it, Kit, I'll be bound," said Joe, "I long for the sports to begin. Fill your glass, my old buck, and here's to the health and happiness of our May-queen, the pretty Kate Markham!"

"Ay, I will drink that toast with all my heart," said Kit, "for England cannot boast of a prettier or more virtuous girl than Kate Markham, the admiration of all who know her, and the pride and comfort of her uncle, under whose protection she has been ever since she had the misfortune to be deprived of her parents."

"Yes, Kit," said Joe, "Kate Markham is a craft that any one might be proud of, and he will be a happy fellow who is destined to become her commander."

"And if I am not much mistaken, that will be no other than our young friend Jack Junk, one of the trimmest and bravest lads in the British navy."

"You may well say that, Kit, and no one admires the boy more than I do, and you know I have known him from his earliest childhood. Here's to the health of Jack Junk, the pride of his majesty's good ship the Defiance, and may he live some day to become an admiral."

"Bravo, Joe," ejaculated his companion; "here's the health of Jack Junk, the tar for all weathers, and may he live to become some day an admiral."

"The tar for all weathers," repeated Joe, "ah, you may say that; fear is a stranger to him, dauntless in the raging storm, bold as a lion in the battle's heat, and merry as a grig at all times; in fact, for singing, laughing, dancing or fighting, find me another that can match him. No, damme, if ever there was a true British sailor, or noble hearted fellow, why, damme, I say it, and I will maintain it too, Jack Junk's the lad. Why, bless you, he was born a sailor, he took to salt water when not half a handspike high as nat'ral as his mother's breast. Kate Markham and he love each other, and I trust that the day is not far distant when they will be happily spliced."

"But Jack has a rival, you know."

"What that lubber, Mark Stanford!" said Joe. "Bah!—he has a pretty good stock of impudence to dare raise his thoughts towards her; but Kate I am certain hates him, and her uncle will give no encouragement to his addresses, so Jack Junk has nothing to fear from him."

"I do not half like that fellow, Farmer Stanford, as he is commonly called," remarked Kit, "there is something in the expression of his features and his manners that convinces me he is a villain at heart. He first took up his residence in this neighbourhood, you know, about five years ago, and no one knew where he came from, and he has been absent at different periods during that time for months together, and no one could discover whither he was gone, but he always returned as suddenly as he departed; this looks very mysterious and suspicious in my opinion, to say the least of it."

"Ay, Ay," replied Joe, "however, it will not do for him to try any tricks here, or he will find himself mistaken, I'll warrant. But let us have some more grog aboard, for I am determined to be merry to-day, if I am never again in my life. Our friends will soon be here no doubt, and then, hey for the dance round the Maypole. Damme, I'll have a dance round it myself, if I break my old wooden pin in the job."

"Ha!—ha!—ha!" laughed Kit Breezely, and he then made his exit into the house in order to bring a fresh supply of grog.

"You have often promised me, Joe," said Kit, on returning and taking his seat, "that you would give me the particulars of the history of our young friend Jack, and I confess I feel a great curiosity to hear it. He is not the son of the late old Jack Junk, whose name he has adopted?"

"Lord love ye, no," answered Joe Trennant, "nor any relation to him. My Jack, as I call him, for he always takes up his quarters with me, whenever he is ashore, since the death of his adopted father, never knew his parents, and it's a great chance if he will do so now."

"No!"

"No. But I will tell you all about it. You see, old Jack Junk and I had long been messmates, and we were sworn friends. It is now about twenty-one years ago, that when homeward-bound from the coast of Guinea, in his majesty's ship Alligator, seventy-four, Captain Summers commander, as brave an officer as ever trod the quarter deck, and for some days we encountered very rough weather, strong gales from N.N.E., latitude and longitude I forget; but at length the wind went down, the weather became more calm, and our vessel made good way on her voyage. It was the mid-watch when the man on board suddenly shouted 'Ship on fire ahead!' All hands immediately hurried on deck, and there, sure enough, we beheld the unfortunate vessel at no great distance ahead of us, enveloped in flames from stem to stern, and we could distinctly hear the shrieks of horror and despair of the poor creatures on board. Oh! Kit, it was an awful sight, such as God forbid that I should ever witness again; but there is not much fear of that. How terrible is a fire at sea! little can the landsmen imagine it. The fierce flames mounting, like giant fiends, to the sky, rendering everything as clear and distinct as in the broad light of day. The ocean for miles appeared one vast sheet of liquid fire, and the crackling of the burning timbers, and the roaring and hissing of the devouring element, as it pursued its dreadful course, was quite frightful to listen to. Destruction seemed inevitable, but we lost no time in rendering all the assistance in our power; boats were launched, and myself, Jack Junk, and several more of the crew put off in them to the burning vessel with the hope of being enabled to save, at any rate, some of the unfortunate creatures. As we approached nearer, the cries for help became more distinct and terrific, and we could plainly see many of them running about in the midst of the flames in the most frantic state; whilst others leaped overboard, but only to meet with a watery grave. But the fatal moment now arrived; there was a terrific crash; the flames had reached the powder-magazine, and every timber of the ill-fated vessel with all the poor souls on board were hurled high in the air, and the work of destruction was complete."

"Awful!" said Kit, "but did they all perish?"

"All with the exception of an infant, whom with its mother, Jack and myself were fortunate enough to pick up just at the moment when they were about to sink for ever. The unfortunate mother was quite dead, but the infant lived. It was a boy, and need I tell you that that boy is our young favourite, the noble-hearted Jack Junk, who has gone by that name ever since? Jack, my messmate, was so interested by the circumstance, and felt so much for the friendless situation of the little stranger, that he requested our captain to be permitted to take him under his protection, until something might occur to lead to a discovery of his connexions, and the captain assented. On arriving in England, Jack took the infant home, and placed it under the care of his wife, and from that time till the day of their death I need not tell you that they brought him up with the same care and affection as if he had been their own son."

"But was the name of the ill-fated ship never known?" inquired Kit.

"Why," answered Joe Trennant, "it was supposed to be the Mary, merchantman, bound for Liverpool; but that was only a matter of conjecture, as nothing was saved from her which could remove all doubt. The clothes of the mother and her infant were of the finest quality, which showed, at any rate, their connections were respectable; but there is not the least probability of the mystery ever being solved; though, for the sake of young Jack, I heartily wish it was. But see, some of our friends approach this way; and after this dismal story, it is needful that we should take some refreshment just to put us in spirits for the pleasures of the day."

"With all my heart," said Kit, and several of the guests then joined them. They gave them a hearty welcome, and retired into the house. They had scarcely disappeared, when a man turned round an abrupt angle of the building, and advancing towards the Maypole, he paused, and folding his arms, contemplated it with a sinister expression of countenance. This was Mark Stanford, the supposed farmer, of whom Kit Breezely and Joe Trennant had spoken in such disparaging terms; and certainly his personal appearance fully corresponded with the portrait they had drawn of him. He was a man apparently between forty and fifty years of age, tall, and of muscular proportions. His features were large and irregular, and his eyes dark and scowling. He was habited as a farmer, but the character seemed but ill to become him; and it required no deep penetration to perceive that it was only assumed to carry out some deep-laid design.

"So," he said, after a pause, "this is the spot chosen for the festivity, and the lovely Kate Markham, who has so scornfully rejected my addresses in favour of Jack Junk, the seaman, is to be the queen of the day. A happy choice; for one so beauteous must shed a lustre around her wherever she goes. I will be present at the sports never fear, though I know that I shall be most unwelcome, and once more feast my eyes on her charms. She scorns me—she despises, she hates me, I know; but I care not; the time shall yet come when she shall learn to feel and tremble at my power. The fools in this neighbourhood little suspect who the supposed farmer, Mark Stanford, as I have chosen to call myself, really is, and I can therefore work out my designs in greater security. What would be the horror of Kate Markham, did she but know that in me she beholds the murderer of her father, whom she supposes to have died a natural death at sea. I cannot marvel at the instinctive hatred she bears towards me. But silence, Mark, you must be more guarded in your speech, lest you should be overheard by some one, in which case your destruction would be inevitable. Let me to my home, and prepare myself to join the rustic festival, and to appear to enter into all the amusements with an hilarity and spirit equal to the rest."

Thus saying, Mark Stanford hurried on his way, and was soon out of sight. Joe Trennant and the others were enjoying themselves freely in the house, and mirth and harmony prevailed to an unlimited extent.

"This is one of the happiest moments of my life," observed old Joe, "and if I do not enjoy myself, may I never taste grog again. My lads, here's to every one's good health. Sweethearts and wives, old and young, gentle and simple; damme! old Joe Trennant does like everybody to be happy. But I wish my young friend, Jack Junk, was here."

"Oh, he will soon arrive, never fear," returned Kit Breezely, "I suppose he is only dallying a little while with his sweetheart, Kate, which is very natural, you know."

"To be sure it is," coincided Joe; "oh, I cannot help picturing to myself how beautiful she will look, to be sure, as our May Queen."

"Kate Markham must look beautiful in any character," observed Kit.

"The wind that blows, the ship that goes,
And the lass that loves a sailor!"

These words were sung in a fine rich manly voice at that moment outside the house, and immediately on hearing them, old Joe Trennant started from his seat with an expression of delight, and exclaimed—

"There he is, the young sea-lion! That's Jack Junk, the pride of the Defiance, and the darling of the crew; hurrah! Jack Junk ahoy!"

"Joe Trennant ahoy!" shouted our hero, in high glee, and immediately afterwards he entered the room, and was received with as much enthusiasm and cordiality by all present as if he had been the admiral of the fleet.

And a fine handsome looking young man was Jack Junk, the hero of our tale; there was grace and activity in every limb, and the very spirit of honour, generosity, and good-humour was enshrined upon his manly brow. His fine black eyes sparkled with vivacity and intelligence, and his hair hung in glossy ringlets down to his shoulders. The neatness of his dress added to the interest of his appearance, and altogether he was a person who, the moment he was seen, could not fail to rivet respect and admiration.

"Thanks, my friends, for this kind reception. I greet ye all," he said; "but I cannot stay with you long for the present—I must make all sail to convoy my dear Kate hither; I am afraid she will have expected me long ere this."

"Jack, you young rascal," said Joe Trennant, "your hand! Here's your health, and may you pass through the voyage of life without ever striking on the quicksands of misfortune."

This toast was heartily responded to by all present; and Jack again returned his acknowledgments in suitable language, and proposed the health of the veteran Joe Trennant, which was done full honour to.

"And now," said our hero. "I must weigh anchor; but I will soon be with you again, my friends, and bring one with me who, I know, will add to the happiness you experience on this day of festivity. Won't the fiddles go to work! and won't we jig it round the merry May-pole till the hour of midnight warns us to our homes? Farewell, for the present—farewell!"

Jack Junk having shaken them all by the hand, took his departure on his joyous errand.

"There's a specimen of old England's brave defenders, my lads," remarked Joe, when he was gone; "why, it's quite a treat to look upon him. While our navy can boast of such noble hearts as that which beats beneath the jacket of young Jack Junk, what has she to fear from foreign enemies? Damme! he is every inch a sailor, and those who are bold enough to deny it must expect a broadside from old Joe Trennant, that's all about it.

'Rule, Britannia, Britannia rules the waves,
For Britons never will be slaves!'"

The old man shouted this at the top of his voice, which, as we have before stated, was one of Stentorian quality, and he was assisted by the other guests. At this moment the company was increased by the appearance of a pompous and important-looking personage, who received the congratulations of the guests with much dignity, and then took his seat amongst them, and tossing off the contents of a glass which was placed before him, seemed determined to make himself quite at home.

"My friends," said the individual, who was no other than Diggory Knobbs, the beadle, "I have the extreme felicity to greet you all on this auspicious first of May."

"Well said. old figure-head of the Gorgon," returned Joe Trennant; a compliment which was received with loud laughter by the persons present, much to the confusion and offended dignity of Mr. Diggory Knobbs himself.

"Mr. Trennant," he observed, "I must desire you to be more circumspect in your language when addressing yourself to me. I trust that every one on this occasion will pay due respect to the high office I have the honour to fill."

"Oh, certainly, my old Trojan," said Joe; "I believe you are to be the master of the ceremonies on this occasion, are you not?"

"I have taken upon myself that high responsibility," replied the beadle, in a dignified tone. "Ahem! if you will pay proper attention, I will read to you the rules and regulations which are to be observed. 'The village festival of the first of May,'" he went on to read, "'will take place as usual, under the following regulations:—Article 1. It must be fine weather—fulfilled. Article 2. Every one will be at liberty to dance—the young, if they choose; the old, if they can; pretty misses, if the whim takes them—their mamma's, if they can find partners. Article 3. Young couples will not be allowed to ramble about in the woods. N.B. Particular caution is recommended to all who are disposed to infringe on this article.' That's all."

"Bravo!" shouted the guests; and Mr. Diggory Knobbs having refreshed his inward man with another glass of wine, folded up the paper, and deposited it in his pocket. The sounds of approaching music and shouts of joy now saluted their ears, and old Joe Trennant started up with the utmost hilarity. and exclaimed—

"Splice my timbers! here they come, full sail. Weigh anchor, my lads; spread every stitch of canvas, and let us away to meet and welcome them."

The guests needed no second invitation, but all of them issued from the house, and the next moment they beheld the rustic procession approaching the scene of festivity to the simple music of the pipe and tabor. It was a joyous and animated sight, and loud were the shouts of gladness that rent the air. First came six young rustic maidens, clad in white, and strewing the path with flowers as they advanced; and then, beneath a canopy of flowers, borne by six youthful mariners, and supported by her lover, appeared the lovely queen of the festivity, the innocent and fascinating Kate Markham, attired in a robe of white, decorated with roses, and a tiara of May flowers encircling her fair and expressive forehead. The remainder of the procession was formed of the numerous persons who intended to take part in the festivities, young and old, and all attired in their holiday gear. Nothing could exceed the beauty of the scene, and when the procession had reached the spot where the pastimes were to take place, and the May-queen had been escorted to a temporary throne erected for the occasion, and our hero had taken his seat upon her right hand, the shouts of joy and welcome which burst from every person present made the air resound again. But how shall we describe the dazzling charms of Kate Markham?—so young and innocent; so modest and retiring; so smiling and so happy. Well indeed did she become the character she assumed, and richly did she merit the homage that was paid to her superior beauty and virtue by the company present. Kate Markham was not yet eighteen, and to all the artless playfulness of the girl was united the calm grace and dignity of the woman. Her features were exquisitely modelled, and her form was symmetry itself—so light, and so airy, and so graceful, that the mind was lost in admiration wherever she appeared. Not one thought that angels need blush to acknowledge had ever entered her breast: all was as intrinsically pure as her person was lovely. No wonder that Jack Junk felt himself the proudest and happiest of individuals in existence in being honoured and blest with her love, and well worthy was that noble-spirited youth of her warmest affections. He would have laid down his life to serve her, and terrible would have been the punishment he would have inflicted on any one who should have dared to insult her. How his heart palpitated with delight as he was thus seated by her side, and beheld her the theme of universal esteem and admiration! The rustic company having paid their homage to the beauteous May queen, several young girls sang the following words, which had been composed for the occasion, the whole of the numerous persons assembled taking part in the chorus:—

" Sound the merry pipe and tabor,
    Gay and happy let us be ;
This day is set apart from labour,
    Keep we now our revelry.
Let the festive dance prevail,
    Trip it lightly, free, and gay ;
Sportive pleasures let us hail,
    To honour Kate, the Queen of May.
Trip it lightly, free, and gay ;
    Honour to the Queen of May !"

The singing of these simple lines had a singularly beautiful and impressive effect, and when they were concluded, the air once more resounded with acclamations of delight. When these demonstrations of pleasure had somewhat subsided, Mrs. Diggory Knobbs, with mock ceremony, proclaimed the rustic festival, and the sports commenced with the greatest spirit, Kate Markham and her lover mingling in the fantastic dance around the Maypole, and still forming the chief magnets of attraction and admiration to all present. How light and graceful were the movements of the lovely Kate; how completely did she, though without any effort on her part, put all her fair companions in the shade, and certainly a more beauteous number of maidens had never been assembled together on one joyous occasion before. Nor was the dancing of our hero less animated and characteristic; for he felt himself so happy that it imparted double energy to his feet, and elasticity to his limbs. Old Joe Trennant was in the highest state of glee, and by the fund of natural humour which he possessed, contributed much to the mirth and harmony of the jovial and happy meeting. It was indeed a pleasant sight, to view the numerous beauteous, the most beauteous of Nature's daughters, and the manly forms that were luxuriating in innocent hilarity there, with a bright sun, and a clear, transparent sky smiling down upon them. Callous and insensible indeed must have been the heart that could not have palpitated in unison with the many joyous hearts that were bounding there. It was forsooth a lovely May morning, and those that were assembled there on that occasion to celebrate its advent did full honour to the glorious season. In the midst of the revelry, Mark Stanford, accompanied by another man, as repulsive in aspect as himself, made their appearance upon the lawn, and standing at a corner of the Old Ship Tavern, where they were not likely to be immediately observed, they for a while contemplated in silence the joyous sports that were proceeding.

" She is here, Pierce," at length said Mark Stanford, pointing in the direction where Kate and her lover were tripping in the dance ; " is she not very beautiful? How chaste, how lovely does she appear as she is now attired. Observe her tiny feet, which nothing but the slipper of a Cinderella could fit ; notice her gracefully turned ankle, Pierce, is she not a being who might move even a stoic's heart to rapture and to admiration?"

" True, true," replied Pierce, " and a rare mate she would be for the Pirate Chief, if he could only gain possession of her !"

" Hush, hush !" said Mark, looking cautiously round him ; " Farmer Stanford, mind you, when I am abroad. Such observations as you have just now been using are dangerous in public, there might be listeners, you know."

" True, true, *Farmer* Stanford," replied Pierce, with a half smile and a wink of the eye ; " but," he added, in an undertone, " entertaining the sentiments you do towards the lass, methinks it must be rather vexatious to you to witness the favour she bestows upon the young sailor, Jack Junk, whom she is now dancing with. See the transport with which he entwines his arm around her slender waist ; the looks of affection which she beams upon him from those sparkling eyes ; by all my hopes, I would sacrifice all that I possess to enjoy the felicity he is now experiencing."

" Hold ! hold ! Pierce," said Stanford, impatiently, " your words set my brain on fire, and I shall forget myself. The time will come, when I will spoil the sports of that stripling, Jack, and he shall know me in my true character. But at present it is only policy on my part to do the amiable. Do you understand me?"

" Oh, yes," answered his companion.

" Pierce," resumed Mark Stanford, after a brief pause, " what would be the feelings of that now happy damsel, whose joyous smiles impart such pleasure to all here assembled, did she but know the real fate of her father; were she aware that his murderer was so near her !"

" His murderer !"

" Ay, it is even so ; you have often heard me allude to that subject, but knowing that I can at least confide in you, I will, on our return home, relate all the particulars. Her father, Horace Markham, as good a seaman as ever trod deck, died by fever at sea ;—ha ! ha ! ha !. His wife was my foster sister. I loved her; she rejected me for him ; I thirsted for revenge; but concealed my thoughts, and deceived them. Years flew by, fortune smiled upon me, while it frowned upon Horace Markham. I became the master and captain of a merchant vessel, Horace, one of my crew, performing several voyages with me, in which I affected to show him all kindness and friendship, but at the same time, as you may be certain, only watching a fitting opportunity to gratify my revenge. My passion for his wife had subsided, and had given place to a feeling of the most inveterate hatred, but I viewed the growing charms of her youthful daughter with the warmest admiration, and at the same time with a firm determination that at one time or other she should be mine."

" Then, of course, Kate Markham, in her more youthful days, knew you well?" said Pierce.

" Yes," replied Stanford, " and believing me to be the sincere friend of her parents, esteemed me."

" And how long is it since the death of her father?" enquired his companion.

" About seven years. Her mother has been dead about five, and since that time she has been under the protection of her uncle."

" Did he ever see you?"

" Not till I came here in my present character."

" But is it possible," said Pierce, " that Kate Markham has never recognised you?"

" No," replied Mark Stanford, " I have so disguised my person as to render that a matter of impossibility. Seven years' buffeting about have changed my features, and this farmer's dress—but stop ; another time—some one approaches, and we must dissemble. I am Farmer Stanford, you remember, and you, plain Giles Homestead, my managing man."

" All right," observed Pierce, winking his eye, and at that moment Mr. Diggory Knobbs advanced towards them, and bowing obsequiously to Mark Stanford, he said—

" Farmer Stanford — a-hem ! Mr. Stanford

you'll pardon me for my temporary forgetfulness of due courtesy, but persons who hold high and responsible situations like myself—a-hem!—are subject to fits of absence of mind; I have the extreme felicity and distinguished honour of welcoming you and your respected agent to our rustic festival, on this glorious first of May."

"Thank you, Master Knobbs," said Mark Stanford, with a gracious smile, "you are a gentleman that I much respect, and I think you shed a lustre upon that town which has the happiness of possessing you as one of its official representatives."

"A-hem!" said the beadle, at the same time being affected with a short cough; "I must beg leave to premise, Mr. Stanford, that gentlemen holding high official situations like that I have the honour to fill, have an aversion to flattery."

"Oh, yes," returned Mark Stanford, smiling complacently, "I understand you; I should have recollected that all high dignitaries are the very quintessence of modesty; I beg leave to apologise, Mr. Knobbs."

"Oh, accepted, my dear sir," said Knobbs, with great condescension, "accepted, I can assure you. Allow me to introduce you and your friend to the august presence of our May-queen. I say, Mr. Stanford, by the by, don't you think she looks very beautiful?"

"Lovely!" replied Stanford.

"Ah!" said the beadle, pulling up his shirt collar, and elevating himself to his full height, "I do not know but if Mrs. Knobbs was defunct, if I should not feel disposed to do Kate Markham the honour of making proposals for her hand."

"Vastly condescending on your part, Mr. Knobbs," returned Stanford, with an ironical smile.

"Well, I really do think that I should have that weakness," observed Mr. Knobbs, "I do, upon the word and honour of an official personage."

"Very good," returned Mark Stanford; "I cannot but express my admiration of your taste, Mr. Knobbs."

"Ah!" said the beadle, "Kate Markham is indeed a rare specimen of Nature's handiworks, and it is a pity that she should throw herself away upon a common sailor like Jack Junk, when she is worthy of becoming the wife even of a beadle—ahem!—an emperor, I meant to say; but for that matter, there is not much distinction that I am aware of."

"Oh, certainly not," replied Stanford and Pierce, in a breath.

"I say, Mr. Stanford," resumed Knobbs, "do you not envy the young sailor the happiness he at present enjoys? See how loving he encircles her waist, as they trip it in the merry dance; how affectionately she smiles upon him; gadzooks! it were worth a whole quarter's salary of a parish dignitary like myself to be favoured with one of those smiles. Eugh! I shall never relish the lips of Mrs. Knobbs again."

"Ha! ha! ha!" laughed Mark Stanford, ironically, "why, I declare you are quite amorous, Mr. Knobbs."

"Amorous!" repeated Knobbs; "men are but mortals, and beadles are but flesh and blood, notwithstanding they wear the embellishments of their high station, and shine resplendent in the glories of gold lace and a cocked hat. I believe, Mr. Stanford, that Kate Markham has made some impression upon your heart, and that you have made overtures for her hand, but have been rejected?"

Mark Stanford nodded assent, and the beadle proceeded—

"Well, well—I must pity her want of taste; but young girls have strange notions, of which they may be cured in time. As Mrs. Knobbs is a remarkably healthy woman, and there is no prospect of her retiring from this life for some years to come I would advise you not to despair. For my own part, I promise you all the influence I possess over Kate and her uncle; for I don't mind telling you in confidence, that I thoroughly detest that upstart boy, Jack Junk, as he is called."

"Indeed!" said Mark Stanford.

"Yes," answered the beadle; "he has never paid proper respect to my person and the high office I hold; and that friend of his, with whom he resides when he is ashore, old Joe Trennant, I mean, had the consummate impudence and presumption to offend my dignity this morning, by applying to me the opprobrious and degrading epithet of the figure-head of the Gorgon!"

"Monstrous!" exclaimed Stanford and his companion, with mock astonishment and indignation.

"'Tis true, I assure you, upon the honour of a parish beadle," replied Knobbs; "but, ah! who have we here? Old Reuben, the wise man, as he is called, as I live, looking as dismal and as ominous as usual. What brings him to this festive scene, I should like to know? Well, if the authorities had only followed my advice, he would have been incarcerated in a jail a long time ago. Why, I declare he is coming towards us, and as I have a particular objection to his company ever since the time when he had the impudence and presumption, because my wife is only fifteen years younger than myself, to tell me I was a contented cuckold, and as the sports cannot possibly get on without my immediate superintendence, I will leave you, gentlemen; perhaps you will allow me to have the honour of introducing you to Kate Markham, the May-queen, in a few minutes?"

With these observations, the parish beadle strutted with much bombastic dignity from the spot, and rejoined the revellers. The individual whom Mr. Knobbs had mentioned advanced towards Mark Stanford and his companion with a slow and measured step, and when he had arrived to within a few paces of them, he stopped, and confronted them. Stanford, in spite of himself, could not help feeling a sensation of uneasiness at the sight of him, but he was unable to speak and to demand his business. He was a very old man, of tall and bony figure, and attired in a costume of a singular character. His face was swarthy and wrinkled; his features sharp and irregular; his eyes small, but particularly penetrating; and his hair, which fell over his shoulders, was as white as silver. He supported himself with a long staff, with which at intervals he described several mysterious figures in the air, but never once removed his eyes from the countenance of Mark Stanford, who felt more uneasy every moment. This singular being resided in a lonely habitation, situated in a remote spot about a mile from the town, and near the sea-side, and was supposed to be enabled to penetrate into the secrets of futurity, and for that reason was looked upon with a kind of superstitious awe by the humble classes of society, and by the more respectable and intelligent portion of the community with some degree of deference. Wonderful were the stories told of him; he had predicted shipwrecks, which had invariably taken place; he had prophesied calamities to individuals, which had never failed to be fulfilled; and on the contrary, he had prognosticated good fortune to certain persons, which had always met with the same result. He was consulted on particular occasions by young and old, rich and poor, and, in fact, was looked upon as the very oracle of the neighbourhood. Had he lived at an earlier period, he would certainly have been burnt as a sorcerer. Whenever the tempest raged the fiercest, and the ocean threatened inevitable destruction to all who were exposed to its perils, old Reuben was to be seen standing on the summit of a lofty rock near his wretched dwelling, laughing in every glee that furious battling of the elements, and his appearance was always considered as the harbinger of some horrible calamity. There he would remain for hours, heedless of the rain, which fell in torrents upon him, or the wind which howled around him; and in such moments as those, no one had ever been known to be bold enough to approach him. Such was the ex'raordinary and mysterious being who now stood before Mark Stanford and his companion, and continued to fix his eyes upon them with the deepest earnestness, which rendered them incapable of uttering a word.

"Hugh Granfield," at length said the old man, addressing himself to the supposed farmer, in solemn and impressive tones; "Hugh Granfield, I greet you."

Mark Stanford, as he called himself, started with astonishment and alarm as he heard his real name thus unexpectedly mentioned, and gazed upon the old man with feelings of the most indescribable character, as he demanded—

"D—n! how is this? How know you my name? Who are you?"

"Reuben of the Hovel," replied the singular old man, "he who ever watches in the storm and the calm, the darkness and the sunshine; whose mind never sleeps; he who penetrates the thoughts of human beings, and who is acquainted with all their secrets. You have seen me oft before, dost doubt me, Hugh Granfield?"

"Strange man, by what means have you become acquainted with my name?" demanded Mark Stanford, as we still think proper to call him; "who are you?"

"Have I not told you?" replied Reuben, "ay, Hugh Granfield, my mind's eye has constantly watched your actions on the boundless deep, and in your greatest privacy on shore. You have been ever present to me in the storm and the calm; there is not a thought that passes in your mind, though thousands of miles may separate us, that can escape my knowledge."

Mark Stanford started, and could not help trembling as he gazed upon the wrinkled countenance of the man who thus addressed him, but the power of utterance was for a few moments denied him.

"She is there," resumed Reuben, in impressive accents, and pointing towards the spot where Kate Markham was standing in the company of her lover and her friends; "she is there, Hugh Granfield, the beautiful and the innocent; her whose father's blood was shed by you, she whom you would doom to destruction; but mark me, assass'n, Kate Markham, though she and her lover are destined to experience many troubles at your hands, shall never become your victim."

"By all my hopes," cried the infuriated Stanford, "I cannot, will not patiently endure this. I will know more of you, and by what means you have arrived at the knowledge you pretend to possess."

"You will know that soon enough to your cost," replied Reuben, with a derisive laugh, "the pirate farmer will in due time be revealed, and his crimes denounced to the world. Look at your hands; is there not blood still upon them? Does not the ghastly countenance of your murdered victim, the unfortunate Horace Markham, appear to your conscience-struck imagination? What if I were now to betray you to those present, would not the retribution that would descend upon your head be as just as it would be terrible?"

"Croaking hound," exclaimed Stanford, "I can endure this no longer!"

As he thus spoke he rushed upon the old man, but in an instant he was felled to the earth by a blow on the head from the staff which he carried, and when Pierce, who was lost in astonishment,

raised him to his feet, he found that Reuben was gone.

"Is this some wild delusion?" he ejaculated, "Pierce, heard you what he said?"

"Undoubtedly I did," replied the latter, "and from the agitation of your manner, I should imagine that he spoke the truth; did he not?"

"Hush! hush!" said Mark Stanford, looking fearfully around him, "for we might be overheard—he did—but I will disclose everything to you anon; which way did he go?"

"That I can scarcely tell you," answered Pierce, "for he vanished so suddenly. Well, I have often heard of the singular character of this mysterious being, but I confess that I never expected to hear what he has this moment revealed respecting you."

"The knowledge he possesses, though by what means he has obtained it, I cannot imagine, is dangerous," remarked Stanford; "he must be secured at all hazards."

"Well," returned Pierce, "that had better be considered at some future time. If you are determined to introduce yourself to Kate, and to join the revellers, you had better endeavour to compose yourself."

"Think you that this awkward affair has been observed?" asked Stanford.

"No," replied Pierce, "it is my opinion that all the persons assembled were too deeply engaged in the sports to take any notice of it."

"It is fortunate if they did not," said Mark, "for it might have excited dangerous suspicions. See the proud and scornful beauty again joins in the dance, and lavishes all her attentions on my hated rival; the sight inflames my brains, and urges me on to deeds of desperation—but my day of triumph shall come, in spite of everything; Kate Markham, you shall yet be mine! Jack Junk, the sanguine hopes you now encourage shall never be realized, and before many weeks have elapsed, you and the pretended farmer, Mark Stanford, shall become better acquainted."

"If all be true that I have heard," remarked Pierce, "the Defiance, to which Jack belongs, will sail from this port in a few weeks, and of course he, as one of the crew, must go with her and leave the girl of his heart behind; had you not better, therefore, wait till she is deprived of his protection, before you attempt to put your designs against her into execution?"

"True," coincided Stanford; "but we will talk further upon that business at a future time; at present I am all impatience to pay my homage to the fair Queen of May. Ha!—ha!—ha!"

"Come, then," said Pierce, "and let us join the sports; and be careful, by your conduct, not to betray the real thoughts that are passing in your mind."

Mark Stanford returned no answer, and they walked together towards the place where Kate and her joyous companions were assembled. Our hero and his lover beheld their approach with no very pleasurable emotions, and Jack, taking her arm, led her to a seat, and took his place by her side.

"Would to Heaven," said Kate, "that that man, whom I cannot look upon without feelings of repugnance, and instinctive and unaccountable horror, had not made his appearance here to-day. His presence will throw a blight upon our festivity."

"Avast there, my lass," replied Jack. "I own that I dislike the swab as much as you can, for I have reason to do so, since he has had the presumption to attempt to supplant me in your affections, and to raise a mutiny in your breast. But you have nothing to fear from the black-looking lubber; he will not dare to insult you while Jack Junk is by your side. Should he do so, I will throw my grappling-irons upon him immediately, and he will soon be glad to cry 'peccavi,' and to sheer off as quick as he can, I'll warrant."

Kate smiled upon him one of her sweetest smiles, and the next moment Mark Stanford and his companion approached, and the former bending one knee to the earth, with mock devotion and humility, said—

"Fair Queen of May, beauteous Kate Markham permit one of the humblest of your admirers, to offer you the sincere homage of his heart on this joyous occasion, and to——"

"Avast heaving there, mate!" interrupted Jack; "belay that palaver, for it neither suits my ears, nor those of my pretty Kate. Mind you, my worthy clodpole, I do not object to your admiring her, as every one must do who knows a handspike from a rope's-end, but no farther; I have had enough of your *friendship* already: you understand me."

Mark Stanford arose, and fixed a look of indignation upon our hero, as he replied—

"Methinks that your observations are rather abrupt and uncalled for; surely I can offer no offence by merely doing that which everybody else present at this rustic festival has been privileged to do?"

"Hark you, Mr. Mark Stanford," returned Jack, "I am a man of few words, but I am never afraid to speak my mind, whether I offend or please. I know very well, in spite of the false colours you now hoist, that you bear me no good will, and for the matter of that I can tell you there is no love lost between us: if Kate is in want of compliments, I dare say I can accommodate her to her heart's content, and, therefore, she has no occasion to come to you for them. Of course you are at liberty to join the company if you like, but I would advise you not to come athwart my hawse, or you will find Jack Junk rather an awkward customer to quarrel with."

"Indeed," said Stanford, with a bitter sneer; "I do not doubt the bravery of Jack Junk, at least so far as his own opinion goes, but I utterly despise his threats, and value not his friendship a farthing; but notwithstanding all that you have said you cannot prevent me from still entertaining what sentiments I please towards Kate Markham."

"Avast there!" cried Jack with rising indignation, "I cannot allow such lingo as that, especially on this occasion. We have met here for mirth and enjoyment, and as I have no wish to quarrel with any one the sooner you slip your cable, messmate, the better."

"Jack Junk," returned Stanford, unable to conceal his rage, "your words are bold and insulting, but the time may come when you will know Mark Stanford better, and it will be well for you then if you do not have reason to regret your present observations."

"Indeed," said our hero, scornfully, "but I plainly tell you, Mr. Mark Stanford, that I have not the least inclination or intention to be on any more intimate terms with you than I am at present; so there is an end to the business."

"No, there is not," returned Stanford, with a sinister expression of countenance; "so you need not flatter yourself with the idea.—You have not a foolish headstrong boy to deal with; which you may discover some day to your cost."

"Mr. Stanford," remonstrated Kate, who was alarmed at the warmth of her lover, and the threats which were conveyed in the observations of his rival; "I must beg of you to desist. I cann't listen to language such as that you have just made use of, and which nothing on earth can justify; the sentiments of Kate Markham can never change, and she possesses too proud and candid a spirit, to seek for a moment to conceal them. Let this answer suffice you, and restrain you from repeating such conduct as that I have now so great a right to complain of."

Stanford bit his lips and frowned, whilst Kate averted her looks with a feeling of disgust, and addressed herself to her lover.

"'Tis well, Kate Markham," said Stanford, in a voice which plainly told the feelings that were passing in his mind; "I obey your commands, peremptory though they be; but there may be a time when you may find it prudent to use far different language to me. Farewell."

Thus saying, Mark Stanford fixed upon our hero a look of scorn and hatred and turned away, walking from the spot, and, with his companion Pierce, mingling among the other persons who were assembled.

"If that fellow is not an arrant scoundrel at heart," said Jack, when Stanford was gone, "I am much mistaken. But I will keep a sharp look-out after the lubber, and if I find him out in any tricks by which he might think to annoy us, I will give him good cause to repent his boldness, never fear."

"Dear Jack," said Kate, "I wish you to avoid coming into collision with him as much as possible. I confess that I cannot help feeling a secret dread of him, and the threats he has held out alarm me. There is a strange mystery about him, which excites my suspicions, and I am strongly inclined to believe that he is not what he represents himself to be."

"Why, for the matter of that, my lass," replied her lover, "I am strangely inclined to be of your opinion; but whoever he is I care not; and as for his threats, I heed them no more than a puddle in a tempest; let him only attempt any wrong against you or me, and I will pour such a broadside in upon him, as will send him to old Davy in the twinkling of a hand spike. But come, my sweet Kate, there has been enough said on this unpleasant subject, and so we had better rejoin our friends in the more agreeable sports of the day."

Kate smiled her assent, and her lover once more entered with the greatest spirit and vivacity into the pleasures of the lively dance, which was kept up with great animation, at different intervals during the day. Evening came, a lovely bright moonlight evening, and still the revels were gay as ever, and seldom had Kate Markham and her lover felt so happy before. Mark Stanford was no where to be seen amongst the throng, so they imagined that, finding his presence was unwelcome, he had taken his departure, which afforded them no little satisfaction. However, they were shortly doomed to discover that they had deceived themselves. It happened that our hero had occasion to retire into the house for a minute, and he therefore left Kate in the company of two of her female friends until his return, never for a moment imagining that any harm could occur to her in such a place, and while so many persons were present. Something, however, attracting the attention of her friends, they suddenly left her, and she found herself alone. She was about to join a party of the festive company who were amusing themselves on another part of the lawn, when she was surprised and alarmed on finding her arm grasped rudely by some person behind, and looking round, her indignation may be imagined, when she beheld Mark Stanford.

"Fair Kate," said Stanford, in assumed accents of respect and admiration, "be not alarmed or look so scornfully upon one. Surely there is nothing so particularly revolting in my appearance as to cause this feeling. Allow me the happiness of a few moments' private conversation with you while my rival is away. I merely ask the favour of an opportunity to explain myself, and I have too high an opinion of the sweet condescension of your nature to imagine for a momet that you will refuse me."

"Unhand me, Mr. Stanford, I command you," said Kate, with a look of resentment, "this boldness is unpardonable. You already know my sentiments, and why should you persist in annoying me?"

"Kate Markham," returned Stanford, "I can endure anything but your scorn; I love you with all the fervour of intense passion; I am prepared to idolize you, to——"

"Hold, sir," interrupted the blushing and indignant girl, "or my cries shall bring those to my assistance who will make you bitterly repent your insolence and unwarrantable presumption. Release me, I say, and begone, or dread the consequences."

She struggled violently as she thus spoke to release herself from his hold, but in vain; and they being now on a part of the lawn where there was no one to observe them, poor Kate began to feel greatly alarmed, and looked anxiously towards the tavern with the hope of seeing her lover approach.

"Nay, beauteous Kate Markham," said Stanford, "your resistance, and the aversion you evince towards me, does but increase my determination, and I will not resign the opportunity I now have of repeating the real thoughts and feelings I entertain towards you, let the consequences be whatever they may. But why thus scorn me, damsel? what is there so superior in the vain boy, Jack Junk, that you should prefer him to me? Shall he monopolize all your affections? Psha! Kate, I wonder at your want of taste in that respect. Hark ye, damsel; Jack is poor—he is but a common seaman, and sailors, you know, find a fresh sweetheart in every port they sail to. He will soon forget you, depend on it, flattering as the promises he now holds out to you. I have the means to make you independent—a lady, Kate; ay, believe me—I make no empty boast, for Mark Stanford is not the humble individual he appears to be. I offer you a heart that nothing can ever change; I lay my fortune at your feet, and——"

"Villain!" cried the disgusted damsel, "I will no longer listen to you; you are totally insensible to every feeling of shame and honour. Detain me not, or you will have bitter cause to rue your boldness. Oh! help! help!"

"Silence!" cried Stanford, still retaining his hold, and endeavouring to imprint a kiss upon her lips; but Kate screamed louder than before, and Stanford, fearing what the consequences of his rash and daring conduct might be, should her cries reach the ears of the assembled guests, with an oath, released his hold, and was flying from the spot, when he saw Jack Junk approaching that way, and found that it would be quite useless to attempt to avoid him. Kate was so overcome by terror that for a moment she was unable to move from the spot, and could with difficulty save herself from fainting. The enraged seaman darted upon Stanford, and grasping him violently by the collar, he said—

"Why, you infernal swab! you confounded pirate! and so you have the daring to bear down upon the fair craft during the absence of her commander? Now, shiver my timbers, if I haven't as good a mind to scuttle your figure-head, as ever I had to drink my allowance of grog. But this time I will suffer you to escape, but as sure as my name's Jack Junk, if ever I catch you on my track again, I will give you such a thrashing that you will never forget it as long as you live. Bah!"

Thus saying, our hero thrust him from him, and Mark Stanford staggered and fell to the earth, but was quickly on his feet again, and foaming with rage, was about to spring upon his youthful rival, when Kate, with a loud cry, rushed into the arms of her lover, and thus prevented the consequences which in all probability would otherwise have taken place.

"Oh, forbear, forbear, I implore you," she said, addressing herself to our hero, "and suffer him to depart."

"The rascally pirate," said the brave young seaman, fixing upon Mark Stanford a look of the utmost indignation; "he dare to insult my Kate—my innocent Kate? Damme! I could kill the lubber for his insolence. Sheer off, ye infernal swab, and think yourself lucky that I have suffered you to escape; but if ever I catch you at the same game again, may I never go aloft again if I do not send you to the devil in less time than the bo'sun could pipe all hands."

"Jack Junk," said Stanford, with a terrible frown, "for the present you may seem to triumph, but my day will come at last, and then you shall have bitter cause to repent the business of this night. From this moment I am your deadly enemy, and tremble at the power I possess, and which you little suspect."

"Let me go, Kate," said her lover; "am I thus to listen, without resenting them, to the insults and threats of this daring scoundrel?"

"Oh, heed them not, dear Jack," she said, "he means not what he says. Mr. Stanford, I beg of you not to provoke this quarrel further, or the consequences may be fatal. You must acknowledge, if you are not quite insensible to every feeling of truth and honour, that you alone are to blame."

"Oh, of course," returned Stanford, with a sneer, "but I go; though I promise you once more, that the time will come when we shall meet again under very different circumstances to the present."

As he thus spoke, he shook his fist menacingly at Jack Junk, and hurried from the spot; Kate being greatly relieved after he had taken his departure.

"The villain!" said Jack; "his words are bold, but I regard them not; the empty boast of the power he possesses I also treat with contempt. I will keep a strict eye upon him however, and should he really contemplate anything wrong, he will find that I am more than a match for him."

Kate returned no answer, and she tried to encourage the same thoughts as those her lover had expressed; but still there was something about the character of Stanford, and the observations he had made use of, which would not suffer her to banish from her mind all apprehensions entirely; and she would have felt much more at her ease had he left the neighbourhood altogether. But how terrible would have been the agony of her mind had she known the dreadful crime of which he had been guilty, and the fate which her father had suffered at his hands. At length, as the hour was getting late, the festivities ceased, and the company separated, our hero conducting Kate home, where they bade each other farewell and parted for the night.

CHAPTER II.

MARK STANFORD'S DWELLING.—THE SECRET.— THE MURDER AT SEA.

THE farm which Mark Stanford, or rather Hugh Granfield, occupied was a very respectable one, and he was looked upon as a prosperous man; though his reserved and repulsive manners gained him but few friends and acquaintances in the neighbourhood, and, for his part, he did not appear at all anxious to cultivate that of any one except the uncle of Kate Markham, and his motives for that need no explanation. There was one part of the farm, however, which none but those in the confidence of Stanford were ever allowed to enter, and which had a secret entrance, known only to a select few. This was at the back of the house, and consisted of two or three spacious apartments of an ancient description, and which were furnished in a manner so as to afford accommodation to several individuals. They were all situated on the ground floor, and it had often been whispered among the servants that they had frequently heard strange noises, mingled with the voices of men, proceed from those rooms, though who the men were, what they met for in so secret a manner, and where they came from, they could not form the slightest conjecture. This circumstance caused no little surprise amongst the servants, but they, fearful of offending their master, never on any occasion ventured to breathe a sentence of it abroad, so that no persons in the neighbourhood knew anything of it. On the night of the festival, after what had taken place between him and Jack, as related in the previous chapter, Mark Stanford, muttering curses to himself, and vowing vengeance against his rival, quickly bent his steps towards home, and on arriving there he walked round to the back of the house, and passing through a low gate, he stopped at one corner of the building, which was thickly clothed in ivy, and where no person who was ignorant of the secret would have imagined for a moment that there were any means of ingress. Stanford, however, took a key from his pocket, and after raking for a second or two among the ivy, he applied it to the lock, and a door in the wall opened and revealed a dark, narrow passage. He stooped and entered, and closing the door after him, he proceeded along the passage till he stopped at another door, which was not fastened, and opened into what was the first of the range of apartments we have just mentioned. After traversing two or three apartments, all of which were furnished, and well supplied with fire-arms and swords, he came to the door of one, from the crevices of which lights might be seen to issue, and the voices of men in earnest conversation might be heard. This door was locked on the inside, but Stanford having knocked three times, the voices ceased, and some one from within demanded who was there?"

"Why, who should it be but me?" replied Stanford.

The door was immediately opened by a rough looking man, and Stanford entered the room, which was furnished in a similar manner to the rest, and contained about half a dozen men of the most repulsive aspects, and who arose from the table at which they had been seated on his entrance, and welcomed him. Stanford took a seat, and hastily swallowed a glass of wine.

"You are late, master," said Pierce, for he was one of the party: "and do not seem to be over well pleased."

"No, confound it," replied Stanford; "but it is no more than I expected, as I told you to-day. The girl is as cold as ice and as proud as an empress; and as for Jack Junk, he holds complete dominion over her, and sets every one at defiance. Perhaps he would alter his tale if he only knew who I really am, and that farmer Stanford as, he is supposed to be, has as gallant a vessel at his command, and as daring a crew to serve under him, as ever braved the perils of the deep."

"True, captain," said Pierce; "the Raven is no cockle-shell, and has weathered many a storm, and triumphed in many hundreds of engagements. But how did you succeed?"

"Why, I contrived to force my conversation upon Kate during the temporary absence of Jack," answered Stanford: but listen."

He then recapitulated that with which the reader is already made acquainted in the last chapter.

"It was a bold venture on your part," remarked Pierce, when he had concluded; "as for the scorn with which the damsel treated you, it was no more than you had a right to expect; but the conduct of the suitor was enough to excite your resentment."

"It was," said Stanford, "but fear not, I will have ample vengeance."

"No doubt of it," returned Pierce.

"Yes, I never forget my friends," observed Mark Stanford, with a sardonic smile. "At present let him flatter himself with the idea that Kate is securely his; his disappointment will be only greater when it comes. When he goes again to sea, which no doubt will be before long, I shall then have an excellent opportunity to put my wishes into effect, and I am perfectly sanguine as to the result. But I wish to speak to you alone, Pierce, on the subject we were talking about this day. Let us retire into another room."

"With all my heart," said Pierce, and they left the room together.

"I do not feel at all easy,' said Stanford when they were seated, "after the observations of that strange being whom we encountered to-day. He evidently knows all the particulars of my history, and might work me harm. I should like to secure him if there were a possibility."

"And I should think there would be no great difficulty in doing that," returned Pierce. "But did he speak the truth?"

"Oh, yes, I cannot deny that," replied Stanford, "but listen to me. You heard him call me by the name of Hugh Granfield?"

"I did; and is that your correct name?"

"Yes," returned Mark, "it is no use denying it to you, though it would not be convenient to let everybody know it. Yes, in me you behold Hugh Granfield, formerly captain of his majesty's brig Neptune, and looked upon on shore with the utmost respect, for I had all the outward polish which attracts regard from the thoughtless, the more numerous portion of mankind. Ashore I was meekness itself, but on the high seas, when loose from the immediate restrictions of the law, my ferocity was unbounded; but I suppose I have no occasion to give this description of my character to you, Pierce!"

The latter returned no verbal answer, but a single look expressed much more than words could have done, and Stanford proceeded—

"It was in such moments as these that the smothered flame of demoniac passion burst forth, and my fury resembled that of raving maniacs in the height of delirium. Offences of the most trivial kind I punished with the greatest severity, and if those opportunities failed, I would supply them with construed crimes or imaginary slights."

"Well, you certainly do not give yourself one of the most amiable of characters, captain." said his companion, with a smile.

"I am not fond of flattery," replied the villain Stanford, "so it is not likely that I am going to flatter myself. Horace Markham was one of my crew, and for a long time I had borne him the most inveterate hatred, and took every opportunity to revenge myself against him, though he had never given me the least cause for offence either by word or deed."

"And was he the father of Kate?" asked Pierce.

Stanford replied in the affirmative, and proceeded—

"My brutal conduct, of course, could not fail to engender an almost universal feeling of detestation towards me. Horace Markham, with more zeal than prudence, ventured to remonstrate with me, and that sealed his fate. The reply he immediately received, was an arrest on the charge of mutiny; all hands were called upon deck, and Markham was ordered to meet instant death by walking the plank."

"And did you carry the sentence into effect?" asked Pierce.

"Did I?" repeated the murderer, "to be sure I did; you ought to know me too well by this time, Pierce, to think that I would fail to keep my word. The sentence was no sooner pronounced than it was executed. A board was poised over the ship's side, and Horace Markham prepared to meet his fate with the most manly firmness, and scorning to ask for mercy, though he well knew that would have been completely useless. Stepping bo'dly forward, a deep plunge announced the completion of his barbarous sentence."

"Did you not put him upon his trial?" inquired Pierce.

"Psha! the only one that is known of at sea—the captain's will. Therein, I suppose, I need not tell you, lie evidence, judge, and jury; sometimes executioner even. But hear me out. On hearing the splash by the fall of Markham, instinctively the eyes of some of the crew wandered over the ship's side, and there they beheld him struggling with the waves, bearing towards the vessel with desperate strength. He implored one of the sailors to throw him a rope; he did so; he seized it; climbed nimbly up, and catching hold of the scantling with one hand, was about to spring on board, when I, snatching up an axe, with my own hand cut off that of Horace Markham. He shrieked—plunged again into the deep, and sunk to rise no more."

"It was a desperate deed," remarked Pierce.

"Yes, it was," coincided the assassin; "but I hated him, and was determined, on that opportunity presenting itself, to gratify my vengeance to the fullest extent. But I must confess that it has often haunted my conscience since; and I have seen the ghastly and supplicating looks of the murdered man, and heard his shriek of agony as he sank into the deep; but, psha! I am getting weak. Fearing that an investigation would take place as to the cause of the death of my unfortunate victim, and knowing that I had no friends among my own crew, I seized an opportunity, on the vessel's arriving in England, to escape."

"But was there no inquiry made?" asked Pierce.

"There was not," answered Stanford.

"That is strange."

"It is, and I cannot account for it," returned Stanford.

"And the brother of Horace Markham, and Kate, did none of the sailors ever make them acquainted with the dreadful and untimely fate that had befallen him?"

"They did not."

"Most extraordinary."

"True, observed Stanford, " but very fortunate for me. It was then I changed my name, and so disguised myself that it would have been next to an impossibility for even my most intimate acquaintances to know me. The manner in which I came on board the Raven, and ultimately your captain, you already know. After an absence of some years, I determined to visit the neighbourhood where I knew the relations of Markham resided, and it was then that I first beheld Kate, and became enamoured of her charms. I made a vow to possess her at all hazards, and I will not break my oath. This farm was to let, and the better to drown suspicion and to effect my plans, I took it, and as for the rest you know. My story is done."

"And a wonderful story it is, captain," remarked Pierce.

"Yes, I thought I should surprise you," said Stanford; "can you any longer wonder that Kate should view me with instinctive feelings o horror?"

"No," replied Pierce, "indeed I do not; but I marvel much, captain, that you should have the boldness to raise your thoughts towards the damsel after what you have told me just now."

"And think you, Pierce," returned Stanford, "that I can resist such transcendent charms as those which Kate Markham possesses, notwithstanding the scorn and repugnance which she evinces towards me? No, that does but inflame my passion the more; and after what has taken place to-day, and the conduct of the sailor, Jack Junk, I am more determined than ever in the designs I have formed for the gratification of my desires. May I perish—may I die the death of a dog, if Kate Markham shall ever be his."

"Well," remarked Pierce, "I must say that I commend your resolution, and I only hope that you may succeed in your designs."

"Succeed!" repeated Stanford, "I cannot—will not fail, however hazardous and doubtful it may appear at present. Did ever you know the daring captain of the Raven of the Sea to fail in anything he has yet undertaken?"

"Never!" answered his companion; "for the last few years, the daring rover of the ocean has excited universal terror and dismay, and many are the wild and romantic tales that are told of the wonderful exploits of him and his bold and desperate crew; little do the lubbers suspect that in Farmer Stanford they behold the man who has caused so much consternation, and whom they are so anxious to get in their clutches."

"True, Pierce," said Stanford; "and it affords me food for exultation when I think of it. But they shall yet have still greater cause to shudder at my name. But there is one circumstance which makes me look upon this youth whom they call Jack Junk, but whose real name is not known, with feelings of still greater detestation, and even with a sensation of dread."

"Of dread, captain?" said Pierce, with a look of surprise.

"Ay," answered the farmer; "the extreme likeness he bears to one whom I deeply injured, and—but I will not repeat that story at present; circumstances may sometime or another render it necessary for me to explain the particulars, till which period I will keep the secret confined to my own breast."

"Very well, captain," observed Pierce; "I have no particular wish to pry into it, though I must confess that your observations have greatly excited my curiosity. Jack is a daring fellow; they call him the tar for all weathers; and if all be true that is told of him, he is well worthy of the title. No danger comes amiss to him; and they say he is as trim and taut a sailor as ever went up aloft."

"That may be," returned Stanford, "I dare say the fellow is well enough for an ordinary seaman; but I am much mistaken if I do not have the opportunity of putting his courage to the test one of these days, and then he will find that the supposed farmer Stanford is not the insignificant swab he at present takes him for. Kate Markham too, the scornful beauty, shall yet be compelled to acknowledge his power, and to submit to his will, however revolting it may be to her feelings; who can resist the terrible power of the Rover of the Seas?—who can thwart his deep-laid schemes?"

"True," coincided Pierce, "but I would that we were on our native element again, braving all its perils with hearts of iron, and seeking for fresh booty to add to our already well-filled coffers; this rural life of indolence but ill accords with my disposition; the battle's heat, and no quarter or surrender, agrees with me much better."

"Well, Pierce, fear not but that your taste shall soon have free indulgence."

"I hope so, captain," said the fellow. "Ah! many a bloody fray have we been in together, in which the Raven has ever come off victorious, though we have had many narrow escapes."

"Yes, but the day is far distant when we shall fail to triumph," remarked Stanford. "Little do they suspect the real character of our vessel which is now lying at anchor in this port, and which is registered as the Enterprise, a fair trader."

"No," replied Pierce: "but still I cannot help thinking that it was rather a bold venture on your part, to put in here, where she might be recogaised by some of those who have tasted our quality to their cost."

"Psha! Pierce," returned Stanford, "the more bold the venture, the less fear of detection, I say. Think you as I am now disguised, that any one could possibly recognise me as Captain Sinclair?"

"Not very easily, I believe."

"No." continued Stanford, "methinks I have played my cards well, and have completely satisfied the authorities; so what have we to apprehend? But come, let us rejoin our companions, and drink success to our future undertakings, and destruction to our enemies."

"With all my heart," answered Pierce, and they then returned to the room where they had left the other men, where they continued to carouse and to talk over the daring and inhuman exploits in which they had been engaged till a late hour.

The real character of the pretended Mark Stanford, the farmer, we imagine has been sufficiently explained to the reader. He it was the atrocious and dauntless captain of the pirate vessel the Raven, who for so many years had been, with his ferocious crew, who never was known to show the least mercy to those whom they overpowered, the terror of the ocean, and who seemed to set detection and defeat at defiance, notwithstanding all the efforts that had been made, and the stratagems that were formed, to overpower them. His crew, which was numerous, consisted of ruffians of the most savage and desperate character, of several nations, English, Spanish, and Portugese, wretches who were ready for the perpetration of any crime, and who dared not to murmur at his command, whatever they might be. So extraordinary and unaccountable were the proceedings of these pirates, and they appeared so suddenly and in different places far apart from each other, when least expected, that many were half inclined to believe their captain to possess some supernatural power which rendered him unconquerable, and they could no', in spite of themselves, 'elp looking upon him with feelings amounting to awe and dread. Such were the schemes he had to metamorphose the appearance of his vessel and his own person, when he chose to put into any port or harbour, that not the slightest suspicion could be excited, and thus he escaped with impunnity As Captain Sinclair of the Enterprise, he was looked upon with the urmost respect when on shore, and received into the most fashionable society, and when alone, and e had re-assumed his disguise as the farmer, Mark Stanford, he would laugh in exultation at the manner in which he was enabled to deceive so many, and the surprise and terror which his numerous deeds had excited. Another advantage he gained by those disguises, was to become acquainted with the numerous plans that were formed to detect him and to crush his power, so that he was ever enabled to frustrate them, and to laugh his enemies to scorn; and thus it was that there seemed not to be the least chance of the daring career of the wild Rover of the Seas would be speedily brought to a close.

———

CHAPTER III.

JACK AND HIS LOVER.—MELANCHOLY INTELLIGENCE.—A SAILOR'S HEART, AND A SAILOR'S COURAGE.—THE MYSTERIOUS INTERVIEW IN THE OLD HOVEL.

IT was about a week after the events which we have related in the previous chapters, that our hero and Kate were seated on a bench beneath the honeysuckled casement of her uncle's dwelling, and from whence was commanded an uninterrupted view of the ocean, and the various stately vessels in the harbour. It was a lovely day, and the sight was animated in the extreme; the bright sun glittered on the white spray as it dashed against the shore, and its golden beams danced upon the gently undulating billows, and the breeze that was wafted from the expansive bosom of the deep, came cool and refreshing to the senses. The marine view that was commanded from this spot was of the most expansive and beautiful description, and here the lover of the wonderful works of nature might have stood for hours, and gazed with feelings of transport and admiration upon all that met his eye. Our hero's arm encircled the slender waist of Kate; her delicate hand was locked in his, and whilst she gazed with a melancholy expression of the most devoted affection into his fine handsome and manly countenance, tears, which she could not restrain, dimmed the lustre of her sparkling eyes, and sighs frequently agitated her gentle bosom. The countenance of Jack, too, although he evidently exerted himself to the utmost to stifle his feelings, was sad, and it needed no keen penetration that something had occurred to interrupt their happiness, and to fill their minds, which lately had been so cheerful, with dismal forebodings. There had been a slight pause in their conversation; but our hero, after a momentary struggle with his feelings, now spoke.

"Kate, my dear girl," he said, "this sudden order for the sailing of the fleet is rather unexpected; but a true British seaman is ready at any time when he is called upon by his country, and never flinches from his duty, however painful it may be for him to leave those he loves so dearly behind him. It is only the lubber who never smelt salt water, or heard the roar of the cannon, that knows either fear or danger; the tar for all weathers is one who is as happy in the storm as in the calm, and who is ready at all times to encounter any peril for the sake of his king and country, and those he so fondly loves. Kate, my lovely Kate, dry your tears, and once more wear those smiles of cheerfulness with which you are are wont to gladden all those who know you, and I trust, with the blessing of the Great Commander above, our separation will not be for long."

"Alas!" sighed Kate, and her tears flowed faster than before, "it may be for ever."

"Oh, say not so, my sweet Kate," returned her lover, imprinting an affectionate kiss upon her fair cheek; I have hitherto escaped unharmed from many a danger, and why should you now despair?"

"Oh, why should the wide and perilous ocean separate two hearts that are so fondly devoted to each other?" said Kate.

"To render their happiness at being united again the more pure and exquisite, my love," replied Jack. "Now, Kate, I tell you what it is, if you continue to give way to this violent grief, you will reduce me to the weakness of a powder monkey, and I know my Kate possesses too much the spirit of an Englishwoman to wish to do that. Come, come—no more crying, lass, but let us be merry, for

'The tar's a jolly tar that can hand, reef, and steer,
Cast off, and nimbly belay!'

Now then for one of your sweetest smiles; and the rememberance of it in the tempest's wrath, or the battle's heat, will act to me as a beacon to glory."

"But when you are gone, dear Jack," again sighed the damsel, "to what insults may I not be exposed to, from the boldness of that man whom I so much abhor, Farmer Stanford?"

"He dare not insult you," said Jack, "the ugly-looking shark; if I thought he would, I would settle his business in less time than I could crack a biscuit. But do not let such thoughts disturb your mind, Kate; he will not be bold enough to venture anything of the kind; and will you not be under the protection of your uncle, and your ether friends, Joe Trennant, Kit Breezely, and many more of them? Cheer up, my lass, for you have nothing to fear from him. See how gallantly my noble vessel, the Defiance, lies at anchor, with the colours of old England flying at her main, and seeming to ride like a proud monarch of the ocean, mocking the idle threats and boastings of the enemies of our native land. Is not that a sight to invigorate the saddest heart, and make it beat with rapture and enthusiasm? But, Kate, now that the day when we must once more part is fast approaching, there is one question that I would ask you, and I feel convinced that you will return me a candid and satisfactory answer."

"What is it, dear Jack?" inquired the lovely Kate Markham, eagerly.

"Will neither absence, time, nor circumstances, dear Kate," replied her lover, "change the sentiments you now so fondly—so fervently avow towards me? May I, in my moments of reflection, cheer myself with the blissful assurance that your heart still beats responsively with my own—that your thoughts are constantly fixed on me, and that when I once more return to my native land, I shall again be welcomed by those radiant smiles which have ever illumined my soul with hope and happiness?"

"And can you—do you doubt me, Jack?" said Kate, with a look of gentle reproach; "do you indeed doubt my fidelity, and believe that any circumstance whatever can ever, alter the sentiments which my heart so fondly encourages for you alone? Oh, surely this is most cruel and ungenerous; but no, I will not upbraid you for hastily and unthinkingly giving utterance to that which I am certain you cannot mean. Dear Jack, how dreary to me will be the time that you are absent from me; how constant and fervent will be the prayers for your safety and welfare; with what torturing anxiety shall I look for your return; and when that time shall providentially arrive, oh, who will be half so happy as Kate Markham?"

"Bless you—bless you, my Kate!" cried her lover, clasping her rapturously to his bosom; "pardon me for what I said, and, believe me, I meant no harm: your sweet assurance will be for ever present to my memory when the wide ocean far divides us, and will gladden my heart, and inspire me with redoubled confidence in the hour of danger. But, hark! did you not hear a voice?"

Kate did indeed hear a muttering sound, which seemed to proceed from behind a cluster of trees at one corner of the house, and close to the place where they were seated. Gradually it became more distinct, and their ears were then saluted by the following remarkable words, spoken in a solemn voice :—

"There is trouble for ye,
Both on land and at sea,
Youth and maiden, deride not the warning;
Oh, dreary the night
That shall on ye alight,
Ere the morn of your bliss shall be dawning!"

Kate Markham clung to her lover with terror, and they both looked towards the spot from whence the sounds seemed to proceed in astonishment, but no human being met their gaze, and all was now again silent.

"Be not alarmed, dear Kate," said our hero, "it's only some harum-scarum lubber or another, who wishes to have a joke at our expense. What ho! there, messmate! all fair and above board is the maxim of Jack Junk; so if you are an honest craft, damme, let's look at your figure head!"

No answer was returned to this, and the fears of Kate increased.

"What!" cried Jack, in louder accents, "what! are you ashamed of your colours?—some infernal pirates cruising off this coast, mayhap. Be not alarmed, Kate; lay by a moment, and I will be alongside of him in no time."

Kate timidly resumed her seat, and our hero darted hastily in among the cluster of trees, and looked anxiously in every direction, but as far as his eyes could stretch, he could not behold a human being, and he returned. to Kate in a state of the most inconceivable surprise and bewilderment.

"Well," he said, "this is one of the most singular adventures that ever I met with. Who could the fellow be, and where could he have gone to?"

"His words alarm me, dear Jack," said the damsel; "did you not notice their singular and mysterious import?"

"Yes, they were remarkable enough, Kate," answered our hero, "but they were hardly worth notice; witches or wizards do not trouble the earth in these days; such yarns may do very well to gull the land lubber with, but no person of common sense will take any heed of them. Think no more about it; and see, just in good time, comes my honest friend and patron, Joe Trennant, making full sail towards us as fast as his old timber toe will let him."

"Jack Junk ahoy! the Kate Markham ahoy!" shouted the old veteran at the top of his voice, as he had hobbled towards them; "yardarm and yardarm, my lad and lass; where are all our messmates? why don't they man the yards, and give three cheers for Jack Junk, Kate Markham, and the British navy? Steady, Joe, steady; I am afraid you have had the grog too much on board this morning, for I find myself beating about like a ship in a head wind, losing on one tack what I gain on the other. My vessel must be in very bad trim, she won't answer the helm. Steady, Joe, steady—she goes. All right! Jack, my lad, your fin; Kate Markham, my dainty lass, my best service to you; upon my soul, you look prettier than ever; if it is not enough to do an old fellow's heart like mine good to gaze at you, and if it was not that I am afraid Jack would be jealous, the young dog, I would steal a kiss from that blushing cheek, as true as my name's Joe Trennant."

Jack laughed heartily at the old man's humour, and Kate smiled, and after they had both welcomed him. he took his seat on the bench by the side of the young seaman.

"So, Jack, my lad," he said, after a pause, "in two days more you again quit old England's shores, and go to help in giving the enemies of your native land a drubbing. Glorious sport, so welcome to the heart of every true blue jacket. There they ride; old England's wooden walls; and there is the gallant Defiance, your own ship, my boy, to which I know you are as much attached as if it were your home. Oh, I wish this old hulk of mine was in proper trim, wouldn't I be one amongst ye? But, holloa, Kate, my lass, why do you look so sad? Ah! I see how it is; it is all at the thoughts of being so soon parted from your lover."

Kate sighed, and covered her blushing face with her handkerchief

"Well," resumed Joe Trennant, "it is very natural; my poor Mary used to feel the same every time I went away. But do not despair, my good girl, there is the same God at sea as ashore, and the hardy mariner has nothing to fear while he puts his trust in Him. Jack will return safe and sound, depend on it."

"Well said, my old friend" replied our hero, "and I trust that we may yet pass many a happy hour together."

"To be sure we shall, my lad," said Joe; "give me your hand, for you are one after my own heart, and will never disgrace the jacket you wear, or the flag you fight under. But I say, Jack, I have a word or two to say to you."

"And what is that, my friend?" asked the young seaman.

"Why, in the first place," replied Joe, "this is the anniversary of the day when my late mess-mate, poor Jack Junk and myself, saved you from an untimely death. It was a fortunate thing, and Jack used to say that everything seemed to prosper with him after he had taken you under his protection, and I believe it did."

"To that good old man," said Jack, fervently, "my lasting gratitude is due, and I must ever cherish his memory as I do my own life; may the Almighty rest his soul in peace. Would to God that the life of her who was doubtless my mother, could also have been preserved."

"Yes," returned Joe, "it was an unfortunate job, poor creature."

"And did you not find anything upon her which might lead to a discovery as to who she was?" asked Kate.

"No," answered Joe Trennant, "but I am certain from her appearance that she was of no mean station of life. But there is one thing I wish particularly to impart to you on this occasion, Jack."

"Proceed," said our hero, "I am all attention."

"On the death of him who adopted you as his son," continued Joe, "he entrusted to my care a locket containing a portion of hair, and the miniature likeness of a gentleman, which he said he had himself found suspended from your neck, but had not thought proper to reveal the circumstance, though from what motive he did not state. This he desired me to deliver to you on the twenty-first anniversary of the day on which you was saved, and not before; he also requested me to enjoin you to take particular care of it, as it might at some future period not improbably lead to a discovery as to whom your parents were."

Jack took the locket, and after gazing steadfastly at it for a few moments, said—

"I will treasure this as I would my own life, although I fear that there is but little probability, after the lapse of so many years, of my ever being able to discover my origin."

"Why, as for that matter, my boy," said Joe, "I do not know. Many more improbable things than that, have happened. But, at any rate, should that be the case, and I should be living, there would be no difficulty in proving your identity. Who knows but the time may come when Jack Junk, the tar for all weathers, may prove to be a gentleman. Splice my timbers, wouldn't that prove a glorious day for the British Navy? What a jollification we would have to be sure! It makes me feel quite young again at the thought, and, damme, if I do not think, even old cripple as I am, that on such an occasion I could dance as well and as merrily as the best of 'em. But, Kate, my lass, you look as dull as a tar without flip again; never despair. Jack will return safe, loaded with honour and brimful of love, and who knows but that the village bells may shortly afterwards be ringing a merry peal for your wedding?"

"Never!" said a loud and coarse voice, which seemed to proceed from the same spot as the singular warning they had received a short time before.

"Holloa!" cried Joe Trennant, starting up, and gazing in amazement around him, "what the devil's in the wind now? Who spoke?"

Kate had sank back on her seat, greatly surprised and terrified, but Jack, without saying a word, hastened to the spot from whence the voice had evidently issued. He soon returned, and his looks sufficiently testified how astonished and bewildered he was.

"What devil is this, that is playing his pranks with us?" he said. "I can see no one."

"No one!" repeated Joe Trennant; "it was the voice of a man, I'll swear, and not a very agreeable one either. How dare he give old Joe Trennant the lie? The lubber, would that I had him here, I would show him that I have not lost any of my courage, though I have two of my limbs."

"It is a most strange adventure," said our hero, "and I cannot understand it at all, unless it is that some of our friends are having a game with us. Be not alarmed, Kate, for no doubt all will be satisfactorily explained by and by."

Kate did look very pale and trembled, but she made no reply, and her lover then proceeded to relate to Joe what had taken place before, previous to his joining them, to which the old seaman listened with profound attention and increased astonishment.

"Why, shiver my topsails!" he cried, when Jack had concluded, "this is one of the strangest things I ever heard of; but it is only a joke; it can only be a joke, and as such I should not let it alarm me. But I suppose you young lovers do not want the company of an old fellow like me, and as I promised to meet Kit Breezely this afternoon, I will weigh anchor, and make all sail thither. Good bye, for the present, Jack; good day, Kate; keep up your spirits, and depend upon it, your lover will be restored safe to your arms, and you will be as happy as one so good and innocent deserves to be."

Kate sighed, and Jack having shaken the old man cordially by the hand, Joe took his departure; and the lovers retired into the house, where our hero exerted himself to the utmost to raise the spirits of Kate, and to banish the dismal forebodings that had taken possession of her mind. They had not been long there, when Constance Markham, the cousin of Kate, who had been absent from home since the morning, returned home, and was cordially welcomed by Kate and her lover. Constance Markham was a sprightly, good tempered girl, about the same age as her cousin, and possessed of considerable personal attractions. Kate and her were as much attached to each other as if they had been even nearer related, and the same sentiments entertained by one were fully responded to by the other; not a thought that passed within their minds but was in perfect harmony. They were seldom apart, and it was only in consequence of Constance having at last accorded to the pressing invitation of an esteemed friend to pass a day or two with her at the residence of her parents, that she was absent from the joyous festival we have described at the commencement of our tale. Constance was possessed of considerable vocal abilities, and the tones of her voice were of the most rich, flexible, and melodious description, riveting the attention, and delighting all who heard her; and her fair cousin Kate being also a most accomplished musician, which since she had been under the protection of her amiable uncle he had taken the greatest pride to cultivate, she frequently accompanied Constance on the harp in one of those beautiful little simple ballads which she sang so sweetly, and with such taste and feeling, and thus they served to beguile many an hour that might otherwise have proved weary and tedious to Mr. Markham.

"Dear Kate," said Constance, after she had received the welcome of her cousin and our hero "I am afraid that you will have thought me a sad truant in absenting myself so long from your society to-day; but the truth is, that I knew you would have the company of Mr. Junk, and I cordially agree with the adage that in respect to lovers, two is company, and three is none. Heigho! what a delightful thing love must be! I wonder when poor Constance will have the felicity of experiencing its pleasures?"

"Why, my pretty Constance," returned Jack, "do you think that all mankind are such arrant lubbers as to suffer so gay and gentle a craft as yourself to be long tossed about in the ocan of neglect, holding out signals of distress, without hastening to your rescue? No, no, my lass, trust me that some worthy lad will yet take your heart in tow, if he has not done so already, and convoy you safely into the port of wedlock."

"Lor! Mr. Junk," returned Constance, playfully, "you really make a poor simple body like myself blush at such observations. But after all I do think, and I must confess it too, that love must be a most beautiful sensation, for it seems to make people so happy; while on the contrary, your frumpish old maid, and crusty old bachelor, I verily believe are two of the most miserable, as they certainly are the most disagreeable, things in creation. Now I do not pretend to say that I possess a heart of stone, enclosed by walls of adamant,—it is not invulnerable to the softer emotions, and if any smart young sailor, with generous feelings, a cheerful disposition, and a noble spirit, as all true British tars possess—oh, I do love a blue jacket as I love myself—were to hail me, and hoist true colours, but I might be induced to accept him as my captain, so long as he appointed me his chief mate. There now, I rather think that is not such a bad bit of nautical for a land lubber, eh?"

"Bravo, Constance, my lass," said Jack, pressing the delicate hand of the merry girl most cordially; "you are born to be the wife of a sailor, or may I never see salt water again, and happy will be the lad who has the honour to take you in tow."

"Ah! Mr. Jack Junk, as you are so familiarly called," replied Constance, with one of her archest smiles, "you are one of the most accomplished flatterers I ever listened to; but bless me, Kate, how sad you look;—what is the matter with you?"

"The truth is, Constance," answered our hero, "my dear Kate here, is sadly down at heart, because my duty to my king and country will compel me to leave her the day after to morrow; but as I tell her, what is the use of meeting troubles half way? I have braved many dangers ere now, and I do not doubt but that the same Providence which protected me then will not desert me now; victory is sure to crown the British navy, and he shall soon return: in the meantime she will have you and her uncle to console her during the time I am away. So cheer up, dear Kate,

"For grieving's a folly, so let us be jolly,
    If there's perils at sea, there are pleasures on
shore.

"Truly spoken, Mr. Junk," remarked Constance, "I perfectly agree with you. Why, my sweet cousin, you, a sailor's betrothed, and shudder at the idea of his being engaged against the enemies of his country? Oh, I only wish I had been a man, wouldn't I have taken a pleasure in becoming one of the naval heroes of my country. Huzza!—huzza! True blue, for ever! England and victory!"

"Oh, Constance," said Kate, "I would that I could experience the same cheerful spirits that you do on this occasion, but indeed I cannot; sad presentiments cross my mind, which have been strengthened by what has occurred to me and Junk during your absence this afternoon."

"Indeed!" said Constance, with much curiosity, "pray tell me what has alarmed you?"

"Why," said our hero, "the fact is, Constance that we have certainly met with rather a romantic nd mysterious adventure this afternoon."

"Oh, do tell it me," said Constance, eagerly, "I am so dotingly fond of anything of the romantic and mysterious. You have not seen the Flying Dutchman in the harbour, have you? or the Wild Rover of the Seas, who sets all power at defiance? or anything more frightful than that strange man, Mark or Farmer Stanford, as he is commonly called? because if you have not, I do not think that my sweet cousin Kate has had anything to alarm her very seriously."

"Pray reserve your bantering, my lively Constance," said Kate, "until the particulars have been explained to you."

"Mum!" returned the playful Constance, with mock solemnity; "Mr. Junk, I beseech you, proceed. I am all attention."

Jack then related, in a few words, what had taken place, and when he had concluded, Constance said—

"Well, my dear Kate, and is this all that has so seriously disturbed you? Why, I declare, I should quite have delighted in the adventure; but it was singular that you could not discover any one on either of the occasions, Mr Junk."

"Yes, it was rather remarkable," replied our hero, "and whoever it was, they must have been sailing with a favourable wind to get so soon out of sight. But what think you of all this, Constance?"

"Why, take my word for it," replied the latter, "the person you heard upon both occasions was no other than that singular being, old Reuben of the Cliff, who seems to take a delight in such pranks as these."

"Well," said Jack, "I shouldn't wonder but you are right in your surmises, my lass; and if so, there is no cause for any fear; the old fellow is perfectly harmless, I believe."

"Oh, yes," answered Constance, "but still they say that he has uttered many predictions that have never failed to come true. He is a strange old man, and I confess I have often been tempted to pay him a visit in his old hovel in order to try his cabalistic art."

"Has it never been ascertained who he really is?" asked Kate.

"No," replied her cousin; "but it is supposed by many persons that he has formerly been connected with the navy, and that some dreadful calamity at sea has impaired his intellects. He has resided in this neighbourhood for many years, and no one knows from whence he came; he lives, as you know, by the benevolence of those who think proper to consult him on the knowledge he professes to possess, and is seen at all hours, and in the most singular and unexpected places; but when the tempest rages in all its most terrific fury, then does Reuben of the Cliff seem to mingle in his native elements—then is he seen on the summit of the loftiest rock which commands the most extensive view of the ocean, and is near his own wretched hovel, with strange gestures, and form erect, apparently bidding defiance to the flashing lightning and the pattering rain, and exulting in the horrors that reign around. No one on such occasions have ever ventured to interrupt him or to approach him; and notwithstanding the excitement it has naturally caused. no person has yet thought it prudent to question his extraordinary and unaccountable conduct."

"Well," observed Jack, "your account of old Reuben, Constance, much surprises me, though I have heard as much before; but after all, we can only say that he is an eccentric being, and they must be very silly and superstitious who pay any serious attention to what he says."

"Oh, as for that. Mr. Junk," replied Constance. "I do not know, I have heard of many singular predictions to which he has given utterance, and which I have been assured, upon good authority, have almost invariably been realized, and although I am by no means superstitious, I do really think that I shall some day venture to pay him a visit, to hear the fate that is in store for me, if it is only for the fun of the thing. But come K to rid yourself of the sad thoughts which you have suffered to take possession of you; assume your accustomed smile of cheerfulness; my father will soon return home, and we must be prepared to greet him with our usual affectionate welcome."

Kate did indeed struggle with the melancholy feelings that had come over her, and the vivacious conversation of her merry cousin did at length succeed to a certain extent, though still the early separation which must take place between her and her lover, and the adventure of the afternoon, continued to prey upon her mind, and to render the spirits she assumed far from genuine. In about another hour Mr. Markham returned home, and having been made acquainted with all the particulars which have just been related, he took the same view of them as our hero and Constance, and endeavoured to banish all apprehensions from the mind of his fair niece.

"Depend upon it, he said, "this is but one of the wild frolics of old Reuben, and as such deserves no serious attention. However, it is only proper that he should be made to confine his eccentricities within due limits, and not to work upon the fears of the weak and the credulous. Jack, my boy, I am sorry that you are compelled so soon to leave us, but it cannot be helped; I trust that Providence will protect you in all the dangers you will have to encounter, and that only a few months will elapse ere you will be restored to us safe and sound."

"Thank you, Mr. Markham," returned the young seaman, "I do not despair but the wishes you have so kindly expressed will be realized, and that is just what I have endeavoured to impress upon the mind of my dear Kate; but she is so doubtful and alarmed, though to be sure, I ought to love her all the better for that, if that were possible. While I am gone she will be under your protection, and beneath the cheering influence of your consolation, and that of your lovely daughter; I trust that she will be happy, and look forward with hope to the future. Hope is the sailor's sheet anchor, you know, and it should also be that of the girl of his heart."

"True—true, my brave lad," said Mr. Markham, "and I do believe that Kate will learn to support the separation that must unavoidably take place between you with fortitude and confidence. Kate is too much of a woman not to feel animated and proud of the glorious struggle in which her lover is about to take his part. What say you, my love?"

"Dear uncle," answered the damsel, "I should be unworthy of the name I bear did not my heart fully, enthusiastically, respond to all that you have said: did I not glory in the noble achievements of the heroes of my native land, who risk their lives to defend its rights and liberties. I am a seaman's daughter, and I feel proud of the honour."

"Nobly spoken, dear Kate!" ejaculated our hero; "I must have a kiss for that, if it is only for the honour of old England. Bless you, my love, the time will soon slip over;—I shall quickly return, and the whole affair will only appear like the dream of a night."

"But still," said Kate, "you, my dear uncle, and all of you, I am certain, will make every allowance for the weakness I may display on this occasion; I should be unworthy of the love I aspire to. could I be indifferent to the sorrow of this parting."

"Spoken like my own sweet Kate, again," said her lover. pressing her affectionately to his bosom; "those words will be constantly in my memory when I am far away, and they will be my shield in the hour of the greatest danger. But let us for the present think no more of this, but endeavour to await the moment of parting with hopeful hearts. Come, Kate, disperse those melancholy looks, and by your sweet smiles assure me that you are happy."

Kate, encouraged by the words of her lover, did indeed become much more calm than could have been expected, and the conversation being diverted to other topics, the remainder of the evening passed agreeably away, to which the vivacity and wit of Constance Markham served not a little to contribute. At length our hero took his departure,

and after some further conversation, the damsels and Mr. Markham separated for the night. But notwithstanding all the efforts which Kate had made to subdue her feelings while in the presence of her lover and her uncle, the sadness of her spirits returned, if possible, with redoubled force, on her and Constance retiring to their chamber, and seating herself by the window, in at which the silvery moonbeams stole, and danced upon the white sails of the stately vessels in the neighbouring harbour, she burst into tears.

"Why, what a silly girl you are, to be sure, cousin Kate," said Constance, "to take on thus. Come, come, I must not allow this, indeed I must not, especially after the promises you have made to me and your lover."

"Ah! Constance," replied her cousin, "you speak without experience, kindly and gratefully though I receive your affectionate remonstrances. As yet your tender heart is not fixed upon one endearing object, whose safety you value more than your own existence, and therefore it is impossible that you can duly appreciate the feelings that agitate my bosom now that the time so rapidly approaches when I and he to whom my whole affections are devoted, are about to separate, perhaps never to meet again."

"Indeed you pay no very flattering compliment to my susceptibility, Kate," said Constance; "but indeed you mistake me, for I fancy myself a remarkably clever judge in such matters, although I have never yet had the felicity of experiencing the tender passion—worse luck for me; poor neglected one! heigho!—I fancy it must be a very delightful sensation; and I suppose my turn will come some day, and when it does, Kate, you shall see with what womanly heroism I will bear the trials of the torturing god!"

In spite of her feelings, Kate could not help smiling at the humour of her playful cousin, and Constance at last succeeded in bringing her to a state of composure.

"But, dear Constance," she observed, after a few moments reflection, "what you have stated this evening respecting old Reuben, has, I confess, excited my curiosity. You said that you should like to visit him, in order that you might put his prophetic powers to the test."

"Nothing would please me better," replied her cousin; "it would really be delightful, if it were only for the romance of the thing."

"You do not think that there is any harm to be apprehended from him?" said Kate.

"Harm! not the least: poor old man," replied Constance; "and who knows but that he might tell us something that might be of the most inestimable advantage to us? For instance, he might reveal to me who is to be my future husband; whether I am to be the happy mother of a lovely family, possessing all their parents' personal beauties and intrinsic virtues, a-hem! That would be delightful, would it not?—What say you,!Kate—shall we visit the old gentleman in his hovel?"

"I feel a most unaccountable curiosity to do so," said Kate, "and yet, should it ever afterwards become known to our friends that we had done so, should we not be laughed at for our folly and superstition?"

"But what occasion have they to know anything at all about it, my dear cousin, if we only keep our own council?" answered Constance; "come, Kate, say the word; shall we go?"

Kate hesitated; but it was evident that she was anxious to agree to the wishes of Constance' notwithstanding some fears and misgivings that beset her mind.

"Ah! I see how it is," observed Constance, "you cannot resist your curiosity; as for myself I am all impatience and anxiety for the adventure, so that point is settled. To-morrow morning, when we take our customary walk, and before the arrival of your lover, we will make our way at once to the old man's hovel, and try whether he is possessed of the gift of foresight that he pretends to be. There is nothing to fear I am certain there is not."

"Well," said Kate, after a pause, "I will e'en venture, although at the same time, I cannot help thinking it is a piece af folly."

"At any rate," remarked her cousin, " it will serve to amuse us, and cannot be productive of any harm. For my own part, if all the tale, that are circulated concerning old Reuben be true I expect to hear wonders. But mind you, Kate you must not mention a word of our intentions to my father in the morning, or he would certainly prohibit us from going."

Kate promised to obey her injunctions, and their plans being all arranged, they retired to bed. But Kate passed a restless night; her imagination was disturbed by the most troublesome dreams, which she was unable in any way to connect, and she awoke in the morning unrefreshed. The morning repast over, Kate and her cousin sallied forth, and after taking their usual path, in order to deceive Mr. Markham, if he should happen to be watching them, they struck off abruptly, and made their way direct towards the cliffs, among which the hovel of Reuben was situated. As they approached nearer towards it, Kate felt her resolution begin to fail her, and had Constance no have been with her, she would have abandone her designs and turned back. Constance, however, read her thoughts, and by every persuasion in her power, urged her on.

"It would be madness to retreat now that we have thus far proceeded," she said; "besides, what have we to fear? We never injured this mysterious and singular being, and therefore what wish can he have to harm us?"

"But may he not be offended at our intruding upon his privacy?" suggested Kate.

"No," answered her companion, "does he not live by the exercise of his extraordinary arts, and has he not been visited frequently by almost ever person in the neighbourhood? I declare I cannot rest until my curiosity is gratified. So let u proceed, Kate, and boldly pursue this adventur to its termination."

Kate raised no further objection, and hastening on their way, they soon afterwards arrived at the base of the cliffs, among which the hovel of old Reuben was situated. It was a wild and dismal scene, and the waves dashed with a deafening sound against the sides of this natural barrier, near which it eemed almost impossible for any human being to exist. Kate again hesitated, and regretted that she had given her consent to accompany her cousin on such a mysterious and singular errand; but Constance took her hand and led her forward towards a rude path which led among the cliffs to the wretched abode in which the old man resided. It was difficult to ascend, even to those who were accustomed to it, and therefore took them s me time to accomplish it, and they were also frequently compelled to pause to rest themselves. At length they arrived in sight of the hovel, and a wretched looking place it was, in which it seemed to be almost impossible that any human being could exist. The roof was thatched with straw, and small loop-holes in the blackened walls supplied both the place of casement, and the means of ventilation. The entrance to it was a low wooden door, which was standing partly open, and before which the two lovely cousins now stood, in order to collect their thoughts before they proceeded any further.

"What a singular fancy any person must have,' observed Constance, " to choose such a wild habitation as this."

"O, let us return," said Kate, " for my heart misgives me."

"Nonsense," replied her companion; " shall we turn cowards now we have proceeded so far? for my own part, Kate, I can tell you that my curiosity is more excited than ever, and I am determined to gratify it, let the consequences be whatever they may. Courage, courage, and my word for it, no harm will come to us. Now to test the power of this wonderful necromancer."

Thus saying, she drew the timid Kate towards the door, at which she knocked, and waited anxiously to receive an answer; but none was returned and all was perfectly silent within.

"He is from home." whispered Kate; " so let us defer our visit till a future time,"

Constance motioned her to silence, and again knocked, more loudly than before, but with no better success; and before Kate could make any offer to prevent her, she thrust the door wide open and entered the hovel, forcng her cousin after her. At first it was so dark that they could not distinguish anything, but at length the dim light admitted at one of the loop-holes before-mentioned, revealed to them the figure of the singular old man, seated in one corner, his chin resting on the top of his staff, and his small but penetrating eyes fixed steadfastly on the faces of his fair visitors. He did not, however, offer to move or to speak a word, and Constance and Kate stood in the centre of the miserable room, irresolute whether to advance or retreat, though Kate would willingly have preferred the latter. A pause of some moments ensued; and still the old man retained his posture and did not offer to speak. Constance at length mustered resolution, and in a firm voice said—"Old man, we pray you pardon this intrusion, but hearing of your marvellous powers, we would fain consult you on our future destiny."

Reuben slowly arose from his seat, and advancing towards them, he paused, and once more gazed earnestly upon them.

"Fair, fair, as innocence itself," he at last ejaculated in a solemn voice; "pity that sorrow should ever be destined to hold dominion o'er two such gentle and guileless bosoms."

Kate shuddered and retreated back a few paces, and even Constance was somewhat startled and daunted by his words; but she remained firm in her determination, and still retained her hold of her cousin's hand, to prevent her from hurrying from the place, which she saw she was inclined to do.

"You would penetrate into the secrets of futurity," resumed the old man; "you would know the destiny that is in store for you; be it so; no person ever applied to me in vain, much as the idle and incredulous may laugh at and deride my power."

As he thus spoke, he lighted a small lamp, and the fair cousins had then a more distinct view of the singular place in which they were. It contained no articles of furniture but a low stool on which Reuben had been seated, and a rudely constructed table, on which stood a globe; and in one corner of the room was a dirty looking mattrass, which was stretched upon the floor without any covering. On the walls were inscribed several mystical characters in chalk, and these were the only things that were worthy of notice. The old man advanced towards a door at the further end of the room, which he unlocked; and holding up the lamp, Kate and her fair cousin, to their astonishment, beheld a flight of stone steps hewn out of the solid rock, and apparently leading to some subterranean apartment.

"Follow me," said Reuben, "and your wishes shall be granted."

Kate shruk back and shuddered.

"Fear not," said the old man, "Reuben of the Cliff never yet did harm to mortal being, and the innocent are the objects of his protection. Follow me, I say, and fear not."

Still Kate hesitated, and was anxious to retire from the place; but Constance, who was encouraged and re-assured by the old man's words, pressed her hand significantly, and urged her forward; and they at once entered the gloomy place. Old Reuben slowly began to descend the steps, frequently looking behind him, in order to ascertain whether Kate and her cousin were following; and as the faint rays emitted by the lamp he carried in his hand fell upon his sallow and wrinkled countenance, they imparted to it a most unearthly appearance, and increased the fears of our heroine, who now more bitterly then ever regretted her having yielded to the persuasions of Constance, and heartily wished herself safe at home again. Notwithstanding the assertions of old Reuben, and his apparent harmlessness, might he not still be acting the part of the hypocrite merely to carry on some nefarious and secret designs? Smugglers and pirates, she well know, in secret infested the coast; it had even been rumoured that the daring and desperate pirate chief of the Raven, had his spies and secret haunts in that neighbourhood, notwithstanding all the vigilance that had been used to discover him; and was it not possible that the singular old man might be in some way or other connected with him, and only assumed his present mysterious character in order to drown suspicion? All these thoughts passed rapidly in in the mind of Kate, as she tremblingly, with her cousin, followed the old man down the rugged steps into an abyss which seemed interminable; but she was fearful to give expression to her feelings; and as they had thus far proceeded, she well knew that there was no other alternative but to await the result of the adventure whatever it might be. The way they was pursuing was circuitous, and it was evident that they had now proceeded to a considerable distance from the hovel of their mysterious conductor, and must be several fathoms below the surface of the earth, and at some distance along the coast from the point at which they started; but at length they paused at a small landing or lodge of rock, and the old man again raising the lamp above his head, they beheld another flight of steps similar to those which they had already descended, but all was buried in the most impenetrable darkness below. Kate trembled still more, and even Constance, in spite of all her efforts to the contrary, could not help feeling some misgivings, and wished the adventure fairly over.

"Whither are you leading us, mysterious man?" Kate at length found courage to demand; "my doubts of the honesty of your intentions increase; I will proceed no further."

"And wherefore, maiden, should you doubt Reuben of the Cliff, who never yet was known to do harm to mortal being?" said the old man, in tones of mild reproach; "he sought not you—he invited you not—to his secret haunt; you come of your own free will, and, therefore, why should you now impugn the motives of his conduct? You would peruse the pages of the Book of Fate, I can reveal to you the past and the future. Ah! maiden, there are many strange things it would be well for you to know; do not then hastily reject the service I offer you, and which will guide you in your future conduct. In a few hours, and he who owns your heart will be far away from you on the measureless waters of the deep; but you have terrible enemies on shore against whom you should be warned. Follow, then, and fear not."

"I do not doubt the integrity of your motives," remarked Constance; "but if it is in your power to reveal anything to us, why did you not do so in your habitation above; what necessity was there for your bringing us to such a place as this, the bare aspect of which is sufficient to excite a feeling of awe and terror in the minds of strangers?"

"Constance Markham," replied Reuben, "the reasons I have for my conduct must not be questioned. Let it suffice you and your fair cousin that I am your friend, and would render you service; do you decline my offer? Say that you do, and

you are welcome to depart immediately, in the same way you entered."

There was so much apparent sincerity in the tones in which the old man spoke these words, that Kate and her companion were re-assured, and motioning Reuben to proceed, they prepared to follow him in silence, fully resolved to see the issue of this extraordinary and romantic adventure. The old man made no further observation, and directly led the way down the other flight of steps, which were exceedingly steep and narrow; and by the dim light which the rays of the lamp emitted, rendered it necessary that the greatest caution should be used, to prevent them from stumbling. The atmosphere was so close and sultry, that Kate and her cousin could scarce'y breathe; but Reuben seemed to experience not the least inconvenience, and led the way with an easy and even agile step. At length they alighted in a low pa sage, which seemed not to have been excavated by human hands, and the rocky sides of which were dripping with unwholesome moisture.

"Have we much farther to go?" demanded Constance, eagerly.

"No damsel," answered Reuben; "the end of this passage will bring us to the place of our destination. It is there that Reuben of the Cliff works his mysterious orgies; many think me mad; but they deceive themselves. But we waste that time which is precious. Follow me!"

His observations encouraged them, and the old man led the way along the passage, until he suddenly stopped before a rudely-constructed door, which was fastened. He took a key from his pocket and unlocked it, and to the astonishment of Kate and her cousin, revealed to them a spacious vault or cavern, hung round with black drapery, on which was worked in white, several mystical characters. The earth was strewn with seaweed, and in the centre was a table covered with crimson clyth, on which was a globe and several mathematical instruments, together with a ponderous volume, which was lying open, and the pages of which revealed a number of singular hieroglyphics. At the further end of the cavern was a long blue curtain, which seemed to conceal some particular object from the view. The astonishment and curiosity of the damsels increased; and when they marked the solemnity of Reuben's demeanour, and noticed all the remarkable characteristics of the place, they could not help feeling a sensation of awe, and awaited the result of the adventure with anxiety and impatience. Reuben seemed to read the thoughts that were passing in their minds, and for some moments he remained silent, and gazed earnestly upon them.

"Damsels," he said at last, in solemn and impressive accents; "you have sought the knowledge of Reuben of the Cliff; you would penetrate the secret of the past and the future; do you place confidence in my power to gratify your wishes?"

Kate was unable to reply, but her cousin said:—

"We do; and I pray you, old man, to proceed, and no longer keep us in suspense, for we are all impatience to hear you."

"Be firm, then," said Reuben, "and interrupt me not."

As he spoke, he placed the lamp in such a position, that its feeble rays were completely obscured and the cavern was involved in profound darkness. Kate clung closer to her cousin, and the most uncontrolable fear took possession of her bosom; but Constance on the contrary felt firm, and awaited what was about to take place with the most breathless impatience. A death-like silence of some moments ensued, and they were unable to distinguish the person of the old man but at length strange mutterings and incoherent sounds saluted their ears, and which seemed to proceed from all parts of the cavern, and increased their astonishment and awe.

"Constance Markham," at length they heard the voice of Reuben ejaculate; "at present it is ordained that I should disclose to you no more than that you will be exposed to temptation; that you will be surrounded by the snares of the guilty and from which it will be well for you if you can escape. Let this warning suffice you, damsel, and treat it not lightly, for the words of Reuben of the Cliff never yet failed to come true. Kate Markham would you have revealed to you the dark deeds of the past?"

"Mysterious man," said our astonished heroine, "my heart misgives me; better had I remain in ignorance of that which may but embitter my future days. Let us begone, Constance: I pray you do not hesitate, for a deadly sensation of horror oppresses me while we remain here. Come, come."

"Nay, Maiden," said the old man, "now you have ventured thus far do not let any foolish weakness induce you to reject the knowledge I tender you, and which may prove of such infinite service to you. Behold!"

A whistling sound like a current of air passing through the cavern, followed the words of Reuben; and then a sickly light faintly illuminated the place; and Kate and her cousin, instinctively directing their eyes towards the end of the cavern, beheld the curtain, by the side of which Reuben stood, gradually disappear, seemingly without being touched, and to their utter amazement, they beheld a large mirror covering the whole space, and which seemed to be enveloped in a thin and shadowey mist. The old man waved his staff above his head, and the mist slowly dispersed, and human forms and other objects became indistinctly visible. Gradually they became more perfect; and then to the astonishment and almost utter incredulity of Kate and her cousin, they beheld the deck of a vessel, crowded with seamen, and against the sides of which dashed the wild waves of the ocean. Suddenly one of the seaman, apparently at the command of the captain, whose features they could not distinguish, was seized by several others, and struggled in vain to release himself. His features were as plainly revealed as if what they beheld was life and reality, and the emotion and astonishment of Kate may be imagined, when she beheld the exact resemblance of her father. She uttered a piercing shriek of terror, and clung still closer to her scarcely less agitated companion.

"Courage, damsel," said Reuben, "and learn the fearful truth."

Kate gazed appauled, and the next moment she beheld a board poised over the ship's side, on which the form which represnted that of her father mounted with a bold step, and proceeded to the end. She saw him precipitated into the sea; she beheld him struggling desperately with the billows, and endeavouring to reach the vessel. He gained it; a rope was thrown out to him by one of the seamen; he caught it, and clambered up the ships side and w about to leap ondeck, when the tall figure of the captain, whose features were still invisible to them, seized an axe, and as his hand was placed upon the scantling, with one blow he severed it from his body, and with a ghastly look he plunged again into the ocean, and the waves closed over him for ever. Horror-struck at this extraordinary vision, which the now apparently supernatural powers of Reuben of the Cliff had conjured up, Kate Markham uttered a loud scream, and sunk almost fainting into the arms of her scarcely less-agitated cousin, and the cavern again became enveoped in complete darkness.

"Such was the fate of Horace Markham, your father, Kate," said the deep-toned and almost unearthly voice of Reuben; "do you any longer doubt my power?"

"Oh, horror! horror!" gasped forth Kate; "but tell me, mysterious man, who was the monster that perpetrated that bloody and inhuman deed?"

"One from whom you and your lover are yet destined to experience many troubles," replied Reuben.

"His name?" eagerly demanded Constance; "Heaven calls aloud for justice on the murderer."

"The time has not come to reveal it," answered the old man; "you must for the present rest satisfied with that which I have already disclosed to you. Kate Markham, turn we now from the dreary past to the future."

Neither Kate or Constence could speak a word, so completely astonished and astounded were they by all they had seen and heard. Reuben once more removed the lamp from the place where he had concealed it, and they then perceived that the curtain was again drawn across the end of the cavern, and everything remained the same as when they had first entered. Reuben took his place behind the table, and seemed to consult the pages of the mystic volume with much earnestness, and Kate and Constance watched his actions with the deepest attention and anxiety.

"Kate Markham," at length said the singular old man, "it is written in the book of fate, that he to whom your affections are devoted is doomed to encounter the most terrible perils by sea and land; storms are gathering that shall overwhelm his happiness, and in which it will be your lot to participate. Oh, maiden, many are the woes that are in store for you both, and which no earthly power can avert. Your father's murderer will pursue you to the brink of destruction; and it is alone by firmness and placing your trust in the goodness of Providence that your innocence can escape his diabolical arts and machinations. To-morrow the British fleet sets sail from these shores, and many and bitter are the sorrows you are destined to experience, ere it again returns. Such are the predictions of the supposed maniac, Reuben of the Cliff, and they will be fulfilled; aye, fulfilled to the very letter."

"Oh, hold! hold! for mercy's sake, strange being," ejaculated the deeply-agitated Kate; "I can hear no more. Let us begone, dear Constance: would to heaven that my unhappy curiosity had not led me hither."

"Mysterious man," said Constance, who was completely bewildered by what had taken place, and could scarcely believe that she was in her senses; "have you anything more to reveal to us?"

"No more at present," replied Reuben. "Bear in mind what I have told you, and should you at any future time require my advice, you have but to seek it and it shall be granted to you, now that you have sufficiently tested my powers you will no longer doubt them. Follow me!"

The extraordinary old man took up the lamp as he spoke, and again leading the way, Kate and her cousin followed him in silence, and completely overpowered by astonishment. After a time they once more gained the hovel, and Reuben, resuming the same attitude in which they had beheld him on their entrance, motioned them to depart; and Constance, taking the arm of her cousin, led her from the place, and they slowly made their way from the cliff, and bent their steps towards home. It would indeed be a difficult task properly to describe the feelings of Kate after this romantic and surprising adventure, as she proceeded towards home; and Constance was scarcely less astonished and agitated than herself.

"Well," she remarked, endeavouring to force a smile, "I must confess that this morning's adventure has nearly cured me of my scepticism; and henceforth I shall almost be inclined to believe in the existence of wizards and witches. Reuben is certainly a most mysterious and extraordinary man, and I am at a loss to fathom his real character. But how distressed you look, my dear Kate; come, come—you mustnot suffer the events of this morning to make too deep an impression on you; for, after all, it may only be some cunning device of old Reuben's to impose upon our credulity. What he revealed to us, extraordinary though it certainly was, could only have been accomplished by some mechanical contrivance, though I must acknowledge it was exceedingly clever."

"Oh, Constance," returned her cousin, I know not what to think; my brain is completely bewildered. Could anything be more true to reality than the fearful scene which Reuben exhibited to us? My God! and is it possible that my poor father can have met with the horrible fate which that singular being has represented to us? My blood freezes at the thought."

"Try to banish it from your mind, Kate," said Constance, "and leave it to time to explain everything."

"Ah, Constance," sighed our heroine, "I have often had a strange presentiment that my poor father came not fairly by his death, for we never could gain any satisfactory account of him from any of the sailors who were on board the same vessel with him; and the captain, you know—Captain Granfield was his name—disappeared in a most mysterious manner, and has never been heard of since."

"It certainly is very mysterious," observed Constance; "but do not suffer it to agitate your mind! for if any foul crime have been committed, depend upon it that Providence, in its own wise time, will bring it to light, and will not permit the guilty to escape from punishment."

"I cannot conquer the feelings that distract my mind," said Kate; "frequently have visions, similar to that we have this morning witnessed, haunted me in my slumbers; and they do but serve to strengthen the horrible apprehensions which the events of this morning have excited in my breast."

"You must struggle with your feelings, dear Kate," said her cousin; "indeed you must. But for the present, I think it would be advisable to keep the strange and unexpected adventure of this morning a secret confined to our own breasts. My father would only chide us for venturing near the hovel of old Reuben, and probably consider that we were only suffering under some weakness and delusion of the senses."

"I will be guided by you, Constance," said her cousin, "although it is impossible that I can think so lightly of this extraordinary business as you affect to do. And then with what feelings of dread do I anticipate my separation from my lover to-morrow; alas! I fear that the predictions of old Reuben will be fearfully realized, and that the greatest troubles are in store for us. Would that I were now his wife and were permitted to share with him all the dangers he will have to encounter on the stormy deep, and in the battle's heat."

"Nay, my dear Kate," said Constance, "again I tell you that you must not encourage such sad thoughts as these; but strive to look forward with hope and cheerfulness to the future. Remember the words of the song 'There's a sweet little cherub that sits up aloft to keep watch for the life of poor Jack,' and depend upon it, that they will be realized on this occasion. Oh, my sweet cousin, you would be unworthy to become a sailor's bride if you were to indulge in such ideas as these. Jack Junk is as brave as he is honourable, and, to speak nautically, I am confident that although he may frequently be cast upon a lee-shore, Providence will never suffer him to founder. So cheer up, Kate, and prepare yourself to meet the separation of to-morrow with womanly fortitude. See

the noble vessels in the harbour, and the proud Defiance rides pre-eminently amongst them all. Oh, it is a glorious sight, and my heart throbs with enthusiasm as I gaze upon it."

"Alas!" sighed our heroine, "when I think of the frightful scenes in which those stately vessels will so shortly be engaged; the many brave fellows that may perish in the dreadful carnage; and that Jack, my dear Jack may be destined to be one of them; my heart sinks within me."

"Fie, Kate," returned Constance; "you a sailor's daughter, and give way to such feelings of weakness as these? But come, let us drop the subject, and endeavour to calm your feelings, so that you may not excite the suspicions of my father when we meet him."

Kate returned no answer, and they continued their way towards home in silence.

CHAPTER IV.

THE PARTING OF THE LOVERS.—THE SAILING OF THE FLEET.—THE STORM.

THE extraordinary scene we have described to have taken place in the hovel of old Reuben of the Cliff in the preceding chapter, may appear to the reader exaggerated and improbable, but it will be satisfactorily explained in the course of our tale. There was a numerous party of sailors and their sweethearts assembled that morning at the Ship, and it seemed as if they were resolved to enjoy themselves, as this was the last day that they would have an opportunity of meeting together for some time. The largest and best room in the inn had been prepared for their accommodation; old Kit Breezely was, as usual, all bustle and altivity in his business; and Joe Trennant shone conspicuous amongst the guests, and created continual mirth by the jokes he cracked and the yarns he spun.

"Belay there!" shouted the veteran; "what cheer, messmates?—yo, ho! Here you are all safe a-board in the twiring of a hand-spike. Now, my hearties, what cheer? Come push about the grog—pipe all hands for mischief. No sad looks to-day, for it may be a long time before we shall meet again; and therefore we must give the grog no quarter at parting. What say you, Kit, you old son of a sea-cork?"

"You are right, Joe," answered Kit, "as you always are; but what say you, lads and lasses; I suppose you will have a dance. It is never too early to commence mirth."

"Ay ay! a dance! a dance!" shouted two or three of the sailors, in a breath.

"Hold! hold!" cried Joe Trennant; "Jack Junk is not alongside of us yet; and for any of you to shake a toe without him would be like going to sea without a jolly-boat."

"Ay," observed one of sailors, "there is no beginning the dance without Jack Junk; though I say it, for a hop and a hearty laugh, there isn't his equal."

"His equal!" repeated Joe; "no, no; I'd back Jack Junk for anything against any lad in the British navy. I suppose he has gone to fetch his sweetheart, and I dare say we shall see them crowding all sail this way presently."

At that moment there was a loud scream heard outside, which seemed to proceed from no great distance from the house, and the guests all started towards the doors and windows.

"Hollo!" cried Joe Trennant; "what's in the wind now? Signals of distress! Clear the gangway and give us sea-room. Crowd all sail, messmates, and bear down upon the enemy, whoever he may be. Yo, ho! yo, ho!"

Several sailors, with old Joe Trennant at their head, hobbling along as fast as he could, immediately left the house, and hastened towards the spot from whence they had heard the cries; and they had not proceeded far when they beheld Jack Junk supporting the insensible form of Kate on his arm, engaged with Mark Stanford in a desperate combat, whilst Constance was standing by, wringing her hands, and making the air resound again with her cries for help.

"Sink my mizen top," exclaimed Joe, "my boy Jack yard arm and yard-arm with that infernal swab; what's the meaning of this? Crowd all sail, my lads, and lay your grappling irons on the rascally pirate! Yo, ho! Jack Junk ahey!"

"Yes, Joe;" replied our hero, "and it is lucky for him that my time for cruising about this coast is so short, or damme he should pay dearly for his tricks; however, the time will come, I have no doubt, when I shall have an opportunity to overhaul him, and I will pour such a broadside in upon his black looking old hulk that will shake every timber. I was bearing down towards the ship, when I heard signals of distress; and reering round a point, I beheld the fellow yard-arm and yard arm with my innocent Kate. Poor girl, he has terribly frightened her; but it is fortunate I happened to be within hail, or there is no knowing what might have happened."

"The d—d scoundrel!" said Joe, warmly; "however, it is all well as it happens, and it strikes me that the swab will not have the courage to hoist his colours again for some time to come. If I am not very much mistaken, this Farmer Stanford, as he calls himself, is not what he represents himself to be; but if a sharp look-out is kept on his actions, his real character will some time or other be discovered. But come, let us hasten to the ship, and see to the recovery of Poor Kate. Constance, my lass, give old Joe Trennant your arm, and he will pilot you safe into port."

Constance, who was much alarmed at what had taken place, complied with the old man's request without making use of any observation, and Jack still supporting the insensible form of his lover in his arms, they made their way to the house of old Kit Breezely, where everything was done to bring about the recovery of Kate, which was speedily effected, and beholding herself in the company of her lover and her friends, she became more composed, though the extraordinary events of the morning, particularly those which had occurred in the hovel of Reuben of the cliff, continued to distract her mind, and to excite her apprehensions of the future.

"My sweet Kate," said our hero,, "how happy do I feel to think I happened to be sailing close at hand when that cowardly shark bore down against you. The fellow has the impudence of the devil, but he must look out, or he may chance to have to dearly pay for his daring. The lubber! to dare to raise his thoughts towards my pretty and innocent Kate. Why damme, there is not a man in the whole British Navy from the poorest devil before the mast to the Lord High Admiral himself, who would presume to rival Jack Junk in the affections of that dear girl to whom his very soul is devoted. But cheer up, my lass, after this slight squall, and look forward to fair weather and a favourable voyage till we anchor safe in the port of matrimony."

Kate sighed, and for a moment hid her blushing face on the shoulder of her lover.

The combat was continuing with unabated spirit and determination on both sides, neither of them being armed with anything more than sticks; but the observations of old Joe Trennant, which were spoken in the loudest tones, immediately reached the ears of Mark Stanford, and looking up, and beholding the fearful odds he would have to contend against if he remained, he considered, under the circumstances, that discretion would be the better part of valour; and giving utterance to a

dreadful oath, he fixed upon the young seaman a threatening look of vengeance, and flying precipitately from the spot, he was quickly out of sight.

"Why, Jack, my young sea-lion," said old Joe Trennant, when he had arrived at the spot where the combat had just taken place, "what's the meaning of all this? Has the lubber dared again to insult your pretty trim built vessel?"

"Alas! Jack," she ejaculated, "the events of this morning have greatly distressed me; and when I reflect how soon the time will arrive when we must part, the dangers to which you will be exposed, and the probability that we may never meet again, I find it impossible to conquer the melancholy forebodings that have taken possession of my bosom."

"Avast—avast, my own sweet Kate," returned our hero, "you must not give way to these sad thoughts; depend upon it, the great commander above will watch over my safety for your sake, and we shall soon meet again. Besides, you will have nothing to fear from the fellow, Mark Stanford; he will not dare to insult you while I am away, for will you not be under the protection of your amiable uncle and your other friends; and who shall dare to entertain a thought against your happiness?"

"Very true," said Kate; "but still, in spite of all my efforts to the contrary, I cannot help feel the greatest dread of Mark Stanford, whom I can never look upon without an instinctive and unaccountable shudder of horror. I feel confident that he is not what he pretends to be, and I have a strange and powerful presentiment that he is destined to be the cause of much misery to us both, and all those connected with us. Would to Heaven that he would quit this neighbourhood, and never return to it again."

"Nay, my lass," said her lover, "indeed you alarm yourself unnecessarily; Stanford is an arrant rascal, I have no doubt of it, but he will not be bold enough to try to put the wishes he entertains towards you into effect by force; for he must be well aware that it could only end in his own defeat and destruction. But come, let us toss dull care overboard, and pipe all hands for mirth. Our friends are assembled here to-day to make merry, for it is the last time we shall have an opportunity of doing so for some months to come, and I know my Kate and her pretty and lively cousin here will not refuse to join them in their cheerful sports."

"Indeed," replied our heroine, "I am in no humour for mirth, and I fear that my presence will but cast a gloom upon the otherwise happy guests. My uncle will expect our return and——"

"Avast—avast there, Kate," interrupted Jack, "I will not hear any excuses; as for your uncle, I will despatch a messenger to him to apprize him where you are, and to invite him to join us, which I know he will do most willingly. Come, my lass, cheer up; bless your pretty eyes, which always sets my heart in a glow whenever I encounter their rays. By heaven! there is not such another figure-head as my bonny Kate's in all his Majesty's navy."

"Right, my lad," cried old Joe Trennant, shaking his hand; "it is a craft that does one's eyes good to look upon; see how gracefully she sails. Come, Kate, my lass, what's the use of hoisting signals of distress in fair weather? Take the advice of your lover, and get the weather-guage of care. Now, lads and lasses, pipe all hands for a dance."

Constance, who had recovered from the alarm into which she had been thrown by the daring and insolent conduct of Mark Stanford, joined her persuasions to those of our hero and the others; and notwithstanding it was most repugnant to her feelings, Kate was at last prevailed upon, and joined her lover in the dance, though her mind was busily occupied with the extraordinary events of the morning, and she could not help giving way to the most dismal forebodings as to the future. After Mark Stanford had so abruptly quitted the spot where he had encountered his rival, bursting with rage and disappointment, and muttering curses to himself, he walked on, meditating on his future plans, but did not feel inclined to return home at present.

"The scornful beauty," he muttered, "she thinks to daunt me in my designs, and to compel me to abandon my wishes; but Hugh Granfield, the pirate, is not the man to be frightened from the execution of any purpose on which he has fixed his mind; and he swears that he will never rest until he has got you securely in his power. Jack Junk, too, the time shall come when you will know me better, and I will fully gratify the feelings of hatred and deadly revenge I entertain towards you. Let me wait patiently, and I do not doubt but the triumph will be mine. To-morrow and you will be separated from her you love, perhaps never more to meet again; and when Kate Markham is deprived of your protection, I shall have every opportunity of putting my designs into execution. What is to prevent me from conveying her on board my gallant vessel? and then will not my triumph be complete? The thought delights me, and fully repays me for all the scorn and insult I have received from her and her lover. She views me with feelings of instinctive horror, and shudders in my presence; I marvel not at it: it is the voice of nature that whispers to her; but what would be her feelings did she but know that in me she beholds her father's murderer!— But that thought daunts me, and fills my mind with terror; let me abandon it, and endeavour to forget the bloody and inhuman deed. Horace Markham, will your foul murder ever be avenged?—Psha! no more of this, or I shall become as weak as an infant. Such feelings as these ill become the daring and reckless Rover of of the Seas."

Looking up, he now found himself on the cliffs; and pausing and folding his arms, he stood and gazed earnestly at the wide waters of the ocean which rolled below, and sparkled in the bright rays of the sun, which was now shining in full meridian splendour. With mingled feelings he contemplated the various stately vessels that were riding at anchor, and from them his eyes wandered towards another ship, which was anchored a short distance from the fleet, and had a stately and noble appearance; and as he fixed his eyes upon it, smiles of satisfaction and triumph animated his features.

"My gallant vessel," he soliloquized; "how proudly do you ride upon the billows, whose fury you have so often braved. You are surrounded by those enemies who would delight in your destruction, but who little suspect your real character; or that the terrible Rover of the Seas, who has hitherto set them all at defiance, is so near a neighbour of theirs. Ha!—ha!—ha!—Who shall be able to baffle the designs or crush the power of Hugh Granfield, the Pirate Chief?"

He started, for at that moment he heard a malicious laugh, and fearful that some person might have overheard what he had said, he turned hastily round, and to his astonishment and confusion he beheld old Reuben standing near him, and supporting himself as usual on his staff.

"How now, old man?" he demanded hastily and peremptorily; "what brings you here?—What would you with me?"

"Merely to congratulate you on the sanguine anticipations you entertain of the future, Hugh Granfield," replied the old man; "but think you that the inhuman pirate will for ever be doomed to triumph? Do you flatter yourself with the idea that retribution will never overtake the murderer

of the unfortunate and ill-fated Horace Markham? Tremble, villain, for the time will come when all the terrible deeds you have committed will recoil upon yourself, and the fate you have so long merited will at last overtake you in the most terrible form. Reuben of the Cliff tells you this, and his words will be realized as surely as your pirate barque, the pretended fair trader, the Enterprise, rides yonder at anchor."

"Babling old hound," cried the astonished and exasperated Stanford; "who are you? and by what means have you become acquainted with my secrets? Tell me, I command you, and if it is gold that you require to keep a still tongue, take it, and begone to your hovel."

"Reuben of the Cliff is not used to be commanded but to command," replied the old man; "it is not gold he seeks, but justice against the guilty: and he will have it too,—mark my words, Hugh Granfield, the dreaded captain of the Raven—he will have it."

"Old man," said the pirate, in a hoarse voice, "have you no fear for yourself? Do you dare to threaten me?"

"Dare to threaten you!" repeated Reuben, scornfully; "ha!—ha!—ha!—Do you dare to brave the power of Reuben of the cliff, whose bare word would hang you like a dog? Remember Horace Markham; let his ghastly countenance as he plunged into the deep to which you, monster, consigned him, continually haunt your imagination, sleeping or awking, and tremble; for the hour of retribution will come, and that when you least expect it, and are the more unprepared to meet it."

"By all the infernal host," exclaimed Stanford, passionately, "I cannot endure this; you know my secrets, and have presumed to threaten me. Beware! for I may deem it necessary for my own security to adopt such measures as may give you bitter cause to repent your boldness."

"Fool!" cried Reuben; "I mock at and defy you. At any time it is in my power to bring you to destruction, and to make your atrocious guilt manifest to the world: but at present it will not answer my purpose to do so, and for a time I suffer you to go in fancied security. But, mark me, the eyes of Reuben of the Cliff will be continually watching you; there is not a single action of yours can escape his knowledge; you have no means of evading him whenever he thinks proper to betray you, and——."

"Liar!" cried the enraged Stanford, suddenly rushing upon the old man, and grasping him fiercely by the throat; "at any rate, I have the power to stop your garrulous tongue, and to render all your further designs abortive, and thus to serve my own safety."

"Rash fool, release your hold!" said the old man: "would you commit another murder?"

"Yes," replied Stanford; "I would rid myself of one who is likely to prove so dangerous an enemy. You have brought this all upon yourself, and must take the consequences."

They struggled violently together, for Reuben was a wonderfully powerful man for his age, and Stanford soon found that unless he strained every nerve, he would be likely to prove more than a match for him. They reached the edge of the cliff, when Reuben's strength seemed to increase, as that of Stanford became exhausted. He released himself from his hold, and bending the form of the pirate completely over the edge of the cliff, he had him completely at his mercy, and rendered powerless to resist him.

"Presumptuous idiot!" exclaimed the old man, 'where is now thy boasted power? Dog! bloodhound! murderer! I hold your life in my hands, and in an instant could hurl thee into the fathomless deep below. Who triumphs now?—Ha!—ha! —ha! but no, I scorn to take thy life and thus to rob the hangman of his due!—Live yet a few years longer, so that thy final punishment may be more prolonged and excruciating!"

As the mysterious old man gave utterance to these words, he hurled Stanford to some distance from him, and fixing upon him a menacing and triumphant look, he hurried from the spot, and was soon lost to the view, leaving Stanford on the earth, in a state of excitement which we need not attempt to describe. Stunned by the violence of the fall he had received, it was some minutes ere he could sufficiently recover himself to rise to his feet; and when he did so, he looked in vain around for Reuben, with mingled feelings of rage and alarm.

"D—n!" he cried, "to be thus dared, insulted, and threatened by this babbling greybeard! It is unendurable! And he knows all my secrets too, and has it in his power at any time to betray me; what a cursed misfortune is this! But I must adopt some means to silence him, or I may be discovered and foiled in my designs when I least expect it. Could I get him by any means on board my vessel, he would never have the opportunity to annoy me again. It shall be done. But who can he really be, and how has he become acquainted with all my secrets? I am at a loss to imagine; but I will know everything before long, and then I shall be enabled to arrange my plans accordingly."

Having thus given expression to his thoughts, he turned away from the spot, and wrapped in deep meditation, bent his steps towards home. On his arrival there he sought the presence of his worthy confidant, Pierce, to whom he communicated all that had taken place, and sought his advice upon the subject.

"I think you acted rather imprudently, captain," remarked Pierce, "in obtruding yourself upon the company of Kate Markham and her cousin; and you may think yourself lucky that you escaped from the vengeance of her lover, Jack Junk, in the manner you did. It would be much better for you to pretend to abandon your designs against her for the present, and thus you will quiet their suspicions and have a better opportunity of accomplishing your wishes, when she is deprived of the protection of your rival."

"Very true," said Stanford; "but this old man?"

"He is an extraordinary being," replied Pierce "and is evidently a dangerous character for you. It is strange how he has become acquainted with your secrets, for you say that you never remember to have seen him till you came to reside in this neighbourhood?"

"Never!" returned Santford.

"It will not be safe for you to suffer him to go at liberty," observed Pierce, "since he has it in his power at any time to denounce you. He must be secured at all hazards, and I do not think there would be much difficulty in accomplishing that."

"No," coincided Stanford, "we can easily surprise him in his old hovel, and if we do not think it safe to convey him on board our vessel, why the readiest means of getting rid of so dangerous an enemy would be to despatch him at once."

"Exactly so" replied Pierce; "and we could do that with perfect safety, for no one would have any suspicion of us."

"That point is then determined upon," remarked Stanford; "and now all that I have to do is, finally to arrange my plans to get Kate Markham in my power."

"And that I imagine you will find to be no very difficult task," said Pierce, "especially after the departure of her lover."

"No," replied Stanford, "and a very few hours will bring about that event; the fleet, you know, sails to-morrow."

"Yes; and I suppose it would afford you no little satisfaction if Jack Junk was never to return again."

"True; but if fortune does not frown upon me, Kate Markham will be in my power long before the young seaman can return to his native shores again?"

"Well," said Pierce, "I do not think there is much doubt of that, if you only act with due precaution. Once on board the Raven, it will be useless for the girl to offer any resistance."

"Yes," observed Stanford, "or for any of her friends to attempt to discover her. Success appears to me to be quite certain, and I exult at the thought. The friends of Kate Markham will yet have reason to shudder at the name of Farmer Stanford. Ha! ha!"

Thus did the villain continue to exult in the sanguine anticipations of the accomplishment of his designs, and arranged his plans for the future. At length the morning dawned on which the British fleet was to set sail from that port, and Jack Junk was to be separated from that fair girl whose happiness was dearer, far dearer to him than his own existence, and who loved him with the most pure and ardent passion that ever reigned within the human breast. It was a sad morning indeed to poor Kate, who had passed a sleepless night, and her cheeks were pale, and her eyes dull and languid with the heavy grief that pressed upon her bosom. The strange scene which herself and Constance had witnessed the day before in the hovel of old Reuben, and the observations he had made use of to her, were impressed upon her memory in the most vivid colours, and added to the fears and sad forebodings which distracted her mind; and it was in vain that Constance endeavoured to compose her feelings, and to inspire her with hope. She could not divest her mind of the melancholy idea that this parting between her and her lover would be for ever; and as the time wore on, her anguish increased. Jack Junk was at the residence of his lover at an early hour in the morning; and although the heart of the gallant youth was full to bursting, at the thought of their speedy separation, he endeavoured to assume all his accustomed gaiety, and to arouse poor Kate to cheerfulness and resignation; but this was a task he found it would be utterly impossible to accomplish, notwithstanding he was aided in his efforts by Mr. Markham and his daughter.

"Cheer thee, cheer thee, my dear Kate," he said, "our parting will not be for long; and surely you can console yourself with the thought that I am performing my duty; and he is unworthy the name of an Englishman, who would shrink from doing the same. Your Jack will still be happy and hopeful, though cruising far away from the dear girl of his heart! for he will know that your prayers will be constantly offered up to Heaven for his safety; and that the prayers of the pure and innocent are never disregarded. Come, come, my lass, do not taken on so, or you will unman me: you are to be a sailor's wife, and you know you must learn to share alike with him in all his cares and pleasures!"

"Truly spoken, Jack, my boy!" said old Joe Trennant, who had accompanied our hero; "besides, absence will only render the joy of meeting again all the greater. Lor! I only wish I was a youngster again, that I might return to my native element—the bright blue waters—and render my aid in thrashing the enemies of our country;—but my day's gone by—

"For the bullets and the gout,
Have so knock'd this hull about,
It will never more be fit for sea."

Cheerly, cheerly, lass! I do not see breakers ahead, and therefore you are not going to founder in the ocean of despair."

"I am afraid that I must appear very weak and silly," said Kate; "but indeed I cannot help it Oh, Jack, dear Jack, how long and dreary will the days and months appear to me that you are away; what doubts and fears will constantly haunt and distract my imagination: I shall hourly see you in the battle's heat, or in the raging storm, surrounded by the greatest horrors, and exposed to the most frightful and untimely death; and then —but the picture is far too torturing; I cannot endure it."

She hid her face upon her lover's shoulder and wept bitterly; for notwithstanding all her efforts to acquire fortitude, she every moment became more melancholy and inconsolable, and the most dismal apprehensions still continued to torment her imagination. Constance, too, in spite of all her endeavours to maintain her usual volatility of spirit, and to reanimate those of her fair cousin, could not help feeling sad and disconsolate at heart, as the time approached when our hero must take his departure, especially after the extraordinary predictions which had been uttered by that very mysterious individual, old Reuben of the Cliff; and she was consequently in a very indifferent disposition to offer the advice she wished to Kate, and which might have tended in some measure to dissipate the forebodings the latter entertained.

"Jack, my dear fellow," at length said Mr. Markham, taking the hand of the young seaman, "this is our day of parting, and knowing the sincerity of the attachment my poor brother's daughter bears towards you, and that you have always hitherto proved yourself worthy of her, I wonder not at her grief on the present occasion; but still we must always try to meet the squalls of life with the best fortitude we can, and therefore I feel assured that my own Kate will bear this trial like a woman. Come, my dear niece, dry your tears, and depend upon it your lover will be restored to you before long, safe and sound. He goes to encounter dangers which might make many hearts quail; but he risks his life in a noble cause, the rights and liberties, the honour and glory of his native land, and the eye of all-gracious Heaven will watch over and protect those who virtuously and nobly struggle to maintain the peace, justice, and tranquillity of his fellow-creatures against oppression and tyranny. Banish those fruitless apprehensions from your breast, I say again, my dear girl, and remember those words, which I know will ever stimulate and encourage Jack Junk, the tar for all weathers, under all circumstances—

"Fear not, but trust in Providence, Wherever thou may'st be!"

The observations of her uncle did indeed tend in a great measure to alleviate the anxiety and distress of Kate's mind, and she sought to assume her wonted smiles, but still she found it utterly impossible to banish entirely the melancholy and powerful presentiments that had taken possession of it.

"Bravo, Markham!" said Joe Trennant; "you are a man entirely after my own heart; what's the use of being capsized altogether by. a mere capful of wind? We cannot expect it to be always a calm, for you know—

"Life's like the sea in constant motion,"

Eh, my old Grampus? But never mind, always keep the weathergage of care, and steer clear off the shoals of injustice, and there is no fear of our making a happy port at last. Kate, my lass, cheer you up; Jack and his messmates sail to-day on a cruise that any brave heart might be proud of, and I only wish that this timber toe, and this iron fin did not prevent me from sharing with him in the glory of the action. But hallo! see the lads and the lasses are crowding all sail to the ship, to have an hour or two's jollification before the parting, and we should become little better than mutineers were we to refuse to join the fleet. What say you, Jack, my lad? You will take pretty Kate in tow, will you not? And myself and Markham and the bonny craft Constance will at once weigh anchor, and act as a convoy!"

Jack smiled at the humour of the old man, and embracing Kate in a most affectionate manner, he whispered in her ear:—

"Come, my dear Kate; grieving's a folly you know, so take courage; sail alongside of hope and by your sweet smiles impart sunshine to the gloom of your poor Jack's heart. Why, I never saw you look so sad before; and yet it is not the first time we have had such interruptions to our happiness, but the day will come, my lass, when we shall anchor safely in the port of wedlock, and neither of us will then care the cracking of a biscuit about the shoals and quick sands we may have, perchance, to encounter in our voyage through life."

Kate blushed, but her heart fully responded to the feelings which animated her lover's bosom; and struggling with her emotions, she smiled sweetly upon him, and suffering him to take her arm, while her cousin also accepted his other, they quitted the house, and made their way towards the ship, old Joe Trennant and Mr. Markham following in the rear. The ship presented the most lively and picturesque scene; sailors and their wives or sweethearts were assembled there in considerable numbers, on that important day; and many was the manly heart that throbbed with the most powerful emotions; many the bright eye that was dimmed with tears at the thought of separation, and the probability of their never more meeting in this world those whom they so fondly loved. But the golden beams of the sun smiled down serenely and cheerfully upon them, as if to inspire them with hope; and the noble vessels in the adjacent harbour seemed to erect their heads more proudly, and to hold out faithful augury of the triumphs the "wooden walls of old England" were about to achieve. It was a sad and yet inspiring scene; and even Kate Markham became inspired by it, and almost forget the probable sorrows of the future in the pleasures of the present. Constance regained her usual vivacity, and aided by the efforts of honest old Kit Breezely who was never in more cheerful mood, albeit he was for an indefinite period about to lose so many excellent customers, the time passed much more happier and convivially away, then under the circumstances could at all have been expected. The dance and the song prevailed alternately; and by degrees Kate became more cheerful, and even entered into the sports of those assembled, much to the delight of her lover, whilst Constance was one of the gayest of the company assembled, and seemed resolved, as far as lay in her power, to contribute to the general mirth, and to banish all the gloomy thoughts which must naturally arise a the event which was about to take place.

"Ah, Constance, my merry lass," said our hero, "it always does my eyes good to see you on such an occasion as this, when by your own sweet smiles, and sprightly disposition, you can lighten the hearts of so many. By the by, you have said, that your heart has never yet been taken in ow; but avast there, what about my old messmate Sam Stedfast, as brave a seaman as ever the British Navy could boast of, and possessing as honest a heart as ever beat beneath a sailors jacket. Poor fellow, he was unfortunately taken prisoner by the enemy, and since then we have heard no more of him; but the time will come when he will jump upon deck again, and—but avast! avast, Jack, you have slipped your cable, and have sailed too much a-head. Pardon me, Constance. I meant not to wound your feelings."

"Poor Steadfast," said Constance, with strong emotion, and dashing a tear from her eye; "shall we ever be destined to meet again?—We were brought up children together—he possessed a noble and generous spirit—he saved my father's life, when he was attacked by ruffians, on his return from market; and I own that I——"

"Love him," rejoined Jack, "that's the plain way of saying it, in spite of your blushes; and no shame either to love one who is deserving of you. Poor Sam, and I love him too, for were we not like brothers? Ah what frolics I and poor Sam have played together in our time. When we were no taller than a grog bucket, and couldn't see over the top of a chicken-coop, there were we trimming our queer little paper vessels side by side, launching them in the same puddle, and towing them to the same bit of rock. When we grew up, we didn't differ in sentiment the space of a spun-yarn. We went to sea together; and though misfortune drafted us into different vessels three years since, I'll warrant, if he has not foundered altogether, which (do not set the pumps to work, Constance,) something assures me he has not, our hearts are as much alongside as ever. Kate, what should you say if, on my return from this voyage, Sam Steadfast, my old companion, and the faithful lover of your cousin, should be in the same vessel with me?"

"Oh, my dear Jack," replied our heroine casting an affectionate glance upon the blushing countenance of Constance, "that would indeed add tenfold pleasure to the transport of your restoration."

"Well said, my dear Kate," remarked our hero, "that's hearts of oak. Ha! who have we here? A pedlar? Let's overhaul your cargo."

The pedlar was a man between fifty and sixty years of age, and there was something rather singular in his appearance; but he affected great good humour, and seemed likely by that means to dispose of his goods freely.

"Ah! said Jack, looking over the handkerchiefs he carried in his pack; "you carry a good assortment, mate—here's a beauty—it reminds me of the sky because it's blue, and it also reminds me of my dear Kate, because it's an emblem of truth and innocence. Dear Kate, I tie this around your neck; it is but a simple gift, but I know it is quite sufficient to remind you of poor Jack when he is far away."

Kate pressed it to her lips in silence, tears at the same time, starting to her eyes and she suffered her lover to place the handkerchief round her neck.

"A very pretty present, a very handsome present," said the pedlar; "and doubtless the young woman would like to make a purchase of somthing to give to you, by which, whenever you looked upon it, you might remember her, and——"

"Avast there, you lubber," interrupted Jack; "think you there is anything Jack Junk requires to remind him of the dear girl of his heart; that she can ever be absent from his memory? Why I shall see her beauteous face in every wave that lashes the ship's side—in every cloud that rides the horizon. Forget my Kate? sink my mizen top; but you are only a land swab, and have never smelt salt water, I——"

"Nay, master," returned the pedlar, interrupting him, "there you are mistaken, for although I am now only what you see me to be, a poor pedlar, who toils hard enough to get a living, I have weathered many a rough gale in the course of my time, notwithstanding. However, I did not mean to offend you, I thought perhaps the young lady might wish to make you a present before you departed, such as a handsome tobacco-box for instance; and by-the-by, I have got such a one as you don't see every day, all silver with a miniature of a gentleman in the lid of it, as much resembling you as ever I saw two peas in a pod. It is very remarkable. I have had it a long time in my possession, and had no particular wish to part with it, only I happen to have been rather unfortunate in business of late, and ready money would be an object to me. I would sell it a bargain."

"Well," said our hero, whose curiosity was somewhat excited by what the pedlar had said, "let us look at this wonderful box."

The pedlar immediately produced from his pocket a handsomely chased silver box which he placed in the hands of our hero, who, opening the lid, gazed with astonishment upon a well-executed miniature enclosed in the interior.

"Why by Heaven!" he exclaimed, "this is the very counterpart of the likeness in the locket which was found suspended from my neck by him from whom I have taken my name, and which was presented to me by old Joe Trennant only the day before yesterday. Compare them, my dear Kate; did you ever see anything more alike?"

Kate examined the miniature in the lid of the box and that in the locket eagerly and ejaculated—

"Astonishing! They are exactly alike; they must both have been done for the same person; and what an extraordinay resemblance they berr to you, my dear Jack."

"Well," returned her lover, "I think there is some likeness. How did this box come into your possession, old man?"

"I found it," answered the pedlar

"Found it?"

"Yes."

"Where?" demanded our hero.

"On the sea-beach many miles from here, where it appeared to have been washed from some wreck. That is more than seven years ago, and I have kept it by me ever since; but I must now part with it, if I can only find a customer; have you any wish to purchase it, master? I will sell it to you cheap."

"What do you require for it?" asked Jack. The pedlar named his price, to which our hero readily agreed, and the box having become his, the pedlar took his departure to endeavour to find fresh customers from the numerous seamen assembled. Jack Junk continued to gaze upon the miniature in the box and that in the locket with the greatest amazement for some minutes, and the longer he did so, the greater his emotion became.

"Well," he remarked at last; "this is certainly one of the most extraordinary circumstances I ever met with. The portraits have evidently been both done for the same individual, and I am lost in mystery. But I will treasure and preserve this box which has come so singularly into my possession, as much as the locket; and some day or other, if Providence so wills it, they may lead to the discovery as to who were my real parents, although it is but too probable that they are both now no more. But, come, my dear Kate, you are again looking as dull as a tar upon six-water-grog. Arouse yourself, my lass, and let us endeavour to pass the few hours we are destined to be together as happily as we can."

"Alas!" sighed his lover, "how hard is the task you would impose upon me; how do I tremble as the fatal moment so rapidly approaches when we must part, perhaps never to meet again. Never did the broad waters of the ocean appear so fearful to me as they do at present, and every stately vessel upon which my eyes now rest, bears to my imagination the gloom and horror of a floating prison. Oh, Jack, were I permitted to share with you the dangers you will have to encounter, methinks I could be content; but who will be left to comfort me when you are far away? And should you perish in the battle's dreadful carnage, what then will be left to your poor Kate but misery and despair?"

"Avast! avast, my love," said Jack, in a hoarse voice, "for your words unman me, and I shall become as weak presently as the veriest lubber that ever plodded his way through life on shore. Talk not of danger, my lass, for that was never yet entered in a sailor's log-book. Shiver my timbers, Kate, would you have me skulking like a porpoise on shore, when there are enemies of our country at sea to assist in drubbing?—Fear not, Jack Junk will live to weather many a storm yet, and before many months have elapsed will again be safely moored in your arms, and we shall both have an opportunity of laughing at all the perils it may be my lot to experience. Who can gaze upon that noble fleet without feeling their bosom glow with enthusiastic delight? Come, Kate, send dull care to old Davy, let us mingle with the brave fellows and their lasses here assembled, and anticipate only happiness for the future."

"Ah, Jack, dear Jack!" again sighed the maiden, "how dreary will the hours wear away that seperate me from you. You may deem me weak and childish, but indeed, I cannot contemplate our parting without still encouraging the most fearful apprehensions. Busy imagination tortures me to madness. Methinks I now behold you engaged in the fury of the bloody strife; I hear the terrific roaring of the cannon; I see the dead and wounded lying in ghastly heaps; I behold you engaged in mortal combat; I see your brave struggles, but you are over-powered by numbers; oh, God! how they press upon you, like savage beasts seeking their prey. Your strength fails you; your arm becomes more feeble; and still onwards, with tenfold fury and deadly determination, they press upon you; you are wounded! a frightful gash appears in your forehead; the crimson blood flows down your pale face from the gaping wound;—your limbs totter—you sink upon the deck completely overpowered, and the dew of death trembling on your brow—I hear you call upon my name, and I am not near to comfort you in your last sad moments; oh Heaven, I——"

"Hold! hold! dear Kate, I implore you," interrupted her agitated lover; "what a frightful picture is this you have permitted your imagination to draw; but it will not be realized, my love, I feel confident it will not: so pray banish such dismal thoughts from your mind. Speak to her, my sweet and gentle Constance; for I know your affectionate and consolatory observations never fail to have the most happy influence over her. You will be her friend, adviser, companion, sister, when her poor Jack is far away; and it is that thought which inspires me with confidence and hope. Now, my beloved Kate, put a bold heart upon the business; never lower your flag to the grim enemy Despair, but have courage and confidence in a just cause, and shout with me—

'Rule Britannia, Britannia rules the waves,
For Britons never, never will be slaves!'"

"Hurrah, Jack!" cried old Joe Trennant; "spoken like a true British sailor, my boy, and I glory in you for it—

'Our country is our ship, d'ye see?
   And a gallant vessel too;
And of his vessel proud is he,
   Who's one of the Albion crew!'"

Constance again endeavoured to tranquillize the feelings of her cousin, and she partially succeeded, and they joined the other guests who were congregated together on that important occasion at "The Ship." The hours passed rapidly away, dismally enough for poor Kate, although her lover and her other friends exerted themselves to the utmost to reanimate her; but at length the melancholy moment arrived; it was time for the gallant seamen to go on board their different vessels, and when they must bid a long farewell to those so dear to them. It was in truth, a sad sight, to behold the young wife and her tender offspring clinging to him who probably ere many weeks had elapsed would be laid low; to see the gentle maiden pressed frantically to the bosom of her lover; to mark the tears that streamed down his manly cheeks; to listen to their half-broken sentences, and hear their mutual vows of eternal love and constancy. Poor Kate's heart sank within her; she felt as if she were parting with her very life; and had it not been for the support of her lover, she must have sunk upon the earth. But the villain Stanford, from a place where he could not be observed, was a gratified spectator of this melancholy scene; and base were the thoughts that crowded upon his guilty mind.

"Cling to him, proud beauty," he muttered to himself, "and pour forth you vows of affection in his gratified ear; for if fortune favours my deep-laid designs, this is the last opportunity you will have of doing so. The Rover of the Seas marks his victim, and will secure her at any cost. Yes, the Black Raven soon shall own as fair a mistress as ever graced a monarch's throne."

With eager eyes the pirate watched them as they slowly bent their way towards the harbour, and then folding a huge mantle around him, which he wore on that occasion, the better to conceal his person from observation, he followed at a distance. The fatal moment more rapidly approached, and poor Kate clung sobbing convulsively to her lover's bosom, and felt as if her heart would break.

"Oh, Jack, dear Jack," she said, "we must not, cannot part; the thought maddens me, and my strength can never support the dreadful trial. Oh, why has cruel destiny decreed that we should be thus separated, and that you should be exposed to such terrible dangers? My heart never felt so full as it does at present, and the most awful forebodings crowd upon my imagination; we shall never meet again."

"Avast! avast! my sweet one," replied our hero, "and bear up against this trial like a woman. It is only a slight breeze, which will soon blow over, and all will be calm and favourable weather for the remainder of our voyage. Not meet again! oh, do not say so—do not think so. Our separation will be but brief, and the happiness of our meeting again will be tenfold. My dear lass, console yourself during my absence, with the assurance that your fond image will ever be moored in my heart—that your Jack's thoughts will ever be fixed upon you; his prayers shall constantly be offered up to the All-merciful Commander aloft for your welfare. Come, come, my dear Kate, dry your tears—let me kiss them from your cheeks. Farewell, sweetest, gentlest, best-beloved of human beings; and oh, great Heaven, hear a sailor's humble, but fervent prayer—watch over and protect her from every danger while I am far away."

"Oh, God!" exclaimed Kate, still clinging frantically to him, "I cannot—my heart will break—my brain is distracted—hark how fiercely the tempest rages—see the foaming billows mount like raging demons to the clouds, o'erwhelming all within their fury in destruction. Jack, dear Jack, you shall not—must not leave me thus;—am I not your affianced bride, and who shall dare to tear you from me? We will not part."

"Kate! Kate!" said the young seaman, in a broken voice, "you—you unman me—you make me a child; nay, nay—this is not like my own bonny Kate; cheerly, cheerly—do not take on so, my poor lass. Constance—Markham, take her, I implore you, for I must away;—this scene is too much for me."

Gently he disengaged himself from her embraces, and with a deep sigh, she sank fainting i the arms of her uncle. Poor Jack fixed one loo of the most intense affection and pity upon her—pressed most fervent kisses upon her pale cheeks and forehead; his heart was too full to suffer him to give utterance to a syllable; and pressing the hands of Constance, Mr. Markham, and Joe Trennant, he rushed hastily from the spot, and was quickly lost to the view among his shipmates who were going on board. Mr. Markham still supported the insensible form of his niece in his arms, and the whole of those on shore gazed anxiously at the fleet, which was now preparing to set sail. In a few minutes the deafening cheers from the sailors on board the different vessels informed them that the time was come, and directly afterwards the gallant fleet steered their course majestically out of the harbour. The eyes of Constance and her father, and Joe Trennant, instinctively fixed themselves upon the Defiance, and there the first object that met their gaze was Jack Junk, who had mounted one of the yards, and with his eyes apparently fixed upon them, was waving the handkerchief which had been given to him by his lover in the air. Mark Stanford stood upon an eminence, from which he could watch everything without interruption, and as the fleet sailed out of the harbour, his heart bounded with exultation.

"They go," he said, "and he, the favoured lover of that fair girl whom I have destined to be my future mistress, will, I trust, never more return to annoy me. May the wild waves engulph his carcase, or the sword of the enemy lay him low. But should Providence restore him in safety to his native land, shall he ever again behold that girl, who is the very idol of his soul? No—I, Hugh Granfield, the pirate captain of the Raven, swear by all the infernal host he shall not. Long ere then she shall be mine, and sailing with me in my gallant barque upon the bright blue waters of the deep, where no help can come to her—no one can rescue her from my power."

Thus soliloquizing, the villain Stanford folded his arms across his broad chest, and continued to watch the departing fleet with eager looks of satisfaction. The firing of the guns aroused our heroine from her state of insensibility, and passing her fair hands across her forehead, as if to collect her thoughts, she gazed wildly and vacantly around her.

"What fearful dream is this that has tortured my imagination?" she ejaculated; "methought that I was separated from my lover, and that the cruel billows bore him from me far away. But no—it cannot be!—who would dare to separate two beings who are so devoted to each other? But he is not here!—I do not hear his voice; why do you hold me thus? Jack—beloved Jack, oh, where are you?"

"Be calm, dear Kate," remonstrated her uncle, "be calm and put your trust in the goodness of Providence, who will not fail to watch over and protect your lover, and to restore him safe to your arms."

"Ah!" exclaimed Kate, suddenly starting, and gazing in the direction of the fleet, which was fast receding from the view; "they have taken him from me; the cruel waves bear him far away, and we shall never meet again. Jack, dear Jack! Oh, Heaven help me!"

The fleet now appeared only as a dim speck upon the distant horizon, and Kate, again overpowered by the intensity of her feelings, uttered a faint cry of despair, and sank insensible in the arms of her uncle.

"Poor lass!" said Joe Trennant; "this trial is too much for her; bear her into the house, friend Markham, and let us see to her recovery. Her spirits have got into the trough of a sea of troubles; I wish I could only lend a hand at the windlass or take in a reef of her canvas if the wind blows too hard."

"Ah, Master Trennant," said Markham, "this is indeed a severe trial for the poor girl who loves Jack Junk so fondly; but may Heaven watch over his safety and once more restore him to her arms."

With these words Mr. Markham bore the insensible form of his niece into the house, and was followed by Constance and the others, Mark Stanford from the place of his concealment watching them with deadly looks of malice as they retired.

"My rival is gone," he muttered to himself, "and if fortune does not frown upon me, they will never meet again. Kate Markham, a few weeks, perhaps only a few short days, shall elapse ere you shall become the prize of the pirate, he whom you so thoroughly hate and despise. Yes, I have marked you for my victim, and by all my hopes, nothing whatever shall save you from my power. Yonder lies my gallant barque at anchor, and ere long I will have you. Kate Markham, I will have you safely there on board, and bear you far away from your native land and beyond the reach of assistance of your friends. Till then, they may continue to despise the supposed Farmer Stanford. Ha! ha! ha! I go to further arrange my plans, which I will not fail, now that my rival is far away, to put into execution as speedily as possible."

He turned to go away as he gave utterance to these words, and beheld the mysterous old man, Reuben of the Cliff, standing at a short distance from him, and leaning on his staff, gazing earnestly upon him. He was fixed immediately in his path, so that he could not avoid him, even if he had been so inclined; and he therefore quickly advanced towards him, and boldly confronted him, the old man not offering to change his attitude the least in the world.

"How now, old man?" sternly demanded Stanford, "why do you again cross my path? What would you with me? Stand aside, I command you, and let me pass!"

"*You* command," repeated Reuben, with a look of ineffable contempt; "pirate, dog, murderer, dare you venture to provoke the wrath of Reuben of the Cliff, who knows all thy dark secrets and holds thy fate in his hands? You think that now your rival has departed, your triumph will be certain, and that nothing can save the innocent Kate Markham, the daughter of that unfortunate man, who perished by your bloody and inhuman hands; but beware, and tremble; for the vengeance of offended Heaven will overtake you when least expected, and terrible will be the retribution that will descend upon your head. Remember my words, and trust me that as sure as you now stand before me, though for a time success may crown your base designs, they will be realized."

"Cease, babbling old wretch!" cried Stanford; "cease your wild predictions and begone. By what means you have become acquainted with my secrets, I cannot imagine; but if I thought you would dare to betray me, I would speedily adopt such means as would silence you for ever!"

"Idiot!" returned Reuben, "dare you threaten me, whose power your guilty blood-stained conscience will not suffer you to deny? Beware, beware; the storm is gathering; black and ponderous clouds darken the horizon, which in due time will burst and overwhelm you with their fury. Think of that, Hugh Granfield, and then exult if thou canst. Remember that I could this moment denounce thee to the world as a pirate and a murderer, and at once bring thy guilty career to a termination; but for the present I will suffer thee to escape the punishment you so richly deserve, for I have deep-laid designs in contemplation, which will inflict upon you tenfold torture and disgrace. Till then you may continue in your fancied triumph; but the day will come, depend upon it, and a terrible day will that be for the pirate chief."

"Strange being!" ejaculated Stanford, who, notwithstanding all his efforts to the contrary, did feel confused and alarmed at the impressive manner and observations of the old man; "I cannot endure those threats; I will know who and what you are, and how you have acquired the knowledge you possess."

"Yes, villain!" replied Reuben, "and you shall know some day to your shame and confusion. The day of retribution will come, and let the anticipation of it fill your guilty soul with terror."

"Away!" exclaimed Stanford, whose patience was completely exhausted, "I will hear no more; I scorn thy boasted power; what witness have you of that of which you accuse me? I defy you and your empty threats? Who will look upon your words any more than as the wild ravings of a wretched maniac?"

"Say you so, Hugh Granfield?" returned the old man; "oh, but you will find yourself most wofully deceived; and it will then be the turn of Reuben of the Cliff to triumph. Yonder rides your pirate barque, the pretended fair trader, the Enterprise, is it not so? Many are the tempests she has braved—many are the perils she has encountered. Her deck has been washed by the crimson blood of brave and innocent men. Terrible are the scenes of carnage that have been enacted on board that dreaded vessel beneath thy savage command; but the day will come when her power will be defeated, and yourself and your inhuman crew be doomed to an ignominious death, amid the execrations of those against whom you have so long waged a cruel and inhuman war of destruction. Tremble, pirate! miscreant! murderer!"

"By all the infernal host!" exclaimed Stanford, unable any longer to contain himself, "I will no longer thus tamely submit to be mocked, taunted, and threatened. Old croaking idiot, begone, I say, and dare not again to cross my path, or tremble at my vengeance. Know you not what it is to incur the wrath of Hugh Granfield, the Rover of the Seas?—he who never yet failed to keep his word—whose aim is sure, whose name the boldest cannot utter without a shudder of horror, and who hitherto has been able to set all power at defiance?"

"I know all," replied the old man, in a calm voice, "and treat your threats with the most ineffable contempt. Nay, you may frown, but I know you tremble at the power of Reuben of the Cliff, although you would fain affect to despise him. I go; but often shall we meet again, and I will never cease to repeat those fearful facts that are so unwelcome to your ears."

Thus saying, the old man turned abruptly away, and darting rapidly down the side of a steep rock, he was out of sight before the villain, Mark Stanford, had recovered from his surprise and confusion.

"D—n!" he at last fiercely exclaimed; "shall I tamely brook this? The infernal shark evidently knows too much, and he is a dangerous customer to be permitted to cruise about this coast. He knows all my secrets—has threatened to foil my designs, and has it in his power at any time to betray me. This must be prevented at all hazards. I must secure the old man, and silence his busy tongue for ever. It can easily be accomplished; and in order to secure my own safety, I must lose no time about it. It shall be done, and that this very night. Idiot he must be, knowing my desperate and determined character, to venture thus boldly to threaten me; but it is well that he has done so, for it has put me on my guard."

Having thus spoken, Mark Stanford once more cast a glance towards the house where Kate and her friends were assembled, and then slowly bent his way towards his home. It was in vain that Constance and her father endeavoured to ameliorate the grief of Kate—the most dismal presentiments continued to haunt and distract her mind,

and she felt, now that her lover had departed, as if she was left alone in the world, and that happiness could never again be her's. At length, feeling restless and uneasy at the tavern, they returned towards home. They had scarcely reached the door of their dwelling, when dark and threatening clouds obscured the horizon; the wind howled in hollow and fitful gusts around, and everything gave token of an approaching storm; and soon the lightning flashed its forked fury—the thunder rolled loudly along the vault of Heaven, and the rain descended in an overwhelming torrent upon the earth. Every moment the tempest increased in fury, and at length it became completely frightful. It blew a perfect hurricane; houses tottered, and stout trees that had stood the storms of many ages, were torn from their roots and carried by the wind to an almost incredible distance. The roaring of the angry waves, as they dashed with deafening fury against the rocks and cliffs, might be heard for miles around; and in fact all nature was convulsed, and it seemed as if the wrath of Heaven had descended in one fell swoop upon the earth. Kate was terrified, and clung to her uncle in speechless agony. She thought of her lover, and her heart sunk with horror when she pictured to herself the dangers to which he was so soon exposed, and from which it was too likely he would not be able to escape.

"Oh, God!" she ejaculated at last, "what will become of him in such a terrible storm as this? What vessel can weather such a frightful tempest? He is lost—he is lost! Alas! how soon are my worst surmises realized. Poor Jack, why did cruel fate thus separate us? We shall never, never meet again, and all the hopes and happiness of Kate Markham are gone for ever."

She wept bitterly as these thoughts arose to her tortured imagination, and Constance and her father in vain endeavoured to console her. More than an hour passed away, and still the storm continued to increase in violence instead of abating, and it was sufficient even to make the stoutest heart quail with terror and awe. It was, indeed, a fearful scene. The earth was enveloped in complete darkness, save at intervals, when the ethereal fire flashed across the sky, rendering the horrors of the scene more impressive. The terror of Kate became more powerful and insupportable, and Constance in vain tried to tranquilise her, and to abate her fears; but at length, as the evening approached, and Kate felt ill and sick at heart, she excused herself to her uncle, and retired to her chamber accompanied by Constance. But not to rest did Kate retire; oh, no—her mind was too busily occupied—too deeply agitated to suffer her to think of that; and she seated herself by the window and watched the horrors of the night with feelings of the most unspeakable anguish. In this manner she continued to sit for hours, and it was not until long after midnight that her cousin could persuade her to go to bed; and when she did, she tried in vain to compose herself to sleep, for the tempest continued to rage with unabated violence throughout the night, and the certainty of the fate which must attend her lover seemed more apparent to her.

"Oh, that I had been permitted to accompany him," she sighed, "to share with him all his dangers; and even though it should have been the will of Heaven that we should have perished in this awful storm, methinks I could have met my fate without a murmur had I been allowed to die in his arms. Oh, Jack—my dear Jack, what is now your situation, tossing about on the wild waters of the deep, on such a night of horror as this? God of Heaven! watch over and protect, I beseech Thee, the life of the poor mariner, and restore him in safety to his native land."

"Be comforted, dear Kate," replied her cousin, "and rest assured that an All-merciful Providence will not fail to listen to and regard your prayers.

The fleet will no doubt put in at the nearest port until this storm has abated, and your lover will be safe. Do not give way to any unnecessary fears, and depend upon it that all will be well."

Kate shook her head and sighed deeply, for it was in vain that she tried to dissipate the melancholy thoughts and forebodings which distracted her mind; and thus they continued to converse at intervals during the night, and the morning found them both languid and unrefreshed.

CHAPTER V.

THE MIDNIGHT MURDER.—THE PIRATE VESSEL.—THE DESIGNS OF MARK STANFORD ARE MORE FULLY DEVELOPED.

THE last meeting with Reuben of the Cliff, and the daring threats he had held out, had made the most powerful impression upon the mind of Mark Stanford; and as he bent his way towards home, he communed deeply with himself upon the subject, and endeavoured to make up his mind as to what was best to be done under the circumstances. However, it needed no second consideration to convince him that it would not be safe for him to suffer such an avowed enemy to remain any longer at large, and he therefore determined to adopt some immediate scheme to get the old man in his power, and to silence his tongue for ever; and he considered that that would be very easy of accomplishment; and that there was no time to be lost. On arriving at home, the storm having overtaken him on the way, he sought the presence of Pierce Raker, to whom he related all that had taken place, and asked his advice on the subject.

"My advice is very soon given, captain," said Pierce; "it is quite evident that this old fellow is no empty boaster, and that he knows all your secrets."

"Yes," coincided Stanford; "I cannot doubt that, though by what means he has acquired his knowledge I am at a loss to conjecture, for I never remember to have seen him before I came to this neighbourhood. He is a dangerous fellow; and should he betray me, I might find it no easy matter to escape; besides, my designs against Kate Markham would thus, in all probability, be frustrated.

"True," remarked Pierce; "and I say, therefore, the only way to make everything secure is, to silence the old man, which can be done without any risk or trouble. It will be easy to surprise the old man in his hovel; and of what use would it then be for him to offer to make any resistance?"

"No," said Stanford; "and I think that the safest plan would be to despatch him at once."

"Certainly; for 'the dead tell no tales,' and the sooner it is done the better."

"That is my opinion," said the pirate; "for I am not safe a moment while old Reuben is suffered to live. This very night we will settle the business."

"Agreed. I am ready to accompany you, for I suppose you have no desire to go alone?"

"No," answered Stanford; "and I might find your assistance necessary. Besides, I have a wish to go a-board our vessel, to see that everything is going on right. In a few days, if all goes on as well as I desire it, I much mistake if Kate Markham will not be safely on board the 'Raven;' and then away to sea in search of fresh adventures, and to endeavour to meet with more booty."

"Ay, captain," observed Pierce; "and for my part, I do not care how soon that time comes, for I am not used to this sort of life; and I long to be on board our gallant barque again, and engaged in business. It is so long since I mixed in the battle, that I am afraid I shall quite get my hand out, if I am suffered to remain skulking on shore much longer."

"Well, Pierce," returned Stanford, "your wishes will soon be gratified, never fear. But what a storm this is—eh? Jack Junk has got rough weather to commence his voyage with; and Kate Markham, no doubt, is fretting her little eyes out in alarm for his safety. May he never experience finer weather!—that's all the harm I wish him, though I do not expect that he will ever have the opportunity to annoy me again; and should he return to England again, it will be to learn that his lover is lost to him for ever, and that she has become the victim of the despised Mark Stanford, the supposed honest farmer. Ha! ha! ha!"

"Ay, captain," remarked Pierce; "you will then indeed have cause to exult, and bitter will be the grief and disappointment of your rival. Kate Markham is a damsel who is every way worthy to become the mistress of the pirate chief; and I congratulate you on your good fortune. But it is finally settled that we shall execute our designs against old Reuben to-night, is it not?"

"It is," answered Stanford; "and that enemy removed, I shall have nothing then to apprehend."

They continued to converse for some time longer, and to arrange their future plans; but it was not until the clock had long since struck the hour of eleven that they started forth on their murderous errand, regardless of the storm which still raged with unabated violence. They soon arrived in the vicinity of the old man's dwelling; and looking round to see that no one was watching them, they walked on, and in a short time stood before the door of the wretched hovel, where they paused and listened; but all was perfectly silent, and the place was buried in profound darkness. Stanford tried the door, but it was fastened on the inside, and they had no doubt that the old man had retired to rest. Pierce, however, pulled a clasp knife out of his pocket, and after some difficulty succeeded in picking the lock, and the door flew open. Having brought a dark lantern with them, they examined the room; but there was nobody there, and they therefore entered the room silently, for they had no doubt that the old man was asleep in some other part of the hovel. Having entered another apartment, which, like the one just mentioned, was quite untenanted, they stopped to listen at an opposite door, and they could then distinctly hear the sounds as of some person breathing heavily. This they had no doubt was Reuben, and they cautiously opened the door and peeped in. They found that they were not mistaken; for, stretched on a wretched mattress in one corner of the room, was the form of old Reuben, and he appeared to sleep soundly.

"'Tis well," said Pierce; "we could not have chosen a better time to put our design into execution. He sleeps soundly enough: one blow, and he will never wake again."

"Yes," whispered Stanford, his eyes flashing wildly with guilty determination; "the old idiot! Where is now his boasted power? Will he now ever have the opportunity to put his threats into execution, and to betray me to the world?"

"No—no," returned Pierce; "his doom is sealed, and nothing can save him. But we waste time: shall I strike the blow?"

"Yes—yes," faltered out Stanford, with an involuntary shudder. "But stay a moment—not yet. It is almost a pity to take the life of the old man, when we could so easily secure his person, and prevent his doing any further mischief."

"Psha!" exclaimed Pierce, impatiently, "why should you spare him? Besides, if we settle him at once, it will save all future trouble, and there will be an end to the business. The old fellow would only be in our way if we were to convey him on board our vessel, and there is nothing like doing things off-hand. Ah!—he wakes!"

They hastily shaded the lantern, and stepped into one corner of the room, where they were not so likely to be observed; and the old man slowly arose from the mattress, and rubbing his eyes, he gazed around him.

"It is past midnight, I should think," he observed; "but I do not care about going to sleep again, for I have had some singular and frightful dreams, and they have left a disagreeable impression upon my mind, which I cannot easily get rid of. It is a wild night. How the thunder rattles and the lightning flashes: and hark how the angry waves roar and bellow! Heaven protect the hardy mariner who is exposed to the horrors of a tempest such as this! Ah!—what sound was that? I am not alone!"

"No, old man," replied Stanford, starting forward; "you are not, indeed, alone. Prepare yourself, for your time is come: you have not many minutes to live."

"Ah!—Hugh Granfield!" exclaimed Reuben, with a look of terror; "blood-stained miscreant, is it indeed you?—What see you here?"

"Your life!" answered the pirate; "and can you marvel that I should do so, after the threats you have held out to me?—Fool! did you suppose that I would suffer you to live to frustrate my designs and to denounce me to the world in my real character? Oh, but you must have considered me a very dolt if you did. Kneel, old man, for this is your last moment."

"Hugh Granfield!" replied the old man, solemnly, though it was evident that his lips quivered with fear; "Hugh Granfield, I say, beware what you do; but you will not dare to take my life. Monster as you are, still I cannot think you capable of such a cowardly and inhuman deed. Forbear, and if you would not have the vengeance of offended Heaven overtake you, abandon your brutal designs and quit this place."

"Oh, no," replied Stanford, "you know too much for me; but had you been wise enough to have kept a still tongue you would never have been suspected, and you might have had an opportunity of betraying me to punishment before I could have been aware of the knowledge you possess. You have worked your own destruction, and——"

"Bah!" impatiently interrupted Pierce, as he brandished a knife, "what's the use of wasting time thus?—Old man, have you got anything particular to say ere I settle the business for you?"

Poor old Reuben was now indeed greatly alarmed at the near prospect of so horrible a death, and clasping his hands together, and gazing alternately at Pierce and Stanford with looks of supplication, he was unable for a moment or two to give utterance to a syllable.

"Mercy! mercy! spare me! spare me!" at length he gasped forth; "I am an old man, a very old man, but yet not fit to die. I—I——"

"Who are you, and how did you acquire your knowledge?" demanded Stanford, impatiently.

"Do not urge such questions," said the singular old man, "for I cannot, will not answer them."

"Obstinate old fool!" cried Stanford, "then you do but hasten your death! Pierce, do your duty!"

"Mercy! mercy!" again shrieked the wretched old man; "help! help!"

"Stop his cries," exclaimed the pirate, "though he calls in vain; the voice of the tempest will be his only answer. Strike, Pierce, strike!"

"No, no," frantically cried old Reuben, endeavouring to arrest the arm of the murderer, but in vain, the next instant the fatal knife was plunged deep in his side, and he sank bleeding and with a deep groan of agony, upon the floor. In a moment or two, however, he staggered on to his knees, and with difficulty crawling towards Mark Stanford; he clasped him by the legs in the agony of death, and fixing his ghastly looks upon his countenance, he said in a hollow solemn voice—

"Murderer, thou hast added another to the long catalogue of thy bloody crimes, but the vengeance of Heaven will yet overtake you, and terrible will be the tortures that will be inflicted. May my dying curse light upon thine head, inhuman wretch, and pursue thee wherever thou goest. May my ghastly form be ever present to your affrighted imagination, whether on sea or land, my dying maledictions ever be ringing in thine ears, and pressing thy guilty soul down to perdition. This hideous crime, and the murder of Horace Markham will yet be avenged, and——"

"Cease, croaking hound!" cried the monster Pierce, as he again plunged his knife into the poor old man's side; who fixed one terrible glance on his murderers, and with a deep frightful groan he sunk on the floor a ghastly corpse. "Well, he is silenced at any rate," said Pierce; "the old fool, had he not been too communicative, he might have saved his life. Bah!—he died hard though."

"Yes," said Stanford, with an involuntary shudder, as he again fixed his eyes upon the ghastly and distorted features of the corpse; the eyes of which, although glazed in death, still seemed to glare upon him with an expression that was enough to appal even the stoutest and most insensible heart. "Would that he had never crossed my path, for I must confess that I would much rather this deed could have been avoided. I like not the words he uttered in his dying moments; his curse still seems to ring in my ear, and—"

"Pshaw, captain," interrupted the ruffian Pierce Raker, impatiently; "I am surprised at you. Would you not have been mad to have suffered one who, was evidently so well acquainted with all your secrets, and who had likewise held out such threats to you, any longer to live?"

"Come—come," said the pirate, still shuddering, and unable to remove his eyes from the ghastly features of the corpse, "let us begone; I do not feel exactly comfortable in remaining here any longer. It is a frightful night!—How the thunder rattles, and the blue lightning, see how it blazes around. The atmosphere of this old hovel is close and oppressive; a leaden weight seems to press upon my brain. I shall be better when we get on board the Raven, and have had a glass or two of grog. Come—come!"

"Shall we leave the carcass of the old fellow here to rot?" demanded the reckless and hardened scoundrel. "I think not; he might be recognised by some one in his true character, and that would perhaps lead to unpleasant and dangerous discoveries; but if we consign his body to the deep, his fate will for ever remain a mystery, and no suspicion can attach to us."

"Do as you please," said the pirate, in a faint voice; "I cannot—dare not touch him."

"Why," said Pierce, looking at the pale countenance and quivering lips of Stanford with surprise; "is it possible that this can be the hitherto desperate and determined rover of the seas, whom nothing could ever before appal? Have you not faced death in all its horrible shapes, and surely you are not now going to quail at the corpse of one who professed himself to be one of your most dangerous enemies? Bah!—stand aside, and see how quickly I, who struck the fatal blow, will finish the business, and remove him from your sight for ever. Ha! ha! ha!" he said "that he should evermore be present to your imagination, sleeping or waking, at sea or on land. Well, we will try whether the words of the old dog will be realized after we have consigned his weather-beaten old hulk to the deep, though it strikes me that it will soon become food for old Mother Carey's chickens."

As the murderer thus spoke, he stooped down, and seizing the corpse of the unfortunate old man, he was about to raise it over his shoulder, when at that moment a broad blaze of lightning filled the wretched apartment, and was succeeded by a terrific peal of thunder, which shook the old hovel to its very foundation, and staggered even the hardened wretch who had just given utterance to such brutal observations. He dropped the corpse upon the floor, and covering his face with his hands, as a strange and almost overpowering sensation darted through his brain, he staggered to one corner of the room, while his guilty companion was transfixed to the spot on which he had been standing, and was unable to utter a word.

"Whewh!" at length said Pierce; "it blows great guns, certainly; but no matter, we are used to such tempests as these, and it is only the landlubber who trembles at them. But captain, how pale you look; come, come, belay there, and take in a reef! Let us tow this old vessel into port, and then crowd all sail to the bonny Raven, and meet the lads there."

"Stop! stop!' said Stanford; "let us be sure that there is no one lurking about who might watch us.

"Why, how qualmish you are, captain," remarked the ruffian; "it is not very likely anyone will be cruising about on such a night as this. Yes, I say, it blows great guns, with all the running gear of thunder and lightning, and rocks, and foggy loomings to the perser's account. But, pardon me, captian. I must say you are on this occasion like a porpoise in a storm, you turn your own way, over and over, and never seem to think of your bearings. However, to satisfy you, I will have a look out."

He went to the door of the hovel as he spoke, and gazed eagerly out upon the tempest, which still continued to rage with the most terrific violence, and seemed as if it would immolate the whole world in one universal scene of destruction. The white spray dashed up the sides of the rocks and cliffs, and even washed the feet of the miscreant as he stood on the threshold of the murdered old man, while the ethereal fire continued to blaze around, rendering the frightful horrors of the night at rapid intervals still more impressively perceptible.

"The coast is clear," said the ruffian, returning in the room; "come, let us finish this business."

Stanford returned no answer, and Pierce Raker raising the lifeless form of their unfortunate victim in his arms, advanced towards the door, the pirate captain following with a trembling step, for in spite of all his efforts to the contrary, he could not conquer the sensation of fear that had come over him, nor could he forget the solemn and impressive words to which poor old Reuben had given utterance in his last moments. More terrifically the thunder rolled, as if to curse them for the hellish and inhuman deed they had committed; but the miscreant Pierce seemed to remain undaunted, and urged on his companion with fearful oaths, until they had reached the very verge of the cliff, and looked down upon the angry and boiling waters.

"To the deep with you!" cried Pierce, in a hoarse voice, as he raised the corpse of his murdered victim in his gaunt arms above his head "and be the secret of your fate for ever buried."

Mark Stanford turned away his head with a sickly and almost overpowering sensation at his heart, and Pierce Raker precipitated the body of Reuben off the Cliff into the deep. In the brief pause of the thunder, the pirate chief heard the heavy splash of the corpse as the dark waters received and engulphed it, and he then, for the first time, ventured to look up. Pierce was standing on the verge of the cliff, and gazing with a look of fiendish triumph and exultation into the deep below, whilst the blue lightning flashed around his tall and athletic form and gave him almost a supernatural appearance.

"The deed is complete," he said, "your old enemy is now food for fishes, captain and the thunder is roaring his funeral dirge. Well, I mean to say that the business has been managed in a workman-like manner, and you ought to consider yourself a lucky fellow to have got rid of such a dangerous old shark; but you seem to be taken all aback;—why, skipper, I am surprised at you. But come, let us weigh anchor immediately and tow ourselves alongside the Raven."

"Avast, Pierce," replied Stanford, "I do indeed feel all aback, and to have lost my reckoning. Let us return home, and defer our visit to the ship till to-morrow; no boat could possibly live in such a sea as this."

"Pshaw, captain!" returned to ruffian, "you surprise me; you that have hitherto been accustomed to laugh at danger, and to punish those who dared to show the least sign of fear. For my own part, I glory in such a night as this; somehow it seems to come quite natural to my feelings. The voice of the thunder sounds no more unpleasant to me than the boatswain's whistle and as for the lightning that dances like a wild demon on the surface of the raging ocean, it affects me no more than a simple flash in the pan, at which I would as willingly light my pipe as I would crack a biscuit. The lads on board our gallant craft expect us to-night; our boat is safely moored in the cave yonder; I will take the helm, and will be answerable for the consequences, so come, captain, a stout heart upon the matter, and we shall soon reach the vessel in safety."

The observations of Pierce Raker aroused the pirate, and without saying a word he allowed himself to be led from the spot, and to yield to the importunities of his daring companion, although to venture in an open boat in such a terrific storm as that which was then raging seemed to be the very height of madness and desperation. The scene which presented itself to the gaze at the moment they stepped into the boat and loosened it from its moorings, was perfectly hideous, and on she dashed with the velocity of an arrow, one moment raised to a fearful height, and anon almost engulphed in the bosom of the mountainous billows. Still more fierce blazed the lightning, and terrific peals of thunder rapidly succeeded each other, every shock threatening inevitable destruction, whilst all attempts to manage the boat being completely futile, Mark Stanford and his guilty companion could do nothing else but to allow it to be carried at random on its wild and mad career, and to leave their fate to chance. Over the wild surging waves the boat was tossed, but still the wind drove her towards the pirate barque, which the elemental fire at intervals revealed, the waters of the deep every instant sweeping over her bulwarks, and threatening immediate destruction. There was one broad sheet of lightning more terrific than any they had yet witnessed, which spread a lurid glare for miles around, and Pierce was startled by a sudden exclamation of horror from his companion; and turning his gaze towards him, he beheld him with fixed eyes staring at a certain part of the ocean, and saw that he was convulsed with the most powerful emotion in every limb, while his face was as pale as that of a corpse.

"Why, captain," said the ruffian, "what the devil's in the breeze now? What are you staring at so intently?"

"Do you not see him!" gasped forth Mark Stanford, in reply.

"See him?—who?" demanded Pierce; "have you turned child again, or are you dreaming?"

"No," returned the pirate-captain, in a hoarse voice; "by h—l he has kept his word! See! see! he approached us, borne on the crest of the billows; and now, oh, horror! the blue lightning's flash, reveal to me distinctly his glassy eyes fixed full upon me. This is no delusion, Pierce, however much you may attempt to brave it out. Do you not see him? You must;—ah! nearer and nearer he comes! He will come in contact with our boat! Look—look, man, and judge for yourself!"

Pierce Raker did indeed follow the direction in which Stanford pointed, and there, in the broad glare of the lightning, and riding erect, breast-high above the waves was the corpse of poor old Reuben of the Cliff, driven rapidly towards the boat, and with its filmy eyes apparently fixed intently upon them, with the same awful expression which had characterised them when he gave utterance to his dying curse.

"By the infernal host!" shouted Pierce, in a voice that might be heard beyond the thunder; "what bitter mockery is this? Shall the deep thus disgorge its food as if to mock and defy us? D—n! the old lubber is bearing down upon us as if he had a design to swamp us altogether. Hold hard, captain, and I will lower his topsail in the twirling of a handspike!"

Onward, and onward, more rapidly came the corpse, while Mark Stanford was completely bound up in horror, and could not find strength to articulate a syllable; and his ferocious companion, although he attempted to pass off the circumstance with such bravado, was scarcely less alarmed, and wished himself safe on shore again. Another instant, and a wave washed it in the same position, directly to the head of the boat, and there, as if by some supernatural agency it became fixed for a minute or two, and its livid features were fully revealed to the two wretches in the boat.

"Fiends of hell!" shouted Stanford, at length worked up to a pitch of distraction; "why torture me thus? Down—down, foul corpse, and no longer sear my eyes with your presence!"

Was it the effect of conscience that worked upon the imagination of the murderers at that moment; or could it be reality? But as Mark Stanford gave utterance to these words, a ghastly smile seemed to overspread the livid features of the corpse; and as the waves dashed the body away from the boat, still erect, and distinctly revealed in the glare of the lightning, a hollow laugh seemed to vibrate in their ears, and was heard above the voice of the tempest until it finally vanished in the distance! All then became profoundly dark; the senses of the pirate captain reeled, and he sank back helplessly in the boat.

More fiercely than ever now raged the storm, and each advancing wave threatened to capsize the frail vessel in which the two villains had hazarded their lives. But Pierce Raker, made desperate with the terrors of their situation, struggled with almost superhuman strength to overcome them; and was enabled, notwithstanding the shock with which this unexpected adventure had given him, to perform wonders. They approached the vessel nearer and nearer, and when they had got to within a short distance of it, perceiving that many of the pirate crew were upon deck, they shouted at the top of their voice for assistance; for the boat was now half full of water, and their destruction seemed to be inevitable. Another tremendous wave dashed them nearly under the ship's bows, and at the same time she filled and was immediately sinking, when a couple of ropes were thrown over the side of the vessel, to which they clung with desperate energy, and were hauled safely on deck.

CHAPTER VI.

THE PIRATE CREW OF THE BLACK RAVEN.— MARK STANFORD'S DETERMINATION TO SEIZE KATE, AND THE CONSEQUENCES.

THE appearance of Mark Stanford and his villanous companion, Pierce Raker, caused the utmost astonishment of the crew of the Raven; for, notwithstanding they had received due intimation of their coming, of course, they had never expected that they would venture in such a storm as that which was then raging, and at such a nocturnal hour.

"Why, captain," observed one of the fellows, "you must have a stouter heart than even we knew you to possess, to brave the ocean in that cockle shell of a craft in such a tempest as this; and you and Pierce may think yourselves devilish lucky that you have reached the ship before you were capsized. But how pale you look—you—"

"Enough!" interrupted Stanford, sternly; "delay your remarks till some more fitting opportunity; I am in no humour to listen to them now. Pierce, follow me below."

The pirate crew retired in obedience to the commands of their captain, and Pierce Raker, taking his arm, accompanied him to his cabin. Stanford threw himself on a seat, and for a few minutes gazed wildly and vacantly around him.

"Why, captain," said Raker, "the adventure of the night seems to have taken you all aback, if it has not capsized you altogether. Arouse yourself, and since we have escaped all the dangers to which we were lately exposed, let us consult what is best now to be done."

"Pierce Raker," replied Stanford, in an agitated voice, "that has occurred to-night which I shall not be able easily to banish from my mind. Methinks I even now behold the ghastly face of the corpse as it was borne erect above the waves in our stormy track; and that I still hear the fearful curses of the murdered man in his dying moments. It was a frightful deed, so earnestly as he prayed for mercy and his life, and I wish it could have been avoided."

"Pshaw!" exclaimed Pierce; "what have we to fear? Would it not have been madness, ay, worse than madness to have suffered him to live after the threats he had held out? You were evidently not safe a moment while you had such an enemy in existence, but now you have nothing to apprehend; the dead tell no tales, I repeat, and who is to become acquainted with the fate which has befallen the old man, or to point the finger of suspicion at us?"

"I would that we had left his carcase to rot in his wretched hovel," said Stanford.

"Ridiculous!" returned Pierce; "surely we adopted the safest and most prudent plan.—Come, come, come, captain, this is a weakness which I did not think you capable of; arouse yourself, I say again, and do not let any of our messmates have any suspicion of what has this night taken place. As for the re-appearance of the corpse of the old man after I had consigned him to the deep, that was a mere accident and is not worthy of a second thought."

"Ah, Pierce," said Stanford, with a shudder, "the circumstances of this night have recalled all the horrors of the past to my memory. Just so did my former victim, Horace Markham, appear, when I had struck the fatal blow which deprived him of life, and he was sinking into the bosom of the ocean to rise no more. Oh, I can never forget his awful looks; the wild shriek of agony to which he gave utterance as the waves enclosed him; and now another——"

"Hold! hold! captain," again interrupted Pierce; "what, you that are so inured to scenes of bloodshed; to whom the expiring groans of agony are so familiar, whose name for years past has inspired such terror in the minds of all who have heard it, to talk thus. Zounds, man! I can scarce believe the evidence of my senses. And yet in spite of all you have fixed your thoughts upon Kate Markham, and have determined to possess her?"

"Yes," replied Stanford; "and strange and

JACK JUNK RESCUES KATE MARKHAM FROM THE DISGUISED PIRATE.

inconsistent though my conduct may appear to be, nothing whatever can alter that determination. The scorn with which the damsel has always treated me, and the affection which she lavishes upon the young sailor, Jack Junk, do but goad me on; and I swear that I will never rest until she is in my power, and safe on board this gallant barque."

"Well said, captain," remarked Pierce, " there you spoke like yourself, and I cannot but commend you for your resolution. Kate Markham will be the pride and ornament of the Black Raven. Oh, where is one more worthy of becoming the pirate's bride? Her presence will urge us on to fresh deeds of daring; and henceforth the fame of the rover of the seas will become more widely spread over the world. Arouse yourself; banish the gloomy thoughts which you have suffered the events of this night to excite in your mind, and unlimited success will crown your most sanguine wishes."

"The storm still howls with unabated fury," said Mark Stanford, after a pause; " it never before had such a powerful effect on me. We cannot venture from the ship until it has abated."

"And why should we?" demanded Pierce; "are we not better where we are, surrounded by our brave crew, and ready for any danger that might threaten us?"

"True," coincided the captain; "but we have nothing to fear. We have long anchored in this port without suspicion, and now that the fleet has departed, we have less reason to apprehend danger than ever.

"Certainly," returned his companion; "besides, I suppose now that Jack Junk is out of the way, and you have got rid of this old Reuben of the Cliff, you will not delay the execution of your designs against Kate Markham any longer than possible?"

"No," answered Stanford; "I am all impatience until they are accomplished, and I have already made up my mind as to the means I will adopt to get the damsel in my power."

"That is well; but what may they be, captain?"

"Oh, simple enough, but sure of success. There is no one, you know, resides with Kate Markham but her uncle and his daughter, Constance. The house is situated in a secluded spot, and at some distance from any other habitation, so what can be more easy than to make an attack on it at night, and bear her away?"

"True," said Pierce, "we have every means to accomplish such a design, and it will be our own faults if we be discovered, or even suspected. In the darkness of night Kate Markham can be borne with perfect safety on board this vessel, and then your triumph will be complete."

"It will," said Stanford, "and I exult at the thought. Oh, what would be the anguish of my hated rival while he is separated far from the girl whom he so fondly loves, did he but know the plot that is in contemplation against her, and be rendered completely powerless to assist her, or to avert the calamity?"

"Ay, captain," remarked Pierce, "that thought is most gratifying to your feelings of revenge; but there is one thing I would suggest to you, and which seems to have escaped your mind."

"And what is that?" demanded Stanford. "Should you retire from the farm immediately after the abduction of Kate, suspicion would naturally alight upon you, and it would not be safe for you to show yourself again in this part of the country."

"Why, that idea is reasonable enough," replied Mark, "and it has before occurred to me.—Such a suspicion must be prevented, if possible, and I will endeavour to hit upon some plan or other which is likely to be attended with the best results. At any rate, it will be advisable for me to remain at the farm for a day or two after the seizure of Kate, or they will at once, as you say, conclude that I am the author of all that has taken place."

"Certainly," said Pierce; "moreover, it is necessary that we should be in readiness to set sail at a minute's warning; for, although we have hitherto been fortunate, there is no knowing how soon something might occur to discover us, and we should find it, perhaps, a difficult job to escape, if the enemy should once get scent of us. You had better give the lads the necessary instructions, to be in readiness, in case of any emergency."

"Yes," agreed Stanford, "and it was for that purpose that I came hither to-night.—However, they will need but little instruction from me; the daring crew of the Black Raven are always prepared to encounter any danger that may threaten them, and to surmount it. But, come, we need some refreshment after the extraordinary and exciting events of the night; so let us rejoin our comrades, and endeavour to banish the effects of them, until this tempest is abated, and we may gain the shore in safety."

To this proposition, of course, Pierce Raker could raise no objection, and they therefore rejoined the remainder of the pirates accordingly, to whom Mark Stanford briefly communicated his designs as regarded Kate, and instructed them to hold themselves in readiness for her reception on board, and likewise to be ready to sail at a moment's notice, for it was not at all unlikely that their real character would after all be suspected, and if they were not on their guard, they might find themselves after their long career of triumph, and their many feats of daring, overpowered by numbers.

The ruffians all applauded the resolution of their captain; and notwithstanding the continued and frightful violence of the storm, they charged and recharged their glasses again and again, and in the most tumultuous manner they pledged the health of their inhuman chief, and his destined victim, and drank success to their future undertakings on the deep. But in spite of all his efforts to the contrary, and of the deep libations of which he so frequently partook, Mark Stanford felt a certain horror and dread at his heart which he could not shake off; and from which all the endeavours of Pierce could not arouse him. The ghastly countenance of the murdered old man as it had appeared to him above the surface of the tempestuous billows was never for a moment absent from his imagination; and even above the deafening voice of the storm, his awful dying curse still seemed to ring in his ears, and to bid him despair. Great as was the danger which the threats of Reuben had implied to him, he would have given the world could he have recalled that hellish deed; and instead of having sacrificed his life in so barbarous a manner he had him now securely in his power on board his pirate craft, and deprived of the means of effecting him any harm. The hours passed dismally and tediously away, and at length the morning dawned; and still the storm had very little abated, much to the annoyance of Mark Stanford, who was anxious to return home, but afraid again to trust himself to the fury of the elements; he was compelled to remain on board until some more favourable opportunity presented itself, and he might return ashore without being observed by any one.

CHAPTER VII.

THE BODY OF REUBEN OF THE CLIFF DISCOVERED.—THE CONSTERNATION.—THE DETERMINATION OF MARK STANFORD AND THE PIRATE CREW.—THE NIGHT OF HORROR.—SEIZURE OF KATE, AND FEARFUL DEATH OF MR. MARKHAM.

THE storm continued its fearful ravages until the middle of the following day, when the wind lulled; the voice of the thunder no longer shook the vault of Heaven; the lightning ceased to flash, and the rain no more descended from the ponderous clouds which had been surcharged with it. Gradually the sun broke forth, and the day became comparatively calm and tranquil. It had been a terrible night for all who resided for miles along the coast; sleep had been a stranger to them, and many were the prayers that were offered up to the Most High for the preservation of the hardy sons of the ocean, who were exposed to all its terrors. Great were the fears that were entertained for the safety of the noble fleet that had sailed on the previous day; and young and old flocked to the beach, in fearful anticipation of the sad havoc that might have been committed among the different vessels that were still anchored in the harbour; for such had been the terrific violence of the late tempest, that it would have been utterly impossible to have ventured to render any assistance, inevitable destruction threatening all those who might have been hardy enough to brave the horrors of the deep on such a frightful occasion. Several of the vessels had been driven from their moorings, and were no where to be seen; while others had boldly braved the storm, and remained apparently comparatively but little injured; and amongst them shone the pirate vessel, the Black Raven, supposed to be the fair trader, the Enterprise.

The spirits of poor Kate gradually revived when she beheld the favourable change in the weather, and devoutly she offered up her prayers to Heaven for the preservation of her lover, and in which she was most earnestly joined by her cousin, the amiable Constance. Old Joe Trennant was early at the house of his friend, Markham, and did his best to quiet the fears of all interested."

"It has been a rough night to be sure," remarked the old veteran; "and seldom in all the voyages I have made, have I witnessed such a storm. Many a brave fellow, I fear, has met with an ocean grave; it is a sad thought; but avast, avast, Joe, it is a noble death, and those who have met it are, I hope, moored in the haven of happiness. Come, Kate, my pretty lass, now, do not again be hoisting those signals of distress, but hold hard by the anchor of hope. Your lover, I trust, is quite safe, and will still be able to steer clear of the shoals of destruction. Jack, my Jack, is a lad of mettle, whom no danger can appal; Jack, why, he is the tar for all weathers! and, damme, he is a lying lubber who dares to say to the contrary."

Kate faintly smiled at the warmth of the honest old seaman; but her mind was still tormented with mingled hopes, doubts, and apprehensions, and it was a completely fruitless task for her to try to regain her wonted composure.

"I cannot remain here," she said; "let us wander to the beach that we may gaze upon that deep which was lately the scene of so many terrors."

"What a strange and extravagant idea, my dear niece," observed Mr. Markham; "you had better abandon it; what good can result from that which must naturally create so many melancholy thoughts?"

"Do not refuse me, my dear sir," said Kate, "for I feel an irresistibile impulse to obey the dictates of my own heart; and something seems to whisper to me that I shall obtain some consolation in the comtemplation of that vast deep on which my poor Jack has embarked his fate. Come, my uncle, Constance, and Mr. Trennant, you will accompany me:—it may appear an extraordinary fancy I am ready to admit, but, at least, do not refuse me from indulging in it."

Finding that it would be useless to attempt to dissuade her, and hoping that it might, as she said, serve to alleviate the anguish of her mind, Mr. Markham and the others no longer raised any objection, and issuing forth from the house they made their way to the sea-beach, trying to divert her mind from the melancholy subjects that engrossed it as they proceeded. On arriving within sight of the cliffs upon which the hovel of the unfortunate and mysterious man, Reuben, was situated, Kate paused, and all the strange events that had occurred to her and Constance at their interview with him, rushed as fresh and vividly upon her memory as if they had only been enacted the previous hour. She could not help shuddering, and she turned very pale; and her uncle, who immediately noticed her emotion, inquired the cause of it.

"Nothing, nothing, my dear uncle," said the damsel, in a faltering voice, and struggling with her feelings; "it was only a weak and unaccountable sensation which suddenly came over me; but it is at an end now. This is a wild and cheerless spot, and——"

"And yet," added Mr. Markham, "that very remarkable old man, Reuben of the Cliff, as he is called, has chosen to take up his residence here. It is stated by some persons that he is possessed of the gift of foresight and can penetrate into the secrets of futurity. Ha! ha! ha! a very likely story, truly; poor old man, his intellects must be deranged, that is very certain; however, from all that I have seen or heard of him, I believe he is perfectly harmless, and, therefore, I do not see why any person should interfere with his singular whims."

"Very true, sir," returned Kate; "but let us proceed; for, I confess, I feel a kind of dread while remaining on this wild spot."

Mr. Markham gazed at her with some degree of astonishment, but made use of no further observation, and they quitted the spot and made their way towards the beach, where, as has been before stated, numerous persons had for some time assembled, and were gazing with anxious eyes across the broad waters of the ocean which had lately been so frightfully convulsed by all the horrors of the storm. Many a sad and foreboding heart was there present, that had been separated from all they held most dear, on the late sailing of the British fleet, and which throbbed with fear and anxiety for the fate which had probably already befallen them, or which might yet be in store for them; but no heart was more sad nor desponding than that which palpitated in the gentle and affectionate bosom of the beauteous Kate Markham. All eyes were directed towards her, and there was not one individual but deeply, and sincerely sympathized in the grief which oppressed her, and banished the roses from her lovely cheeks. With the most melancholy expression she fixed her gaze upon the deep blue waters; distracting thoughts crowded with tumultuous and overwhelming rapidity upon her brain, and tears gushing to her eyes, and streamed down her cheeks. Mr. Markham and his fair daughter marked her emotion with the most profound and heartfelt pity, but they did not offer to interrupt her thoughts, as they knew, full well, that her grief was more likely to be ameliorated by her being suffered to give free indulgence to them.

Suddenly their attention was attracted by something that was being drifted on the surface of the ocean towards the shore, and on its approaching nearer, they perceived it was a long track of sea-weed, in which the body of a human being seemed to be entangled, and was floating with the head uppermost. It was dashed more rapidly onwards, and at length a powerful wave washed it on the beach, immediately at the feet of Kate Markham and her friends. She uttered a faint scream of mingled astonishment and terror, and several of the other persons assembled, rushed to the spot, and stooping down, the ghastly and distorted features of the ill-fated Reuben of the Cliff, with his eyes wide open, revealed themselves to the horror-struck gaze of all present.

A deadly sickness came over our heroine, and she could not remove her eyes from the corpse, but Mr. Markham and the others, examining it more minutely, beheld the frightful and gaping wounds in the side, and then the horrible fate which had befallen the unfortunate old man became perfectly apparent.

"A foul and cowardly murder has been committed," said Mr. Markham; "what wretch or wretches have done this?"

"Oh, horror!" gasped forth Kate; "so soon, too, after——wretched old man, could not thy gray hairs stay the hand of the inhuman assassin?—I cannot gaze upon the ghastly and mutilated corpse. Oh, let us begone!—May Heaven visit the monsters who have perpetrated this hideous crime with its most terrible vengeance!"

She covered her face with her hands, to shut out the revolting sight, and the deepest anguish agitated her gentle and susceptible bosom.

"Let the corpse of the ill-fated man be conveyed to his miserable hovel," said Mr. Markham, and the proper authorities being informed of the dreadful circumstance, every inquiry must, immediately be made, which may lead to the detection and punishment of the murderer or murderers."

Several of the persons assembled on the spot, who all expressed their horror, raised the mangled body from the earth, and in obedience to the instructions of Mr. Markham, they conveyed it to the hovel which Reuben had occupied while living; and Mr. Markham and Constance taking the arm of our heroine, supported her trembling form towards home, where, on arriving, it was some time ere she could recover from the shock her feelings had sustained.

The savage murder of poor old Reuben of the Cliff caused the greatest sensation in the neighbourhood, and every means that reason could suggest were adopted to discover the atrocious assassins, but without any prospect of success, for such was the secrecy with which it had been perpetrated, that it was impossible for suspicion to alight on any one; and it seemed more than likely that the dreadful circumstance would ever remain involved in mystery. A strict search was made in the hovel, but nothing whatever was discovered which was calculated to lead to any idea as to who the old man really was, and what could be his motives for taking up to so singular a course of life. In vain did Kate try to banish his image and the extraordinary and awful scene which herself and Constance had witnessed in his wretched abode from her memory; and she more than ever regretted his melancholy death, since there now seemed to be little or no chance of the mystery connected with herself ever being unravelled; and if her father had really met with the horrible fate which Reuben had represented him to have done, all chance of his brutal murderer being detected and brought to condign punishment seemed to be at an end. These thoughts distracted her brain almost beyond endurance, and she was several times on the point of revealing the whole of the circumstances to her uncle, but something prevented her, and Constance persuaded her not to do so for the present, but to seek to divert her thoughts to other subjects.

In the meantime Mark Stanford and the other pirates exulted in the thought of the impenetrable mystery that prevailed as to who were the real assassins of the unfortunate Reuben; and they felt perfectly satisfied that, if they kept their own counsel, there was no possibility of its ever being discovered. But the guilty conscience of the monster, Stanford, was far from being at ease, and the dying words and ghastly looks of the murdered man continually haunted his imagination. He, however, determined to persevere in his diabolical designs against Kate Markham, and he had not the least doubt but that he would meet with all the success he could wish. For the last few days he had not ventured much from the house, and he had always most sedulously avoided the presence of Kate or her friends, so that any suspicions of his intentions might be stifled; but he lost not a moment in maturing his plans, and the time seemed now to be rapidly approaching when he might safely put them into execution.

It was night, and Mark Stanford and his worthy colleague, Pierce, were seated together in one of the secret rooms before described, at the back of the house. This was about a fortnight after the departure of our hero, and the events taking place which we have described in the previous pages.

"There is no other way of accomplishing it, captain," observed Pierce, in continuation of the conversation; "to be crowned with success in any desperate undertaking, desperate and determined means must always be adopted. There is no chance of our being enabled to ensnare the girl into our power, and therefore our only way is to seize her by a *coup de main*. One bold effort and she is yours, and once on board the Raven, we may set pursuit and discovery at defiance."

"True," said Stanford; "and if we make an attack upon the house at midnight, there is no danger, I should think, of our being interrupted."

"Not the least," answered Pierce, "if we can only manage to elude the preventive service, which, by common prudence and precaution, we can easily do. The house where Kate resides, is situated in the most lonely part, and there is no one but old Markham to protect her, so what chance is there of our plans being defeated?"

"None that I see at present," said Mark. "I feel the greatest confidence in my triumph though had the British fleet still been in the harbour, the attempt would have been a daring one, and might easily have been discovered and defeated."

"Yes, captain," coincided Pierce, "you acted wisely in deferring the execution of your plot till after the departure of the enemy; and, moreover, I think we adopted the safest course in putting that babbling old fool, Reuben of the Cliff, out of the way altogether. He knew too much for us, and would not have failed to betray us at the earliest opportunity, depend upon it."

Mark Stanford shuddered, with an involuntary feeling of horror, and did not return any immediate answer.

"Why do you continually remind me of that fearful circumstance, Pierce?" he said at length; "I can never recal it to my memory without a feeling of trembling and dread coming over me."

"Pshaw!" exclaimed Pierce, impatiently, "I am surprised at you, captain; such feelings as those you have just now expressed are unworthy of your daring character."

"You may deride me, Pierce," returned the pirate, "and think that I have become weak and superstitious; but do you imagine that I can recal the dying words of the murdered man to my memory with indifference, or that I can ever cease to remember the awful events that succeeded his death, with any other sentiments than those of horror? His pale face and reproachful eyes have been present to my imagination ever since that fatal night, when the terrific voice of the storm seemed to thunder curses on the bloody deed, and——"

"Hold! hold! captain!" interrupted his guilty companion; "I can scarcely believe it is yourself to whom I am listening. But enough of this; at present let our whole thoughts be devoted to the accomplishment of our deep-laid designs. All is prepared on board our vessel for the reception of the girl, I believe?"

"Everything," answered Stanford, having hastily quaffed off the contents of a glass in order to revive his courage.

"Then the sooner we set about the execution of our plot the better."

"Exactly so."

"When do you, then, propose that it shall be?"

"The night after to-morrow at the latest; and in the meantime, I will finally make up my mind what it would be wisest to do in respect to this farm."

"Ay," observed Pierce, "it would be by no means pleasant or convenient to abandon a place so well adapted for our secret purposes altogether; and yet, after what has already taken place between you and Kate Markham, suspicion might be excited against you, should you remain here after her abduction, and inquiries might be made which would probably lead to unpleasant discoveries."

"Right!" replied Stanford, "but I cannot for a moment think of resigning the farm, for that would be too great a sacrifice. An idea, however, strikes me."

"And what is that?" demanded Pierce.

"Why, would it not be easy to make it appear, in order to account for my sudden disappearance, that particular and private reasons had induced me to let the farm on lease for a certain number of years? One of our crew could personate the in-coming tenant without suspicion, and thus they would be completely deceived and taken off their guard, eh?"

"An excellent idea, captain," said Pierce.

"Yes, I think that would baffle them."

"But in order to carry out that scheme with safety, it will be necessary to delay the seizure of Kate for a short time longer," remarked Pierce.

"Well, suppose we say a week from the present time? A few days will not make such a vast deal of differance."

"Very true, be it so. That then is decided on."

"It is," replied Mark Stanford, "and in the meantime, in order the better to forward my plot, I will play the hypocrite, visit old Markham in a friendly way, pretend to feel regret for my past boldness, solicit his forgiveness, and that of his fair niece, and bid them farewell. Ha! ha! ha! if that do not deceive them and remove suspicion from me, I don't know what will."

"Ay, captain," said Pierce, "it is well contrived, and I have not the least doubt that you will execute it with your usual ability."

The two villains having thus arranged their infamous plans to their mutual satisfactions, after some further conversation, retired for the night.

Two or three days elapsed without anything particular occurring worthy of being recorded in these pages, and the melancholy of Kate suffered but little abatement, though Constance and her father did all they could to console her, and to inspire her with hope. Her thoughts were continually fixed upon her lover, and the most dismal forebodings constantly distracted her mind, especially when she thought of the extraordinary predictions of Reuben of the Cliff, and his awful and untimely fate, which was still involved in so much mystery.

Kate and her cousin and Markham, were seated one afternoon in the parlour of their dwelling, engaged in conversation, when they were suddenly startled and surprised by the appearance of Mark Stanford, who they had hoped would never have the boldness to obtrude upon their society again. Immediately on his entrance Kate and her cousin arose from their seats, and curtseying coldly, they abruptly quitted the room. Stanford bit his lips, but concealed his chagrin as well as he could, and bowing to Mr. Markham with studied politeness, he inquired respectfully after his health. Mr. Markham returned a suitable reply, and then added:

"To what may I be indebted for the honour of this visit, Mr. Stanford?"

"The honour is mine, Mr. Markham," replied the pirate, with a gracious smile.   "I have to apologize to you for what may at first appear to you the boldness of this visit ; but I come to request a favour of you, and I have too high an opinion of your condescension and generosity to entertain the least apprehension that you will refuse me."

"A favour from me, sir ?" said Markham, with a look of surprise.

"Yes, Mr. Markham," answered Stanford ; "and I have to request your patience while I explain myself."

Mr. Markham handed him a chair, and then awaited with much curiosity to hear what he had to say.

"Mr. Markham," began the pirate, "I am fully aware that the subject on which I am about to address you is a most delicate one, and that circumstances have occurred which unfortunately are calculated to prejudice you against my character ; but I will endeavour to be as brief as I can."

"Proceed, sir," said Mr. Markham rather impatiently.

"I need not inform you, Mr. Markham," continued Stanford ; "that the great personal and intrinsic charms of your amiable niece, captivated my heart from the first moment I beheld her, and——"

"Sir?" interrupted Mr. Markham, and rising angrily.

"Bear with me, my dear sir, a few moments, I beg of you," returned Stanford, "and do not misunderstand me. I repeat that I loved your niece, but her heart was unfortunately another's, and there was nothing left to me but despair ; but still so powerful was the passion that reigned within my breast, that I could not readily resign my hopes ;—I confessed my love, was rejected, but still I ventured to prosecute my suit ; in that I own I was wrong, very wrong, and it is for that I have to supplicate your forgiveness, and that of Miss Markham, your niece. From this time you nor she will never again receive any annoyance from me ; circumstances have compelled me to dispose of the farm and retire to a distant land. It is quite uncertain whether this country will ever behold me again ; but wherever I am, I assure you that I shall never cease to remember yourself, the amiable Kate, and her fair cousin, with the most unfeigned respect, and to feel the most poignant regret that I should ever have caused her or any one connected with her, a moment's uneasiness."

Mr. Markham looked at him narrowly : his words surprised him ; but they were spoken with so much apparent sincerity, that he could not doubt him.

"Mr. Stanford," he remarked, "I accept your apology with the same frankness with which it appears to be given ; and as it is a subject which cannot be altogether pleasing to either of us, we will say no more upon it. I bear you no ill will, neither, I am certain, will my gentle niece do so, nothwithstanding all that has taken place. I wish you prosperity, sir, wherever you may go."

"Thank you, Mr. Markham, for your kind wishes," returned Stanford, with the same assumption of respect : "my course is bent to a far distant land, and as it is not likely that we shall ever meet again, it will afford me much gratification to know that, at any rate, we do not part bad friends. May I request you to convey my sentiments to your amiable niece?"

"I will do so," answered Mr. Markham ; "and I feel convinced that she will receive them with much satisfaction, and will bury the past in oblivion ."

Mark Stanford again returned his acknowledgments, and after a few more observations, he politely took his leave, secretly exulting at the success of his scheme, and the manner in which he had deceived Mr. Markham.

"The fool," he muttered to himself, as he proceeded towards his home, "he little imagines the deep-laid scheme I have in contemplation ; and that, so far from abandoning my designs against the scornful beauty, his niece, I have so matured my plans that she cannot possibly escape me. I go to a distant land, far across the bright blue waters, true ; but Kate Markham shall be the companion of my voyage ; she shall become the pirate's mistress, and I will fully revenge myself for the scorn and hatred with which she has hitherto treated me. Jack Junk, should you ever return again to your native land, it will be to meet sorrow and disappointment. The fair and innocent girl, in whom your whole affections are centred, you shall never behold again, unless it be as the fallen and degraded mistress of the daring Rover of the Seas, whose very name for years past has struck terror into the minds of all who heard it. I triumph !—I triumph !"

Thus soliloquizing with himself, the villain reached his home, where he found Pierce Raker anxiously awaiting him.

"Well, what success, captain?" he inquired.

"All that I could wish," replied Stanford. "I have played my cards with my usual skill, and old Markham is completely deceived. He thinks me a very paragon of penitence and humility, and no doubt, after what I have said, he will persuade his niece to think the same of me.   Ha! ha! ha!"

"'Tis well," said Pierce: "then they will be thrown completely off their guard, and our plot cannot fail of being crowned with success."

"It cannot," said Stanford; "in a day or two we will put our design into execution, and Kate Markham will be securely in my power, and safely on board the Black Raven. The thought inspires me with delight, and will fully repay me for the scorn with which she has hiterto treated me.   Our arrangements are all complete, and at the earliest opportunity they shall be put into effect.   Once safe on board our gallant vessel, we may set discovery at defiance, and I care not whether suspicion lights upon me."

"And yet," said Pierce ; " it would be as well if it did not ; but I think you have adopted the proper course to prevent that."

To this opinion Stanford agreed, and the conversation for the present dropped.

The plausibility of Stanford's statement and his manners had indeed completely deceived Mr. Markham, and he felt satisfied at the resolution he had formed, and the prospect of his so soon leaving the neighbourhood, his bold advances towards his niece having hitherto proved a source of such annoyance to them all.   Kate and Constance also heard the purport of his visit with no little surprise and satisfaction ; but still the former could not help entertaining some doubts as to the sincerity of his professions, and she had also some misgivings that he had some sinister design in view, which it would be necessary for them to guard against.   Two days afterwards, however, all their suspicions were set at rest, when they were made acquainted with the departure of Mark Stanford, and that the farm had come into the occupation of another man, who was a total stranger in the neighbourhood, so skilfully and so secretly had Stanford arranged all his plans, that it was almost impossible that the least suspicion should be excited, and the success of his nefarious design seemed quite certain.   The reader, however, will not need to be informed that he had not quitted the neighbourhood, but he kept himself closely confined to the house, only venturing forth at night, and then so disguised that it would have been almost impossible for any one to have recognised him.   In this manner he suffered another week to elapse, and suspicion was now completely set at an end, and he then determined at once to put his designs into execution.

Kate had now become more tranquillised in her mind, though she could not help at times feeling some strange and sad presentiments, that some misfortune was about to befal them which they would find it impossible to avert.   Her favourite walk was on the beach, where she would wander for hours, and while she gazed upon the broad waters of the deep, her thoughts would constantly dwell upon her lover, and she would picture to her imagination in vivid colours his situation, and offer up the most fervent prayers to Heaven for his preservation, and look forward with the most painful anxiety to the time when they might meet again ; although she often entertained the most terrible apprehensions that he would perish in the battle's heat, and at such times it was in vain that her uncle and Constance sought to impart consolation to her.

It was night, and Kate and her cousin had sought their chamber, but neither of them felt inclined for rest, but sat conversing together till a late hour.   Kate had felt more than usually melancholy during the day, and the most dismal forebodings tortured her mind, which in spite of all her efforts she could not conquer ; and now her fears gradually seemed to increase, until she became so violently agitated that it was with the utmost difficulty she could support herself. The night too was dark and cheerless, and the wind howled mournfully at intervals round the house ; but still Kate could not think of retiring to rest, notwithstanding the lateness of the hour, and the pursuasions of her cousin.

"Why do you persist in encouraging such painful apprehensions, my dear cousin?" said Constance ; "what danger should you fear ?   The only one whom you had cause to dread was Stanford ; but he is now far away, and I feel confident that he will never annoy you again. Come, come, arouse yourself, and endeavour to look forward to the future with hope and tranquillity."

"Alas, Constance," replied our heroine ; "you may deem me weak and foolish, but indeed I find it impossible to conquer the melancholy feelings that have occupied my mind throughout the day.   I fear to go to rest, for it seems to me as if some fearful calamity were impending over me, and which it will be totally impossible for me to avert.   I wish to Heaven it was morning."

"How extraordinary and unaccountable is this," remarked Constance ; "what danger should threaten you ?   But the gloom of the night has taken this dismal effect upon your spirits ; and certainly it is by no means calculated to inspire the most lively thoughts.   But come let us seek our pillow, and sleep will banish these gloomy ideas from your brain."

"No Constance," returned our heroine ; "I do not feel the least inclined for sleep ; I will

THE PIRATE CONSIGNING THE DEAD BODY TO THE WAVES.

sit here till daylight. But do not let me detain you from your bed ; I shall find sufficient society in the communion of my own thoughts."

"Would that I could persuade you," said Constance, "for, really, such ideas appear to me most unreasonable."

"They may appear so," said Kate ; "but I find that it is completely useless for me to try to divest my mind of them.   Hark ! what noise was that below ?"

"Nonsense, Kate," replied her cousin, "you are suffering your imagination to deceive you. I heard nothing."

"Oh, I am certain I could not have been mistaken," returned our heroine ; "it sounded like the hasty closing of a door below."

"It was nothing but the wind, depend upon it, which is   tainly very high and boisterous. Come, come, arouse yourself."

Kate shook her head, and her countenance, which was very pale, showed plainly the emotions which tortured her bosom, and which gained strength every moment. The night became more intensely dark, and everything gave warning of an approaching storm; but still Kate continued in the same condition, and could not for a moment think of retiring to rest; and Constance saw that it was entirely useless to endeavour to persuade her, and she therefore tried to divert her thoughts from the dismal subject that engrossed them.

The storm which had so long threatened now commenced with great violence, and the rain pattered loudly against the windows, and the wind blew so violently that it shook the very house to its foundation. But amid the pauses of the blast, Kate frequently imagined that she heard strange noises, and her cousin fruitlessly sought to persuade her to the contrary; in fact, she was herself at times half inclined to think that Kate was not mistaken, though she could not bring herself to believe that the sounds proceeded from any other cause than the fury of the storm. In this manner another quarter of an hour of painful suspense passed away, and still Kate kept imagining she heard strange noises proceeding from below, and her apprehensions became at last so powerful that she almost dreaded to look around her.

"Would that my uncle had not retired to rest," she said; "or that the morning was here. Something terrible, I feel convinced, is about to happen."

"Ridiculous!" said Constance; "I really shall lose all patience with you, my dear Kate, if you thus persist in giving way to such idle and groundless fears."

"Hist! hist!" ejaculated her cousin, in a faint voice, and suddenly laying her hand upon her arm; "There! there! did you not hear that?"

"I heard nothing but the wind," replied Constance.

"Oh, no," gasped forth Kate, "I am certain I was not mistaken. It sounded like the suppressed mutterings of human voices, and the cautious treading of footsteps on the stairs There again—you must hear that."

Constance did, indeed, at that moment distinctly hear sounds such as Kate had described; and they clung together, and held their breath in a state of the greatest alarm and astonishment. Louder and louder the sounds became, until they appeared to be immediately outside the door. Worked up to a pitch of the greatest terror, the fair cousins uttered a simultaneous scream, and the next instant the room door was burst open, and several of the pirates wearing black masks, and all armed, appeared on the threshold.

"Cease your cries, for they are useless!" exclaimed the well known voice of Mark Stanford, seizing the horror-struck Kate in his arms; "resistance is in vain. Constance Markham, the prize I seek is your fair, though scornful cousin, and not you! Away, lads, and leave the other girl to console her father for his loss!—Mark Stanford's moment of triumph has arrived, and in another hour the lovely Kate shall be on board his gallant pirate barque!"

"Oh, help!—help!" shrieked Constance; "monsters! release your senseless victim, or the vengeance of Heaven will overtake you, even unprotected though we are!"

"Ha! ha! ha!" laughed Stanford, scornfully; "I heed not your threats, weak girl; and you may think yourself fortunate that I do not desire you to accompany us. But we waste time! Quick, my lads, quick!"

Poor Kate had fainted, and Constance was now so overpowered with horror that she also sank on the floor insensible. Stanford, throwing the light and graceful form of his intended victim across his shoulder, quitted the room, followed by Pearce and the other pirates, and hastily descended the stairs towards the back of the house, at which they had effected their entrance; but the noise had aroused Mr. Markham, who, unfortunately, at that moment made his appearance in his dressing-gown on the landing, and on beholding the pirates, and the insensible form of his niece, he started back a few paces in terror and amazement; but he recovered himself in an instant, and, rushing desperately on Stanford he exclaimed—

"Villain! miscreant! midnight robber and assassin, release this innocent girl, or my cries shall rend the air, and——"

"Madman!" interrupted Mark Stanford in a savage voice; "stand back, and do not offer a fruitless resistance, or take the consequences."

"Ah! Mark Stanford," cried the old man, "is it you? Ah, wretch! wretch! But I will resist your diabolical purpose, however feeble my arm may be."

As he thus spoke, he again rushed on the pirate, and endeavoured to seize him by the throat.

"Headstrong fool!" shouted Pierce, "are you determined to brave your fate? Then take the consequences."

"Hold! hold!" cried Stanford; "take not his life, but secure him and stop his noise."

He spoke too late, however, for at that instant the miscreant, Pierce, dealt the unfortunate Mr. Markham a terrible blow with his sword upon the head, and he sank bleeding and insensible upon the floor.

"By h——l! you have slain him!" exclaimed Mark Stanford, "this is cursed unfortunate. But away! and let us make all speed to the place where the boat awaits to carry us on board."

He rushed down the stairs as he thus spoke, still bearing the insensible Kate in his arms, and followed by Pierce and the other pirates, and soon emerged from the house. The coast was quite clear, and the ruffians hurried on with the greatest rapidity, and were soon far beyond the spot.

"Fortune be praised!" ejaculated Stanford, as they proceeded; "I triumph! The girl is mine, and nothing can again rescue her from my power; but I would that you had not been so hasty, Pierce; I would that the old man's life had been spared."

"He brought his fate upon himself by his obstinacy," answered Pierce, "and what's the use of regretting it now? But perhaps after all he may not be dead."

"I hope not," said Stanford; "but quick, while the girl still remains insensible."

Pierce made no reply, and they pursued their way with increased speed, and totally regardless of the fury of the battling elements. Having arrived at the rocks they made their way through a rude opening to the beach, where the boat was moored ready to convey them to the pirate vessel. In two or three minutes they were dashing rapidly over the deep, and at length the boat came alongside the ship, and they all got safely on board, where they were welcomed by the shouts of the pirates. Stanford conveyed the insensible form of his destined victim to a cabin which had been prepared for her reception, and having kissed the poor girl rapturously, he left her in charge of a female, and returned on deck to give orders for the anchor to be weighed immediately. In less than a quarter of an hour, all was ready, and the pirate vessel was dashing swiftly, like a gigantic bird of ill omen, over the deep.

"Hurrah!" shouted the pirate chief, throwing aside his disguise and appearing in his true character. "Hugh Granfied is again upon his native element, proud and triumphant! Kate Markham, you will see your native land no more, nor those so dear to you. You are now the mistress of the Buccaneer, and must learn to submit to no other will but his. Rejoice, my lads, shout long life and prosperity to your captain and his lovely mate."

The rude and boisterous shouts of the daring crew of the Black Raven rent the air, and Mark Stanford allowed them to give free indulgence to their hilarity. Before our heroine had recovered her senses, the pretended Enterprise was far away over the dark waters, and her fate seemed to be inevitable. The motion of the vessel, and the noise of the crew at length aroused Kate, and opening her eyes and starting to her feet, she gazed with astonishment and horror around her.

"God of Heaven!" she exclaimed, clasping her aching temples; "what is the meaning of this? Where am I? Where are my friends, and what has brought me hither?"

The woman in whose care she had been left, now advanced towards her, but Kate started back alarmed at the sight of her, and in frantic accents repeated her questions.

"Why, Miss Markham," replied the woman, "for that is your name, I believe, I should think it would not take you much trouble to discover that you are on board a ship, and as gallant a vessel as ever stemmed the wave. The Black Raven must be your future home, and the rover of the seas, he whom you have hitherto known only as Farmer Stanford claims you for his mistress!"

No sooner did the unfortunate damsel hear the terrible announcement than she gave utterance to a piercing shriek, and again became insensible.

CHAPTER VIII.

THE CATASTROPHE—THE DISTRACTION OF CONSTANCE MARKHAM.

RETURN we now to the scene where the monstrous outrage we have been describing was perpetrated. It was not until several minutes after the departure of the pirates with their unfortunate victim, that Constance was awakened to consciousness; and her brain was then tortured to madness as the dreadful truth flashed upon her memory, and she found herself alone. Screaming aloud for help, and calling upon the name of her cousin, she rushed from the chamber, and made her way down the stairs till she came to the landing, when the bleeding form of her unfortunate parent met her appalled sight; and, with a loud cry of horror, she sank upon the floor by his side, and once more her senses left her. It was some time before she recovered; and with what feelings of distraction and horror did she then raise the form of her father and gaze upon his ghastly, blood-stained countenance.

"Father! father!" she groaned; "oh, speak to me!—Almighty God! the monsters have murdered him!"

She pressed the poor old man in her arms, and eagerly laid her hand upon his heart; but she could not feel it beat; and life appeared to be quite extinct.

"Horror! horror!" she cried, in delirious accents; "he is no more! the fiends have slain him! and I am a friendless, wretched orphan! Heaven, I invoke your most terrible retribution for this frightful, this hideous crime!—Father! dear father! art thou, indeed, no more? and wilt thou never speak to me again?—I shall go mad—Oh, God! this trial is surely too severe!"

She started, and uttered a mingled exclamation of hope and fear, for at that moment a faint groan escaped the bosom of her father, and he opened his eyes and fixed them upon her with such an expression of pity and regret, as she could never forget.

"Ah! all merciful Heaven!" she cried, "I thank thee.—He still lives!—Father, dear unfortunate father!—but one word! oh, let your poor child but hear you speak again, and appease the horror that distracts my soul!"

He made several painful efforts to speak, but in vain—it was too late; the dew of death already stood upon his brow; his eyes grew dim; he pressed the hand of his daughter convulsively, breathed one groan of agony, and sank back a corpse. A frightful shriek of agony and despair, which might have been heard far around, burst from the lips of Constance; her brain swam round; her limbs tottered under her, and she fell by the side of the corpse totally unconscious. Morning dawned, and still the poor girl remained in the same state of stupor; and it did not seem likely that she would ever recover again; and it was not till old Joe Trennant came to the house to pay his customary morning visit, that the dreadful occurrence was discovered. We need not attempt to describe the horror of the kind hearted old veteran at the ghastly sight; and it was not till after the lapse of a few minutes that he could recover himself sufficiently to decide how to act.

"My poor old friend dead—murdered!" he faltered out, in a broken voice; "can I believe my eyes? or is it only some frightful dream? What monster in human form has done this? Poor girl, it will be the death of her.—But where is Kate—the pretty innocent Kate?—Ah! what strange fear is this that suddenly comes over me? Kate, my lass, why are you not here? Kit Breezely! messmates! all, why do you not come to my assistance?—I—I—oh, shiver my timbers, if I couldn't cry like a lubberly boy!"

He drew the cuff of his coat across his eyes; and for a few minutes he could not move or give utterance to a syllable; but at length he raised the insensible form of poor Constance from the floor, and conveyed her into the apartment, placing her on a sofa. He then, with a heavy heart, also removed the body of his ill-fated friend into another room, and rushed frantically over the house, calling upon the name of Kate; but his anguish and despair were almost insupportable when he discovered that she was not there.

"It is clear enough," he said; "some infernal villains have borne down upon the poor girl, forced her from her moorings, and her poor uncle has lost his life in attempting to defend her. I am taken all aback.—I—I—I shall go mad! Let me alarm the neighbourhood, and see whether we cannot overhaul this terrible mystery. Oh, Jack, my poor lad, what would be your anguish did you but know what has taken place!"

He rushed out of the house, and made his way with all the speed he could to the inn, in order that he might make old Kit acquainted with the dreadful event; and the consternation of Kit and everybody else who heard it may be readily imagined. Old Joe was accompanied back to the house by Breezely and several others, and the utmost horror was expressed by every one at the ghastly sight which presented itself. Constance was still in the same state of unconsciousness as she was when Joe Trennant first discovered her and the body of her murdered father; but a person was immediately despatched for the assistance of a medical man, who immediately announced that Mr. Markham must have been dead for some time; and he then used his best exertions to restore poor Constance to sensibility, for they were all anxiety until they heard from her lips an explanation of the awful circumstance. Some time, however, elapsed, before any visible effects attended the doctor's efforts, and the whole of the parties present were in a state of the most painful suspense and apprehension, lest the shock the poor girl had sustained from the dreadful and unexpected calamity might prove too much for her strength to support; but at length a deep sigh escaped her bosom, and gave token of returning life. In another moment she opened her eyes, and gazed wildly and vacantly around upon the individuals present. Poor old Joe Trennant approached her with the kindness of a parent, and taking her hand, in a voice of the greatest gentleness and sympathy, he said—

" Cheer thee, cheer thee, my poor lass: you are surrounded by your friends, and——"

Constance started at the sound of his voice, and interrupting him, exclaimed—

" Ah! who are you that thus addresses me? Where am I? Why am I thus surrounded? Who are you al? Oh, horror! I remember now! Father! father! Monsters! They have torn you from me! It is in vain to attempt to deceive me! I pressed his lifeless, mangled corpse in my arms! I saw the clotted blood upon his brow! They have murdered him! Father! father! Oh, God!——"

She could say no more, but with a frenzied shriek, she again sank insensible upon the sofa.

" Unfortunate girl," remarked Trennant, " this awful blow will prove too much for her. She will never be able to survive so frightful a catastrophe. Kate Markham too; oh, what has become of her? The monsters who have done this will surely be visited with the most terrible retribution of heaven!"

Every one present looked on for a few moments in a state of the greatest consternation, but at length the doctor advised the removal of Constance to her chamber where she was left in the charge of himself and two of the females, and the authorities of the district were made acquainted with the dreadful particulars, so that every prompt search might be made after the perpetrators of so atrocious an outrage.

We need not attempt to describe the painful sensation which was created in the vicinity as soon as the frightful event became generally known, and every exertion was immediately made which might lead to any discovery, but at present with little prospect of success. The house was strictly examined, and from the imprint of several feet on the stairs and in the ground attached to the house, it was quickly concluded that there had been an attack made upon it by ruffians, who had seized our heroine and borne her away, and savagely murdered her ill-fated uncle in a fruitless attempt to resist them. What created no little astonishment too, was the sudden and unexpected disappearance of the Enterprise in the night. Suspicion almost immediately fell upon Mark Stanford, and a strict search was made at the farm, but nothing was there elicited which was calculated to throw the least light upon the mysterious and awful subject, which cast an universal gloom over the neighbourhood.

For two days poor Constance remained in a state of torpor, and the doctor despaired of her recovery; and when at last a change took place, it was found that her senses wandered; she raved wildly, but sufficient could be gathered from what she said to confirm their suspicions that the miscreant Stanford was the author of this hideous outrage, and also the unfortunate Kate had fallen into his power. It was likewise strongly suspected that he was in some way connected with the Enterprise, which had made its disappearance so suddenly from the harbour, and all these various conjectures, kept up the excitement to such an intolerable degree that it became perfectly painful.

The poor bereaved Constance Markham remained in the same condition, and it was quite melancholy to listen to the wild and rambling observations which emanated from her disordered brain. The murdered man was buried with all due respect to his memory, by those by whom he had been so justly esteemed for a long series of years; and a sad day it was in the neighbourhood on that occasion, especially when taking into consideration the all but hopeless condition of Constance, and the loss of her who had been the soul, the life-spring of all who had the pleasure of knowing her, and the dreadful uncertainty of the fate that had befallen her. Unremitting were all in their exertions to discover the authors of so much misery and to bring them to punishment, but with little hope of success; and thus passed away another week, and without any favourable change taking place in the appearance of the malady which had seized upon the intellect of Constance Markham. She was removed, as soon as it was safe to do so, to the house of Kit Breezely, where she might be under the immediate attention of the wife and daughter of the latter; and old Joe Trennant was a constant visitor, as he observed, merely to watch the bearings of the fair craft, who had struck on a lee shore, and to keep a sharp look out for th' infernal pirates who had caused this terrible wreck. Everything that humanity could suggest was done for her, but her malady underwent no favourable change, and it seemed but too probable that her reason would never again be restored to her; which could not be wondered at after the melancholy bereavement she had experienced, and the terrible circumstances under which it had taken place.

What a painful change had a few short days brought in the neighbourhood, Jack Junk was far away encountering all the perils of the deep, the fair girl, whom he so ardently loved was torn from her home, and taken, Heaven only knows whither, the ill-fated Mr. Markham had met with a cruel and untimely death, while poor Constance was in the most deplorable state that it was possible for any person to be. The desolating hand of fate had indeed dealt a terrible blow, and the heaviest gloom prevailed around. The most unremitting exertions were however, continued to be made to discover the fate of Kate, but all to no purpose; not the least clue could be obtained, although, when all the circumstances were taken into consideration, that she was in the power of the villain, Mark Stanford, was generally believed, and it was feared that she would thus be irrecoverably lost; and every one felt the calamity severely for her amiable and gentle manners, and her numerous virtues had endeared her to them all.

CHAPTER IX.

THE PERSECUTION OF KATE ON BOARD THE PIRATE VESSEL.

THROUGHOUT that day Kate Markham remained in the same state of stupefaction, but not at all to the surprise of the pirate captain, although he could not but feel somewhat alarmed lest the terror of her seizure, and the prospect of the fate that was in store for her, might prove too much for her strength to support. He paid her frequent visits during the day, and as he gazed upon her pale but lovely features, and reflected that she was now entirely at his mercy, his exultation knew no bounds. Often did the villain dare to polute her lips with his unholy kisses; and as he continued to feast his eyes upon her matchless charms, his digusting passion every moment increased.

"Proud, scornful beauty!" he ejaculated, "who triumphs now, the pirate captain or his favoured rival? Oh, the thought is delightful! and I would not resign the present opportunity of gratifying my wishes, even though a kingdom was offered to my acceptance for doing so. Jack Junk!—ah!—ah!—ah!—Should it be your fate ever to be restored to your native land, what will be the torture and disappointment of your mind when you find that the beauteous and innocent maiden to whom your heart is indissolubly attached is torn from you, and most probably for ever? How terrible will be your anguish at the uncertainty of the fate which has befallen her! Yes, and long ere that time arrives, Kate Markham, she, the village pride, the beautiful and innocent, to whom all hearts were willing to pay homage, the admired of all, will have become the victim of the dreaded pirate chief; her degradation will be complete; and though her heart should break under the dreadful trial, nothing whatever can rescue her from the shame and misery that is in store for her. That thought affords the most exquisite gratification to my soul. And yet," he continued, "I would much rather that Pierce Raker had not been so hasty in the desperate blow he dealt her uncle, which I am afraid has proved fatal. I would rather that his blood as well as that of her father did not rest upon my head; and even now, when I recal all the fearful circumstances to my memory, I—'psha!—away with this cowardly weakness—it is unworthy of the daring rover of the deep! Let me think only of the gratification of my desires, and give unlimited indulgence to the completion of my triumph!"

Again he pressed the warmest kisses upon the lips of the unconscious damsel, and then once more summoning the attendance of the female, he left poor Kate in her care, and quitted the cabin.

The weather continued anything but favourable, and the pirate ship made but indifferent progress, and contrary winds arising, she was driven completely out of her course, much to the annoyance of Stanford. He paced the quarter-deck impatiently, giving his orders in a hurried and disturbed manner; casting his eyes anxiously over the ocean, and muttering curses to himself at intervals, although he saw nothing particularly to alarm him. Pierce Raker at length joined him, and they entered into conversation together.

"It is d——d unfortunate," observed Stanford; "the Black Raven makes no way at all; and unless the wind changes, it will be a long time before we shall be likely to reach the place of our destination."

"Oh, fear not, captain," replied Raker; "it strikes me forcibly that we shall not long be exposed to these contrary winds; besides, we have got good sea-room, and have nothing to apprehend. But how fares your lovely prize?"

"Why," answered Stanford, "she is much in the same condition, and she does not seem likely to recover very soon."

"Well," observed Pierce, "perhaps it is all the better that she should remain in this state of insensibility until we have proceeded farther on our voyage. We have nothing to fear from pursuit now."

"True," coincided the pirate; "although our progress has hitherto been but slow, we are far enough out of the reach of that, and we are fully prepared to encounter any foe that might have the hardihood to attack us. By this time, I imagine, a pretty strong suspicion is entertained of the real character of our vessel, and a rare sensation our abrupt departure from the harbour, no doubt, has caused."

"Ay, ay, captain," returned Pierce, "and most marvellous will be the stories the lubbers now will doubtless invent about us. Ha! ha! ha! But the time may come when they will

...ave a much better opportunity of judging of our quality. It is fortunate that old Reuben of the Cliff was put out of the way, or he might have revealed much more than would have been at all convenient to us."

"Hold, Pierce," said the pirate chief, with some agitation; "why do you persist in recalling to my memory the fate of that old man?—I never hear his name mentioned without a shudder of horror; and I would much rather that his life had been spared, and that instead he had been safely conveyed on board."

"You surprise me," said his companion; "of what value was the life of the old dog? and after the threats he held out, you should feel no regret at its being sacrificed. But this is a weakness which, I trust, you will soon learn to overcome. You that have waded through so much human blood, and performed such desperate deeds to accomplish your wishes, to give way to such thoughts as these, seems to be impossible and preposterous. But come, no more of this; a long career of triumph is still in store for you, and the success which has attended your designs against Kate Markham ought to augur well for the future."

In spite of the arguments of Pierce, however, after the allusions which he had made to the brutal assassination of old Reuben, Mark Stanford felt anything but easy and satisfied in his own mind; and it was not until he had partaken freely of the intoxicating beverage, that he was enabled to regain his wonted composure and self-possession. In the course of the night the wind changed, and the vessel now proceeded rapidly on her course, and the remainder of the voyage seemed likely to be performed with safety and expedition.

It was not till long after midnight that our heroine was completely restored to consciousness, and she then found herself alone, and reclining on a sofa which had been fixed for her accommodation. With a sensation of the most unconquerable horror she started to her feet, and clasping her fair hands vehemently together, gazed fearfully around her. The black clouds that had hitherto hung upon the Heavens, had now dispersed;—the moon had burst forth in all her chaste and mellow splendour, and shone brightly in at the cabin windows. The sound of the waves, as they dashed against the sides of the vessel, and the voices of the men on deck, quickly smote the ears of the unfortunate damsel, and fully convinced her of the horrible reality of her situation, if she could longer have entertained any doubts upon the subject. She uttered a cry of agony and despair, and then staggered towards the door of the cabin, which she hastily tried, but it was securely fastened on the outside, and the fearful position in which she was placed became clearly apparent. She sank on her knees, and with her eyes filled with tears, remained for some minutes totally incapable of giving utterance to a syllable.

"God of Heaven!" she at length ejaculated; "oh, watch over and protect me, I beseech thee, for without thy merciful interposition, I am lost! The monsters! to tear me thus violently from my home, and to doom me to a fate which I cannot even contemplate without emotions of the most inexpressible horror! Oh, my beloved friends! what has become of you?—Shall I never behold you again?—my lover, too! my faithful, my affectionate Jack!—Too fearfully are my most dreadful surmises realized, and we are parted to meet no more! If you have not already perished in the battle's heat, or in the merciless fury of the tempest, your thoughts are, doubtless, at this very moment fixed on me; your prayers are offered up to Heaven for my preservation, and you are picturing to yourself the fond transport of that hour when we should meet again—that hour which I fear, alas! is never destined to arrive. How torturing, how insupportable would be your anguish did you but know the horrors of my situation? Oh, God! that thought distracts me!—my heart is full to bursting!—I shall go mad!—Almighty Father have mercy upon me! Do not, I humbly, but earnestly implore thee, try me beyond my strength!"

She pressed her hands upon her burning temples, and sobbed as if her heart would break.— The motion of the vessel to which she was so unused made her feel sick and giddy, and it was not without the greatest difficulty that she could support her trembling limbs. No one offered to come near her, and she was left entirely to the horror and anguish of her own thoughts.— Then she recalled to her memory the observations of the female whom she had on first regaining her senses, found in attendance upon her; she had told her that she was in the power of pirates and villains of the most brutal and desperate character; and if such were, indeed, the fact, which she could not for an instant doubt, her fate appeared to be inevitable. She groaned bitterly in her despair, and then screamed aloud for help; but no answer was returned to her cries, and the hollow murmuring of the waves seemed to mock her sufferings. But, at length, completely worn out with the intensity of her anguish, she sank back on her seat, and again fell into a kind of stupor of forgetfulness, which, perhaps, under the horror of the circumstances in which she was placed, was a mercy to her.

How long she had remained in this situation she had no means of judging, but at length she was aroused by hearing some person at the door of the cabin in which she was confined, and directly afterwards it was thrown open, and the female before mentioned entered, bringing with her some provisions and a portion of wine. Kate started on beholding her, and looked eagerly upon her, but she could not speak,—and the woman, after looking attentively at her for a few moments, said :—

"I am glad to see that you have recovered and are looking so much better, and no doubt our captain will be equally gratified when he is made acquainted with it.   You had better partake of these refreshments, for you must need them after your long abstinence."

"Oh, God!" ejaculated our heroine, in a faint voice ; "it is too true then that I am a prisoner on the perilous deep, and by this time far away from my home and those kind friends who are so dear to me."

"You have guessed perfectly right," replied the female, "and so you may as well make your mind contented, as you cannot help yourself."

"What is the name of the vessel in which I am ?" demanded Kate, in a tremulous voice, "and who is the vil'ain who has thus dared to commit so brutal an outrage against an innocent and unprotected girl?   Speak, I conjure you, for certainty is far less terrible than this awful state of suspense?"

"This vessel is the pretended fair trader, the 'Enterprise;'" answered the woman; "but as you are anxious to know its real name, I do not scruple to inform you it is the much dreaded 'Black Raven,' which has long ruled the empire of the seas; its captain, whom you have hitherto known and despised as Farmer Stanford, is no other than Hugh Granfield the Pirate Chief, whose name has ever struck awe and terror into the minds of all who have heard it. Who shall dare defy his power, or seek to penetrate his dark secrets, by which that power is maintained?   He sails triumphant in the tempest or the calm ; no danger can appal him ; no means, however subtle, can defeat his purpose, and woe to those whom he and his gallant crew encounter.   You are his destined mistress, girl, and nought can interpose to rescue you from the fate that is in store for you."

"Oh, horror !" groaned our heroine, covering her face with her hands, and trembling all over; "what have I done ?   Why has Heaven reserved me for such a hideous fate as this ? But it cannot be ; the thought is too monstrous to entertain.   Great God ! upon Thy mercy I throw myself, and will not, cannot believe that Thou wilt permit my brutal enemy to triumph."

She looked up when she had given utterance to these words, and to her astonishment beheld that the female was gone, and that she was left to all the anguish of her own thoughts. What language could do adequate justice to them?—She clasped her hands vehemently together, and the most violent sobs escaped her bosom; then she threw herself on the sofa, and for some time became completely absorbed in the intensity of her grief and despair.

"It is all over!" she sighed at length; "the cup of my misery is filled to the brim, and a fate far more terrible than the most torturing of deaths is in store for me!—In the power of the fearful Pirate Chief!—Gracious Heaven! can it be true, or do my disordered senses only deceive me?   Alas ! alas ! and are there no means of escaping from the fate with which I am threatened?—Alas! no ! here on the boundless deep, and in the power of such desperate wretches, there is not the least hope for me.   Beloved friends, farewell for ever ! we shall never, never meet again."

The violence of her grief and anguish choked her further utterance, and again covering her face with her hands, she gave herself up to despair.   In this manner two or three hours of the most indescribable misery passed away, when poor Kate was once more started from her lethargy by hearing the door of the cabin unfastened, and the next moment the much dreaded pirate captain stood before her appalled gaze, in his true character, and with a smile of triumph upon his repulsive features.   The unfortunate damsel could not help uttering a cry of horror on beholding him, and she shrank trembling to the remotest corner of the cabin.   Stanford, however, nothing daunted or abashed by the reception she gave him, and which he had fully anticipated, advanced boldly towards her, and even attempted to take her hand, but had a serpent stung her, she could not have recoiled with greater terror and disgust ; and unable to meet the gaze of the villain, she averted her eyes, and awaited the result of this visit in a state of the most agonizing suspense.

"So, beauteous Kate," began the pirate, "at length we meet under those circumstances I have so long been anxious for.   My hopes are realized, my wishes will soon be gratified to their fullest extent.   Here there is no one to interrupt me in the prosecution of that suit which you so scornfully rejected. Farmer Stanford, alias Hugh Granfield the Pirate Chief, bids you welcome to his gallant barque; he salutes his future mistress with a proud and exulting heart.   The blue waves are below us, the clear sky above us, favouring winds waft us to a far distant land, where no eye can discover you or rescue you from my power.   I'm afloat ! I'm afloat ! And the Rover is free !"

"Look down upon me, oh Heaven!" cried our heroine, clasping her hands, " and guard me from this monster in human form !   Oh——"

"Kate Markham," interrupted Stanford, in a determined voice, "this is no time for useless

THE PIRATES DISCUSSING THEIR DESIGNS AGAINST KATE.

prayers or invocations; the pirate captain is not the man on whom they are likely to have the least effect; fate has made you mine, and you must learn to submit with patience to its power; ay, girl, start not nor recoile from me with such repugnance and horror. The time is past for the expression of such feelings. They might do very well while you were under the protection of your uncle, and the young seaman, Jack Junk, but, henceforth, they must be strangers to your thoughts, and you must learn to love me as your future lord and master!"

"Love you!" repeated the poor girl, in a half-stifled voice of the greatest disgust and emotion.

"Ay, me!" returned Stanford. "Mark me, girl, you have no weak or irresolute boy to tamper with, but one who was never yet known to be defeated in his designs. But think not that the heart of the daring rover of the seas is insensible to the influence of beauty. No, he is prepared to lavish upon you such a passion as never yet ruled the breast of man! You shall be the most affectionate object of his soul—his goddess, his queen! Away then, with these feelings of pride and scorn, and yield submissively to that will it would be useless for you to attempt to oppose. The pirate claims his mistress, and who shall dare dispute his right?"

"Hold! hold! heartless man, if such I may indeed call you, unless you would see me a corpse at your feet!" cried our heroine, still more terrified by the boldness and determination of his manner; "when I think of all the awful and sanguinary crimes you have perpetrated, I cannot ever gaze upon you without a shudder. Alas! I know too well that I am in your power, and how little I have to expect from your mercy, but I will not yield myself up entirely to despair. I feel myself strong in conscious innocence and virtue, and putting my trust in the goodness of the Supreme, whose laws you have so monstrously outraged, I will still set your boasted power at defiance."

"What a pity it is," replied Stanford, with a bitter sneer, "that such fondly expressed hopes should be doomed to be disappointed; what folly it is that one so lovely should thus waste her time in offering this useless opposition. Damsel, here my will is supreme, and who was ever yet known to be bold enough to resist it? But enough of this; you know me now in my real character, no longer the humble rustic, farmer Stanford, but the bold and reckless buccaneer, Hugh Granfield, whom all must fear, and none dare disobey. You have heard my determination, and know, proud beauty, that to attempt to resist it would be as fruitless a task as to seek to silence the voice of the tempest. Ay, I repeat, it, girl; I say to you once more, and wish to impress it on your memory that you may no longer deceive yourself with false hopes, that no words, no tears, no supplications, no sophistry you can call to your aid, will work their influence upon me. I am invulnerable, callous, reckless;—talk to the roaring wind and bid it abate its fury, when its hurricanes whelm, in one prodigious ruin, all within the vortex of their powers! bid the angry waters, when they burst their flood-gates, formed by the rocks of ages, to retire and seek their bed, it would be as fruitless as to attempt to stem the torrent of the passions that now rage in my bosom towards you; to daunt the resolution I have formed to accomplish those wishes which have already cost me so much pains and perseverance to achieve. You tremble, maiden, and turn pale, but roses must supersede the pallor of your cheeks, and smiles of love and gladness usurp the place of those frowns of disapprobation and scorn which at this moment disfigure your fair brow!—Remember, that in Hugh Granfield, the pirate chief, you have no boy like Jack Junk to tamper with, but a man of determination, and who never yet gave utterance to a word but what he meant to carry out to the very letter."

"Oh, horrible!" groaned the terrified damsel; "must I be sacrificed to such a monster, as this?"

"I can bear with your epithets, sweet Kate Markham," returned Stanford, with an ironical smile; "they do but serve to amuse me—they are no more than I fully expected; in fact, I enjoy them; methinks you look even prettier in your anger than your smiles, fascinating even though they are; but, my lovely Kate, why thus take such pains to make yourself wretched since you cannot possibly combat with the fate which is marked out for you?—A proud position is offered to you; I am sovereign of the seas; all have hitherto been compelled to acknowledge and succumb to my power!—I have chosen you my queen! The 'Black Raven,' is our palace; and the measureless waters of the deep our dominions; and thus, with this fond embrace, this kiss of transport and of love, do I seal the compact."

As the daring villain gave utterance to these fearful words, he darted towards our heroine and endeavoured to enfold her in his arms; but she retreated to the further end of the cabin, and by the dignity of her demeanour, for a few moments held him at defiance.

"Hold! miscreant!" she exclaimed in a voice of firmness, and erecting her arm in an attitude of command; "dare not to advance a step towards me, lest the vengeance of the Almighty Protector of innocence at once descend upon your head!"

"Obstinate girl!" cried the ruffian, recovering from the momentary confusion into which the resolution of her manner had thrown him; "of what avail are your words, or your opposition? This moment could I at once sacrifice you to my will, and who is there here to interpose to rescue you? But so far you will find me act with more forbearance than you seem disposed to give me credit for. For a few days I will respite you from that fate which I have marked out for you, and from which nothing can save you; but thus, again I say, do I seal the compact!"

Once more the miscreant advanced towards her, and enfolded her delicate and beautiful form in his arms, endeavouring at the same time to pollute her lips with his odious kisses; but she once more succeeded in releasing herself from him, and retreating to one end of the cabin, she raised her hands and eyes solemnly towards Heaven, and fervently ejaculated—

"Spirit of my father, now in Heaven! thy poor child humbly beseeches thee to look down upon her in this hour of danger, and to supplicate the merciful interposition of the Supreme to save her from the brutal designs of the monster who holds her in his power. Spirit of my father, I again most humbly but devoutly implore you!"

A sudden change came over the pirate as she gave utterance to these words; he started back aghast, as if he had encountered some fearful object, his limbs trembled in every joint, his face was bloodless, his lips quivered, his eyes seemed ready to start from their sockets, and stared upon vacancy, and his whole demeanour was that of a man who had just been convicted at the bar of justice of a most heinous and horrible crime. Even Kate herself gazed at him amazed and almost incredulous.

"Fiends of h—l!" he at length exclaimed, in a hoarse voice, "what could have suggested those words to you, girl? Who could have told you that—but I rave!—What madness is this that seizes upon my brain? D—n! shall the dead rise again to confront me? He is there! I see him now as plainly as when—oh, horror!"

Was it merely the effect of the murderer's guilty conscience, or was it reality? but at that moment he imagined he beheld the awful form of the murdered Horace Markham, the father of his destined victim, standing between him and her; his glassy eyes and ghastly features fixed full upon him, and his long, bony fingers pointed towards him. The assassin for a few moments stood appalled; his lips moved, but they cou'd give utterance to no sound, and at length, without venturing to cast another glance towards our heroine, or to speak a word, he rushed hurriedly from the cabin, and closed the door, leaving Kate in a state of the utmost amazement and alarm. In this manner he made his way upon deck, where he encountered Pierce Raker, who noticed the agitation of his manner, and the paleness of his looks, with no little astonishment.

"Why, how is this, captain?" demanded the ruffian; "you look as pale as a corpse, and you tremble in every limb. This is not exactly the demeanour you should assume, methinks, after an interview of love."

"By all the infernal host," ejaculated Stanford, looking around him with an expression of the utmost fear; "I have seen him!"

"Seen him! who? are you mad?" said Pierce.

"No—no!" faltered out the pirate, "I am not mad—I—I—but my eyes could not deceive me; there he stood, as distinctly as I saw him in life!"

"Who do you mean?" again demanded Pierce, impatiently.

"The murdered man, Horace Markham," replied Stanford, in a hollow voice, and still trembling violently.

"Pshaw!" returned Pierce, "you are dreaming; you are labouring under some delusion; arouse yourself; this is worse than childish, and totally unworthy of you."

"No, no, Pierce," replied Stanford, "you may mock me, but I am not dreaming, neither am I labouring under a delusion. I saw him plainly; he stood before me, between me and Kate, when she so solemnly invoked his spirit."

"Bah! I have no patience with this," said Pierce Raker.

"I tell you, Pierce," returned Stanford, "that I saw him as distinctly as I see you now. He fixed upon me the same look as he did in his dying moments. Oh, can I ever forget the awful night of his brutal murder? It was a night of tempest, fit time for the perpetration of such a hellish deed! The heaven's winds seemed to have conspired with ocean's gulphs to that destruction which the hapless mariner deemed inevitable. I have not forgotten the long protracted groan, which, gurgling, burst from my victims lips, as he sank beneath the toppling billow, which curled to foaming terror o'er his head. Who, when the miserable wretch, with the gigantic strength which departing life gives to the murdered, rose above his watery grave, grappled with him, pressed his heaving throat, and thrust him down beneath the brine? It was I—It was I! and now his grim shade comes here to haunt me with it. Pierce! I—I——"

"This is sheer madness," interrupted Raker, "and such as I could never have believed Hugh Granfield, the daring and much dreaded captain of the pirate barque to be capable of. Ghosts live but in the minds of the timid and superstitious. Bethink yourself, and recover your right position. Is this the way to win the girl, Kate, to your purpose? You will, by your weakness, betray the whole of your secrets to her, and should anything occur to rescue her from your power, you will be entirely at her mercy. Come, come! a glass of grog will revive you."

Stanford returned no answer, but taking the arm of his lieutenant, he suffered himself to be led to his cabin, where, having partaken of a glass or two of the invigorating spirit, he related to Pierce all that had transpired between him and our heroine, after which they both rejoined a portion of the crew who were in the midst of their revelry.   Immediately on their entrance, they commenced singing the following chorus, in tones that made the air resound again—

"Sons of the sea,
So daring are we,
    Fear unto us is a stranger;
The billows may roll,
The tempest may howl,
    But the pirate can laugh at all danger!
        Hurrah!
    Hoist it high! hoist it high!
    The symbol of death, let it fly,
    The pirate can laugh at all danger!

Behold o'er the sea,
The Raven skims she,
    A terror to all who beho'd her;
Her captain is brave—
The king of the wave,
    And the crew he commands, who are bolder!
        Hurrah!
    Hoist it high! hoist it high!
    The symbol of death let it fly!
    The pirate can laugh at all danger!"

This rude chorus revived the spirits of Stanford, and the circumstances of the past were dissipated from his mind.

"Bravo, my lads!" he exclaimed; "the words of your song speak the sentiments of my mind!—What fear ever appalled the hearts or daunted the spirits of the captain of the Black Raven and his crew?   Let the foe threaten—they do but encounter us to be defeated, and to have death and terror spread amongst them.   See how gallantly the Black Raven breasts the billows, bidding defiance to whatever tempests may arise, and anxiously seeking that prey which must fall within her power!   Drink, my bold hearts, and shout success to the Black Raven, and the gallant crew who man her, in all their undertakings!"

"Success to the Black Raven, and the gallant crew who man her, in all their undertakings!" responded the pirates, and they resumed their revelry with increased spirit, in which Stanford and Pierce heartily joined, and continued with them for some time.   But when the pirate captain retired to his own cabin, and was alone, he could not help giving way to the same feelings which had impressed themselves upon his mind on his late interview with our heroine; nor could he persuade himself that he was only suffering under the influence of his own guilty conscience.   He could have sworn that the phantom of the murdered Horace Markham stood between him and Kate at the very moment when she invoked his spirit, and he almost feared to look around him, lest he should encounter it again.

"But can such things be?" he muttered to himself; "can the yawning deep yield up its dead to scare the eyes of the murderer?   Bah! it is impossible!   I have suffered my eyes to deceive me, and I have become a coward and a slave to my imagination!   Let me shake off these sickly and foolish thoughts, and become again the daring pirate captain, reckless to the past and the future, and resolute to the purpose upon which he has fixed his mind.   Should I betray such weakness before the girl, she will not fail to take advantage of it, and notwithstanding I have her securely in my power, and may safely set discovery at defiance, she may yet find means to oppose my will.   I must be firm, or the prize I have risked so much to obtain possession of, may yet contrive to escape me.   Pshaw! I talk madly.   What power has she to resist me?   Who is there at hand to stand up in her defence?   What chance has she of being rescued from my power?   She is securely mine, and why should I let any ridiculous fear or imagination for a moment divert me from my purpose?   Why should I heed her words—her reproaches?   They are but wind, and are no more than what I had a right to anticipate.   In a few days I will consummate my wishes, let whatever may be the consequences."

Thus determined, Mark Stanford shook off the fears that had before taken possession of his mind, and was fully resolved that the destruction of the innocence of the unfortunate Kate should be accomplished without delay.

The agitation of our heroine after Stanford had left her, was of the most violent description, and it was some time ere she could bring herself to anything like a degree of composure.—The boldness of his manner, and the threats he had held out, and which she knew he was so well competent to fulfil, filled her with the most terrible alarm, as may readily be imagined, and she could not but look forward to her fate as inevitable.   Who was there that could save her?—was she not torn far away from her friends, a prisoner on the boundless ocean and entirely at the mercy of the daring and inhuman villain who held her in his power ? The thought was horrible ; but, alas ! it was too true. And then the strange observations of Stanford, when she appealed to the spirit of her father ; the terror he had evinced, and the abrupt manner in which he had quitted the cabin, recurred to her recollection and bewildered her brain. "What can be the meaning of all this ?" she said ;—" what could have excited him in such a moment to so extraordinary a degree ?—It must have been the effect of his guilty conscience He imagined that the ghastly shade of one of his murdered victims stood before him, and yet I saw nothing. I am lost in amazement. But oh, God! surely Thou wilt not suffer me to fall a victim to such an atrocious villain ! Rather let me die than meet with such a fate. I shudder with horror at the bare thought. Heaven support me throughout this dreadful trial or I am lost for ever ! Oh, my beloved friend, my dear Jack, what would be the horror and anguish of your feelings did you but know the terrible danger of my present situation !—and you have no power to assist me even if you were acquainted with all the facts. And shall I never behold you again ? Alas, I fear not, or if I do, it will only be as a poor degraded being. I shall go mad ; never can I support such horrible thoughts as these.''

She wrung her hands and sank back on her seat, completely overwhelmed with fear and grief. In this manner several hours passed away, and she was unable to obtain the least composure ; and the rude voices of the pirates, which in their boisterous revelry distinctly reached her ears, tended to increase her fears, and to make more apparent the horrors and hopelessness of her situation. Night came on, and no one again attempted to intrude upon her. Again a storm arose, and soon it raged with alarming violence, the solemn darkness around only being interrupted by the repeated flashes of lightning, The waves swelled to a tremendous height, threatening inevitable destruction to all who were exposed to their wrath, and the vessel was tossed about at their mercy like a straw. The roaring of the thunder, and the voices of the men, which might be heard above the storm, increased the horrors of the moment, and filled the bosom of our hapless heroine with terror and dismay. She sank upon her knees, and clasped her hands in despair, whilst the heaving of the ship, as it battled with the angry waters, made her so ill that she could scarcely support herself. It seemed almost impossible that any vessel could live in such a storm, and poor Kate expected an awful and untimely death every moment. But even the horror of the fate with which she was threatened by Mark Stanford, sank for a time into comparative insignificance at the prospect of immediate death ; such is the tenacity with which we all, under any circumstances, cling to life. Devoutly she implored the mercy of Heaven, but even at that moment her anxiety was more for her lover and her friends than herself.

"But why should I tremble at the prospect of death," she said at length, "dreadfully situated as I am ? Surely it would be a mercy to me, rather than to become the victim of such an atrocious miscreant as Stanford ! Oh, God ! I beseech you to inspire me with fortitude and resignation ; I submit to your Almighty will, whatever it may be. Lover, friends, a long farewell till we meet again in that glorious eternity were sorrow never enters."

She clasped her hands more vehemently together as she gave utterance to these words, and she then sank into a state of comparative insensibility. But the voice of the storm, and the noise of the pirates, as they rushed about in the execution of their duty, soon aroused her, and she started to her feet, expecting every moment that the vessel was about to founder. More than an hour of the most terrible suspense and anxiety elapsed, and still the storm continued to threaten inevitable destruction. It was truly frightful, and it was in vain that our heroine sought to compose herself. Every peal of the thunder seemed to be the tremendous voice of despair. No one approached her, and it seemed as if they had remorselessly and brutally consigned her to her fate. But from whom could she expect pity or consolation ? There was no hope for her, nothing but misery and despair. Again she threw herself upon her knees, and supplicating the mercy of the Supreme, endeavoured to resign herself to her fate.

It would be a fruitless task to endeavour to describe all the horrors of that night ; but the pirate vessel weathered the storm bravely, and as the morning approached it gradually abated, until at length it entirely subsided, and all danger was at an end. Fervently did Kate return her thanks to Heaven ; but then all the terrors of the fate with which Stanford had threatened her returned to her imagination with tenfold force, and her mind again became the abode of the most poignant anguish. She was interrupted in the midst of her gloomy meditations by the entrance of Margaret, the woman who was deputed to attend upon her, and who, having placed the provisions she had brought with her on a table, inquired with more civility than had hitherto distinguished her, how she was, and how she had weathered the storm.

"It has certainly been a rough night," she added ; "but it did not at all alarm me ;—I have experienced many such a tempest in my time, and it is not a trifle that the Black Raven is prepared to encounter."

Emboldened by her manner, Kate ventured to appeal to her for pity, but the countenance of Margarat changed, and she replied in her usual repulsive tones—

"One would have thought that you must at once have seen the utter inutility of appealing to me, for how could I assist you if I had even the will?—I am but the servant of the captain, and bound to do his bidding. You are completely in his power and at his m ercy, and situated as you are, there is nothing left to you but to learn to submit to your fate."

"Horrible thought!" ejaculated Kate, tears starting to her eyes; "how can I ever resign myself to a fate so revolting?—Alas! alas! is there no hope for me?"

"None whatever," replied Margaret, "if you imagine that Hugh Granfield will ever abandon his designs. He must be mad indeed if he were to do so after all the trouble he has been at to obtain possession of you, and now you are so completely in his power. The pirate chief is a man of his word, and that you will soon find, or I am much mistaken. However, that is no business of mine; I suppose you can dispense with my society?"

Kate was too much agitated and disgusted to return any answer, and Margaret, without making use of any further observations, quitted the cabin. When she was gone, our heroine again clasped her hands and remained for some time totally absorbed in the violence of her grief.

"Oh, God!" she ejaculated; "this is surely too much; it is insupportable. My fate is sealed, and better, far better would it have been for me had I perished in the storm! Inhuman ruffian, and will you indeed be allowed to triumph in your diabolical designs?—Must I become your wretched victim? Is there no power to save me?

Oh, shade of my dear father, and must I entirely give myself up to despair! I can scarcely encourage so fearful a thought. And what, oh, God! is the fate of my dear uncle, and my amiable and affectionate Constance?—I shudder even to follow up the imagination. Alas! alas!—mine is, indeed, a sad destiny! But," and the noble spirited Kate after a moment or two's reflection, added, with an energy that was perfectly characteristic of her, "I am a woman, I trust, endowed with all the firmness, so far as my sex will admit of, that my dear Jack possesses, and I will not sink beneath the threats of the wretch who holds me in his power; I will die, but never submit to his will."

Such were the thoughts which occupied the mind of Kate for many, many dreary hours, and, as the time elapsed, when her fate seemed more likely to be brought to a crisis, her determination received fresh strength, and Providence seemed to arm her against the deadly enemy that was battling against her innocence.

*　　　*　　　*　　　*　　　*　　　*

It was the mid-watch, and the pirate captain was pacing the deck of his vessel in an agitated manner, when his lieutenant, Pierce, joined him.

"'Tis a sullen night, captain," said Pierce; "our ship wears heavily, and from the appearance of yon star which alone peeps out from the ocean of clouds upon the black horizon, we shall have a tempest ere long. But, how is this?—Why do you look so gloomy and so reflective? you have the girl on board with you; you have her at your will—she must submit to it; we are far beyond our pursuers, and even if they had overtaken us, it strikes me that the Raven could very soon have proved to them that she had lost none of her usual abilities."

"Pierce," answered Stanford, "I feel sad at heart."

"Sad at heart!" repeated Pierce, "What from the reception you met with, I suppose, from the damsel herself. Ha! ha! ha! One of the tricks of the fair craft! Depend on it, she loves you, sir, only she has her own peculiar way of showing it; at any rate, you have her under your command, and if you do not make her obey orders, it is your own fault, that's all I can say about it."

"Ay, she is beautiful," said Stanford, in a half abstracted manner; "but yet, how has she been won? Look! look! Pierce! do you not see that star, how it bursts through the dense mist of clouds, and shows a lumen on the ocean?—do you not see it, man, like a will-o'-the-wisp, it dances above and around our vessel; and now it skims o'er the surface like a comet descended from the Heavens, bearing blood in its track, I'm faint; Pierce—I'm sick!"

"Pardon me, captain," said Pierce, "but, if I may form a just opinion from your language, you seem to be going mad. What has caused this strange and cowardly nervous feeling to come over you?"

"I saw him, Pierce; there is nothing will convince me to the contrary."

"Saw him! who?"

"The last murdered!"

"Pshaw!"

"Do not treat it indifferently, I saw him, I tell you, again, and his brother too · Horace

Markham's shade interposed between me and his daughter, while that of his brother stood by his side, and—"

"Ha! ha! ha! laughed the pirate, ironically; "a devilish good joke! Ha! ha! ha!"

"Pierce!" said Stanford, partially recovering himself, and fixing upon his reckless lieutenant a stern look; "this is no trifling; if you value my favour or my friendship, you will not treat with idle levity that which I again solemnly protest to be true. I saw them both as plainly as when they appeared in life; and then when I rushed away from the spot turning my head over the bows, as if by some inscrutable, uncontrollable power, I beheld the ghastly and blood-stained countenance of Reuben of the Cliff. I covered my eyes with my hands!—but it was fruitless; had the earth enclosed me in its innermost bowels, I must have seen those awful spectres. Were all the thunders that ever pealed from the lofty arch of Heaven to have poured the full torrent of their fury upon my trembling senses, I tell you, Pierce, they could not have drowned the dying curses of Reuben of the Cliff, as they were uttered on the night of his murder!"

"Ha! ha! ha!"

"Again you laugh!" said Mark Stanford; "but you, even you will be convinced it is no idle delusion, ere long. Whoever knew Hugh Granfield, the pirate chief of the Black Raven to be a coward? Did you? No! and think you then, that I am to be daunted, intimidated by mere delusions? I tell you, man, that when I looked over the bows of our vessel, I saw the ghastly and blood-stained face of that old man, the same as it appeared to me soaring above the billows on the night where he was assassinated, and the glassy eyes were fixed upon me with the same expression. I saw the lips move, and by h—l!"

"Bah!" interrupted Pierce, impatiently, "I am perfectly sick of this nonsense; I shall begin to think that it is some countefeit, and not the daring Pirate Chief, Hugh Granfield, who holds the command of this vessel, if you go on at such a rate. Let us below, and see what grog will do to dissipate these fallacies."

Stanford for a moment or two appeared to take no notice of him, or to understand what he said, but walked away folding his arms across his chest, fixing his eyes upon the vast expanse of waters, and seemingly entirely lost in his own meditations. The only star that had been visible in the horizon, now disappeared altogether, and the darkness became intense. At the same time the wind arose and howled fitful ominous gusts around the vessel, sweeping in sullen murmurs over the more distant billows. Independantly of this there was a stillness which reigned over everything and rendered the moment particularly solemn.

Pierce did not offer to interrupt the pirate captain, but retained his position, and watched him stedfastly; but suddenly he was startled by an exclamation of horror from Stanford, and, at the same moment a supernatural light seemed to surround the vessel, and cast its reflection far over the wide waters of the deep. Such a phenomenon for a minute or two completely paralysed the reckless pirate, but recovering himself, he rushed towards Stanford, and grasping his arm, demanded what it was that had excited or alarmed him in so extraordinary a manner. The expression of Mark Stanford's countenance under the sickly reflection of the strange and unaccountable light, was ghastly in the extreme, and for a minute or two he seemed to be totally unconscious of any person addressing him, but continued with his eyes earnestly fixed upon a certain part of the ocean, and which in the lurid, and almost supernatural glare, was rendered as distinctly visible as if it had been noon-day. But although he appeared to be thus insensible to the presence of his guilty companion, his muscular frame was violently agitated, and large drops of perspiration stood upon his quivering brow.

"Why, how now, captain?" demanded Pierce, approaching him; "why do you fix your gaze so intently upon one particular spot?—This is rather a remarkable phenomenon, I confess, and such an one as I never before witnessed all the years that I have ploughed the salt deep, and—but you tremble!—You start!—Pshaw!—your——"

"By h—l!" interrupted Stanford, in a hollow voice, and suddenly grasping the arm of his companion, while he pointed with the other hand over the ocean; "the re can be no delusion in this!"

"What do you mean?"

"Do you not see?"

"See what?—Have your senses entirely left you?" demanded the ruffian impatiently;—"I see nothing but this strange light; an Aurora Borealis, no doubt, and a good friend it may be to us, for that single star formed but a faint lamp to light us on our course."

"No—no—no!" ejaculated the pirate captain, trembling more violently than before, and still keeping his eyes fixed upon the same spot;—"not that, not that!—Pierce, are you blind? or do you pretend to be so, in order to torture me?"

"Torture you?"

"Yes!—yes! 'tis there! by all the infernal host 'tis there!"

"What madness is this?"

"No—no—'tis not madness! You must be blind if you do not see it, and—and—it is coming this way!"

"What is coming this way?" again demanded Pierce; "you speak in riddles."

"There! there!" replied Stanford, "is it not as clear as the sun at noon-day?—The ghastly countenance of the murdered man, of Reuben of the Cliff, the same as it appeared shortly after you had consigned his body to the deep!—His glassy eyes are even at this moment fixed full upon me, and seem to eat into my very soul; by h—l! he has kept his word!"

Startled by the words of Stanford, and the earnestness of his manner, Pierce gazed more steadfastly towards that part of the ocean to which he indicated; and as he did so an exclamation of mingled surprise and horror escaped him, and he became scarcely less agitated than the captain. Could it be fancy or only the workings of a guilty conscience? No, it was there, the corpse of Old Reuben of the Cliff, drifting upright towards the vessel as palpable as the most incontrovertible fact could appear to be; the ghastly countenance and glaring glassy eyes distinctly shown in the broad and sickly glare of the supernatural light.

"Demons of h—l!" cried Pierce; "what bitter mockery is this? If the graves yield up their ghastly tenants, shall not the waters of the deep cover their mutilated remains? Our senses must be leaving us!"

"Ha! ha! you do see him then!" said Mark Stanford in hoarse and frightful tones; "it is no wild illusion of the disordered brain, then!—Horror! horror! he approaches this way! He has kept his word—he has kept his word! The murdered victim pursues his cowardly assassins and will do so to the day of Judgment!"

The villains clung to each other with all the terror and cowardice that their guilty imagination had conjured up, and continued with their eyes fixed upon the awful phantom, without being able to utter another word! On—on it came, now mounting high upon the waves, and anon partially hidden in their bosom, but still the head always erect, and the countenance plainly visible, the sepulchral glance never removed from their blanched and quivering faces. The strange light grew stronger, and a dead and awful stillness seemed to rest upon them. The murmuring of the waves even seemed to be hushed, and not the slightest sound disturbed the painful and solemn silence of the moment. Mark Stanford and his guilty companion tried to speak to each other, but could not, and they awaited the issue of this strange and awful adventure with trembling anxiety, being completely rivetted to the spot on which they were standing. Still, on and on came the fearful spectre of the deep, until it had arrived immediately at the side of the pirate ship, and there for a minute or two it became stationary, and its livid countenance, and filmy eyes were fixed full upon the faces of the murderers, or it was their terrified imaginations that believed them to be so. Still they could not stir—they could not speak, all their faculties, for the moment, seemed to have deserted them! A hollow wailing sound at length smote their ears—the spectre drifted along, past the vessel, and vanished in the distance—the supernatural light faded gradually away, and all was once more involved in darkness and obscurity. The wind now arose—the waves sullenly murmured as they dashed against the sides of the ship, like souls in purgatory, and the horror of Mark Stanford and Pierce was worked up to the highest and most insupportable pitch.

"The friends have conspired against us," at length stammered out Stanford, in accents that fully betokened the horror and agony of his feelings. "Pierce, can you now be bold enough to assert that I am mad!—that I was deceived? You saw him—you saw him—I know you did! Your pale face and trembling limbs convince me of it. And must we thus be pursued? —will not the waves hide from our sight the victim of our bloody crime?"

"'Tis strange! 'tis unaccountable!—'tis almost past belief!" replied Pierce, in a faint voice.

"Past belief!" repeated Stanford;—"Oh, no, that is impossible. It is an awful, an incontrovertible fact.—The dying words of Reuben of the Cliff are fulfilled, he will ever more be present to our sight. Oh, why did you not stay your accursed hand when I commanded you to do so?'

"What!" replied Pierce, sternly, "and by so doing consign us all to the gallows. Bah! this is a weakness totally unworthy of men of our desperate character. We must have suffered our distempered imaginations to deceive us, and must not give way to such fancies."

"Fancies, fool? we should indeed be fools were we to call a fact so fearfully palpable mere idle fancy, the wild chimera of the brain. You saw him as plainly as I did, I know it, by the terror under which you laboured, and why then seek to deny it?"

"Come, come, let us below;" urged Pierce, "and endeavour to conquer this worse than womanish feeling. Again I say that some sickly delusion has wrought upon our imaginations."

KATE MARKHAM IN THE CABIN OF THE PIRATE CRAFT.

" 'Tis false ! 'tis you who would seek to deceive me and yourself," returned Stanford, " but it is useless ;—I see by the expression of your eyes, and the quivering of your lips, however much you may seek to conquer your feelings, that your fears are equal to my own."

" What useless folly is this !"

" Call it by whatever name you please, Pierce," returned the pirate chief, " but I know that I speak the truth."

" Pshaw ! we will talk of this another time."

" No, now !—now !"

" We are neither of us in a proper frame of mind to do so ; let us below, and, perhaps, the influence of the grog may tend to remove the strange and unpleasant fancies that have taken possession of our brains."

" No—no, I will remain here."

"Ridiculous! what good can that do?" demanded Pierce.

"It is my will," returned Stanford; "you may retire if you like."

"Not without you.   Come, come!"

"Oh, Pierce, did you not notice his un ex adaverous features? Did you not observe the ghastly glare of his hollow eyes?—There was clotted blood, too, upon his brow; I saw it distinctly."

"Cease, cease!" cried Pierce, who in vain tried to conceal the inward terror under which he was labouring; "do not thus unman yourself!"

"I must be more than man or devil," returned Mark Stanford, "could I thus so easily try to banish from my recollection what has happened."

"And what good will dwelling upon so dismal a theme do you?" demanded Pierce.

"You cannot forget it, though you may affect to do so;" said Stanford.

"Well, well, I will not argue that point with you at present," answered his companion.

"It is useless for you to attempt to do so. Would you indeed persuade me that I am mad, that I have entirely lost the evidence of my eyes? Did we not both watch it for several minutes? —Was not the ghastly phantom fixed before us as a statue for some moments? Idiot! of what avail are your arguments or persuasions?"

"Well—well; I will abandon the task since I see it is entirely useless. But what good will it do to give way to these terrors?—The crew would think it strange to see you thus unnerved, and I suppose you have no particular wish to enter into any explanation with them upon the subject."

"True, true;" replied Stanford, bethinking himself.

"It might create some very idle and unpleasant speculations amongst them," added Pierce.

"That is correct, we must endeavour to conceal what has happened from them."

"Certainly, or it might lower you in their estimation, or otherwise daunt their courage."

"Your advice is worthy of attention, Pierce;" said Mark Stanford, becoming more cool and collected.

"I never presume to offer any, especially to you, captain, without the most mature deliberation."

"I believe so, I place every confidence in you, Pierce, for I have hitherto always found you faithful."

"And pretty correct in my conjectures?"

"True, true."

"And so you ever shall find me," remarked Pierce.

"I have no doubt of it," returned Stanford.

"Well then, as that is the case I suppose there is an end to the matter. Come, come resume your wanted appearance, for the crew would be rather surprised, methinks, to see the daring captain of the Raven with that blanched face and that wandering eye. After all, I say again, we may have suffered our imagination to work upon our reason."

"No, no," replied Stanford, "that is impossible."

"We must be mad indeed to encourage such idle superstitions."

"Pshaw!" exclaimed the pirate, impatiently, "you believe not what you would seek to persuade me to."

"Indeed I do."

"Nonsense! do not persist in such useless and erroneous folly."

"You may deem it so, captain," answered Pierce, "but I speak the truth."

"Well, well, let us drop the subject, and endeavour to banish, for the present, from our minds what has taken place."

"With all my heart," returned Pierce, "I am most anxious to do so. Our safety demanded the sacrifice of the old man's life, who knew all your secrets, it was quite evident."

"Well, that may be so," said Stanford; "his words, and the threats he dared to give utterance to, I must confess proved him to be a dangerous character, but still it would have been much better could we have secured him on board our craft."

"Death is always the best remedy to silence such dangerous customers," said the ruffian Pierce.

"Markham too," said the pirate captain with an involuntary shudder; "I fear your rash hand also dealt him his death blow."

"And how could it be avoided?" demanded Pierce; "was it not his own seeking?"

"He was indeed rash—mad to attempt to resist us;" replied Stanford.

"He was, had he remained silent, and confined to his own chamber he might still have been living. However, it ought to satisfy you that you have got the girl securely in your power, and henceforth you should devote the whole of your thoughts to the completion of your designs against her."

"I will do so, and not all her tears, her supplications, or bitter reproaches shall have the power to move me from my purpose."

"Well said," observed his companion;—"and what means has she of resisting you?"

"None whatever," answered the pirate chief,—"oh, she is a rich prize, and one that I would not have minded making any sacrifice to obtain possession of. How different is her situation to what it was when she shone so conspicuous and so lovely as the may-day queen."

"And you received the insults of her lover, Jack Junk."

"Very true, the thought is triumph to me."

"What would be the agony of the young seaman's mind, did he but know that that fair being on whom his affections are so ardently fixed is in the power of her most dreaded foe."

"Ay," replied Stanford; "I told him that I would be revenged for the insults he heaped upon me, and the scorn with which Kate Markham treated my vows, and I have kept my word. He shall never behold her again, unless it is after she has fallen the victim to my designs, and the torture that it will inflict upon him will increase my triumph; but I wish that I had him on board our ship, that he might be witness to her sufferings, and that I might further gratify the feelings of hatred I bear towards him."

"Fear not, captain," observed Pierce, "the time may come when your wishes will be realized."

"I trust it will," returned Stanford.

"But come," said Pierce, "all goes well upon deck; so let us below, and try what effect a glass of grog will have after the strange events of the night."

"Ay," answered Mark Stanford; "we need some refreshment to recruit our spirits. Come come!"

They now quitted the deck, and hastening to the captain's cabin, they seated themselves, and endeavoured to recruit their spirits with a glass or two of liquors; but notwithstanding all the efforts of Stanford and the arguments of his companion, he found it in vain to seek to shake off the effects of the awful event of the night, nor could he get rid of the impression that it was the spectre of the murdered man which he and Pierce had seen.

"I tell you, Pierce," he replied to some argument which his companion had made use of, "it is no use seeking to persuade me against my reason, and I am convinced that you yourself do not entertain the opinion you profess. I could not have been deceived, and did you not also behold it?"

"I must have been mistaken," said Pierce, "it was the impression which the fears you expressed, that must have worked the influence upon me. Such superstitious apprehensions are totally unworthy of men, and especially of men of our determined and reckless character."

"You may call it superstition, if you please," said Stanford; "but I am satisfied you are far from meaning what you say."

"Well, well, let us say no more upon the subject;" remarked Pierce, for it does not appear that we shall agree upon it at present. You ought to make your mind perfectly easy now that you have got the girl completely in your power, and at your mercy. Come, I will give you a toast, to which I think you will heartily respond. Here's the health of the beauteous Kate Markham, and success to your future undertakings."

"Ay," replied the pirate chief, "I will drink that toast with all my heart. She is a fair girl, is she not?"

"Most lovely;" coincided Pierce, "and so is her cousin, Constance Markham."

"True."

"I confess, captain, that the charms of that girl made no little impression on me," said Pierce, "and I should have had no objection to her having also been the companion of our voyage."

"Why then did you not mention it?" demanded Stanford; "she could easily have been secured at the same time as her cousin."

"Well, it matters not, and perhaps it is quite as well that we did not do so at present. We probably may have an opportunity of securing her at some future period."

"Yes," said Stanford, "and of course you may command my assistance."

"You are then resolved not to delay the accomplishment of you designs against Kate Markham?"

"I am," replied the pirate, "and now that she is entirely in my power, of what use will any resistance on her part be?"

"None whatever, and of course you will not be deterred by her remonstrances or reproaches."

"It is not very likely. I was fully prepared for them before hand. But it is late, and I shall now retire to my berth. Good night."

"Good night," repeated Pierce, and they separated. But in spite of all that Pierce had said, Mark Stanford found it utterly impossible to banish from his mind the impression which the awful event of the night had made upon it, and for several hours he courted sleep in vain.

and still to his disordered imagination did the phantom of the murdered man appear before him ; still did he behold his ghastly and cadaverous features, and in imagination he heard the words he had given utterance to in his dying moments and which seemed so likely to come true. Callous and hardened as the villain's heart was, he could not help feeling the utmost dread and terror when he reflected upon all the circumstances, and he deeply regretted that the life of old Reuben of the Cliff and that of Mr. Markham had been sacrificed, though he was unable to deny the force and truth of Pierce's argument, namely, that it might have been fraught with the greatest danger to himself had they, especially Reuben, been suffered to live.

Such were the thoughts that continued to rack the Pirate's mind, and it was some time before he could compose himself to sleep, and then his imagination was disturbed by the most frightful and torturing visions.

After the interview which had taken place between herself and Mark Stanford, suffer the ings four heroine may most readily be imagined, and she gave herself up almost entirely to despair. What chance indeed was there of her escaping? It was evident that Stanfor would not fail to put his diabolical threats into execution without delay, now that he had her completely at his mercy, and unless a merciful Providence should interpose to save her, she was irrecoverably lost. Her tears flowed fast when she thought of the sufferrings that her uncle and Constance would in all probability be at present enduring at the terrible loss they had sustained, and the uncertainty of the fate that had befallen her. Then her thoughts would revert to her lover ; the perils and dangers to which he was exposed, and the little likelihood there was of their ever meeting again. These thoughts were almost too much for her strength to support, and she gave herself up to all the intense anguish of her feelings. But still she resolved to resist the villanous advances of her guilty persecutor with all the strength and firmness at her command, and to brave anything, even the most torturing death, rather than. quietly yield to so revolting a fate as that with which he threatened her.

That night passed drearily away, and sleep never once closed the eyelids of the distracted damsel. The vessel proceeded rapidly on its way, and her anguish and despair increased every moment.

The morning came, and the woman who was deputed to attend on her made her appearance, to bring her provisions; but Kate was too sick at heart to enter into any conversation with her, if even she had been so inclined ; and she quickly again retired from the cabin, and left our heroine to her own melancholy reflections, the nature of which may be easily conceived, She was not long, however, permitted to be alone, for the cabin door was suddenly thrown open. and the pirate chief again stood before her. She started with a feeling of horror on first beholding him, and trembled; for she well knew her helpless situation : but struggling with her feelings, she soon recovered herself and met him with a dauntless eye and demeanour. He stood for a few moments and contemplated her in silence, while the expression of his features, plainly showed the feelings of triumph and delight which predominated in his mind.

"Fair Kate," at length he said, "your sworn slave and admirer again comes to pay the homage of his love and devotion at the shrine of your beauty. Nay, frown not, for I am fully prepared to meet your scorn and reproaches, and heed them not; they are useless, which upon reasonable and mature reflection you must be fully convinced of. Here on board my gallant barque, riding proudly on the broad waters of the ocean, and surrounded by my daring and intrepid crew you are securely in my power, and entirely at my will. I have chosen you for the empress of my heart; I love you with all the ardour of the most fervent passion, and pirate though I am, there is no happiness, no indulgence, short of liberty, which I am not prepared most willingly to lavish upon you. Henceforth you are mine, my beauteous mistress, and nought can save you. Banish then your feelings of repugnance, and learn to look upon me in uture as your lord and fondest admirer."

"Brutal man !" exclaimed Kate, shrinking from him, and at the same time fixing upon him a look of the utmost disgust and horror; "cease your guilty observations, and no longer shock my feelings by your odious presence. Alas! I know too well that I am entirely in your power, and at your mercy, and that I can expect no forbearance from one who is so complete a stranger to pity or humanity: but there is one above in whom I will put my trust, who will throw the shield of his Almighty protection around me, and who will not suffer you to triumph in your diabolical designs."

"Ha, ha, ha!" laughed the pirate, scornfully, "what madness is this? But we shall see how far your sanguine hopes will be realized. The power you have invoked, and on whom you place your dependance, I scorn, and nothing that you can say, no reproaches that you can heap upon me, shall deter me from my purpose. The contempt with which you treat me, the hatred with which you view me, does but urge me on the more to the completion of my wishes, and by all my hopes I will accomplish them, let the consequences be whatever they may. Abandon all thoughts of home and the friends so dear to you, for never will you behold them again; henceforward you are the chosen mistress of the rover of the seas; and who is there can rescue you from his power? Did I not tell you and the proud boy to whom you have devoted your affections, that Farmer Stanford's hour of triumph would quickly arrive, and have I not kept my promise? Oh, yes, the pirate chief never fails to keep his word."

"Oh, horrible!" ejaculated the poor girl, "must I listen to language so revolting as this? Will nothing interpose to save me from the awful fate with which this hardened miscreant threatens me?"

"Nothing, beauteous damsel," replied Stanford exultingly, "of that you may rest assured. What prospect is there of you being able to escape, or of my designs being frustrated? It would be worse than madness to entertain such an idea. But fear not; again I tell you that I will lavish upon you every fondness, and that in future I will bow the willing slave to your superior charms. There is not a wish that you can indulge, independant of liberty, that shall remain ungratified; your power on board this vessel shall be supreme; you shall be its queen, and all the daring spirits under my command shall bow to you in obedience. Oh, what a life of freedom and enjoyment shall ours be. Away then with the doubts and fears that now distract your mind, and yield yourself entirely to love and happiness."

"Away!" cried our heroine, "your words disgust and terrify me, and I shudder in your presence. Dare you blaspheme the sacred name of love, villain, by giving utterance to it?"

"Even so, sweet monitor," replied the pirate; "and by all my hopes, I will yet conquer your proud and scornful spirit, and induce you to look upon me with the same sentiments as those I entertain towards you. Obstinate resistance will avail you not; reproaches will only be wasted on me: the pirate's determination is fixed, and no mortal power shall move him from it. Oh, how have I longed for this hour of triumph! But it has come at last, and I will not fail to take every advantage of the opportunity that is afforded me to gratify my most sanguine wishes. Beauteous damsel, the pirate chief, he whose name has spread terror over the whole expanse of ocean, claims you for his future mistress, and thus, by this fond embrace, this rapturous kiss, he seals the compact."

As the miscreant thus spoke he encircled the lovely form of Kate Markham in his rude embrace, and in spite of her screams and struggles, again and again he polluted her lips with his odious kisses. Blushing with shame and indignation, she at length released herself from his hold, and rushing to the farther end of the cabin, she exclaimed:—

"Monster! will no sense of pitty for my forlorn and helpless situation deter you from this brutal outrage upon my feelings? Cowardly ruffian, begone, or may the most terrible vengeance of offended Heaven descend upon your head."

"Pshaw!" replied Stanford, "I scorn your words. Have I not before told you that I defy the power you invoke? How lovely you look even in your resentment! By the infernal host I would not resign this triumph for all the riches that this world contains. Leave you! Yes for the present I will obey you, but prepare yourself, fair maiden, for ere many days have elapsed you must yield entirely to my will, and naught can save you!"

"Oh, God, look down in pity upon me!" cried our distracted heroine, clasping her hands together in agony and despair.

"You pray in vain," returned the pirate chief; "my mind is made up, and nothing whatever can move me from my settled purpose. Mark Stanford is no empty boaster, and so you will find."

"Oh, forbear! forbear! spare me! spare me!" supplicated the poor girl, sinking on her knees at the pirate's feet, and tears of anguish streaming from her eyes. "Hard of heart, and callous though you be, you surely cannot, will not persist in consigning me to so horrible a fate! Rather sacrifice my life; young even as I am, I am prepared to die rather than to meet so frightful, so revolting a doom."

"Die!" repeated Mark Stanford, "oh, no; you shall live to be my pride and solace in my reckless and perilous life. I have purchased thee at every risk, and never again will I resign thee!"

"God of Heaven help me then," gasped forth the maiden, "for without Thy merciful interposition I am indeed lost."

"All hope of your escaping from me is useless, I repeat," said the ruffian; "and, therefore, you may as well make up your mind to a fate which you will find it impossible to evade. The sea now far divides you from your friends and your relations, and there is no one to help you. How fruitless, then, is your obduracy!—how vain is all resistance! I now leave you to your own thoughts; but remember what I have said, and rest assured that I will not fail to put my threats into execution."

"Monster!" cried Kate, with renewed energy, "whom no entreaties can move to forbearance, I will no longer appeal to you; but I will place my sole reliance in the goodness of that Supreme Power whose laws you have ever so brutally outraged, and still set you at defiance."

"Your words make not the slightest impression on me," said Stanford: "you will soon find how completely futile they are. But beware! for your obstinacy may induce me to behave far differently towards you than I wish to do. I am prepared to love you, to worship you, and it will, therefore, be your own fault if I merely keep you as the victim of my passions. Bear that in mind if you are wise or prudent, and be cautious how you act."

"Alas! alas!" sighed Kate, wringing her hands in despair, "I am, indeed, helpless. Oh, what have I done that I should be subjected to such a fate as this? Would to Heaven that I were dead, or that I had never been born. But I will hold no further converse with you, villain—my heart sickens with horror and disgust at your presence; murder, rapine, and destruction are stamped upon your brow. I know you for a wretch capable of performing all you have threatened, and—"

"You do me but justice by that supposition, damsel," interrupted Mark Stanford; "and I am glad you entertain such an estimate of my character, for you will not so readily be inclined to encourage hopes that could only be deemed to disappointment. No prayers, no supplications will prevail upon me to abandon my designs; so you may, therefore, as well save yourself the trouble to remonstrate with me."

"Begone!" commanded one heroine, "and no longer shock my ears with your ruffianly language."

"I would utter words of love and adoration," replied the villain, "but your scorn provokes me to less becoming language. However, I have no doubt that you will think better of this; and at our future meetings, see the necessity of acting with more prudence. For the present, farewell. To-morrow we meet again."

Kate had not the strength to return any answer to this, and the pirate captain quitted the cabin, securing the door after him. When he was gone, our heroine, completely overpowered, sank on her knees, and for several minutes she resigned herself entirely to the violence of her emotions.

"Oh, God! Oh, God!" she ejaculated; "what will become of me? How shall I escape the dreadful fate which seems to be impending over me? The monster will not fail to put his diabolical threats into execution, and without the merciful interposition of Providence, my destruction is inevitable. But surely that will not desert me in the terrible hour of danger! The Almighty will never suffer me to fall a victim to this brutal miscreant. Oh, my beloved friend—dear Jack! shall I never behold you again? Alas! what must be the anguish you are enduring, and how doubly severe would it be did you but know the misery and degradation to which I am subjected! Heaven give me fortitude, or I shall never be able to endure and combat this dreadful trial!"

In this state of mind poor Kate Markham continued throughout the day, and was unable to obtain the least consolation. No one intruded upon her after Stanford had quitted her, and she was thus left entirely to the misery of her own thoughts; but she well knew there was no one on board from whom she could expect the slightest sympathy or who could render her the least assistance, and she was therefore satisfied to remain alone, that she might give uninterrupted indulgence to her reflections. The voices of the pirates frequently saluted her ears, and filled her bosom with a sensation of unconquerable dread, for she every moment feared that some of them would have the daring to obtrude themselves upon her privacy; but she was soon convinced that these apprehensions were perfectly groundless, and at length by dint of great exertion, she became considerably more calm, and tried to acquire confidence in the goodness and protection of Providence.

The day wore tediously away, without anything more worth recording occurring, and night again approached, dark, gloomy, and tempestuous. In a short time it blew a perfect hurricane; the waves swelled to a tremendous height, and the violent motion of the vessel caused the damsel considerable alarm. The tumultuous shouts of the crew added to her terrors; and when she gazed upon the tempestuous ocean from the window of her cabin, the scene was so frightful that she shrank appalled, and it seemed as though their destruction was inevitable.

Throughout the night the storm raged with the most terrific violence; but towards the middle of the following day it abated and gradually ceased altogether, and the ship pursued her course calmly and steadily, having received no injury in the late tempest.

CHAPTER X.

JACK JUNK AGAIN.—THE PERILS OF THE DEEP.—THE SHIPWRECK.—THE ISLAND.— THE MANIAC.

THE reader will doubtless by this time be anxious that we should follow the fortunes of the hero of our tale.

The British fleet had scarcely set sail from the shores of old England, when it met with most disastrous weather, and for several days and nights the tempest never ceased; but alarming as the weather was the courage of Jack Junk never forsook him, for he put his trust in that Providence which mercifully protects the hardy mariner through the greatest perils, and guides him to a port of safety at last. His thoughts were constantly fixed upon the beloved girl he had left behind him; and many were the fervent prayers the noble-hearted youth offered up to Heaven for her safety; but when he remembered the observations she had made at parting, he could not at times help some dismal forebodings and apprehensions to take possession of his mind; these, however, soon vanished, and he looked forward to the future with the most sanguine hopes. With what feelings of delight would he gaze upon the token Kate had given him at parting, and again and again he would press it with the most indescribable transport to his lips, and invoke the blessings of Heaven on her head. There was, however, in spite of all his efforts to the contrary, a strong, an insurmountable presentiment on his mind that some danger threatened his beloved Kate, and a thousand times he wished that the expedition was o'er, that he might once more return to her, and be ready to protect her against any danger that might threaten.

The tempest continued, as we have before stated, to rage with unabated violence for several days; and the different vessels had the greatest difficulty of keeping company. On the evening of the seventh day that the fleet had been at sea, the storm somewhat abated, but then a dense fog arose, and the wind veering at the same time, the vessels became completely separated, and lost hail of each other.

The fog increased, and the tempest raged with renewed and redoubled violence. The Defiance, noble craft as she was, battled bravely against the infuriated elements, but was driven completely out of her latitude. Several times she fired signals of distress, but receiving no reply from the other portion of the fleet or any vessel, it was clear that they were parted, and the most painful apprehensions were naturally entertained as to the fate which might have befallen them. All was darkness and horror around, and the storm every moment increasing in its frightful wrath, the most powerful fears began to take possession even of the bold hearts that were on board. A night of horror ensued, all persons dreading the result, while each man worked at his post bravely and vigorously, but with no prospect of success to cheer them on. To penetrate through the dense mist was impossible, and they were driven entirely at the mercy of the waves, which tossed them every moment to the clouds, and anon engulphed them in their bosoms, seeming to threaten inevitable destruction. During the whole of this awful time there was no one on board the gallant Defiance who maintained such cool courage and determination, or who displayed greater energy and perseverance, than Jack Junk. Where the greatest peril was to be encountered, wherever it required the greatest skill and perception to overcome a difficulty, there was Jack to be found. Should his messmates begin to droop from sheer despair, Jack was the first to revive them and to cheer them on to fresh exertions, and with all his constant good humour and manly flow of spirits was sufficient to modify, if not entirely to banish the influence which the horrors of the time naturally engendered. But amidst all, and the confusion which prevailed even when death seemed to be inevitable, when it appeared next to impossible that the ship could weather the fearful tempest to which she was exposed, the thoughts of our hero were constantly fixed upon his beloved Kate, and many were the mental prayers he offered up to Heaven for her safety and welfare, while at the same time a strong hope predominated in his breast that he should be permitted to see her again, and that their happiness would be rendered complete. It was these thoughts that upheld him, and made him look with almost a feeling of indifference upon the frightful dangers by which he was at the time surrounded.

"Dear lass!" he ejaculated, as he pressed the token she had given him to his lips, "I feel a sweet reliance in the goodness of that 'little cherub that's perched up aloft, to keep watch for the life of poor Jack,' to pilot me safe again to your arms, and that we shall be enabled to laugh at the dangers and troubles we have both been allotted to encounter during our separation. My fair craft!—it would be a libel on the mercy and goodness of the Great Commander aloft, to suppose that He would suffer two such fond and faithful hearts to be cast away altogether, and ultimately to strike upon the quicksands of despair!—No, we shall meet again, my lass, in spite of all your dismal forebodings, and—Pshaw! what coast am I off now?—I've been beating about in a fog till all reckoning's lost, and the devil a chance is there of taking an observation. Not meet my Kate again! Lord love the purser's mother's cat's aunt—ha, ridiculous! I'll let that go by the board, ay, and lend a hand to cut the rattlins. However, after all mine is no easy voyage through life. I've often thought of the fate of my poor mother, buried beneath the ocean billows. My old benefactor, bless his memory, raised an imaginary grave for her cold remains in the old churchyard; ah! and when a boy I used to sit and deck that humble mound of earth, persuading myself that the ashes of her who bore me rested beneath, and picturing to myself the day when I should be man enough and rich enough to buy it, that I might built a palace over it bigger than the church itself, in honour of her whom I never knew, but whom I am certain would have taught me to *feel* honest, and to hope in integrity. But, pshaw! I'm getting as weak as a powder monkey."

Such were the thoughts that occupied the mind of our hero during the raging of the tempest, but at the same time, instead of decreasing his energies, they, on the contrary, stimulated him on to fresh exertions.

The danger every moment became more apparent, the storm increased in violence, the fog abated not, they were driven they knew not whither, all hope of assistance seemed to be at end, and destruction appeared to be inevitable. In the middle of the night the ship gave a heavy lurch, and it was then discovered that she had sprung a leak, and that there were several feet of water in the hold. All hands that could be spared from the other duties, were immediately called to the pumps, and the anxiety and alarm became intense, but throughout the whole of the proceedings and the dangers by which they were surrounded, Jack Junk retained his self-possession and most indomitable courage, and wherever danger was the greatest, he was to be seen the foremost and the most prominent. But what would have been the anguish of his feelings, had he at that time have been aware of the perilous situation of the beauteous damsel on whom his whole affections were placed, in whose welfare he felt by far a greater anxiety than the preservation of his own life? One after one the guns were thrown overboard in order to lighten the vessel, but without any visable effect, and at length, in a dreadful gale of wind, the mainmast went by the board, and universal consternation seized upon the crew. The leak increased, the pumps were choked, and speedy death stared them all in the face. About another half hour of the most indescribable horror ensued, when a frightful shock took place, the waters rushed furiously in at every side, and it was immediately evident to every one that the ill-fated vessel had struck upon some hidden rock, and that she was fast sinking. A simultaneous cry was now raised to launch the boats, and in a few moments a large majority of the crew leaped overboard into them, and committing themselves to the mercy of the tempestuous ocean, deserted the ship. The next moment she went down with the whole of the unfortunate individuals who had remained on board of her.

The fog now suddenly dispersed, and the full horrors of the scene were made clearly visable to them. Jack still maintained his coolness, courage, and self-possession, and exerted himself to the utmost in the perilous and awful situation to which they were all exposed; but the other boat was so overloaded, that it quickly capsized, and the whole of its unfortunate inmates were instantly consigned to a watery grave.

Land appeared in sight at no very considerable distance, and they laboured hard to reach it but the raging ocean was against them, and every instant death stared them in the face; it, seemed utterly impossible that the boat could live in such a storm. Our hero offered up a prayer for the welfare of Kate, and committed himself to its mercy. Every wave that swelled over them filled the boat with water, and it was also so crowded that there seemed to be no chance of its being able to reach the land in safety, although it was drifted that way. A few minutes more, and one tremendous wave engulphed them all at one fell swoop, and our hero found himself struggling desperately for life, and the whole of his unfortunate companions gone. He had, before entering the boat, thrown off his jacket and shirt; and being an excellent swimmer, and thus released from any incumbrance, he found himself at full liberty to exert himself for the preservation of his life. Still, however, so great was the fatigue he had already undergone, and so many were the difficulties he had to contend against, that he almost despaired of being able to reach the land that was in sight. He struggled, however, with Herculean strength, and breasted the turbulent billows manfully, which dashed him on with furious speed, and almost deprived him of breath and reason. He gained upon his point. A few minutes more, and he gained a rock, to which he clung; and clambering up, he reached a spot where he was free from danger, and then sank overpowered and senseless.

How long he had remained in that condition he had no correct means of ascertaining, but when he again awakened to consciousness, he found that the sun was streaming over the broad surface of the deep, the storm had entirely subsided, and it was therefore quite evident that he must have been in that state of insensibility for some considerable time. He arose with difficulty upon his feet, and gazed despairingly around him. There was not, indeed, anything to raise his hopes. Nothing met his gaze but the wide waters of the boundless sea as far as his eyes could stretch, and not the slightest prospect whatever of relief; but still the fortitude of the hardy young seaman never for a moment forsook him, and devoutly committing himself to the mercy of Providence, he clambered up the rock until he had reached its summit, and then found himself upon an island, apparently of some extent, and not entirely barren. He threw himself upon his knees and supplicated the mercy and assistance of the Supreme, and then completely exhausted he stretched himself upon the earth, and in spite of the anxiety of

JACK JUNK'S FEARFUL STRUGGLE WITH THE MANIAC.

his mind, sleep gradually stole upon his senses, in which he remained for an hour or two, and on awakening felt refreshed and imbued with fresh spirit. With anxious looks he gazed over the deep ; but nothing whatever appeared to excite his hopes, and he saw no prospect before him, unless relief speedily arrived, but that of certain starvation. However, he resolved to explore the island farther with the hope of finding it inhabited, and he started forward at a steady pace. He had not proceeded far when he came upon a spring of pure water, which was a god-send to him in his situation; and slaking his thirst freely, he felt much refreshed and inspired with fresh courage.

As he further advanced, the aspect of the island became more favourable, and he found several trees bearing a delicious fruit, so that his fears of immediate starvation were quite set at rest ; but still no signs of a human habitation met his sight, and he had every reason to suppose that he was the only individual on the island : and of the situation of that island he could not form the slightest conjecture. At length, tired with walking, he seated himself on the ground, and gave himself up to the painful thoughts and apprehensions which crowded upon his mind. His chief anxiety, however, was for his beloved Kate, whom his heart misgave him was placed in some position of danger, and whom he feared he should never behold again.

"My poor lass," he ejaculated, "what would be your agony of mind did you but know the present desperate and hopeless situation of him to whom your affections are so sincerely and fervently devoted. Alas! the dismal presentiments that tortured your mind on our separation were not without foundation, and too much I now have reason to apprehend that we shall never meet again. Heaven watch over you, my beloved girl, and give you strength to support this dreadful trial with fortitude and resignation, and may the fate of him to whom your soul is devoted if it should ever reach your knowledge, be speedily eradicated from your memory. May God, in His infinite mercy, protect you from every danger that may threaten you, and frustrate any of the guilty designs that your enemies may have in contemplation. But this cannot be; we shall not be parted thus, untoward and hopeless though our prospects may at present appear. I will not give myself up entirely to despair; Providence has hitherto protected your faithful Jack through numerous dangers, and I cannot believe that it will now desert me. Courage, courage, Jack Junk, and all will yet be well."

As these thoughts crossed his mind, fresh fortitude nerved him, and he once more arose to his feet, and pursued his way further across the island. He had not advanced many yards when, casting his eyes to the ground, he was startled and astonished on beholding the footprints of a human being distinctly visible in the earth.

"Ah! by Heaven!" he exclaimed, "I am not alone; there are other individuals on the island, and yet I may meet with some relief. But, alas! perhaps it is only some unfortunate being like myself, whom Fate has cast hither, and who is placed in the same hopeless situation."

He started, for at that moment casting his gaze forward, he was almost certain that he beheld the form of a man in the distance, but it vanished behind a cluster of trees with the speed of a phantom, and he was left in a state of doubt and uncertainty, and was almost inclined to think that he had suffered his excited imagination to deceive him; however, when he had somewhat recovered himself, he hurried on towards the spot where he thought he had seen the human form, and arriving at it, he was perfectly satisfied that he had not been mistaken, for he beheld at no great distance from him, a rude hut, which was backed by trees, and near which there was not another human habitation.

"Thank God!" exclaimed the young seaman, fervently; "I am not entirely alone, and here perhaps, I may find shelter and relief until assistance arrives to rescue me from this island."

He walked on towards the hut with an impatient step, and on arriving at the door, he stopped to listen, before he ventured to knock or to obtrude himself. All within, however, was perfectly still, and imagining that the individual, whoever he was, was absent, he ventured to open the door quietly, and entered. He gazed around the singular room he now found himself in, with curiosity and amazement. The interior corresponded completely with the rude aspect of the outside, but the place had all the appearance of having been erected for some years. The walls were hung round with the skins of various animals, and the furniture consisted only of a clumsy table and a stool formed out of the arms of a tree, whilst in one corner was a heap of leaves and sea-weed, which seemed to answer the purpose of a bed. The embers of a wood fire were smouldering in a rudely-constructed fire-place, over which was suspended an iron pot, that seemed to have been only recently put in use. On the table was some dried fish, a jug of water, and a quantity of fruit. The amazement of our hero as he marked all these things may easily be imagined, and for some minutes he found it impossible to remove his eyes from them.

"What brother in misfortune can have sought a shelter here?" he ejaculated. "Surely it cannot have been choice that has induced any one to take up their residence in this desolate place, so far remote from any human being?"

Conjecture was vain; for the longer he reflected, the more he became bewildered; but feeling himself very hungry, he seated himself at the table, and partook greedily of the fish before him, every moment expecting the return of the occupant of this strange place, whom he had no doubt was the same individual of whom he had caught a slight glance a short time before, and who he imagined was some poor shipwrecked seaman like himself, who had been cast on this island, and had ever since taken up his residence upon it from necessity, but certainly not from choice. Half an hour, at the least, however, passed away, and no one made their appearance, and Jack was beginning to grow impatient, when he was startled by hearing some one at the door, and he concealed himself behind a certain part of the room, from whence he could see who entered, and all that passed, without being observed himself. The next moment the door was thrown open, and a being entered, whose wild and singular appearance filled the mind of our hero with the utmost astonishment.

A closer resemblance to Robinson Crusoe could not well be imagined. He was a man of athletic frame, apparently between fifty and sixty years of age, and a long beard, as white as snow, descended to his breast. His body was clothed in the skins of wild animals, but his legs and feet were completely bare. His features were regularly formed, but much sunburnt, and he had evidently in his more youthful days been what might be justly termed a handsome man. There was a wild and restless expression about his eyes, however, which seemed to betoken a wandering mind. He carried in his hand a long staff, with the blade of an old knife, sharpened at the point, fixed in one end, and across his back was strapped a canvas bag, which seemed to contain provisions.

He looked anxiously around his rude apartments for a few moments, and then approaching the table, started on beholding the decrease in the provisions he had left behind him, and gave utterance to an exclamation of astonishment. Our hero continued in the same position he had taken up, and watched all the actions of the singular man, with the greatest curiosity, and with the hope of being able to elicit something which might give him an opportunity of judging more correctly what the exact character of the recluse was.

Having muttered some incoherent words to himself, and appearing very much dissatisfied at the disappearance of the food, which he had left behind him on the table, he walked two or three times backwards and forwards across the room, and laughed in a wild manner, at the same time at intervals continuing to give utterance to undistinguishable words to himself. He then re-seated himself at the table, and removing the wallet, or bag, from his back, he took from it a quantity of fish and wild fowl, at which he gazed for a few moments with the most intense earnestness, and then depositing it in one corner of the room, he once more took his place at the table, and finished what provisions there were on the table. After this he knelt solemnly down before a crucifix, hung at one side of the apartment, and seemed to pray devoutly, and our hero had now an opportunity of more attentively observing his features, and the contemplation excited redoubled interest in his bosom.

The features of this extraordinary man were remarkably handsome and expressive; yet there was a wildness—a restlessness in the eyes, which plainly indicated the wandering of the mind; and the furrows in his cheeks and on his brow, too clearly evinced the sea of troubles it had been his hard lot in life to encounter.

While our hero continued to gaze, and scarcely daring to breathe, lest he should interrupt him, a most extraordinary feeling came over him, for which, for a minute or two, he could scarcely account, and the features of the man struck him as those of some individual he had seen before, but where he could not for the instant recal to his memory. At last he recollected the locket which old Joe Trennant had presented to him a day or two before the sailing of the fleet, and which was still suspended from his neck; and looking at it, he was completely astounded at the wonderful resemblance there was between it and the recluse; in fact, the only difference was the age, and the long beard, and the other outre appearances of the man; the features were, in every respect, the same.

As Jack Junk noticed these particulars, his emotion and curiosity increased, and he could scarcely refrain from rushing forward from his place of concealment, and at once revealing himself; but anxious to observe how he would farther proceed, he still kept himself quiet, and watched his actions narrowly.

The strange being continued on his knees for some time before the crucifix, but at length he slowly arose, and having crossed himself devoutly, he seated himself on the earth, in that particular part of the room where our hero was concealed. For some moments he remained inactive, and apparently wrapped in deep thought; but at length, he drew from his bosom a picture, and gazing at it steadfastly, sighed deeply. As he held it before him, the subject was plainly visible to our hero, and he gazed at it intently, and with a great deal of interest.

The subject was that of a tempest at sea; the horizon in the background was black as pitch, save where the forked flashes of lightning relieved the density. A large full-rigged vessel appeared struggling with the breakers, and evidently upon the point of foundering. She seemed to have been cast on her beam-ends, and numerous individuals were represented rushing about her deck in the most frantic state of despair, while others were clinging to her various spars, or leaping wildly into the foaming ocean, only to meet with a more immediate death.

Amongst all this heterogeneous mass of characters there was one figure which was particularly prominent, and on which the sole attention of the man seemed to be fixed. It also particularly drew the observation of our hero. It was that of a female of exquisite form, and the utmost delicacy of features, distracted though they were by the desperate situation in which she was pourtrayed to be placed. She bore in her arms an infant, and appeared to bo in the act to spring overboard, but was prevented from doing so by one of the seamen holding her by a portion of her dress.

At this picture the recluse of the unknown island, upon which our hero had been cast, continued to gaze for many minutes with the most intense earnestness, and his whole soul seemed to be absorbed in the subject; but at length, after kissing it in a frantic manner, he burst into a wild laugh, again deposited it in his bosom, and rising from his seat, traversed the room for a few seconds, muttering strange and incoherent sentences to himself.

" Poor fellow !" thought the young seaman ; " he has doubtless met with some strange and awful calamities ; his has been a rough voyage through life, and it has wrecked his intellect."

He paused, for at that moment the subject of his thoughts stopped, and, folding his arms across his chest, spoke distinctly—

" Poor thing ! poor thing !—child of innocence, but misfortune !" he said, in the most melancholy accents, every word of which went to the heart of our hero, and made a lasting impression upon it ; " poor thing, poor child ! sweet innocent partner of my bosom !—yes, that must assuredly have been your fate, and so have I depicted it. How many years have elapsed since that frightful calamity has taken place, and which has ever since rendered my mind a blank— a useless void ! Ah ! and what was the name of the ship in which she—oh, it is useless ! I— I cannot recollect. Let me see; there was she and her child—a sweet smiling infant— both discarded—both sent away through my accursed means, and—God! my mind wanders !

Like a hideous dream my solitude is haunted, and yet there is no one here to upbraid me, or remind me of the past. No, I am the monarch of everything here! The land my dominions —the animals who range its surface, my subjects—the wide ocean bounds me on every side, and its inmates own me master—sovereign! Ha, ha, ha!—And yet men who might see me now would call me madman! Fools! they know not what it is to suffer! Idiots! they have never experienced the trials that I have. They are infants in the school of life, and yet they would presume to call me madman! Ha! ha! ha! I am not mad—I am not mad !"

It would be impossible to describe adequately the effect which these wild words had upon our hero ; but he still remained concealed, and watched with the utmost anxiety and the most painful interest the actions of the recluse, who now again seated himself at the table and seemed for some minutes entirely lost in the most painful meditation. At length he again arose, and stalked hurriedly across the room, laughing and chattering to himself in indistinct tones.

" My Emilia !" he said at last, aloud ; " shall I ever behold you again, or your innocent babe ? No—no, you have both perished ! Instinct tells me that, and I am a murderer ! Yes—yes, it was I who drove you both from the bosom that should have succoured you under all circumstances, and all through the poisonous breath of that fiend in human form who—God—why hast thou not deprived me of thought? Why not have rendered my memory more barren than the island on which Thou hast cast me? Oh, wretch! wretch! atrocious wretch that I have been ! I deserve not to live. All that was pure and innocent, fond and loving, I cast ruthlessly away from me, and consigned to an untimely fate ; and why, forsooth? Was it an act of justice that I did so? He told me it was, wretch! miscreant! and greater monster I to believe him, and to act upon his advice. Oh! that I had him now within my grasp! by Heaven, I would not release my hand from his throat until I had choked the life's breath out of him! But why do I continue to live? I, the primary cause of all this misery and crime ; I, the isolated member of society, upon whose brow is stamped more than the guilt of Cain ! No—no I have the means at hand—it is but a plunge and all his buried in oblivion. All will be effaced from the earth—the guilty and the innocent. My nerves are strung, my resolution is fixed, and thus I accomplish my purpose. Farewell—farewell to all; spirit of my injured wife ! plead for me at the throne of mercy for forgiveness !"

Thus wildly speaking, the wretched and unfortunate man, still carrying his staff in his hand, rushed from the hovel, leaving our hero in that state of amazement and bewilderment which needs no description from us.

" Poor fellow !" said Jack, now coming forward from his place of concealment, " his senses have slipped their cable to a certainty, and his mind is driven quite aback ! What's he intend to do?—To make a hole in the ocean to a certainty ; but that must be prevented ! We must never see a vessel founder when we have the means of rendering assistance in our power. Lor', lor' ! what a singular adventure this is to be sure ! Helm's a-lee, messmate !—Mr. Madman ! —Sir—brother tar—ahoy !—What's your name ? ahoy! yo ho ! —Heave a head, Jack !"

Thus saying, Jack Junk, hitching up his trousers, darted with the speed of lightning from the hut, pursuing the way which he imagined the unfortunate man to have taken, and shouting all the way at the top of his voice.

CHAPTER XI.

THE INTERPOSITION.—JACK AND THE RECLUSE.—STRANGE AND MYSTERIOUS CONDUCT OF THE LATTER.—HOPE REVIVES.—THE APPEARANCE OF A VESSEL OFF THE ISLAND.—THE FLIGHT OF THE MANIAC, DESTRUCTION OF HIS COTTAGE, AND CAPTURE OF OUR HERO BY THE PIRATES.

JACK JUNK hurried on, still calling as loud as he could upon the unfortunate man to stop but at first he could perceive nothing of him ; however, at last turning round a rise in the island, he beheld him running at the top of his speed, and wildly flourishing his staff in the air, as if he were bidding defiance to the Supreme power to counteract him in his desperate design. Still our hero shouted more loudly, if possible, than before, but the recluse seemed not to hear him, or at any rate, he took no notice of him, but continued on his mad flight towards the sea, with a velocity that quite surprised Jack, he taking into consideration his age. In fact, our hero was almost out-winded, and he began to fear that the object of his interest would outstrip him, and that he would be enabled to complete his desperate design before he had the power to prevent him. However, something obstructed the wretched man's path, and he stumbled, and while he was recovering his feet, Jack gained upon him. But in spite of this accident, the man seemed to regain his strength in the most extraordinary manner, and resumed his flight with even increased rapidity, still waving his staff in the air, and giving utterance to the most wild and strange exclamations. He reached the rocks that bounded that part of the island, and ascending to the summit of one of the loftiest of them, he paused, and our hero had now an opportunity of coming up to him, an advantage which he did not fail to avail himself of. He also reached the rock, and ascending it, he fixed himself immediately behind the unfortunate man, by whom he was unobserved, but whom he watched with the most vigilant eye, and was ready in an instant to frustrate the fatal design which he seemed to have in contemplation. The poor maniac maintained the same attitude for several minutes without uttering a word, but gazed earnestly across the ocean, and seemed to be wrapped in meditations of the most solemn description, and sighed deeply at intervals, as though his heart were bursting.

"Majestic ocean," he at length ejaculated in the same wandering strain ; "thou art there in all your grandeur, and with the same power of destruction, which has crushed so many hopes and immolated so many innocent victims. But thou art calm now, when the poor wretch, whose life has been a curse to his fellow creatures, comes to seek a grave beneath your billows. How is this ?—Why should you relent in your fury when the guilty approach? It was not so when the good and innocent were exposed to your mercy!—No!—then you raged in all your mighty wrath, and all the prayers that doubtless ascended to Heaven could not have the effect of staying you in your work of destruction. Yes ! yes !—I feel it here ! it is at my heart ! it is upon my brain !—It burns there with the fire of hell !—It was your relentless bosom that swallowed up my poor discarded wife and her helpless innocent offspring. Their cries for help or mercy could not prevail with you ! they are dead !—they have perished through my diabolical means, and shall I still continue to live ?—No ! no ! justice demands the sacrifice, that justice which I, coward-like, have too long evaded ; and thus I——"

As he spoke he was about to precipitate himself from the summit of the rock into the deep, but our hero, starting forward, seized him by the arm, and arrested his deadly purpose, at the same time exclaiming—

"Hold ! wretched man, would you rush unbidden into the presence of that Almighty judge whose laws, to judge by what you have said, you have already so greatly broken ? Forbear, forbear ! and by a life of penitence earn that mercy which you would now in a moment of rashness and madness forfeit for ever."

The unfortunate man started round at this unexpected interruption to the accomplishment of his desperate purpose, and fixed his wild eyes with an expression of astonishment and incredulity upon the face of our hero that was perfectly indescribable.

"Ah !" he cried, " who art thou ?—How came you here ?—What devil sent you hither, to obstruct a miserable wretch in the execution of his purpose ?—Art thou man ? mortal ?—Release your hold of me, or we both perish together."

As he spoke he grappled with the young seaman, and endeavoured to force him to the extreme verge of the rock on which they were standing, but although his strength was great, even wonderful for his age, it could not compete with that of our hero, and he held him as firmly and securely as if he had been in the hands of a giant.

"Compose yourself," he said, "and allow me to lead you from this spot to your own dwelling which I accidentally have discovered, and followed you hither !"

"Ah! a man!" cried the unknown, in the same wild accents; "discovered! I, who have for so many years lived secluded from mortal gaze! The curse of God has at last descended upon me! Release your hold, boy!—I am not mad!—I am not mad! I am king of these spacious territories, and who dare dispute my authority? Ha, ha, ha! Off! off!"

"Come, come," said our hero, coaxingly, "we will talk of this anon."

"You have the voice, the features of a human being," said the poor maniac, looking still more narrowly at him, "and should therefore shun me as something loathsome and contagious. Why do you not let me seek her and my child in the deep? Who shall dare restrain my wishes? Off, I say, or——"

"Come, come," interrupted Jack, in the same soothing tones; "we do but waste valuable time while remaining here. Let us to the cottage; I am your friend, I have consolation to offer; I have much to say to you."

"To me—to me!" ejaculated the maniac; "'tis false! All men should shun me, as I have done them, for many, many years! It is a bitter mockery! You would deceive me! Begone!"

"No, by heaven!" replied our hero, still urging him from the rock. "Fate has cast us together on a lee shore, and it is not likely that I am going to desert you. Come, what is the use of all this resistance to me, who perhaps am almost as unfortunate as yourself, and who, at any rate intends you no wrong?"

"Unfortunate!" repeated the unknown, looking still more steadfastly in his face, and passing his hand across his own brow, as if to recal his scattered memory; "unfortunate! are there still other poor wretches in the world like myself? Yes—yes; I have been unfortunate; no—no too fortunate to be permitted to long to live to repent the past. See you yon boundless deep? Beneath its surging billows, lie buried all that was good, and pure, and innocent, and helpless, and plunged thither by these relentless hands. Had the child lived, he would now have been as stalwart a man as you, but I—oh! I have been a wretch! a monster! Why do you hold me? Let me hasten to my fate; I am not fit to live!"

"Old man!" rejoined our hero, solemnly, "and if you have that on your conscience which you have just now stated, think you you are fit to die?"

"Die—die!" repeated the maniac with a wild shriek, and his features assuming an expression which was almost frightful to behold; "who talks to me of death? Who would usher me into the presence of that Eternal Judge whose laws I have so greatly outraged! No—no! it was not I! Who dare accuse me? Who knows the fearful secret? The distant land denies it; the waves conceal it! It was he! yes, it was he! the wretch! the fiend! He it was who caused it all! Where is he? Oh! that I had him now within my grasp; methinks that I should possess more than a lion's strength and determination to wreak my vengeance on his head!"

"No more, my good friend," said Jack, who was much interested by the wandering observations of the unfortunate man, and who at the moment would have given anything could he have penetrated into the secret of his history; "we will talk upon that subject at some future period, and when your feelings have become more calm. Let us now away from this spot, and——"

"Who are you," interrupted the maniac, "that dare thus to dictate to me?"

"One who would do you no harm," replied our hero, "but who is on the contrary the victim of misfortune, like yourself. The vessel in which I sailed was wrecked just off this island in the fearful storm of last night, and I am the only one amongst all the crew whose life was preserved. Chance led me to your habitation, and I was induced to watch your footsteps hither."

The unfortunate man appeared to have but a faint comprehension of what the young seaman said; however, his manner evidently made a favourable impression on him, and he suffered him to lead him from the spot, without saying a word. After they had proceeded a short distance, however, he suddenly paused, and looking earnestly in the face of our hero, he sighed heavily, and said—

"I have seen those features before; no—no, it must be a dream. Oh, my poor wandering brain! You are a sailor, and have been upon the remorseless and devouring ocean when the tempest raged in all its wrath; when the clouds were as black as a funeral pall; when the heavenly lion roared its mes deaf'ening thunder, and the lightning flashed with forked fury, splitting masts and all with which it came in contact; but did you ever witness a young mother and her infant offspring perish? No, no, that terrible sight has only been reserved for few eyes! thank God! I have not witnessed it in reality, but for many, many years it has been vivid to my imagination, it has constantly been present to my mind's eye in my waking moments, and has haunted me in my dreams. But why should I harrow up your feelings by the dreadful tale? You are young, you look honest, generous; you will not harm poor Herbert? No, no, I am sure you will not. Come, come, I will take you to my palace; yes, I am king here, and who is there to dispute my power or authority? You shall live with me, I will make you my prime minister, and we will bo so happy! Come, come!"

"Poor fellow," thought Jack, "his mind is certainly a wreck."

Humouring him, however, and glad that he had succeeded so much better than he had at first expected, he took his arm and led him from the spot, and took the way which conducted them towards his cottage. As they proceeded, the unfortunate man continued to give utterance to the most incoherent and wild observations, alternately laughing, and then moaning in the most dismal tones, but still keeping his eyes fixed with the most intense earnestness upon the countenance of our hero.

"Ah!" he sighed, as they walked on, "had fate ordained that he should have lived, he would have been just about the age of you, and equally noble-looking no doubt. But no, Heaven in its wrath destroyed both him and his beauteous mother, and—oh, my heart—my heart, it will break! Come, come, let us go home; you will not leave me again, will you?"

"We will not separate again," replied our hero, "until Providence has happily enabled me to see you to a place of safety."

"No, no," said Herbert quickly, "I will not quit this island again; it is my future home, my kingdom, as it has been for many years; I shall not be safe anywhere else, and who is there that would be bold enough to depose me from my throne? Come, come, to my palace, and if you are faithful to me I will not seek the deep bosom of the ocean for my grave yet!"

"Well, well, my friend," replied Jack, who felt more deeply interested every moment in the misfortunes of his hapless companion, "I will continue with you, and endeavour to soothe you in your troubles."

"Your words are kind," said the maniac in more rational tones than he had hitherto spoken; "I will trust you. Oh, you will find mine is a rare life, hunting the wild goats, and dragging the fish from their watery home. There is no one here to interrupt me, or to work me harm. Come, come, this way, this way!"

They walked on at a quickened pace, and soon arrived once more at the hut of the recluse, where the latter insisted upon our hero taking a seat at the table, and appeared to take much notice of him, and to be deeply interested in him. He placed before him the remains of the fish, and some fruit, and motioned him to eat, with which request the young seaman complied, in order to humour him, although he had already appeased his hunger; and Herbert seemed much pleased, and taking a seat opposite to him, watched him with eager and satisfied looks, laughing at intervals, and then muttering some unintelligible words to himself.

"You are very good—you are very brave," he said at length. "You will not leave me, will you?"

"No, no," replied our hero. "Alas! where can the poor shipwrecked seaman go? Oh Kate! Kate! beloved of my heart, what would be the excruciating anguish you would endure, did you but know my present melancholy and hopeless situation!"

"Ah!" said the maniac, as a sudden thought seemed to flash upon his benighted brain; "you love! Is she to whom your heart is devoted young, and innocent, and lovely?"

"Ah, she is most good and lovely!" replied our hero, with energy.

"Cherish her! treasure her! do not let the insidious voice of scandal prejudice your mind against her!" said the recluse. "Trust not to friends, for they are false and treacherous. Oh! how fearfully have I experienced all this! and you see me now what I am! I had one who was pure, lovely and confiding, but I banished her from me with her infant, and they are both now angels in Heaven!"

The observations of Herbert, as he had called himself, made a still deeper impression upon the mind of Jack, and he felt the most burning curiosity to become acquainted with the particulars of his history; but while his mind remained in the same wandering state, he saw not the least chance of being able to do so. He could not remove his eyes from his countenance, and watched his every action with the greatest anxiety.

"Have you been long on this island?" he said at length, when Herbert seemed to be somewhat in a more rational state of mind.

"Oh, yes, yes," replied the maniac; "many, many years. Let me see—how many? No no—my poor memory is gone! But still I recollect that frightful night, when the wind howled, and the thunder roared; the vivid lightning blazed across the sky; and the waves swelled, and dashed, and hurried on like hideous monsters! In vain the vessel struggled against the fury of the tempest! Her masts, her rigging—all are gone! The waters rush into her on every side! One fearful, simultaneous shriek is heard to arise on from the poor wretches on board, and she sinks! I struggle with the waves! I am dashed upon the shore, and—and—I remember no more! Oh, yes! I do bethink me now. The next day I picked up some portions of the wreck, and some provisions, and by the most extraordinary exertions I was enabled to build this hut, where I have lived ever since, and never till you came here have I gazed on mortal being!"

"And was your wife, she to whom you have alluded, and her child, whom you loved, on board the unfortunate ship?" anxiously asked our hero.

"No, no," replied his wretched companion, with a wild look. "They had gone—perished before. I drove them from me—villain, monster that I was! Say not that I loved them, for it is false as hell, or the voice of a fiend in human form could never have induced me to discard them. No, no! I must have hated them both, or I never would have believed him. And I was rich, too, and prosperous; I had a palace to live in, and numerous slaves at my command; but I have lost all!—I am a wretched, lonely outcast; but I deserve all that I have suffered, and, oh, much more—much more! But do not think me mad! No, no, my senses are as acute as ever they were, or I could not remember all that I have told you."

"But how do you know that your wife and your child are not still living?" inquired Jack, eagerly.

"Living!" replied the maniac, impatiently. "No, no, that is impossible; do not attempt to flatter me with false hopes and delusions. Am I not as sure of their fate as if I had witnessed it? Have I not seen it times and oft in my troubled dreams? They were buried beneath the ocean's billows, and this picture which my imagination drew represents the awful scene!"

As he thus spoke, he took from the drawer in the table the same rude painting which our hero had seen him gazing at on his first entrance into the cottage, and exhibited it to him.

"It is there," he continued, in the same wild and wandering accents; "see you not how fiercely the storm rages—how the ill-fated ship is tossed about in the midst of the breakers, with no hope of rescue? And there! behold you, not that female form with the little innocent at her breast? It is they!—it is they! They are constantly present to my mind's eye!—Oh, God!—oh, God!"

He covered his face with his hands, and groaned in the utmost agony of his feelings, and our hero for a few moments did not offer to interrupt him, but at last, with the hope of diverting his thoughts to other subjects, he said—

"Come, my friend, let us take a stroll over the island, for I wish much to see the wonders of your dominions."

Herbert seemed to be highly pleased at the suggestion, and replied—

"Yes, yes; we will go, and I will show you all. Oh, it is a rare place; come—come!"

Thus saying he took up his staff, and laying hold of the arm of Jack, urged him forward. When they had got from the cottage, he bounded on before him, with the most astonishing activity, every now and then looking back as though he were fearful of losing him. The farther they proceeded, the more the surprise of our hero increased; for he was totally unprepared to meet with what he saw. The island was of considerable extent, and was remarkably fertile. Trees, bearing the most delicious fruit, abounded, and they met with several springs of pure water. At length, however, the maniac suddenly stopped, and beckoned to our hero eagerly to approach him. Jack obeyed, and found him standing before a rude cross which he had erected on a mound of earth, and which was surrounded with wild flowers of every variety of beautiful hue, and which breathed a delicious odour On it were inscribed the names of Emilia and Alfred.

"Kneel with me," said the recluse, "and let us together invoke the spirits of the dead!"

Our hero felt a most solemn and impressive sensation steal over him, and he immediately complied with the request of his singular companion, who continued for several minutes in silent prayer, in which Jack could not help joining, and at the same time he fervently invoked the protection of Heaven for his beloved Kate, and ardently prayed that the Supreme would mercifully interpose to restore them to each other. At length the maniac slowly arose from his knees, and our hero followed his example; they then moved away from the spot, and took a wide circuit of the island, until Herbert evidently feeling tired, they bent their steps back towards the hut, which they did not reach till towards the evening. Herbert now seemed more composed in his mind; and having kindled a fire by the same means that Robinson Crusoe is represented to have done, namely, by rubbing two pieces of a peculiar wood together, he placed upon it a fish, and made other preparations for a meal with due formality and precision. He also roasted two or three of a vegetable which very much resembled the potato, and when all was done, he placed the repast upon two wooden trenchers on the table, and equally divided them with a rude knife, constructed out of a piece of iron hoop; this done, he motioned our hero to eat, and commenced heartily doing so himself. The strange meal passed over in silence; and Herbert having cleared all away, resumed his seat, and for some moments continued to gaze earnestly at Jack, without saying a word.

THE STORM, AND PERILOUS POSITION OF THE BLACK RAVEN.

"Is not this a jovial life?" he said at length, with a wild laugh; "what princes or kings can have more at their command than we? Are you not happy?"

"Yes," answered our hero, "quite so," though he was far from feeling what he said, when he thought of his beauteous and beloved Kate, and the probability there was that they would never meet again.

"Oh, I am so glad to hear that," said the poor maniac, in tones of the most unfeigned delight;—"this is our place, and all upon this island is ours, and we will enjoy ourselves to our hearts' content. We will visit the cross I have erected to the memory of my Emilia and her child every day, and we will be so happy, so very happy together. But you will not leave me?"

"Oh, no," answered Jack, "you need not be under any apprehensions on that score, there is no chance of my being able to do so if even I were so inclined. But tell me, have you never seen a vessel approach this island since you have been here?"

"Oh, yes, yes, often;" replied Herbert;—"and I have run and hid myself, lest I should be discovered. I will never, never more quit my proud dominions;—and who shall dare to force me away from them?"

"But have you no relations, no dear friends in the world, whom you would like to behold again?" asked our hero, eagerly.

"None, none," replied Herbert, solemnly; "they are all gone;—all perished; this must be my future world."

"And which is your native country?"

"England!" answered the maniac, "and there I have proud estates! but I value them not; I will never more claim them;—I could never enjoy them; I must loathe them now that she and her child are no more."

"Unfortunate man," said Jack, compassionately, "may God help you!"

"You are kind, very kind," said Herbert, with something like an expression of reason and pressing his hand; "you pity Herbert? you pray God's mercy for him? you will not prove false and treacherous? and I will pray Heaven's blessings on your head. Ah! had he lived, just such another youth as you would he now have been. I will endeavour to fancy you are he, and call you son; and will you not look upon me as your father?"

Our hero felt greatly affected by the singular earnestness of his manners, and his observations, and he pressed his hand in silence.

"Son! son!" repeated Herbert, in the same wild, wandering strain; "oh, it is a sweet name. Do you not like it?"

"Oh, yes," replied Jack; "and I will reverence you as a father."

"Will you?" said the maniac, his eyes glistening with pleasure; "oh, what happiness is this—but who are your parents?"

"I never knew any," replied Jack.

"Ah!" ejaculated Herbert, with a look of surprise and curiosity; "no parents! Let me think!——"

"I have every reason to believe my mother perished at sea," said our hero.

"Perished at sea?" repeated Herbert, starting, and looking more narrowly in the face of the young seaman, "and you preserved? Gracious Heaven! how like—but no, it cannot be—my brain is distracted; let us talk no more about it!"

Jack did not urge the subject, since he saw plainly that it might have the most unfavourable effect upon the mind of his unfortunate companion at present; but he could not help feeling the most powerful emotion, and the greatest curiosity to become better acquainted with the particulars of his history.

Thus the time wore away, and Herbert having made up a bed for Jack in another corner of the room, retired to rest, and was soon wrapped in a sound sleep. Our hero's mind was, however, too violently agitated with the extraordinary events of the last few hours to suffer him to think of retiring to rest, and he sat thinking upon all that Herbert had said, and gazing earnestly upon him for some time. The expression of his features struck him forcibly; and taking the locket from his bosom, he compared it with the countenance of Herbert, and was most powerfully struck with the strong resemblance there was between them. But the longer he reflected on this, the more bewildered he became. But now all his thoughts reverted to Kate, and when he reflected upon his present situation, despair fell upon his heart, and he feared that he should never behold her again. And to what troubles and dangers might she not be exposed during his absence? He did not forget the threats which Mark Stanford had held out, and he had the most powerful misgivings that now he (Jack) was away, he would not fail to persevere in his designs, and that he might be more successful than he had hitherto been.

"But the fellow will not surely dare to insult her while she is under the protection of her uncle," he said; "no—no; I will not torture myself with any such thoughts. Providence will, I trust, watch over and protect her, and some time or other restore us to each other's arms. My poor Kate, could I think otherwise, what a wretched being I should be; life would become a burthen to me, and it would have been better for me had I shared the same fate as my unfortunate messmates. Courage, Jack, and all will yet be well."

Thus he continued to ruminate for some time longer, but at length feeling tired and drowsy, he offered up his prayers to Heaven, and stretching himself on the rude bed, he soon sunk off to sleep. He did not awake till the morning, and opening his eyes, he beheld Herbert standing over him, and earnestly contemplating him. He immediately arose to his feet, and pressing the hand of the maniac fervently, he greeted him in the most kind and friendly manner, which seemed to make the most favourable impression upon him.

"You have not left me, then?" he said; "you will not desert poor Herbert, and leave him to the misery of his own wandering thoughts? Good youth—good youth! Heaven will reward you for this."

"And I trust it will also extend its mercy to you, my unfortunate friend," replied our hero.

"Ah, no!" ejaculated the recluse, in a melancholy voice, "there is no hope for me—no hope! no hope! They are gone, they are dead. But I will not leave this island; it has long been my home, and it must continue to be so till my eyes are closed in death. But we will be so happy together, will we not?"

"I fervently trust that we shall," replied Jack.

"Oh, yes, I know we shall," said Herbert, his eyes glistening with hope; "but come, let us partake of our humble meal, and then we will again walk forth and pay our devotions at the shrine of my poor Emilia and her offspring, and view the vast beauties of my dominions. Do you not think them very beautiful, my son?"

"Oh, yes," replied our hero, humouring the unfortunate man; "and we ought to feel ourselves particularly happy and grateful that we have such a beautiful spot to reside in, far away from the evil machinations of the guilty and designing."

"Ah!" exclaimed Herbert, quickly, "what know you of the evil designs—the persecutions, and the treachery of mankind, boy? You are too young to have suffered yet—but I have done so; oh, yes, bitterly, cruelly! God help me! Tell me, did you ever yet see that being on whom your whole soul's affections have become rivetted—one whom you were prepared to worship—to sacrifice your life for? One whom you thought all pure and innocent as the angels in Heaven! Did you ever have a pretended friend?—a smooth-tongued, insidious, deep-plotting and wily sycophant, who wormed himself into your esteem and confidence but to work destruction, and to instil that poison—that deadly poison into your mind, that must throw an eternal blight over your prospects of happiness—destroy your hopes—lay waste the fair scene that Providence had created for your enjoyment, and left the venom to rankle at your heart, and scorch your brain for ever? Boy! boy! I have experienced all this, and if you have not, you know nothing of what the black-hearted treachery of mankind is."

"Come, come, my good friend," said the young seaman soothingly, fearful of the effect which the excitement of these torturing retrospections might have upon his wretched companion's mind, "we will talk more upon this painful subject anon. Let us partake of our repast, and then I will accompany you on your ramble."

"Good lad! good lad!" said the poor maniac, pressing his hand fervently; "yes, yes: I will do all that you wish, for I know that you are sent by the Almighty in His mercy to be a comfort to me in my solitude. Oh! the time will yet come when we shall learn to forget the fearful past, and to resign ourselves entirely to the pleasures of the future. And I will talk to you of my poor Emilia and her infant, Alfred, and we will together invoke their gentle spirits in Heaven, and supplicate them to intercede to God for mercy to us both!"

"We will," ejaculated our hero, "and no doubt our mutual prayers will avail with that Supreme Being, whose laws are founded in justice and mercy to the humblest of His creatures!"

Herbert made no reply, but the observations of Jack Junk seemed to make the most sensible impression upon him, and his looks expressed far more than language could possibly have done. They seated themselves at the table, and took their frugal meal in silence. Whilst this proceeded, our hero watched the countenance of the unfortunate recluse minutely, and while he did so, the deep interest which he had created in his bosom increased every moment. Wild, and unconnected as his observations had been, he imagined that he could pretty clearly read his melancholy history, and he deeply sympathised with him in the heavy misfortunes he had evidently endured, and which from all he had been enabled to elicit, appeared to have been brought about through the treacherous designs and deep laid artifices of some pretended friend. But there was such a remarkable coincidence in the circumstances he had gathered as connected with the misfortunes of the recluse with his own history, that the longer he reflected on them the more powerful became his emotion, and the greater his curiosity. He supposed his wife and her offspring to have perished at sea, and how similar was that to the circumstances attending his own destiny and that of her whom he had no reason to doubt was his mother! And then the extraordinary likeness there was between Herbert and the miniature which he wore in his bosom, increased his astonishment and agitation tenfold, and gave rise to certain thoughts and speculations that bewildered his brain. However, he sought to control his feelings as much as possible lest they should be observed by his companion, and tend to add to the melancholy malady under which he laboured. The simple meal passed over without any remarks on either side, and when it was concluded, Herbert took up his staff, fixed his wallet across his shoulders, and taking the arm of our hero, said—

"Come, come, let us forth; there is rare sport in store for us; the wild goats await the taking of their monarch, the trees droop beneath the weight of the delicious fruit they bear in such abundance for him. The turtle lies helpless on the sands; there is plenty everywhere; oh, this is a rare kingdom; come, come!"

Jack smiled in the most friendly and compassionate manner upon the unfortunate maniac, and they quitted the hut together. They had not proceeded far when Jack beheld a number of wild goats and deer sporting in the distance before them, and Herbert, with an exclamation of delight, releasing his arm from his, bounded off with a rapidity that would have exceeded all belief, had not our hero beheld it. Any one so fleet of foot he had never beheld before, and he stood for some moments to watch the result, feeling the deepest interest in the same. Still, on Herbert bounded, laughing wildly all the time, when Jack imagined, from the velocity with which he proceeded, that it was almost an impossibility for any human being to retain their breath for even any brief period of time. At length, the recluse gained fast upon one of the goats, and hurling his staff at it with wonderful precision, it entered its side, and the poor animal sank to the earth, apparently dead, from the wound inflicted by the blade we have before stated was attached to one end of the staff which Herbert always carried. He turned round to our hero, and pointing to his fallen victim, he laughed exultingly, and then beckoned Jack to approach. He did so, and they both went to the spot where the goat was lying, dead from the wound it had received.

"Ha, ha, ha!" laughed the maniac; "see how they are all compelled to submit to the power of their sovereign! They would call me mad, but can they do that which I have just now done? No, no; I am not mad—I am not mad!"

Jack smiled complacently and soothingly upon him; and throwing the carcass of the slaughtered goat across his shoulders, they proceeded on their way.

At length they once more arrived at the rude cross erected to the memory of the unfortunate maniac's wife and his child, and Herbert paused, and the expression of his countenance became solemn in the extreme. He motioned our hero to place the goat upon the ground, with which he immediately complied, and the maniac kneeling solemnly before the cross, Jack followed his example, while at the same time he once more felt the most strange and powerful emotions come over him, and fervently joined in the silent prayers which the recluse offered up to Heaven. It seemed to him that there could not be a thought which might at that moment be passing in the maniac's mind, to which his own heart did not fully and ardently respond; and at the same time, with that feeling was coupled the image of his beloved Kate, and many were the devout and earnest blessings he invoked of the Supreme upon her head.

At length, Herbert once more slowly ascended from his knees, and our hero did the same, and the former then leant in the most melancholy attitude over the cross for a few minutes, sighed deeply, and appeared to be absorbed in the most torturing meditation. Suddenly, however, he turned away from the cross, and grasping the arm of our hero, his eyes flashing with a wild and extraordinary expression, he pointed towards the sea, and exclaimed,—

"There! do you not see it? Do you not mark it? The storm toiled vessel! How she struggles with the angry billows. But it is useless—she must perish, she cannot live in such a storm as this! Behold how the lightning blazes around her. God!—it will strike her creaking masts, and consume her rigging! Hark! how the thunder rattles; peal after peal, in rapid succession, shaking the very vault of Heaven, and convulsing the earth to its centre! Do you not mark how the stupendous rocks and cliffs totter and tremble, like so many infants in their feebleness when exposed to the majestic and terrible wrath of the elements. And now that appalling shriek, which may be heard even above the voice of the tempest! It comes from the despairing bosom of a discarded mother, when there is none to help her. Where is he who swore at the altar, and in the presence of God, to cherish and protect her? Villain! villain! And now that fair form that rushed with frantic wildness to the side of the fast sinking ship, with the innocent child clasped to her bosom, and her silken hair fluttering wild and dishevelled in the tempestuous air! See how wildly her eyes flash in their burning sockets; how frenzied are her looks, as she views the inevitable fate that is in store for her and her child! Oh, Heaven! ed st tdon lhnaand to hhere her, no one to rescue her and that tender babe from so awful a doom! Hark that simultaneous shriek of despair, which sinks the voice of the storm into insignificance; the water rushes over the sides of the vessel!—the moment of destruction has arrived! She sinks!—she sinks!—and all is over!"

Once more the wretched man fell on his knees, and clasping his hands vehemently together, and raising his eyes towards Heaven. Our hero stood by, and for a few moment did not offer to interrupt him, but gazed at him with the deepest interest and commiseration. At length he ventured to place his hand gently on his shoulder, and Herbert started, and gazing at him wildly and vacantly, exclaimed—

"Do you not see it? Do you not behold the work of destruction and death? And yet you stand tamely and passively by, and do not offer to render any assistance in the terrible hour of need. Is your heart callous and inhuman like the rest of mankind? Away, away! you have deceived me, or you would have plunged at once into the deep, and rescued them from their fate! Begone! I will not again believe you! False! false you all are, as the fiends of hell!"

"Herbert!" said our hero, in a compassionate voice, "do you not know me? I am your friend. Let us leave this spot."

"My friend," repeated the maniac, starting to his feet, and staring vacantly in the young seaman's face. "Who dare repeat that name to me? It is mockery—bitter mockery, and given utterance to only to mislead me, and to answer some dark and guilty purpose! Had I, indeed, friends, would they have seen them perish? Would they not have stretched forth a hand to have rescued them from so awful a fate? Begone, I say, and mock me not in the tempest of my despair!"

"Come, come," said our hero, in the same soothing accents; "let us return home, and invoke Heaven's mercy for the future."

"Heaven's mercy!" reiterated Herbert. "No, no; it has none for me. I am the abandoned of God and man! I tell you so again—and who dare dispute it? The curse of Heaven is upon me, for I deserted them, and left them to their fate! And think you that a wretch like me can presume to look for mercy? Psha! there is madness in the thought! Boy—boy! you would deceive me: I will no longer trust you! Begone, I say, and let me meet the doom that is inevitably in store for me alone! And yet," he continued, after a brief pause, "I will not upbraid you; it would be wrong in me to do so, for you look kind, and honest, and generous, and I remember that you have permitted me to call you son! Ah, me! how my brain wanders! What a tempest rages in my mind—scattering all my reasoning faculties to the winds! Is it not very dark? Are there not strange sounds in the air? Do you not hear cries for help? Do you not behold her pale face and reproachful eyes? And now she supplicates to me for help! No, no—it is all imagination! I am mad! I am mad! Come, come—let's away!"

Jack took his arm in silence, deeply affected by all he had said, and gently led him from the spot, while the wretched maniac continued to matter broken and incoherent sentences to himself as they proceeded, but offered not to disobey him. In a short time they reached the hut: and having entered it, Herbert threw himself on a seat, and covering his face with his hands, for some minutes seemed to be completely immersed in the most wild and racking thoughts; but at length he raised his eyes, and beckoning our hero to him, he laid his hand upon his arm, and said—

"Oh, she was so very beautiful! You should have seen her in her youth and innocence, as I first beheld her! You must have worshipped her as a superior being! Oh, monster that I must be to believe the false and guilty tales that were got up to her prejudice, and to discard her from my bosom! She who was so fondly devoted to me, and whom I had sworn to love and to protect, even at the hazard of my life! Youth! do you not commiserate in her fate?"

"Yes, yes," replied Jack, "I do sincerely: but think no more upon the painful subject at present."

"Think no more!" cried the maniac fiercely; "who are you that would presume to check the thoughts which have for so many years taken possession of my mind, and which neither time nor circumstances can banish? Fool! hold your peace, and seek not to arouse the demon in my breast! Are they not ever present to my mind's eye, and can anything banish them from it?—No! no!—I should indeed be mad, were I to encourage such an idea!—I see their pale and ghastly faces even at this moment fixed upon me! I hear her shriek for hope and mercy, when there are neither at hand. I am am a murderer! a cold blooded assassin, and the curse of God is upon me! Do not interrupt me, boy, or I will not be answerable what in the frenzy of my feelings I may be tempted to do."

As the unfortunate man gave utterance to these wild observations, he arose from his seat, and traversing the room with hasty and disordered steps, he tore his hair and beat his breast in the most piteous manner; our hero standing by and watching him with the most earnest emotion and anxiety, but at the same time fearful of interrupting him or remonstrating with him; and thinking that for a time it would be better to leave him to the free indulgence of his own feelings.

At length he became more composed, and again resuming his seat, appeared to ponder for a few minutes in deep silence.

"Come hither, boy," he said at last, "you do not mind me; you will bear with me? I am but a poor old man, borne down with the weight of care and suffering. You will not leave me, will you?"

"No, no," answered our hero, in soothing and persuasive accents; "set your mind at rest I beseech you; I will remain with you, and do all in my humble power to tranquillise your feelings."

"Oh, thank you for that assurance," said the maniac, his features becoming re-animated with hope and confidence; "you are very good; I can see it by your looks and words; and I will be grateful, too; yes, so very, very grateful."

Our hero continued to humour him, and then in order to divert his mind, assisted him to dress the goat, and when the time came round they once more sat down to refresh themselves, and both of them partook of a hearty meal.

During the remainder of the day Herbert remained pretty tranquil, only at intervals relapsing into the same melancholy state of mind under which he so painfully laboured; but from all the observations he made use of, Jack was unable to elicit anything which was at all calculated to throw any further light upon the particulars of his dismal and unfortunate history. Every moment he seemed to grow in favour with him, and Herbert scarcely for a moment removed his eyes from his countenance, though he frequently sighed deeply, and seemed to connect his likeness with some particular subject that was nearest his heart. In this manner the day passed away much the same as the previous one, and the most melancholy thoughts at times disturbed the brain of the young seaman, and many were the apprehensions he entertained for the future, and the misgivings he had that he should never behold his beauteous Kate, and all those friends so dear to him again. When he retired to rest, these thoughts kept him waking for some time, and many were the prayers he offered up to Heaven for their protection, and that something would yet before long occur to restore him to his native land and to realise all those bright visions of happiness he had for so many years indulged in.

"Beloved Kate," he said, "bereft of you, life would indeed become a curse to me, for all my hopes would be annihilated, and I could look forward to nothing but misery and despair. But I dare not think that Providence will so desert me, or I should go mad. No, no, Jack keep up your spirits; although you are at present tossed about in a sea of troubles, and I have no doubt that the good Pilot Above will enable you to weather the storm. Jack Junk, the tar for all weathers, is never destined to meet with such a fate as this. Poor fellow!" he added, fixing his eyes upon the maniac, who was sleeping soundly; "your's I fear has been a sad destiny, and when I compare it with mine own, why should I murmur? May the Almighty look down upon you with mercy, and restore you once more to reason and happiness. He said that he was noble and rich, and his appearance and manners, wild though they be, fully confirms it; what strange calamities can have brought him to his present melancholy condition? Would that I had the means of becoming acquainted with the whole particulars of his history, but at present I see not the least chance of my being enabled to do so. I feel the greatest interest in his fate, and would fain hope that I may yet be made the humble instrument in the hands of Providence, of recalling his wandering senses, and likewise of restoring him to any relations or friends whom he may still have in existence."

Tired with thinking, our hero at last succeeded in composing his mind to sleep, but visions of the most varied character flitted before his imagination during the night. At one time he saw his beloved Kate struggling in the arms of a frightful monster, whose form was too *outre* to admit of description, while he felt himself bound and fettered as it seemed by some inscrutable power, although his limbs were at full liberty. He was completely powerless to render her any aid, and felt, as it were, chained and rivetted to the spot on which he was standing, and compelled inactively, passively, to witness all the agonies, the struggles she endured to release herself from the embraces of the frightful being that held her in his power. He thought at the same time that the elements were battling in their utmost fury, and yet the shrieks of her he so fondly loved could be heard far above the tempest's most terrific voice. It was a wild scene too, in which all this was being enacted; a barren space, inclosed by an amphitheatre of craggy rocks, between which might be seen the gurgling sea, red as blood with the lurid reflection cast upon it from the overcharged atmosphere. Not a human being but themselves was to be seen as far as the eye could stretch. All was desolate and hopeless! How the cries of the maiden went to our hero's heart, and how desperate were the efforts he made to release himself from the power which held him, and to fly to her rescue, but in vain. And how piteous and supplicating were the looks which Kate fixed upon him. Suddenly the form and features of the monster that thus held the person of his lover underwent a remarkable metamorphosis, and the villain, Mark Stanford, stood confessed before him; but his costume was very different from that in which he had hitherto seen him. The simple dress of the farmer had yielded to that of the daring buccaneer, and his person seemed to dilate with the change in his apparel. He turned one look of malice and exultation upon Jack, and pointing significantly to the weapons of death which he carried in the broad leathern belt around his waist, mocked and derided his sufferings. Still our hero imagined in his dream that he felt as helpless as an infant, and appeared totally unable to move a single step from the spot on which he was fixed, while the agonized looks of Kate seemed to reproach him with his inactivity and non-interference. His heart swelled to bursting, and he struggled with a giant's strength to release himself from the mysterious power that enchained him, but all to no purpose. The strength of his lover seemed to be now exhausted, and her face became ghastly pale; her eyes closed, and she sank inanimate in the arms of the ruffian who held her, and whose loud laugh of triumph our hero imagined in his dream he heard resound upon the air, and re-echoed from the cavities of the surrounding rocks. Then Stanford dared to pollute the beauteous cheeks of Kate with his kisses, and throwing her fair and insensible form across his shoulder, he made his way with his lovely burthen towards one of the openings in the rocks, and from which Jack could perceive a large dark vessel riding at anchor at no great distance, and from the mast-head of which floated the black flag. A boat was moored off the beach, in which two men were awaiting the arrival of Stanford and his victim, and into which having stepped, it was pushed off towards the ship. And yet our hero imagined that notwithstanding he used every exertion in his power, he could not stir from the spot, or offer the least interference. The boat now reached the vessel, and at that moment an extraordinary and supernatural light seemed to illumine the ocean, and Jack could behold every object as distinctly as if it had been noonday, and he had been close upon the spot. He saw the deck of the ship crowded with the most ferocious looking men, and in the midst of them stood Mark Stanford, still holding in his arms the delicate and gentle form of Kate, and his looks, which were plainly discernable, expressive of every triumph. The damsel stretched forth her arms for help towards her lover, and her looks evinced the most awful agony of mind. But in vain were her supplications; the vessel weighed anchor; with most astonishing rapidity it faded away in the distance; and in the anguish of his feelings our hero awoke.

For a few moments, such was the powerful impression which this remarkable dream had upon his mind, that Jack could not persuade himself but what it had actually occurred, and for some time his mind was so bewildered that he could not imagine where he was. But at length he rubbed his eyes, and looking around him, remembrance returned to him, and he started to his feet in a state of the greatest agitation.

"Was it then but a dream?" he cried; "but oh, should that dream be realized;—no—no—it cannot, will not be, Providence will never permit it. That infernal shark, Mark Stanford, should he indeed turn out to be what he was represented to be in this singular vision, Kate, I fear, has much to apprehend from him, now that she is deprived of may protection. The black looking swab, I always had strong suspicions that he hoisted false colours, but if I had only had any suspicion of the truth, I would have taken good care to have spoilt his sports. My poor lass! it seems we are both destined to be tossed about on the tempestuous sea of life, but I trust that Heaven will not allow us to founder altogether, but that we shall at lenght be enabled to reach the haven of our hopes, and to lie in ordinary for the future in the port of happiness and content."

These thoughts somewhat restored the spirits of the young sailor, but still he found it impossible to banish from his mind the impression which the extraordinary dream had made upon it. Herbert still slept, and Jack now once more turned his attention towards him, he not feeling at all disposed to compose himself again to rest. As he contemplated the expressive features of the unfortunate recluse, he could not but feel his sympathy and curiosity increase, which feeling was much strengthened by the remarkable resemblance that existed between him and the portrait which had been delivered to him by old Joe Trennant on his leaving his native shores. It seemed quite evident to Jack Junk, that Herbert was a man who had sprang from no mean station of society, and that he had received a most liberal education, and the longer he reflected upon all the circumstances of their meeting, and what had taken place since, the more anxious did he feel to penetrate into all the secrets of his past life.

As our hero still gazed upon the features of the sleeping man, he suddenly remembered the box which he had accidentally purchased of the pedlar on the day of the sailing of the fleet, and the miniature in the lid of which so strongly resembled that which was contained in the locket before so often alluded to. He had not removed his trousers since the wreck, and it struck him for the moment, that it was still in one of the pockets; but feeling in them all, to his disappointment and vexation, he found that it was not in either of them, and upon mere mature reflection he recollected that he had placed it in his chest a short time before the fatal storm commenced, and consequently, he concluded that it was lost to him for ever. This was a source of great uneasiness to him, not from the mere intrinsic value of the box, but that he could not help thing from the remarkable coincidence of the likeness between the two miniatures that they had been painted from one and the same individual, and had he had them both in his possession, they might at some time or other have tended to have thrown some light upon the mystery as to who were the authors of his being. However, it was useless to regret that loss now, and he therefore sought to think no more of it; though the more he dwelt upon the countenance of Herbert, the more forcibly did the extraordinary likeness which it bore to both portraits strike him, and impress itself upon his mind. Could he but even for a short time recall his mind to reason, he might probably be enabled to elicit such facts from him of the particulars of his history, as would be of the utmost importance to them both; but at present, at any rate, he saw no chance of being enabled to do so, and consequently, he gave up the idea in despair.

The day had now dawned, and as Herbert did not seem likely to awaken for some time, in order to relieve his thoughts, our hero determined to leave the hut for a short time, and to take a solitary ramble to the sea-shore, with a faint hope of being able to discover some prospect of relief.

He walked on towards the rocks up which he had made his escape from the wreck, and seating himself on the summit of one of the loftiest, he gazed anxiously across the wide expanse of ocean; but nothing whatever met the poor mariner's gaze to inspire him with hope. It was a beautiful morning; not a cloud obscured the horizon; the sea was perfectly calm, and the sun shed his golden rays full upon its surface. A gentle breeze was stirring, scarcely sufficient to ruffle the waves the least in the world, and all was as serene and refreshing as the heart could wish. The thoughts of our hero naturally reverted to his poor Kate, from whom he was separated by so many, many miles, and whom he never might behold again; and these reflections caused his heart to be crowded by the deepest care and anguish.

"Alas!" he sighed, "to what dangers may you not be at present exposed, and I not at hand to rescue you or to stand up in your defence? Should my dream be realized, what have I not to apprehend?—But avast, Jack! surely you are not becoming so weak as to give way to any such idle notions? No, no—I will banish them from my mind, and endeavour to stick to the sailor's sheet-anchor—hope! Though the wide waves divide us, and your Jack is cast adrift and has lost his reckonings, he will not give way to despair. His vessel will yet be righted; he will ere long find safe anchorage, and learn to laugh at the troubles of the past. The lubber, Mark Stanford, will not dare to insult you, protected as you are by your uncle and your other friends, and therefore, whatever his thoughts and wishes may be, they will be defeated, and himself be glad to sheer off! Oh, my sweet Kate! with what fond transport I look forward to that moment when we shall meet again, and I shall have the felicity of your lovely and innocent smiles to compensate me for all the troubles and vicissitudes I have endured."

He was interrupted in the midst of these reflections by an exclamation from immediately behind him, and turning round, to his no small astonishment, he beheld Herbert standing close to him, leaning upon his staff, and gazing earnestly upon him. Jack started to his feet, and presented his hand in a friendly manner, but the maniac drew back a few paces and eyeing him with a mingled expression of reproach and sorrow, he said—

"So, you would leave me—you would desert poor old Herbert, after all the solemn promises you have made to remain with him in his solitude, to be the partner of his kingdom, the participator in all his glories and his fortunes, and to call him father! Oh, thou art false, cruel, treacherous, like the rest of ungrateful mankind!"

"My good Herbert," replied our hero, kindly, and persuasively, "you do me wrong, indeed you do; I meant not to desert you; no thought of ingratitude ever entered my mind, indeed it did not; but you slept, and as the morning was fine and I wished not to disturb you, I thought I would ramble forth for awhile to——"

"Sleep! sleep!" interrupted Herbert, hastily; "no, no, I never sleep! All is ever fresh an vivid in my mind's eye, though my senses may seem to be steeped in forgetfulness. Oh, th I could sleep; that I could find an oblivion to my thoughts; but it will not be. You say the morn is calm and lovely, but it is not so; do you not mark how black the Heavens are? Black, black, even as pitch. Do you not hear the thunder? Do you not see the lightning's vivid flash? Hear you not the roaring waves? See you not the storm-tossed bark? There—there she is, struggling with the mountainous billows! See how vainly she battles with the furious elements that every moment threaten her with destruction; and there is no one at hand to render her the least assistance. Oh, God—oh, God! and she and her child, too, are on board. Why do you gaze thus indifferently and inactively? Do you not see that the ship is fast sinking, and that a few minutes more must engulph her in the ocean's bosom? Do you not hear that frantic cry for help? Will no one stretch forth the hand of mercy towards them? Will no one fly to save them? Wretches! must they perish thus? No, by Heaven they shall not! I—I alone will brave the perils of the angry deep, and thus I hasten on my errand of mercy, and will succeed or perish with them."

As the unfortunate man thus spoke, he darted to the extreme verge of the rock, and would have precipitated himself into the deep, had not our hero grasped his arm, and forcibly detained him.

"My good Herbert," remarked the young seaman, in his most gentle and persuasive accents,

JACK JUNK.

"what would you do ? Come, come; this is all a wild delusion; there is nothing whatever to disturb you thus."

"A delusion !" repeated the unhappy maniac, pressing his hand to his forehead; "does not the tempest rage, then ? Do they not cry for help and succour in their terrible calamity? Do not seek to deceive me, or, old as I am, it shall cost you dear !"

"No, no, Herbert," replied our hero; "I would not for the world seek to deceive you; all is calm here as an infant's slumber. Come, let us return home."

"Home !" cried Herbert. "Yes, we have a home—a rare home—a palace, and you are to be my future companion ! You will not abandon me ?"

"I will not," replied our hero, emphatically; "but will watch over you and reverence you the same as if you were my father."

The eyes of the poor maniac glistened with pleasure; and pressing the hand of Jack vehemently to his lips, he said—

"Ah! now you do, indeed, speak kind, and I will believe you and trust to you. We will be so happy together, too; and who is there to interrupt us? Come, come! to our palace—to our palace!"

Our hero uttered not another word; and taking the arm of the recluse, he led him from the spot, and they made their way towards the hut.

During the remainder of that day nothing more worthy of recording took place, and they did not offer to quit their habitation, Jack doing all that he could to divert the wandering mind of his unfortunate companion from the many cares that beset it. He soon worked a most powerful influence over his mind, and he became more calm and somewhat more rational; but still Jack was unable to elicit any more particulars of his melancholy and extraordinary history than those he had already been enabled to obtain from him by accident.

In this manner more than a fortnight passed away, and the daily avocations of our hero and the recluse continued the same, and the former began to despair that anything would occur to release him from the island, or to restore him to his native land, and those he held so dear. He had become so quickly inured to the wild sports of Herbert, that he could enter into them as dexterously as he could, and they had always an ample supply of provisions, which under all the circumstances in which he had been cast upon the island was a most providential thing, and the seaman felt sufficiently grateful for it; but still his thoughts were always most painfully and naturally fixed on Kate, and many were the prayers he offered up to heaven for her safety and protection, and that something might shortly occur to restore them again to each other's arms.

One afternoon, however, they had wandered to the rocks, and they had no sooner arrived there than our hero, casting his eyes as usual eagerly across the ocean, started back with an exclamation of surprise and delight on beholding a vessel at no great distance, which had apparently cast her anchor, and at that moment a boat put off from her filled with several men, and made towards the island, though, whether they had been observed or not, Jack at that time, of course, had no means of ascertaining.

"Ah! by Heaven, we are saved!" he exclaimed, joyfully, grasping the arm of the maniac, and directing his attention to the vessel, and the approaching boat. "Courage, Herbert, and we shall quickly be rescued from our present situation."

The maniac uttered a wild exclamation when he beheld the vessel, and with a powerful effort released himself from the hold of our hero.

"Ah!" he cried,—"a ship!—They come to tear me from my dominions! The wretches! —The villains!—But they shall not have me!—No! I will fly, and conceal myself in the deepest bowels of the earth first. Emilia,—my child! Ye are lost to me for ever, and who shall dare again to drag me into the world?—I go! I fly!—and pursuit will be in vain!"

Before Jack had any opportunity to offer to prevent him, the unfortunate Herbert fled from the spot with the rapidity of lightning, and was almost instantaneously out of sight. Confused and bewildered, Jack knew not how to act, and was unable to attempt to go in pursuit, and he now awaited the result of this adventure with the utmost impatience and anxiety, and watched the approach of the boat with the greatest eagerness. It came nearer, and our hero shouted as loud as he could to them, and waved his handkerchief above his head. They beheld him, and returned his salute, and then pulling harder than ever made their way into a small creek, secured the boat, and ascending the rock, soon stood before our hero, who was almost overpowered by the numerous feelings that took possession of his breast at the speedy prospect of deliverance. They were, however, ferocious looking fellows, and such as at any other time Jack would not have felt much prepossessed in favour of.

"We put in here for fresh water," said one of them; "but, hollo, mess-mate, how is it we find you here?"

"I was one of the crew of the unfortunate vessel, His Majesty's ship, Defiance, which was wrecked off this island about a fortnight since, and I am the only one who was saved," answered our hero.

"The Defiance!" repeated the man; "let us inspect your figure-head more narrowly. Ah! by Neptune, mess-mates, 'tis he! Do you not know him? 'Tis Jack Junk!"

"Known!" cried our hero, in a tone of the utmost astonishment;—"What is the meaning of this?—Why do you look so triumphantly and savagely upon me? Who are ye? and what is the name of the ship to which you long?"

"Softly! softly, my salt-water tar," said the man with a sneer; "you will have an opportunity of overhauling our papers soon enough. Secure him, and two of you keep watch over him, while I and my comrades go in search of the other lubber whom we saw with him on the rock!"

"Villains!" exclaimed the alarmed seaman, struggling. "What would you do?—Who are you?"

"Heed not his words," said the ruffian who had hitherto spoken; "our captain will, no doubt, feel highly honoured and gratified by his company!"

In a moment our hero was bound hand and foot and thrown upon the earth, and the horror, surprise, and consternation of his feelings at that moment may readily be imagined. He could have no doubt for an instant that he was in the hands of pirates; but who they could be, and how they had become acquainted with his name he could form not the least idea of. His mind was distracted at this unexpected misfortune, and it was some time after the departure of the other men before he could give utterance to a word.

"Why is this outrage committed upon me?" he at length said; "why am I thus violently seized?"

"Oh, you will be satisfied upon that point, all in good time, messmate, I dare say," replied one of the ruffians. "But for the present you may as well put your jawing tackle under hatches."

"What is the name of your vessel," demanded Jack; "and who is your captain?"

"Why, if it will afford you any satisfaction to know," answered the fellow, "the name of our vessel is the Black Raven, and her captain is Hugh Granfield, the daring Rover of the Seas."

"Ah!" ejaculated our hero, "in the power of that reckless monster! Then, I am, indeed, lost!"

He groaned in the extreme anguish and horror of his feelings, and was unable to utter another word. In this manner nearly half an hour elapsed, when the other pirates returned, but unaccompanied by Herbert.

"The swab has deluded us, and we have not time to waste in search of him," said one of them; "but we discovered his hut, and have levelled it with the ground, so the poor devil will stand a good chance of perishing."

"Wretches!" exclaimed Jack.

"Oh, you may talk, my master," replied the pirate, "it is all you can do now. We have found plenty of fresh water. Away with him to the boat, and let us put off with all speed to the vessel; there will be a pleasant meeting between him and our captain, no doubt; ha, ha, ha!"

Jack made no reply, for he saw it would be useless, and having made up his mind to the worst as well as he could, he was carried to the boat, into which he was thrown like a dog, and the pirates having entered it, they pulled away with all their might to the Black Raven.

CHAPTER XII.

JACK JUNK ON BOARD THE PIRATE VESSEL.—THE MEETING OF THE LOVERS.—THEIR SUFFERINGS.

WE will not seek to describe the feelings of our hero as the boat proceeded on its way to the ship, for the reader will be able to imagine them; but his separation from Herbert, and the destruction of the habitation of the wretched maniac, if possible, excited him more than all, so great was the interest that the mystery connected with his history had created in his mind. The boat soon reached the ship, and Jack was handed on board, and was then released from the cords which bound him. The men hastened to inform their captain of what had taken place, and the astonishment and satisfaction of Stanford on hearing the particulars exceeded all bounds.

"By all the infernal host!" he ejaculated, "this is most fortunate; Jack in my power as well as Kate, my triumph is complete. Bring him hither immediately, that he may have the pleasure of seeing who his rival, farmer Stanford, really is."

The men immediately departed, and presently returned, bringing in our hero, who started with amazement and consternation when he recognised in the much dreaded pirate chief, Mark Stanford, the supposed farmer, and his rival in the affections of Kate Markham.

"You seem surprised, my worthy Jack Junk," said the pirate, with a bitter sneer; "and no doubt you did not expect that we should meet again so soon, and under such circumstances. I bid you welcome to the Black Raven!"

"Villain!" exclaimed our hero, indignantly.

"Better language, my young spark," said the pirate, "you will recollect that here I am master, and that you are entirely at my mercy."

"Your mercy, you lubber," repeated Jack, scornfully, "think you I will crave for it? No! But oh, I only wish you would give me a fair chance, and if I would not sink your piratical craft in less time than a man could cry peccavi, my name's not Jack Junk."

"Poor devil!" said Stanford with a sneer, "I can make every allowance for your excitement, and treat your observations with perfect indifference. Did I not tell you that the time would come when you would know Mark Stanford better, and when you might have reason to tremble at his power? You find that I have kept my word. But I must acknowledge that I little anticipated that pleasure so soon. Again I bid you welcome to the pirate ship, the Raven, whose captain, fear not, will study everything for your accommodation."

"Why you infernal shark!" said the young seaman, "now do you not think that you deserve to be strung up to the yard-arm, like a dog, as richly as any rascal that ever embellished a gibbet-post? But I defy you, you lubber; although fate has placed me, it is true, in your power, yet I do not fear that Providence will protect me, and ere long release me from your clutches."

"Indeed!" said Stanford, "I am glad to see you so sanguine, for it will only render your disappointment the greater. But I have information for you that probably may serve to depress your spirits. Kate Markham ——"

"Ah! what of her?" demanded Jack, starting and staring anxiously and indignantly upon Standford.

"Why," replied the latter, coolly, "I merely wish to inform you, for I thought, perhaps, it might interest you to know, that she is at present in my power, and destined to become my future mistress!"

"Liar!" cried Jack, bursting with resentment.

"Tush, tush, man, what is the use of your contradicting me?" said the pirate, "if you have any doubts upon the subject, I will soon give you an opportunity of convincing yourself that your beloved Kate is not only in my power, but that she is also at this very moment on board this vessel."

"On board this vessel!" repeated our hero, with a shudder of horror, yet still looking at the pirate incredulously.

"'Tis even so, my gallant sea lion," returned Stanford, "and in a short time you will have the opportunity of satisfying yourself by beholding her."

"Oh, God!" cried the young sailor, in the greatest agony of mind; "this is too much. Mark Stanford, do you indeed speak the truth?"

"Fool! why should you doubt my word? Mark Stanford, or Hugh Granfield the pirate, is not in the habit of making empty boasts. The beauteous Kate is in my power; and is destined to become my victim. I will fully avenge myself for her scorn and hatred. Think you that I would ever abandon the hopes upon which I had fixed my mind? think you that I, the dreaded rover of the seas, would suffer myself to be foiled in my designs? Oh, no! my plans were all maturely laid from the first, and I felt certain of success. You insulted me, struck me, called me villain, and I will not fail to make you pay dearly for it."

"Mark Stanford," said our hero, in a subdued tone, for the words of his bitter enemy filled his mind with despair; "for myself I care not, do with me as you please, heap upon me any indignity; but oh, I implore your mercy for that fair and innocent girl whom I love far dearer than my very existence. You cannot, even hardened villain as you are, dare to put your disgusting and terrible threats against her into execution."

"Ha! ha! ha!" laughed the pirate scornfully and triumphantly; "and think you that after I have dared so much, and have succeeded in getting the damsel in my power I will hesitate for a moment in fully accomplishing all my designs against her? Mark Stanford is no weak boy to trifle with the good fortune that has been placed in his hands. She is mine, my future mistress, and nought can save her from the fate that I have marked out for her. You shall be witness of my triumph, and in your agony I will find a tenfold gratification to my revenge."

"Miscreant!" exclaimed our hero, "can nothing move your savage heart to pity and forbearance?"

"No," replied the pirate, scornfully. "Mark Stanford is not subject to the melting mood, and so you will find to your cost. Doubt not but that I will fulfil my promise to the very letter. I will gratify my revenge against you and the fair girl whom you so fondly love to the fullest extent. Oh, she is a lovely girl, and right worthy of becoming the mistress of the Pirate Chief!"

"Cowardly ruffian!" cried Jack, his manly bosom swelling with the most uncontrolable indignation and anguish; "to appeal to you I find is useless; but still I will not yield myself to despair. No, there is a power which however much you may affect to despise, will not suffer you to triumph in your guilty and brutal designs."

"Capital!" said Stanford, with an ironical laugh; "you would make an excellent ship's chaplain, only we do not require one on board this craft, its captain and crew being all such strictly moral characters! Ha! ha! ha!—But I confess that I did not expect to meet you again so soon and under such circumstances, and I cannot properly express the pleasure it affords me. You will find that I have excellent accommodation on board for you."

"You may at present appear to triumph, villain!" said our hero; "but depend upon it the time will come, and that before long, an when justice will overtake you, and you will have to answer dearly for the many atrocious crimes you have committed."

"Pshaw!" exclaimed Stanford, impatiently, "what idle talk is this? Think you that I am to be intimidated, or that anything can daunt me from my purpose? Hugh Granfield, the pirate chief, sets all power at defiance, and laughs the future to scorn. Has he not for years been the master of the seas; and who has yet been able to conquer him? But I waste words with you—bear the lubber below."

"Beware!" said Jack, "and reflect before you proceed to extremities."

"Reflect be d—d!" replied the ruffian, "it needs no reflection. My decisions are always prompt and resolute, and I need not tell you that I have fully made up my mind as regards you and Kate Markham. Away with him, lads, and perhaps an hour or two's solitary meditation may serve to cool his courage, and convince him of the hopelessness of his situation."

"Cowardly wretch!" said Jack, "in spite of your threats you shall find me firm. Oh, that I had you alone and the means of defence in my hands, I would soon inflict upon you that punishment that your atrocities merit."

"Poor fool!" returned Stanford; "but I will e'en suffer you to talk, as you are powerless to do anything else. You will recollect that I have you entirely at my mercy, and that it is I who have the means of punishment in my hands. It will be rare sport for me to see you lashed to the gratings, and writhing under the agony of the cat. Ha! ha! ha! Think of that my gallant tar, and luxuriate in anticipation of the pleasures that are in store for you. Away with him!"

Jack was too much overpowered by his feelings to be enabled to make any reply, and the pirates having seized him, forced him from the cabin in obedience to the commands of their captain.

"By h—l this is a fortunate circumstance, Pierce, and one which I didn't expect," remarked Stanford when he was gone; "now that my rival is in my power, my triumph is doubly complete."

"Ay, you may say that, captain," replied Pierce; "how strange that our men should put in at the very island on which he had been cast."

"It was," said Stanford, "and fortune evidently favours me in my designs. What will be the anguish of Kate when she beholds her lover in my power?"

"True; but may it not have the most dangerous effect upon her and retard the gratification of your wishes?"

"Oh, I will leave everything to chance, and at all hazards will not fail to obtain the full accomplishment of all my wishes. Of course I must expect that the girl will offer all the resistance in her power, but what will that avail her? It is impossible that she can escape the fate that I have destined her to."

"Why, no, I do not see any chance of her being able to do that," said Pierce; "but still your wishes would be greatly disappointed, I should imagine, should she sink under the weight of her sufferings."

"Certainly," returned Stanford, "that would be much more than I bargained for. However I will not give way to any such fears, and I have no doubt that I shall succeed as well as I could wish; a few days shall witness the completion of my designs, and the triumph of my wishes. Kate Markham the proud and scornful beauty, who looks upon me with horror and detestation, shall become my victim, and no power can rescue her from the fate to which I have doomed her. But let us crowd all sail, for I am anxious to reach the place to which we are bound as quickly as possible."

Pierce and the captain now separated, and the latter sought his cabin, where he gave himself up to feelings of the greatest exultation at the unexpected adventure that had taken place.

Jack Junk was confined in a cabin of the smallest dimensions, and when he was alone he gave himself up to all those feelings of anguish which the reader must be aware distracted his bosom. But to know that his beloved Kate was also in the power of the terrible pirate chief tortured him more than all; and it was some time ere he could bring his mind to anything like a degree of composure. That Stanford would not fail to put his diabolical threats into execution to the very letter he could not entertain the least doubt, and unless providence interposed to save her, her destruction seemed to be inevitable. How he shuddered as this terrible and revolting thought crossed his mind, and he beat his breast in the utmost agony of despair. And what must be the horrors of that poor girl's feelings, and how greatly would her anguish be increased when she became aware that he also had fallen into the power of the pirate captain. She could never, he thought, find fortitude to support the shock.

"Oh, Kate, my unfortunate Kate!" he ejaculated, "that you, so young, so good, so innocent, should ever be subjected to such misery, and exposed to such a terrible and revolting fate. Heaven protect you, or you are lost for ever! But it will not, cannot allow such a daring and brutal miscreant to triumph. It would be monstrous to entertain such a thought. Notwithstanding the gloominess of our present prospects, I will not give myself up entirely to despair. Oh, that I that I had known the real character of the pretended Farmer Stanford before I left England, he might then have been secured and all these misfortunes prevented. Too fatally have the melancholy misgivings of Kate been realised, and I shudder when I think of the dangers to which she is exposed."

Such were the thoughts that continued to torture the mind of our hero, and it was in vain that he endeavoured to obtain the least tranquillity. He also reflected upon the unfortunate maniac, Herbert, with the greatest anxiety; and great was the regret he felt at being parted from him, and that he should never have had an opportunity of eliciting the whole particulars of his melancholy and mysterious history; but situated as he now was there did not seem to be any probability of their ever meeting again.

In the same state of mind Jack continued for several hours, and no one offered to interrup him. The vessel was proceeding at a rapid rate, and the voices of the pirates frequently met his ears, and tended to increase the anguish and despair of his feelings. Worn out with care and anxiety, at length, he stretched his reary limbs upon the floor of the cabin, and tried to compose himself to sleep, but that was impossible, and he at length gave up the task in despair, and he once more resigned himself to the most painful thoughts.

The reader may form a ready idea of the sufferings poor Kate had been enduring throughout the voyage, and how vainly she had sought to inspire herself with consolation and hope. It was wonderful how she could find fortitude to support herself under the terrible circumstances in which she was placed, and when she contemplated the dismal prospect before her. Constantly she offered up her prayers to the Supreme, and supplicated His mercy and protection; and earnestly did she long for death, rather than be consigned to the dreadful fate with which she was threatened. Her thoughts were constantly fixed upon her lover, and many were the fearful conjectures she formed as to the fate which had befallen him, and the sad misgivings that she had that they would never meet again. When such thoughts afflicted her mind the poor girl's tears would flow fast, and she gave herself up to all the anguish of the most insupportable despair. The villain Stanford visited her every day, and tortured and disgusted her with his odious addresses, and it was in vain she tried to move him to pity and forbearance; he seemed determined to persist in the accomplishment of his diabolical designs, and unless by some miraculous interposition of the Almighty, she saw no means of escaping from destruction. The thought was madness, and her strength almost gave way under it. In this manner, some time elapsed, and every day she expected that the miscreant Stanford would put his threats into execution; but he still forbore to do so, and she began to hope that something might yet occur to rescue her from his power.

On the day on which our hero had been seized and brought on board the pirate ship, Kate had felt her spirits even more than usually depressed, and the most dismal presentiments disturbed her mind, for which she was unable to account, but which she found it impossible to control or to conquer. It seemed to her as if something of the most extraordinary and fatal description was about to happen, and she started and trembled at every sound which met her ears from the deck. At length she heard the boat which had been sent to procure fresh water, return to the ship, and soon afterwards there was a great bustle and confusion on deck; but Kate was, of course, unable to form the least conjecture as to what had happened, though she felt convinced that it was something extraordinary; and a most melancholy feeling came over her, which made her tremble in every limb, though why she did so she could not imagine. After a short time all became silent again, and the vessel proceeded on its way; but Kate could not banish from her mind the dismal thoughts that had taken possession of it. What would have been her anguish had she known that her lover was at that time on board the same vessel with her!

Night came on, but the mind of Kate was too violently agitated to suffer her to sleep, and the most strange and distracting thoughts continued to disturb her imagination, and to bewilder her brain. The image of her lover was constantly before her eyes, and it was in vain that she endeavoured to divest her mind of the idea that something fatal was about to take place.

In this manner the night passed away, and the morning came, and in a short time the cabin door was unfastened, and Mark Stanford made his appearance. There was an expression of more than usual exultation on the countenance of the villain, and it required no deep penetration to discover that something had happened which afforded him considerable satisfaction. Kate averted her looks from him with a feeling of shame and disgust, and could not help shuddering with fear; but she started when he advanced towards her, and took her hand.

"How fares the lovely Kate this morning?" said the villain, in assumed accents of affection; "by all my hopes, you look more beautiful than ever; such charms as these, so glowing and so exquisite, are sufficient to warm the heart of a stoic. Nay, frown not, damsel; for it is with smiles of pleasure and welcome alone that you should greet your fond admirer."

"Mr. Stanford," replied the indignant girl; "are you destitute of every manly feeling that you can thus delight to insult and torture me? Leave me, I beseech you, for your presence is odious to me."

"Indeed!" sneered the brutal ruffian;—"but it matters not; hateful though my presence may be to you, you must learn to endure it, ay, and to welcome it, too. Phsaw, girl! of what use is this prudish obduracy? Think you it will intimidate me from my purpose?—No! the passion with which your transcendant charms have inspired me nothing can subdue, and your opposition does but serve to inflame it. You may flatter yourself with the wild hope that you will yet be able to escape me; but to encourage such a thought would be worse than madness. You are mine—irrevocably mine, and a few days only shall witness the completion of my triumph."

"Oh, God forbid!" ejaculated, Kate fervently; "but I will not despair: I will put my trust in Him, and He will not fail to frustrate your guilty designs at the very moment when you flatter yourself that your triumph is most certain.'

"Well, my scornful beauty," returned the pirate, with anironical grin, "you are at perfect liberty to entertain such hopes, but I am much mistaken if they are not doomed to disappointment. I will not, however argue that point with you now; I came here for a different purpose; I bring you news."

"News!" repeated Kate, with a look of astonishment and doubt.

"Yes," answered Stanford, "though I am not quite certain whether it will cause you happiness or regret."

"Oh, keep me not in suspense," said our heroine, eagerly; "tell me what is it you have to communicate."

"Oh, certainly," remarked the pirate, coolly; "I do not know why I should hesitate. Your lover, Jack Junk——"

"Ah!" cried Kate; "why do you mention his name? Speak! speak! what of him?"

"By a most fortunate accident," replied Stanford, "he has fallen into my hands, and is at present on board this vessel."

"Great God!" exclaimed the distracted girl, sinking on her knees, clasping her hands vehemently together, and raising her hands towards Heaven; "can this indeed be true?"

"You need not doubt my word," said the pirate; "I tell you again that Jack Junk is in my power; he was brought on board yesterday; and by-and-by I will convince you of the truth of what I say, by introducing you to him."

"Alas! alas!" groaned the agonized Kate, "then my misery is complete. Oh, my beloved Jack, by what extraordinary fatality have you thus fallen into the hands of your most cruel enemy?—God protect you, or your destruction is inevitable. But oh, Stanford," she continued, "what is your intention towards him?"

"Why, as to that," replied the pirate, "I have not exactly made up my mind, but it depends entirely on your conduct. My sweet Kate, you have it in your power to save your lover, and to win my fondest, my most fervent devotion. Why do you, then, still remain foolishly obstinate? Why not yield that to persuasion, which otherwise must be accomplished by force?"

"Oh, God," groaned the unfortunate damsel, clasping her hands energetically, and averting her gaze in disgust from the pirate; "I humbly implore thee to interpose in my behalf, and not to suffer this miscreant to triumph in his villanous designs."

"Of what use, may I ask you, Kate Markham," said Stanford, who with difficulty could conceal the rage her scorn created in his breast; "of what use, I repeat, is it to make use of those epithets to me, who hold you and my hated rival in my power, and when I have your lives, ay, your very lives in my hands? Beware, girl; provoke me not too much."

"Mark Stanford," said our heroine, solemnly, "you may pride yourself upon *your* power, but have you no dread of the Almighty power of the Supreme, who——"

"Bah!" interrupted the pirate, impatiently, "ought you not by this time to have learnt that I completely scorn the power you invoke? But I will deal more mercifully with you than you seem to give me the credit for, and not resent the insults you have offered me upon your lover, though, I am free to admit, he will have to answer severely to me for those which he has heaped upon me."

Our heroine shuddered when she heard these observations, and saw the malicious expression of countenance with which they were made.

"Oh, Stanford," she ejaculated, " do not suffer your resentment, I implore you, to carry you to any brutal extremes. 'Twould be cowardly, 'twould be monstrous, against one who is power-less to offer you any resistance."

" I am glad my, scornful beauty," said the pirate with a sardonic grin, "I am extremely glad to hear you at last talk so sensibly. As I have before said, my treatment of your beloved Jack Junk will be guided entirely by your own conduct; you have his very life in your hands: it rests with you, whether or not by your own pervesity you seal his death-warrant."

"You would not, surely," said Kate, with a look of horror, "carry your feelings of revenge so far as to sacrifice his life?"

"My simple answer to that is," replied the pirate, coolly and deliberately, "are you prepared to yield willingly to my wishes, to become my mistress, to love me?"

"To love you! Oh, horrible, revolting thought!" replied our heroine.

" Well then," returned the pirate captain, "since you are so obdurate, my beauteous damsel, you must e'en take the consequences, and your lover will have reason, I should imagine, to feel grateful to you for your firmness."

"Miscreant!" cried Kate, "notwithstanding your assertions, I will not even now believe that he to whom my heart is devoted is in your power."

"Indeed!" returned the villain, with a bitter sneer, "then you shall soon have your doubts upon that subject removed. This afternoon I will allow you to meet in my presence. I now leave you, and afford you an opportunity calmly to reflect upon what I have said, and to decide upon the course you may deem it most prudent to adopt."

Thus saying, he was about to stalk out of the cabin in which Kate was confined, when wound up to a pitch of frenzy and despair, she laid her fair hand upon his arm, and gently detained him, at the same time observing—

" Mr. Stanford, I once more supplicate you to be merciful, as you hope for mercy from your fellowman, or that Supreme Power which your affect to despise, but must acknowledge notwith-standing your reckless and desperate life."

" Girl," returned the ruffian, "why persist in making these useless appeals to me? Have I not before told you that the power you affect to venerate, I despise? Have I not, moreover, told you what are my determinations? It is for you to use your own discretion. For the pre-sent, farewell; in an hour or two we shall meet again, and the presence of your lover will cor-roborate my assertions."

He said no more, but Kate having placed her fair hands across her brow, he left her, exulting in his cowardly triumph.

It was some time before Kate recovered from the state of emotion into which she had been thrown by the brutal observations and threats of the miscreat, Stanford ; but when she did acquire the least degree of composure, she threw herself upon her knees and devoutly implored the interposition of the Most High to rescue herself and our hero from the hard fate which was at present impending over them ; and without whose Almighty interference there seemed at pre-sent to be no probable chance of their escaping.

" Dear Jack," she remarked, " and can it indeed be true that you are in the power of our remorseless enemy? Fain would I endeavour to persuade myself that such is not the case, but that is impossible. Oh, God! I humbly beseech Thee to look mercifully down upon us both, and to thwart the monstrous designs of our brutal enemy. Suffer him not to triumph. But Thou wilt not! No, I place too much reliance in Thine infinite mercy and goodness to believe Thou wilt. Jack, dear Jack, we shall meet again; and notwithstanding it be under such dread ful and alarming circumstances, it shall still afford me some satisfaction to convince you that ur Kate has the fortitude to resist the miscreant who holds us both in his power.

Dear Jack, your Kate has not broken the vows pledged to you ; her heart, under any circum-stances, notwithstanding every trial, however severe, to which she may be subjected, must ever remain the same. We can die together, if such be the fate that the will of the Supreme has marked out for us, but never, no never prove unfaithful to each other's vows."

It was thus that she sought to console herself, and to await with patience the time when she would be brought into contact with our here, although she could not, at the same time; at inter-vals, help entertaing some doubts as to the truth of the assertions of Mark Stanford. The story of his capture of Jack, seemed to be altogether so improbable, that it was perfectly incredible ; and yet it was not for a moment to be imagined that Stanford would make such statements unless he was in a position to corroborate what he said.

"Oh, no," Kate observed, clasping her hands in a state of the greatest agony; "it is too true ; I must be mad any longer to doubt it, and all that I can do is to place my trust in that Almighty Being who never deserts the innocent and afflicted in the time of their need. Look down upon us, oh God! I again humbly supplicate Thee, and render the iniquiteus designs of this monster in human form abortive."

THE RECLUSE OFFERING UP A SACRIFICE.

She wrung her hands in the agony of spirit that the words of her brutal jailer had produced, and wept piteously for a time, after which she became more firm, and better enabled to withstand the trials that she knew were in store for her.

Our hero, Jack Junk, was at the same time suffering all the martyrdom of suspense that the reader can imagine as to the amount of insult and indignity that the lubber, Landford, as Jack called him, had inflicted on his beloved Kate. He imagined her suffering everything that his worst anticipations could conjure up, and calling upon him for assistance, while he was manacled and unable to release himself or fly to her rescue. The thought was maddening; yet endure it he must, for what could he do, powerless as his enemies had made him?

"Oh, that I were released," he said, "I would soon show them what a British sailor could do. I would soon settle the whole crew of ruffianly rascals, six at a time, with their leader at their head. But that I am a poor, wretched captive is too true, and that unless The Great Commander interferes, which I trust he will, there is no hope for you or her."

The young seaman beat his breast in the agony of his thoughts as he gave utterance to these words, and continued to pace the cabin in the most agitated manner. All, for a time, was comparatively silent on board the pirate vessel; but at length the coarse voices of the lawless crew, as they bandied their ribald jests one amongst each other, saluted his ears, and at last he heard several of them singing the following chorus:

"Toss the flip! toss the flip!—
　Oh, the pirates life is free;
Find on board fair trader's ship
　A crew that boasts such lads as we!
O'er the wave, o'er the wave,
　How we skim it light and bold;
Nothing have we got to crave,
　Plenty, pleasure, hoards of gold;
Toss the flip! toss the flip!
　Oh, the pirates life is free;
Find on board fair trader's ship
　A crew that boasts such lads as we.

"Who shall dare our courage test,
　Hard the contest they will find;
Fighting is what we like best,
　And wounds or bloodshed do not mind.
Pistols cock'd and sword in hand,
　Each man feels himself a lord;
Like a lion takes his stand,
　Death or conquest, is the word!
Toss the flip! toss the flip!
　Oh, the pirates life is free;
Find on board fair trader's ship
　A crew that boasts such lads as we."

"You d—d lubberly scoundrels!" said Jack, as the ruffians concluded this rude chorus; "I only wish I had you two, three, ay, four at a time, and it strikes me forcibly that I should soon be able to convince you that there were at any rate something like better lads than you to be found among the crew of a fair trader. But, pshaw! this is like throwing salt junk to crocodiles! Avast heaving, Jack; you are not exactly thrown on your beam-ends yet. You are not going to hoist signals of distress in such a squall as this! a mere puddle in a tempest! Bah! a mere powder monkey would make weigh in a rougher storm.

'There's a sweet little cherub sits perch'd up aloft,
　A sweet little cherub sits perch'd up aloft,
　To keep watch for the life of poor Jack.'"

He was interrupted by hearing the door of the cabin in which he was confined unlocked, and Mark Stanford entered. Our hero boldly confronted him.

"I am glad to find you so particularly cheerful, my young sea-lion," remarked the pirate captain with a sardonic and ironical grin.

"The same to you, devil's imp—you infernal figure-head of the Gorgon!" replied our hero. "Now ain't you a pretty fellow to attempt to pass compliments? Why, d—me! if I had the opportunity of doing so, if I would not make you dance as pretty a hornpipe in fetters as ever was performed by a gallows bird since gibbets were invented."

"You are extremely witty, too," said Mark Stanford, sarcastically, but biting his lips with vexation at the same time; "but you might as well be cautious in your observations, lest I should avail myself of the suggestions you thus throw out."

"You—you be d—d!" returned Jack, with a look of scorn; "I defy you, you cowardly, rascally swab! Give me a bit of steel, and stand before me, you and another half-dozen of your infernal crew, and see whether I do not quickly teach you the respect that ought to be paid to a British tar and a gentleman."

"Fool!" retorted the pirate; "belay your jawing tackle, or you may chance to find yourself lashed to the gratings, and receiving a round dozen or two in less time than the twirling of a hand-spike."

"You dare not thus degrade and outrage a British seamen," said our hero.

"I dare not?" repeated Stanford; "are you mad, that you thus venture to set my power at defiance? However, I will not waste words with you in such an argument. I came to converse with you on a different subject. I have informed you that Kate Markham is in my power, that she is on board this vessel, and is destined to become my future mistress."

"Liar! villian!" exclaimed Jack, indignantly; "I will not even believe that you hold her in your power until I behold her."

"Oh, very well," laughed the pirate, coolly and triumphantly; "continue sceptical, if you think proper, but you shall soon be convinced to your confusion."

"Mark Stanford," said Jack, somewhat subdued by the earnestness of the pirate's manner, and the agony of his own feelings, "if it indeed be true what you say—if you have anything at all approaching the man left in your nature, you will abandon your monstrous designs, and never attempt to injure or pollute that innocent girl."

"Indeed!—But methinks by such a supposition, my young spark, you entertain a far better opinion of my character than it deserves."

"Inflict on me what tortures your cruelty may suggest; I trust that I shall find fortitude sufficient to endure them all; but oh, spare her."

"Ha! ha! ha!" laughed the villain, ironically; "this is indeed a triumph. And from I, the scorned, the detested, the insulted, you expect mercy and forbearance, do you?—Oh, you shall have it, to your heart's content you shall have it. Did I not tell you that the day of Mark Stanford's triumph would arrive? That the time would come when you should have ample reason to repent the insults you have at different periods heaped upon my head?—I did—I did! and have I not kept my word?—Yes; and I will continue to do so to the very letter. You are both my prisoners; your very lives are in my hands; we are on the wide and boundless deep; far, far away from any of your friends, there is no one who can fly to your assistance, if even they had the power, and it shall be my delight to witness your helpless agony, when Kate Markham is compelled to yield to my will, and you shall behold her degradation. Oh, how lovely she looked as the May-Queen, did she not?—Do you remember the looks of scorn she flashed upon *Farmer* Stanford?—The opprobrious epithets you applied to him? The blow you struck him, thinking him some poor helpless, passive cur who had no means to retaliate?—Do you remember all this? You must! Ha! ha! ha! and now the poor humble *Farmer* Stanford stands confessed before you as Hugh Granfield, the terrible and invulnerable rover of the seas."

"You will not suffer your vengeance to carry you to such desperate lengths as those which you threaten?" said our hero, whose soul shrank appalled at the fearful observations of the pirate chief, and he felt his courage almost entirely forsake him.

"Indeed," returned the ruffian, with a bitter sneer, "but you will find yourself mistaken; you presume far too much on my clemency."

"Villain!" cried our hero, his eyes flashing with the indignation that swelled his bosom.

"Ay," replied Mark Stanford, coolly, "villain if you please, but you might as well keep your temper, for I am totally indifferent as to the epithets you may think proper to apply to me. You will recollect, however, that you are not on board the Defiance now, but the Black Raven and that I am commander here, and perhaps that recollection will teach you better manners; if not, we may probably try what effect the cat will have upon your temper, and that too, administered in the presence of your beloved Kate."

"Monster!" said Jack, "you dare attempt such an outrage!"

"I dare not? ha, ha, ha! what is there that Hugh Granfield, the pirate chief dare not do?—But you still doubt that Kate is in my power?"

"I cannot believe that Providence would ever permit you so far to triumph in your villanous designs," answered our hero.

"Well, it is my intention to convince you in a few minutes. I have just left her."

"Alas!" said the young sailor, in tones of despair, for he now felt too certain that Mark Stanford spoke the truth; "and is she aware that I am also your prisoner?"

"Oh yes," replied the pirate, "you may be sure that I did not fail to impart to her that gratifying intelligence."

"Oh, God!" groaned Jack, unable to restrain his feelings; "how terrible must be her anguish and despair."

"Why, you may be sure that the information has not altogether exhilarated her spirits. Do you any longer doubt my triumph?"

"Oh, no," answered our hero; "'tis true that you triumph now in your villany, but the time will come when justice will not fail to overtake you."

"Bah!" ejaculated Mark Stanford; "what think you I heed about such threats?"

"I know full well that you are remorseless and determined; but still I can but entertain the idea that the innocence of my beloved Kate will subdue even your hardened and reckless heart."

"You flatter yourself to no purpose," replied Stanford; "you will find that everything I have promised I will fulfil to the very letter. Kate Markham, the beautiful and innocent, is in my power; she is my destined victim, and nothing can save her."

"By Heaven I will still defy you!" returned Jack. "Hopeless as her situation and that of mine may appear to be at present, I will not despair, but put my trust in the merciful interpo-sition of Providence to counteract all your diabolical designs, and to bring you to that con-dign punishment, which your numerous atrocious crimes so richly merit."

"Idiot!" said Mark Stanford, "what empty boasting is this. What prospect have you of deliverance?—But I waste words with you; I go to bring Kate Markham into your presence, and no doubt the interview will be a highly interesting and gratifying one to both of you."

"Will nothing move you to relent, at least in your conduct towards her?" demanded our hero, eagerly.

"Nothing that you can say," answered the pirate, exultingly. "I should be worse than a fool to be influenced by your observations or supplications."

"Hardened villain, I will no longer degrade myself by remonstrating with you; but the time will yet come when it will be my turn to triumph, and in that confidence I will endea-vour to support, with the fortitude that becomes a man, the sufferings to which I am at pre-sent exposed."

"Ha! ha! ha! you talk boldly, young man, but I know full well that it comes not from your heart, and that I shall yet find the means to cool your courage."

"I defy you!"

"How can you help yourself? and what means has the fair and scornful Kate of resisting my will?—I have you both securely in my power, and I will not fail to take advantage of my triumph. Oh, my gallant young spark, it gladdens me to think I have so nicely caged you, after all the insults I received from you, when you thought me weak and powerless. You little expected whom you had to deal with."

"I expected I had a devil at heart," replied our hero, "though he was too much of a cur to show his cloven-foot on shore. Oh! but damme, I will not waste my jawing tackle on any such infernal, cowardly shark as yourself."

"You do well to belay your abuse," said Mark Stanford, "as I might feel disposed to give you a taste of my quality sooner than I had intended. But I leave you for awhile to your own reflections; in a short time you shall have the pleasure of beholding Kate Markham, my fair prisoner and future mistress."

Thus saying Mark Stanford, fixing upon his prisoner a look of triumph, quitted the cabin. We need not seek to pourtray minutely the feelings of both the prisoners, for the reader will be well able to form his own conception of them. Jack continued to pace the cabin with hasty and disordered steps, and to lament his hard fate, but more especially that of her he so fondly loved, and for whose sake he would so willingly have sacrificed his own life. That the pirate would not fail to keep his word, he could not entertain the least doubt, and therefore did he give himself up entirely to despair, and the manly fortitude which usualy sustained him almost forsook him.

"Poor girl—door girl!" he cried in a melancholy voice, "and must you indeed fall a victim to such a heartless and daring miscreant as this? Horrible thought! I cannot entertain it with any degree of patience. But it will not, cannot be. Providence in its infinite mercy will never permit so monstrous a sacrifice. Dear Kate, you will yet be rescued from the terrible ate with which you are at present threatened, and we shall both again be happy. But oh, what a painful meeting will this be. May Heaven give you strength and fortitude to support it. Alas! too fataly have the melancholy misgivings that haunted your mind on the day we parted been realised."

Thus he continued to soliloquise in the same dismal manner for some time, and in vain en-deavoured to tranquilize his feelings. He awaited with the utmost impatience and anxiety the time when he should meet his beloved and unfortunate Kate, and sought to prepare himself to meet the trial with becoming composure, so that the triumph of Mark Stanford might not be rendered altogether complete.

In the meantime the anguish of mind which poor Kate was enduring was of the most tortur-ing and insupportable description, and in vain she endeavoured to find the least ray of conso-lation and hope. She wrung her hands and wept bitterly, then in the most piteous and earnest accents she implored the mercy and protection of Heaven. Every sound that she heard on board the vessel—the coarse voices of the pirate crew, which ever and anon smote her ears, struck terror to her heart, and inspired her with the greatest apprehensions, and it was in vain that she tried to obtain the least composure. At length she heard the bolt of the cabin door in which she was confined being withdrawn, and the next moment the villain Mark Stanfo d again stood before her. He fixed upon her a malicious look of triumph, and folding his arms across his broad chest, stood contemplating her for several minutes in silence. She turned from him with feelings of the most unbounded terror and disgust, and awaited what he had to say in the greatest apprehension and suspense.

"So my fair Kate, fair but scornful empress of my soul," he said at length in his usual disagreeable tones, and again attempting to take her hand, which she however, succeeded in withdrawing, and retreated to the father end of the cabin, "so we meet again, and I am once more enchanted by the contemplation of these superlative charms which have captivated my very soul, and of which in future I must be the supreme lord and master. Nay, frown not so scornfully upon me, for it is useless, and can have no other effect upon me than to urge me on in my former design against you. By all my hopes you look more beautiful than ever even in the midst of your scorn, and I would not resign my hopes of you, even if by so doing I could become the inheritor of a kingdom."

"Heartless man," ejaculated the damsel, in tones of the bitterest reproach, "forbear, nor dare any longer thus to insult and disgust my ears by your brutal observations. Have you no sense of manly feeling or decency? Have you entirely closed your heart to pity or forbearance?"

"You have heard my will," returned the villain, "and of this you may rest assured that I will not fail to keep my word. The time is fast approaching when my triumph will be complete, and Kate Markham will become the pirate's mistress."

"Oh, monstrous!" said our heroine, with a shudder of horror, "but I will still defy you and put my trust in Providence, who will not desert me in this the terrible hour of my need."

"Ha, ha, ha," laughed the pirate scornfully; "you do well to entertain such sanguine hopes my beauteous Kate, but it is a pity they are doomed to be disappointed. What chance have you of escaping from the fate to which I have destined you? Are we not both upon the boundless ocean, in my gallant vessel, and surrounded by my daring and trusty crew? Of what use is it then, your offering any resistance to my will? Pshaw, girl—the very idea is preposterous."

"I will nevertheless not give way to despair," said Kate with increased firmness, "desperate and hopeless though my situation seems to be. There is an all-merciful Power above, who will protect me and render all your guilty plans abortive."

"That Power you invoke, I need not tell you, I scorn," remarked Stanford; "I set it at defiance, and will persist in my determination let the consequences be whatever they may. But are you prepared for the meeting I promised you? Are you not most anxious again to behold your lover, whom I have apprised of the intended interview?"

"Mark Stanford," said the damsel with a look of terror and supplication, "surely you cannot speak the truth?—You only make the assertion in order to torture my feelings; Providence can never have permitted he whom I so fondly love to fall into your power, and to be placed at your mercy. I cannot, will not believe it!"

"What ridiculous nonsense is this," said the pirate, "am I not about to satisfy you of the truth of what I say, and of what use is it for you any longer to entertain a doubt?"

"My God," exclaimed Kate, "then is my misery indeed complete! But, oh, Stanford, do not, I beseech you, let me appeal to you in vain, or great as your triumph may appear at present to be, you will have bitter cause to repent it, when it will be too late.—Spare that unfortunate man who never gave you cause for offence, unless it was in loving me too well, and receiving a return of my affections."

"Ah!" returned Stanford; "there it is, girl; it is for that I view him with a deadly hatred and have determined to have ample vengeance."

"On my knees I implore you to forbear," said Kate, sinking at his feet with clasped hands and piteous looks.

"What would you have me do?" demanded the pirate with a look of scorn.

"To spare my lover," replied Kate, "and by showing him mercy, prove that you are not entirely destitute of every feeling of humanity."

"You plead in vain," returned the ruffian;—"he insulted me, taunted me, struck me a vile blow, and now that fate has placed him in my power, it shall be my delight to torture him."

"Oh, you cannot, will not be so monstrous!" said our heroine.

"What reason have you to doubt my word?" said the pirate, sarcastically; "Mark Stanford is not the man to make promises which he does not mean to fulfil. Did I not tell him that the time should come when he would have reason to dread me, much as he then pretended to despise me? And that time has now come, and he shall find that I will fulfil my threats to the very letter."

"God help him, then!" ejaculated Kate; "for unless He interferes, he is lost. Oh, by what cruel fate was he ever placed at the mercy of such a miscreant as this?"

"You would do well to abstain from such epithets as that which you have just made use of Kate Markham," said Stanford, "which can answer no other purpose, which can serve no other, purpose than to tend to exasperate me. But I waste words: I go to bring your lover to you.'

And without saying another word he abruptly quitted the cabin, leaving our heroine in a state of mind which the reader will find no difficulty in imagining. She sank on her knees, and clasping her hands and raising her eyes towards Heaven, for a few moments the violence of her grief completely choked her utterance.

"All Merciful Father," she said at length, "I humbly implore Thee to look down with pity upon me and my unfortunate lover, and to frustrate the diabolical designs of the villain who holds us in his power. But surely Thou wilt never permit him to triumph—my heart shudders with terror at the thought. Alas, should this brutal man put his savage threats into execution—and can I any longer doubt, after what he has said, that he will keep his word?—what will become of us both? Beloved Jack, little did I imagine that we should ever meet under such dreadful circumstance. How shall I find strength sufficient to sustain the trying interview? But let me not give way entirely to despair. No! Providence will yet interpose in our behalf, and will rescue us from the hands of this hardened miscreant."

She was interrupted by hearing the sound of footsteps approaching. Her heart palpitated violently against her side as she arose hastily from her knees and fixed her eyes upon the cabin door, which was immediately afterwards opened and the next instant the unfortunate lovers were clasped frantically in each other's arms, Stanford standing by, and gazing upon them with an expression of the most diabolical exultation.

"Kate, my beloved, unfortunate Kate," cried our hero in a voice of the deepest emotion, and pressing her beauteous form still closer to his bosom—"and do we again meet under such fearful circumstances? By Heaven, this trial is more, much more than I can find fortitude to support. I shall go mad!"

"My poor Jack," sobbed the maiden, "never did I imagine that such unmerited misfortunes as these would befal us. But I care not so much for myself as the terrible fate with which you are threatened."

"And which you may rest assured I will fulfil to the very letter," remarked the pirate with a look of triumph and fierce determination. "Do you any longer doubt the power I hold in my hands?"

"Mark Stanford," said our hero, "what are your intentions?"

"Have I not already told you?" replied Stanford: "you cannot surely require any further explanation."

"For myself I care not," said the sailor, "for I trust that Providence will give me fortitude to endure any indignities and outrages you may think proper to inflict upon me; but I condescend to implore your mercy for this innocent maiden, whom I love far dearer than my own existence."

"I know it," returned the pirate, "and it is that which urges me on in my designs. Think you that now I have you both in my power that I will be moved to abandon my designs? Mercy? what mercy can you expect from Hugh Granfield the pirate chief, who hates with a malice such as fiends alone can feel? Oh, I will wring your heart, and glory in your anguish. This beauteous girl is mine, and you shall be the daily witness of her degradation."

"Monster!" exclaimed our hero.

"Beware!" returned Stanford, "or I will inflict upon you such a punishment as you little dream of."

"You dare not, villain."

"I dare not!" repeated the pirate, with a look of scorn and laughing triumphantly; "fool, what is there that Hugh Granfield, the reckless rover of the seas, dare not do? Trust me, I will soon find a way to subdue that proud spirit."

"Mark Stanford," ejaculated Kate; "are you a man that you can talk thus? Have you no fear of the consequences that may follow your brutal conduct?"

"Fear? Ha—ha—ha!" he laughed, "what have I to fear? It is you that should fear my wrath, for terrible is the vengeance that Hugh Granfield never fails to wreak upon the heads of those who venture to offend him, or to set his power at defiance."

"Hold, Kate," said her lover, "do not degrade yourself by appealing to such a heartless miscreant as this. Courage, my poor girl; there is a just God above, on whom we can safely rely, and who will not suffer our persecutor to triumph altogether in his diabolical designs."

"I am glad to find that you entertain such sanguine hopes, my worthy young friend," observed Stanford, ironically, "for your disappointment will afford me the greater satisfaction."

"Alas—alas!" sighed our heroine, burying her face in her lover's bosom, "what will become of us? Oh, what have we ever done that we should be subjected to such misery as this?"

"Calm your feelings, my beloved Kate," said Jack; "and fear not but that we shall yet be rescued from the power of this cowardly miscreant, and learn to smile at the misfortunes of the past. Believe me I do not despair, and that I shall find fortitude sufficient to bear any outrages which he may dare to inflict upon me."

"Indeed!" sneered the pirate; "and depend upon it I will not fail to put your boasted courage to the test."

"Alas! alas!" sighed Kate, "that we should ever meet thus, dear Jack. But are there no means of escaping?—Shall we never again see our native land?"

"It strikes me rather forcibly that you will not," answered Stanford; "as for escaping, bah! it would be worse than madness to entertain such a thought."

"Will nothing induce you to take pity on us?" said the wretched damsel.

"Pity and Hugh Granfield are perfect strangers to each other," replied the pirate; "you should be fully convinced of that ere this. But enough of this; I have kept my word—I have introduced you to each other, and your interview must now terminate."

"Oh, no!" cried Kate, clinging still closer to her lover; "but a little longer. Oh, Jack, dear Jack, what will become of us at the mercy of such a man as this?"

"Courage, Kate, or you will render his triumph the more complete," said our hero.

"Away with you," commanded the ruffian, "and in solitude reflect upon the happy prospect before you."

"Villain!" cried our hero, passionately, "I will still set your boasted power at defiance. You shall not separate us thus!"

"How!" exclaimed Mark Stanford, fiercely; "do you dare to turn mutinous already, dog?"

"Nay," returned Jack, boldly, "I am not to be daunted by your fierce looks, nor intimidated by your threats."

"Fool!" cried Stanford; "know you the danger into which you are plunging yourself? But your courage shall shortly be put to the test, I promise you; and it strikes me that you will soon be glad to alter your tone."

"Oh, spare him, I implore you," said Kate. "Is it not enough that you hold him in your power, and that you also have me at your mercy? Why should you seek to torture him thus?"

"Because it delights me to do so," replied Stanford, with a malicious grin; "oh, I have such tortures in store for him as he can little imagine."

"Heartless scoundrel!" exclaimed our hero.

"No more!" cried Stanford, seizing Kate by the arm, and endeavouring to force her from him; "the meeting is at end. I have indulged you long enough."

"Oh, villain!" said Jack, "would that you would furnish me with the means, and I would quickly punish you for your brutality. But you dare not, coward as you are, you dare not I say."

"Ha! ha! ha!" laughed the pirate, "these are bold words, methinks, for one in your situation. However, I answer for it that I shall soon find the way to cool your courage, much as you boast at present."

"Oh, forbear!" ejaculated Kate; "you surely will not carry your vengeance to such deadly, such dreadful lengths?"

"Appeal not to him, my poor lass," said her lover, "for his savage heart is insensible to pity. Heaven bless you and watch over you, my dear girl; my prayers shall be constantly offered up to the Almighty for your safety; and I will still hope that the time will come when we shall be restored to happiness."

"Alas!" sobbed Kate, "I cannot, dare not entertain such a thought after what has happened, and the dangers with which we are at present surrounded. Oh, I can never find fortitude to endure this. God help us both! for without His merciful interposition, I feel too well convinced that we are both lost."

"Bah!" exclaimed the pirate, impatiently, "what sickening cant is this? But your interview is at an end, I again tell you. Follow me, Master Junk, and leave the girl to her own reflections, which doubtless will be of the most pleasant description."

Kate still clung frantically to her lover; but the pirate, losing all patience, seized her, rudely endeavouring to force her from her lover's embrace. Swelling with rage and indignation, our hero could no longer contain himself, but aimed a violent blow at the head of Stanford with his clenched fist, which, however, took but little effect, and Kate, screaming with terror, darted in between them.

"Ah!" cried the pirate, fiercely, "dare you thus set me at defiance?—Oh, but you shall dearly repent this. What ho! there!"

In a minute Pierce and two or three other pirates rushed into the cabin, and awaited the stern orders of their captain.

"The dog has dared to strike me!" said Mark. "Seize him! place him in irons immediately, and then await my further orders."

The villains instantly obeyed, and Jack struggled violently, but to no purpose; while the distracted Kate threw herself on her knees at the feet of Stanford, as she exclaimed—

"Oh, mercy!—mercy!—It was done in a moment of thoughtlessness and impetuosity; he——"

"Away with him!" sternly interrupted the villain, "and do as I have commanded you."

"My poor Kate!" said our hero, as they forced him away, "may Heaven protect you!—Fear not for me; I defy the deadly malice of my cowardly enemy. As for you, you lubberly swabs, if I only had my liberty for a few minutes, I would give you all as sound a drubbing as ever you had in your lives. Kate, my beloved, my faithful Kate, farewell. We shall meet again ere long, and Providence will not desert us."

"Jack! Jack!" cried Kate, in distracted accents, and endeavouring to rush after him, but the pirate prevented her; and overpowered by the violence of her feelings, she sank fainting in the arms of Stanford. Jack was retaken to the cabin in which he had been before confined; and placed in heavy irons, was left to the misery of his own thoughts.

"This is unbearable!" he exclaimed; "and must I and the innocent and helpless Kate be thus subjected to the cruelty of this fiend in human form? Will not Providence interpose to save us from the revolting fate with which we are threatened? I shall go mad! And yet it was rash and imprudent in me to suffer my indignation to get the better of my reason. There is no knowing to what lengths the vengeance of Stanford may urge him to go."

He beat his breast in despair, as these thoughts flashed across his brain, and in vain he tried to tranquillise his feelings or to gain the least consolation. The fetters with which his limbs were loaded were so heavy, that he could scarcely rise from his seat, and they served to add to the misery which distracted his mind. In this manner he remained for about an hour, when the door of the cabin was thrown open, and Mark Stanford entered. For a few moments he stood and gazed at him with an expression of fiendish triumph. and our hero returned his looks with one of the utmost scorn.

"So, my gallant rival," said the pirate, in accents of irony, "you are placed in the bilboes at last! Those darbies become you amazingly; I have no doubt that they will tend to cure you of some of your mad tricks."

"Cowardly villian!" returned our hero; "I scorn and despise you. It is true, I am in your power, and that I have no means to help myself; but I do not despair that the time will shortly come when both myself and the innocent, much-wronged Kate will be rescued, and the retribution of offended justice will descend upon your head."

"Idiot!" exclaimed Stanford, "what prospect is there of your hopes being realized?— But I came to congratulate you on your present happy situation! Think you that a round dozen or so would not be a proper punishment for the blow you struck me?"

"You would not dare to degrade me thus!" replied the young seaman, his eyes flashing with resentment.

"Psha!—of what use is it your talking thus largely?" said the pirate, with a sneer. "I have but to utter the word, and you would find yourself immediately lashed to the gratings, and receiving the punishment I have hinted at. However, to show that I can be merciful, though it is more for the sake of Kate Markham than your own, I will forgive you this time."

"Mark Stanford," said Jack, "I again tell you that for myself I care but little; but I implore you to act with mercy and forbearance towards the innocent Kate, if you are not entirely lost to every feeling of humanity."

"Humph!" returned Stanford; "and may I ask what right you have to expect that I should pay any respect to your supplications? However, I will not deceive you with false hopes on that subject. You may depend upon it, that all I have promised I will perform. In a few days Kate Markham must yield to my desires, and I need not tell you that there is not theassurastchace of her escaping, or the slightest use in her offering any resistance. Perhaps thient„s alnce may serve to remove any doubts you may have suffered to take possession of your mind."

"Hardened miscreant!" exclaimed our hero, "think not to daunt me by any threats you may hold out to me. I should, indeed, be a disgrace to the British Navy, lor' love it, and every praise to it, if I could be intimidated by such a lubber as yon. However it is only like throwing sprats to sharks to waste words with you."

"Bravely spoken, my young sea-lion," retorted Stanford, and laughing sarcastically, "but it rather strikes me you will change your tone before long. You feel the greatest sympathy, or profess to do, with your beloved Kate, as you term her; might you not then be a little more temperate in your language towards the man who holds her in his power?"

"You will not dare to attempt to wrong her, Mark Stanford, or Hugh Granfield, or whatever else your name may be, even villain as you are," said our hero; "no damme. I will give even you the credit of possessing too much manly feeling about you than to sacrifice to your guilty passions, one so young and innocent. Fetter me, scourge me, torture me, in whatever way you like, but at least spare her."

JACK JUNK BROUGHT BEFORE THE PIRATE.

"Oh, fear not," replied Stanford, "I am too gallant not to treat my future mistress with becoming gallantry,"

"Your future mistress!" repeated Jack, his manly breast swelling with indignation; "oh, no, that can never be; the Lord High Admiral aloft will never permit such a rascally swab as you to triumph in your diabolical and nefarious designs."

"Indeed," sneered Mark Stanford, "but you will find that in spite of the confidence you assume to place in that power you invoke, that I will fulfil every promise I have made to you. There is not one single torture that my mind can suggest—that the feelings of the greatest monster (as you have been pleased to call me) could conceive, that I will not inflict upon you; and when I see you writhing in the midst of your agony it will afford me the greatest satisfaction. I, as Farmer Stanford, the humble, unpretending Farmer Stanford—ha—ha—ha! I told you that the day would come when even the proud spirits of both you and Kate should be tamed; and have I not been faithful to the very letter in my promise? I have you here, dog; Providence does not appear to have done much for you in that respect—I have her that you so fondly love in my power, and therefore what a bitter mockery it is upon reason to talk of defiance. Rather learn humility, and beg to me for the amelioration of that which you cannot otherwise avoid."

"*Beg to you?*" said the young seaman, indignantly; "why—why I would sooner become nurse to a powder monkey; sooner—damme, I say again, and I think that resembles swearing, than I, Jack Junk, the tar for all weathers, would condescend to beg to such a lubberly, lop-sided ill-trimmed, badly-taut, unbuilt, slop-made hulk like you? Take these manacles off my wrist, let us stand man to man, or rather man to monkey, and see if I do not render you a good account of myself."

While our irritated hero was thus delivering himself, Mark Stanford stood by with his arms folded across his ample chest, and received all he had to say with the utmost coolness imaginable, at the same time a sardonic grin distorted his otherwise repulsive features; and when he had concluded, he said:—

"Well, shipmate, you certainly give it me fore and aft, with a vengeance; however, there is not much seamanship in your bearings under the circumstances. But, notwithstanding, I scorn to take advantage of your bad temper, and leave you to enjoy the pleasant reflections and feelings that must result from it, merely with this gentle intimation that more circumspect language might probably save you from an early infliction of the lash. Do you mark that, Jack Junk, *the Tar for all weathers*, eh?"

Rage for a few moments stifled the utterance of our hero, but the look he fixed upon the villain Mark Stanford, expressed much more than words could possibly have done, and at length he replied:—

"Miscreant, devil! Damme, I don't know what epithet to apply to you that is black enough! do you think to daunt me by the threats you hold out to me? No, I will in spite of all still set you at defiance. You dare not, pirate though you are, thus degrade one of His Majesty's seamen."

"I dare not, fool!" returned Stanford; "beware what you say. Provoke me not too far, or you may be taught to your cost, how far the daring of the pirate chief may lead him. Idiot have I not you entirely at my mercy? Could I not at this moment consign you to death, and why then thus endeavour to exasperate me?"

"Alas, Jack," said our hero, pressing his hand in an agitated manner upon his forehead, "you are indeed cast upon a lee shore, and all that you can do is to hoist signals of distress. But avast heaving; I will not slip from the sheet anchor of Hope yet. Master Stanford, Hugh Granfield, or what the d—l your name may be, I will no longer condescend to sue to you, for I find you are insensible, totally insensible to every manly feeling; but I caution you to beware how you act, for great as your triumph may for the present seem to be, depend upon it, as true as my name is Jack Junk, you will be brought to a severe account for your conduct."

"I am, I suppose I need scarcely tell you, fully prepared to take all the responsibility of my conduct on my own shoulders," replied the pirate; "satisfied as I am that I may safely set the power on which you so mainly seem to rely at defiance. But I will waste no more words upon you. Poor d—l! I think I have got you pretty safe at last, and can, therefore, afford to put up with your empty and useless blusterings. I go now to hold a few minutes converse with your lovely devoted, the fair Kate Markham, and to prepare her for that ceremony which in a few days shall take place, which will make her mine, ay, and my gallant Jack Junk, my bold rival at the May-day revels, it shall take place in your presence. No doubt it will be a day of great enjoyment to you, and you will then be fully convinced that Mark Stanford, alias Hugh Granfield, is a man of his word."

"I will not condescend, I repeat," said our hero, "for you are a man destitute of every spark of honour or humanity; but I will put my trust in that Supreme Power whom you affect to despise, and I have but very little doubt as to what the result will be."

"Well, do as you think proper," said the pirate, with a look of malice mingled with satisfaction; "but mark my words, and rest yourself satisfied that I make no idle assertion, you will yet find that all those sanguine hopes which you so freely express, will be doomed to be disappointed. I go once more to visit the lovely Kate Markham, and to again prepare her for the fate to which I have destined her."

"Villain!" exclaimed the indignant young sailor, "do you dare to call yourself a man, and yet make it your boast and glory to triumph over female innocence and to exult in its misery? Damme, if you are not an infamous scandal upon the sex; but the time will come, of that I feel fully convinced, when you will be justly punished for all your atrocious acts, and those whom you have so deeply injured will receive full atonement for the misery you have heaped upon their heads. But it is only a waste of words to talk to such an arrant rascal as you. Leave me."

Mark Stanford laughed scornfully, and pointing significantly and triumphantly to the fetters with which he had loaded his limbs, abruptly quitted the cabin.

Notwithstanding the fortitude with which our hero had endeavoured to support this interview, and the indifference and defiance with which he had pretended to view the threats of Stanford, when he was gone he gave himself up to all those poignant feelings of anguish and despair to which the situation in which himself and his beloved Kate naturally gave rise, and for a considerable time he was totally unable to bring his mind to anything like a degree of composure. That the pirate captain would not fail to put his diabolical threats into execution, and unless by some miraculous accident the fate of Kate would undoubtedly be sealed for ever. From such a prospect Jack could not help shrinking with feelings of the most indescribable disgust and horror, but it was in vain that he sought to encourage the hope that something would yet occur to rescue them both from the fate with which they were both threatened, and that they would be once more restored to happiness.

It required all the energy he could muster to endure these painful thoughts with anything like a degree of patience.

"Oh, that one so young, so lovely, and so innocent, should be subjected to so painful a trial," he observed; "what has she ever done to merit such sufferings? For myself I care not; but kind Heaven, in Thine infinite mercy do not suffer her to fall a victim to a fate so terrible. Sooner, methinks, could I witness her death than her degradation."

Thus he continued to soliloquise for some time, and no one again offered to interrupt him; but at length, tired of thinking, and worn out by the power of his feelings, he sank into a state bordering upon apathy; and his mind became lost and bewildered.

In the meantime the sufferings of poor Kate were of that torturing nature that it would be almost impossible to do adequate justice to them in description. On being restored to her senses, she found herself under the care of Margaret. and she had but an indistinct recollection of what had taken place; but pressing her fair and delicate hands for an instant on her temples, the whole truth flashed in a moment upon her memory, and turning upon the woman a look of the utmost agony and dismay, she ejaculated:

"Ah, where is he?—What has become of him, whose peace and welfare are far more precious to me than my very existence? The miscreant Stanford threatened him with his deadly vengeance, and dragged forcibly from my sight; but he will not, dare not proceed to such inhuman lengths. Oh, no; I will not believe it."

"What he is capable of doing, Kate Markham," replied Margaret, "methinks you should by this time be fully satisfied of. It is not a little that will intimidate him from the execution of any purpose upon which he may have fixed his mind; and the conduct of your lover was by no means calculated to change his determination. He struck him a blow, and the only thing that surprises me is that the captain did not consign him to instant death."

"Oh, horrible!" groaned our heroine, in an agony of grief; "and are there no means of escaping from this cruelty and oppression? Must we continue to be subjected to such unmerited troubles!"

"To think of escaping," returned the woman, in tones of the utmost coolness and indifference, "would be little short of madness. Do you think that Hugh Granfield, the rover of the seas, will so easily sacrifice the hopes on which he has fixed his mind, and which he has run so many risks to gratify? Oh, no; he would be worthy of the utmost derision only if he did."

"Oh, what cruel observations are these from one who wears the form of woman," said the unfortunate Kate; tears of anguish starting to her eyes.

"Nay," said Margaret, in subdued and much milder accents, "I have no wish to add to the anguish of your mind by anything that I may accidentally say; though I am ready to confess that the rude scenes to which I have for so many years been exposed have not by any means served to soften my nature. However, you may as well calm your feelings and try to meet the captain with less coolness and disdain, if you have the interest and safety of Jack Junk at heart."

"Oh, how can I meet so hardened and brutal a ruffian as Mark Stanford, with any other feelings than those of the most unconquerable disgust and horror?" demanded the damsel.

"Then you must take the consequences," returned Margaret, "that's all I can say about it You may depend upon this, however, that Mark Stanford, as you call the captain, is the wrong man to be trifled with or insulted,"

"Alas! alas!" sighed Kate, and she wrung her hands in despair. "Oh, God! look down I implore thee, with pity upon us both. But tell me, Margaret, I beg of you; what has become of my unfortunate and much injured lover?"

"He has been removed to the cabin in which he was before confined; and the captain, I believe, is at this present moment with him," answered Margaret.

"Oh, Heaven!" gasped forth our heroine; "to what suffering's and degradations may he not be subjected to gratify the deadly hatred and revenge of our cruel persecutor."

"That principally depends on yourself," said Margaret; "and if you persist in remaining obstinate, why, you must e'en take the consequences that are almost sure to follow. If you really love this Jack Junk with the warmth and sincerity you profess to do, you will not hesitate for a moment what course to pursue."

"What!" cried our heroine, with a look of resentment and offended modesty, " and would you then have me tamely submit to the monstrous wishes of the pirate chief? Can you un-blushingly hint at such a thing to one of your own sex? By Heaven! sooner would I meet with the most horrible death that could be inflicted on me, than become a being so lost and degraded."

"Well," remarked Margaret, "you know best of course it is not my province to argue the subject with you. I only tell you that Mark Standford is determined, and that if you do not yield your consent, force will shortly make you his and may be the means of inflicting addi-tional suffering on your lover. It is no use trying to trifle with the pirate captain, or to move him to pity; he is a stranger to any such feelings, and you might as well talk to the idle winds."

"Alas!" sighed Kate, "too well am I convinced of the truth of what you assert, and I can-not but look at the dreary prospect before me with feelings of dread; but still I will remain firm, and if I fall it shall not be without a desperate effort, nor will I long survive my disgrace."

"Nay, Miss Markham," returned Margaret, "allow me to say that you talk wildly and to no purpose."

"And think you," demanded our heroine proudly, and crimson blushes suffusing her cheeks as she spoke, "that I would ever live to become the degraded mistress of such a monster as Mark Stanford? Oh, no, no, no, my soul shrinks from the bare contemplation of such a fate with feelings of the most indescribable horror."

"Nevertheless, such your fate will unquestionably be, unless something very little short of a miracle should occur to rescue you," replied Margaret.

"Oh, no!" sighed the distracted Kate; "it must not, cannot be! I will not sink alto-gether with despair, but endeavour to meet the trials that probably are in store for me with firmness and determination."

"Well, Kate Markham," observed her attendant, "I see plainly enough that it is useless to try to persuade you; so I will leave you to the indulgence of your own thoughts, and with a hope that you may not find yourself most disagreeably disappointed in the wild expectations you seem to have formed. No doubt you will shortly behold Stanford again, and I therefore leave you to make what kind of impression upon him you can."

Without saying another word, Margaret left her, and for a few minutes after she was gone, poor Kate covered her blushing face with her hands, and gave herself up to the most terrible and racking thoughts.

"All hope is at an end," she sobbed forth;—"I am lost! lost! entirely lost; and nothing whatever can save me or him to whom my very soul is devoted, from the fate with which we are at present threatened by this fiend in human shape!—Alas! alas!—why was I ever born since it seems that I am destined to such misery and likewise to bring trouble upon the heads of all those who become in any way connected with me. Dear Jack! how terrible I feel con-vinced, are the tortures you are now enduring, more on my account than on your own. What cursed fate placed you in the power of our bitter and implacable enemy? He will delight to torture you; he has threatened to do so; and after what has taken place alread, I cannot for a moment suppose that he will fail to keep his word. You cannot help yourself, and pity is unknown the wretches on board this vessel; therefore what hope is there for you? My brain is distracted; and it seems as if Providence had entirely deserted me and abandoned me to my fate."

She was interrupted in the midst of these meditations, by hearing some one at the door of the cabin, and guessing who it was, she made a hasty effort to recover herself, but could not help shuddering with a feeling of dread. She had not, however, much time given to her for reflec-tion, for the door was thrown open, and the villain Stanford again presented himself before her. His features wore their usual disagreeable expression, and there was a look of recklessness, and determination in the glances which flashed from his large and penetrating eyes, as he fixed them earnestly upon her, which made her tremble with apprehension.

"So, my fair Kate," he said, "you see I have soon returned to you, for really it is quite annoying to be deprived of your sweet society for even the shortest interval. I am glad to see that you have recovered from your late agitation, and that——"

"Cease, cruel man!" interrupted our heroine, her fair bosom swelling with shame ;—"cease your fulsome and insulting observations, and leave me to myself."

"Not yet, my lovely Kate," said the ruffian ; "indeed I cannot. You must again listen to the fervent declaration of that love with which you have inspired me, and which gains strength every moment that I gaze upon you. But why will you still look upon me with such scorn, when it is in your power to make me your complete slave ?—Oh! there is not a pleasure which this world contains that shall not be at your command ; who shall possess more power than the pirate chief's mistress, the beauteous Kate Markham ?"

"Monster !" exclaimed the disgusted damsel, "are you completely insensible to every feeling of shame or common decency? But why do I ask that question? Why do I appeal to one who disgraces the form of man ?"

"Softly, softly, my scornful fair one," returned the pirate, with a sardonic grin ; "better word would best become those lips, and moreover they would be more likely to be productive of a favourable effect upon my mind. You seem to forget that your lover is also in my power and at my mercy."

"Oh, no," replied Kate, with a look of the greatest agony ; "alas ! I know it too well. But oh, tell me, I earnestly supplicate you ; what fresh miseries and indignities have you inflicted upon him ? What are your intentions towards him ?"

"At present," said Stanford, "I have merely placed him in irons for the assault he dared to inflict upon me, and for which many a better man than he has lost his life ; as to your second question, I have to inform you that it depends entirely upon your own conduct."

Kate Markham clasped her hands together in an agony of despair, and returned no answer.

"Come, come, girl," continued Stanford, "what is the use of offering this foolish opposition to my will? Had you not better yield to a fate that is inevitable, and——"

"Never ! never!" interrupted our heroine, and her fine eyes flashed with an almost indescribable expression ; "you may stretch me a corpse at your feet, but never shall you triumph in the diabolical designs your have in contemplation."

"Indeed ?" sneered the pirate ; "but I would advise you not to be too confident, lest the disappointment should prove more powerful than you can find fortitude to bear. I have repeatedly told you that I never fail to keep my word, and you shall shortly be convinced of it if you longer entertain any doubt. Prepare yourself, for before the week has elapsed, you shall become mine. I will no longer defer the gratification of my wishes."

"Oh, horror !" ejaculated our heroine, trembling in every limb ; "no! no! no!—You will think better of this, hardened though you are, you will not proceed to such monstrous extremities."

"You entertain a very erroneous opinion of my character if you imagine that I will not," said Stanford.

"Alas, then," sighed Kate, "it is in vain for me to appeal to you, and I will no longer degrade myself by doing so ; but rely upon the mercy and goodness of that Supreme who never forsakes those who have not offended his laws and who put their trust in him."

"Well," returned Mark Stanford, cooly, "do as you think proper ; you have heard my determination, and you may therefore prepare yourself, for you cannot escape from it. In the meantime, you perhaps may reflect more maturely upon the effect which your conduct may have upon me as far as regards your lover. Remember, that I will be entirely guided by the manner in which you behave towards me, and that the misery, nay the very life of Jack Junk is in your hands."

Kate raised her eyes towards Heaven with the utmost emotion, and uttered not a word. The villain Stanford continued to watch her with the most bold, insulting looks ; and the anguish of mind, the deep despair, and shame she was too plainly suffering, afforded the hardened miscreant the means of the most unnatural and ruffianly satisfaction.

"Three days, no more," he resumed at last, "I will allow you for consideration ; and at the expiration of that time, I swear by all my hopes, let the consequences be whatever they may, as true as I am Hugh Granfield, the rover and terror of the seas, and captain of the invulnerable Black Raven, I will put my designs into execution. Reflect then upon all that I have said, and it strikes me you will yet be disposed to alter your mind."

"I have reflected maturely already," replied our heroine, with renewed courage and energy, "and my resolution is formed—nothing whatever can shake it. Death, death in preference to dishonour."

"Bold words, my fair Kate," said the pirate, with a sneer ; "however, I heed them not ; my triumph is certain, and your resistance is the very height of folly and uselessness. Were you on land, and your admirer at liberty, instead of being situated as you both are, there might indeed be some small chance for you, but as it is, your case is utterly hopeless, however much you may flatter yourself to the contrary. We are now many hundreds of miles away from your native land : we are bound to a distant and wild region of the globe where my power is all but supreme, and by all the infernal host I swear that I will exercise that power to its utmost limits, that nothing shall stay me in my firm resolves."

"Then," ejaculated our heroine, solemnly, and raising her hands in an imposing manner towards Heaven, "may the curses of Almighty God descend upon your head, and crush you, monster, in your career of crime."

"Ha! ha! ha!" laughed Stanford, scornfully, "you do but waste your breath, fair damsel in giving utterance to these invocations. I set the power you mention at defiance; I have never obeyed His laws; let drivelling fools do that; I should despise myself were I to follow their example. Thus you see how useless it is for you to address me after that fashion. Hugh Granfield, the pirate, is as reckless as the rude billows over which his gallant vessel rides, and he has hitherto proved that his power is not to be subdued."

"But it will be ultimately, depend upon it," returned Kate; "confident though you now are."

"Pshaw!" returned the pirate impatiently, "think you girl, to intimidate me by any such predictions? What a bitter mockery is this. 'Tis not by such means you will deter me from the full accomplishment of my purpose. No, I swear by all the powers of darkness that at the time I have mentioned, you shall become mine."

"Look down with pity and compassion upon me, oh, All-Merciful God, I beseech Thee," cried our heroine, fervently, "for to thy care I commit myself. Spirit of my father, I again invoke thee, and——"

"Hold babbling girl!" interrupted the pirate chief fiercely, and trembling with the most violent emotion, at the same time that he clutched the arm of Kate, and stared wildly in her face; "what fiend of h—l has again suggested that idea to your mind?"

"What means this violent agitation at the mention of my parent?" demanded our heroine, with a look of surprise, "and why do you gaze so wildly upon me? Release my arm from your hold, brutal man; you hurt me.

"Am I thus to be reminded of the past?" muttered Stanford to himself, but sufficiently loud enough for Kate to hear what he said; "girl!" he added, turning abruptly towards her, and fixing upon her a savage look; "beware what you say, for you have one to deal with who knows no mercy."

"Alas!" sighed Kate in reply, "too well do I know that, but Heaven will yet protect me; and notwithstanding your guilty threats, I will still be firm in the confidence of innocence and virtue.

"You talk boldly Kate Markham," said Stanford, somewhat regaining his usual composure "but have you no fear for the consequences you may, by your conduct, bring upon the head o him you profess to love so fondly?

"Ah!" sighed the damsel; "poor Jack, 'tis for thee I care more than all; but Mark Stanford, notwithstanding all the threats you have held out against that unoffending man, I cannot, will not bring my mind to believe that you will put them into execution.

"Indeed!" returned the other with an ironical grin, "you give me credit for much more clemency and forbearance than I can boast of possessing. However, we have talked quite enough on that subject, and I should imagine that I have given you sufficient proof that I can and will fulfil my promises to the very letter. Reflect calmly upon that; and I flatter myself that you will be induced to give a more favourable answer to my suit when next we meet.

"Oh, no, no, eagerly replied Kate, shuddering and averting her blushing face; "nothing whatever can alter my mind upon that disgusting subject. It would be monstrous to suppose it could.

"Well, then," returned the pirate, coolly, "you know the fate of yourself and Junk, so that ends the matter; for the present I leave you. Farewell, beauteous Kate Markham, my future mistress."

"Heaven forbid!" ejaculated the innocent damsel, with a look of horror, and clasping her hands vehemently together, "may death rather put an end to my sufferings than that I should be consigned to such a revolting fate."

Mark Stanford returned no answer, but smiling triumphantly upon her he quitted the place. When he had gone, Kate knelt down and solemnly besought the protection of the Supreme Power, and after some time passed in this manner, she resumed her seat, and by dint of great exertion she did succeed in tranquillising her feelings.

"My situation is awful," she ejaculated, "but still I will not give way to despair, for something whispers me that I and he to whom my heart is devoted will yet be rescued from the power of this heartless villain, and that the clouds which at present obscure the horizon of our happiness will be dispersed. Oh, hope, sweet hope, what a gentle soother of our afflictions art thou. And shall I evermore behold those kind friends and relations so dear to me?"

A shuddering sensation came over her, as a vague presentiment of something dreadful having happened to them occurred to her mind; but tears came to her rel {and she soon became more composed.

"Dear uncle; beloved Constance!" she ejaculated, "how terrible must be the anguish you are now enduring at the uncertainty of the fate which has befallen me, though, alas! you must anticipate the worst. And even if you knew my present situation and that of poor Junk, what assistance could you render to rescue us from the dreadful fate with which we are threatened? None whatever, far away as we are from you, and the impossibility of any vessel that might be despatched, overtaking us ere the threats which the miscreant Stanford has held out could be put into execution. That thought is terrible and enough to distract my brain. But I will not give way to it. No, something wil yet occur when we least expect it, to frustrate the cruel designs of our inhuman persecutor, and to restore us, uninjured, to liberty and our friends."

The latter thoughts revived her spirits, and she became more calm than under the circumstances could at all have been expected.

In spite of all his efforts, however, the allusion which our heroine had made to her murdered father, had made the most powerful impression on Mark Stanford's mind.

His guilty conscience smote him bitterly, and caused the most violent emotions in his breast, and for some time after he had quitted her presence, he continued to reflect upon the words she had utterred with mingled feelings of doubt and fear, in spite of the boast he had so repeatedly made of his utter indifference to everything.

"Can she have become acquainted with the fate that her father met with, and that it was by my hand he fell?" he soliloquised; "oh, no, it is not so, or she would ere now have accused me of it and reproached me with it. And even if she knew it, of what consequence would it be? She could not help herself any the more, and she could not view me with greater disgust and horror than she does at present. Psha! why should I torture my brain by any such reflections as these? They are both in my power and I have nothing to dread. At the time I have fixed, the girl shall become mine, though all the internal host stood in the way to obstruct me in the accomplishment of my purpose. Let that thought assure me, and inspire me with confidence."

"At that moment Pierce entered the cabin in which Mark Stanford was seated.

"How now, captain,' he said; "all goes on well I suppose?"

"Yes, yes," hastily replied Stanford; "how should it do otherwise?"

"Very true," remarked Pierce; "we have both the girl and her lover secure enough, and nothing can prevent the completion of your designs."

"Nothing," answered the pirate captain.

"Ah! captain," said Pierce; "Kate Markham is a rare prize, and you ought to think yourself a lucky man that you have got possession of her. But I must say that I should have felt much more satisfied if her fair cousin, the beauteous Constance, had also fallen into my power."

"She might have done so easily enough had you made me acquainted with your wishes," returned Stanford.

"Well, it is too late to think of that matter now," observed Pierce, "but the time may come when I shall have another opportunity of gratifying my wishes."

"No doubt of it."

"But you look rather agitated, captain," said his ruffianly companion, "has anything particular occurred to disturb you?"

"No—no," answered Stanford, hesitating; "and yet——"

"Yet, what?" demanded Pierce.

"I do feel myself somewhat ruffled by some expressions which Kate made use of," answered Stanford.

"And what were they, captain?" asked the other.

Stanford informed him, and Pierce listened to him impatiently, and when he had concluded he said,—

"And is it possible that you can suffer such a trifle as this to disturb you for an instant?"

"I like not such allusions, Pierce."

"Psha! Captain, why, I declare you get quite qualmish of late."

"Should Kate, by any means, have become acquainted with the murder of her father."

"And what if she should have done so; I imagine it can make very little difference in the sentiments she entertains towards you," replied Pierce; "but what chance is there of her having done so, unless you have divulged the secret yourself?"

"You may be certain," returned Stanford, "that I should be too cautious to do that."

"I should think you would," observed Pierce; "however, it matters little in my opinion."

"Her uncle, too, I believe, received his death blow from your hand."

"And it was entirely his own fault that he did so," answered the ruffian; "had he not offered a foolish and useless resistance, he would have escaped. But Kate knows not of his death."

"She does not, and it is fortunate that she does not; for it would probably have such an effect upon her mind that she would never be able to survive the shock. Oh, Pierce, I should have been more satisfied had this not have happened; and also if the life of old Reuben had been spared."

"Why do you suffer that old officious idiot who held out such threats to you to continually haunt your mind?" said Pierce; "did he not convince you that he was in the possession of all your secrets? consequently, common prudence suggested that he should be disposed of to prevent him from doing any mischief."

"True," answered the captain; "but still that might have been effected by securing him on board our vessel."

"And he would then have been a constant source of annoyance to you," said Pierce. "It is much better that he should have been quieted altogether. But I have no patience with this subject. Let us drop it altogether."

"The ghastly countenance of that singular being as it appeared in his last moments is continually present to my imagination, and his words are constantly in my ears," said Stanford "it is in vain I try to banish them from my memory."

"Why what contemptible weakness is this!" said Pierce, impatiently; "come, arouse yourself; it is totally unworthy of you; I can scarcely believe that it is the desperate Rover of the Sea that I am talking to."

"You do me an injustice, Pierce," replied Stanford, with some expression of displeasure, "if you imagine that I have lost any of my natural courage and determination."

"Then why give utterance to such sentiments as those you have just made use of?" demanded Pierce. "But come, we will talk no more upon such a ridiculous subject as this. You have again seen Jack Junk, have you not?"

"I have," replied Stanford; "and taunted him to my heart's content. Oh, it is a glorious opportunity for the gratification of my revenge."

"And how does he seem to fancy himself while in the bilboes?" asked Pierce, with a laugh.

"No better than you can imagine," replied the pirate captain; "at first we talked boldly but when I reminded him that Kate was in my power, and that I had destined her to become, my mistress, at a certain time, his courage became daunted and he condescended to lower his tone and to sue to me for mercy."

"Ha! ha! ha!" laughed the miscreant, Pierce, "no doubt we shall be able to reduce this "gallant tar for all weathers" to his proper level, before long. I suppose you do not mean to spare him?"

"You may depend upon that," replied Stanford; "if he expects any mercy or forbearance from me, he will find himself very much mistaken."

"Well spoken, captain," returned his villanous companion; "I admire you for that determination. You have no reason to entertain much respect towards him."

"Respect!" repeated the pirate; "I loathe him more bitterly than any other being in existence, and it shall be my delight to torture him. Oh, little did he anticipate that it would ever come to this, when he only knew me as simple Farmer Stanford. He had little idea that in Farmer Stanford he beheld the much-dreaded Hugh Granfield, the Rover of the Seas, and the terror of every fair trader. He would not then have dared to insult me, and provoke my wrath in the manner he did. However, it is perhaps as well that he was ignorant as to who I was, or we might have been betrayed and trepanned, and we should have found it difficult to resist the force that would sure to have been opposed to us."

"Very true," coincided Pierce; "everything has turned out for the best, and if you only keep firm to the determination you at present express, your triumph is certain."

"There is nothing to prevent it."

"And the girl?"

"Oh, she remains as inflexible as ever'."

"I expected that."

"True," returned Mark Stanford; "but of what use is her opposition to my will?"

"None whatever," said Pierce; "resistance from any one on board the Black Raven is nothing better than sheer madness, and is sure to bring down our utmost vengeance upon their heads."

THE RUFFIANLY CREW OF THE BLACK RAVEN.

"It is sheer madness to resist us on board our own bonny bark; whatever amount of hardiness and stubborness may be shown us on shore, there we were quiet and tolerably peaceably inclined for our own sakes; but when we are afloat, it is a very different matter, indeed; for it is then that we are in power, and relentlessly rule the deep, blue ocean, which is the home and delight of the rover of the seas. We can toss our grog, sing our jovial songs, ride and sleep, and lead a merry life. Here we want for nothing while the brave lads stick true to their captain, and true to one another."

"A better life princes need not wish to lead," said Pierce; "and if you would cast from you those gloomy forebodings that at times force themselves on your mind, you would be much more comfortable, and lively. It is worse than folly to picture to your mind what will never happen, and fancy you see and hear things that have no existence. What should Hugh Granfield care for the ravings of a dying maniac? If we listened to every malediction uttered by lunatics, we should live in fear to the end of our days. Avoid these things, and who shall dispute your power?"

"Ay, you say right, my faithful Pierce, and so my enemies shall always find, much as they may affect to despise my power. Jack Junk will be convinced of that in a few days, should any doubts remain upon his mind."

"I should think he would," replied Pierce, with a malicious expresssion of countenance.

"There can be no doubt of that," remarked the pirate captain; "I will keep all the promises I have made to him most strictly, to his cost. I have also informed Kate, that in three days from the present, notwithstanding her repugnance, she may make up her mind to become mine; and that no tears, no supplications, will have the power to move me from my purpose."

"A noble resolution, captain," observed the ruffian, Pierce; "a monarch might envy you such a mistress."

"True; and I will not fail to exercise to the fullest extent the authority I have obtained over her. At the expiration of that time, if the wind still continues in our favour, we may expect to arrive at the place of our destination, and there the ceremony can take place with the *eclat* it deserves."

"Yes," said his companion, "it is fitting that the pirate captain should have such a revel as the occasion demands. Is it your determination that Jack Junk should be present at it?"

"Undoubtedly it is," answered Stanford, "or my triumph would be only half complete. Oh! how excruciating will be his agony on that occasion, and what satisfaction it will afford me to witness his sufferings! How I will laugh and exult at his futile ravings; and when his agony and despair are at the greatest pitch, my satisfaction will be the more complete. It will be a glorious day for me, Pierce—a glorious day, indeed!"

As the hardened ruffian gave utterance to this brutal speech, the expression of his repulsive features was scarcely that of a human being; and it was perfectly evident that he was fully determined to carry out his atrocious designs to the very letter.

"You speak exactly the sentiments of my mind, captain," said Pierce; "and I shall exult on the occasion no less than yourself. But it was a most fortunate circumstance which threw Jack Junk accidentally in our way."

"It was," answered Stanford, "and one that I never anticipated."

"But I wonder who it was who was his companion on the island, and who so successfully eluded our chase."

"I cannot form the slightest conjecture, but I suppose it was only some shipwrecked-seaman like himself. Our men said he was a strange, wild-looking individual."

"True," replied Pierce, "and probably his misfortunes had turned his brain. But I dare say we shall be able to elicit some particulars concerning him from Junk in a short time."

"I doubt that," said Stanford, "however, it is not of much consequence, and I do not see why we should feel any interest in the subject. The man could have been of no use to us."

"Certainly not. Poor devil, it was almost too bad to destroy his habitation."

"It was a just punishment for him for presuming to treat us so uncivily by shunning our company. But come, we have other business to attend to, and we have talked sufficiently long upon this subject."

"Ay," replied Pierce, "and yet it is one in which you feel the greatest gratification, I know."

"None more so," said Stanford; and they then departed from the cabin.

Jack Junk continued in the same state of mind, with little intermission, and miserably and drearily the hours passed away. No one came to visit him, and his thoughts, therefore, received no interruption. Torturing indeed were those thoughts, and he could not obatin the least consolation, for which ever way he turned his mind, nothing but the most abject misery and despair met his imagination. The last interview he had had with the villain, Stanford, confirmed his worst fears, and fully convinced him, if anything had been wanting before, of the dreadful situation in which himself and his beloved, but unfortunate Kate were placed in. When he thought of the sufferings, the terrible anguish of mind she must be enduring, he could scarcely contain himself within the bounds of reason, and for a few minutes he gave utterance to the most bitter lamentations, and cursed their hard fate, which neither of them at all merited. Had he only been permitted to be near her, that he might seek to impart consolation to her, and to inspire her with hope, he might have been more content; but, alas! there was no hope of that: it would have been preposterous to encourage such an idea, and he, therefore, gave himself up to the utmost despair.

"Oh, Kate—Kate! companion of my childhood!" he said, "how little, in our youthful days, did we anticipate such a fate as this: how little have we deserved to be left to the mercy of such a miscreant as he who now holds us in his power. But no; I say again, I will not despair. God is all good and merciful, and He will not allow us to become the victims of the cruel enemy who laughs at our sufferings, and affects to dispise and to set at defiance that Power to which I now appeal. I will endeavour to be firm, and thus defeat, by all possible means, the monstrous designs of the reckless wretch who sets all laws, human and divine, at naught. Jack Junk, you have hitherto weathered many a storm, and the Great Commander has permitted you to escape unscathed. In that same Almighty and just Providence I will still put my trust, and doubt not that it will guide both myself and her whose happiness is far more precious to me than my own existance, to a happy port at last. My sweet Kate," he resumed, after a pause, " what a fearful change has come over our prospects since, in the days of our blissful childhood, when care was a stranger to us, and we used to sport it o'er the sunny meads, and gambols up and down the lofty hills which bound the circuit of our native home. But no change in our hearts, my dear girl, no, no: savage man, alone, has done that which has obscured the horizon of our bliss, and rendered us the miserable beings that we at present are. Oh, how bright and radiant were the sunbeams that then showered their influence upon us! how sweet was the perfume of the various flowers! what exhilarating influence had the various seasons upon us! how joyous our laugh—how little we though of care ! No: it was then indeed, the time of our halcyon days. But—but—" continued the honest, warm hearted young seaman, dashing a tear away from his eye, which his manly feelings and sad retrospection of the past had called forth, " damme, Jack, your scuppers are streaming over. This must not be. You are a man, and yet enabled to brave all such lubbers as the rascally one who now holds you in his power. You must not hoist those signals of distress. Be firm—be firm, and you will yet be enabled to put this lubberly pirate on his beam ends. I will be firm, ay, firm as a rock, against which the most furious sea may battle in its utmost wrath !

He paused, for his emotions and the excitement under which he naturally laboured, almost overpowered him ; but at length his feelings become considerably more composed, and remained or some time in a state of meditation. He then in the fervency and sincerity of his heart, offered up a prayer to the Supreme, for the preservation of himself and our heroine, from the dangers with which they were then threatened, and as the night approached, endeavoured to compose his mind to sleep. But this, independent of the many torturing cares that pressed upon his mind, was a most difficult task, from the weight of the fetters with which his limbs were loaded. He could not place himself in any position which was at all likely to furnish him with repose, and again he got up, and as we'l as he could traversed the narrow limits of the cabin in which he was confined, in a state of mind which the reader will have no occasion to be described to them. Again and again he lamented the hard fate which had befallen himself, and she who was so precious to him, and invoked the bitterest curses upon the head of their cowardly and heartless oppressor ; and that afforded him, questionable even as it was, some little relief. After the conversation he had had with Stanford, at their last interview, he imagined all kinds of horrible things, and could entertain no other idea than that his worst fears would be realized. And yet his manly heart, " the heart of a true British Sailor," sought to bear up with becoming fortitude against the perils with which they were both threatened, and to hold the threats which the miscreant, Stanford had so frequently given utterance to, to scorn. But it was all to no purpose; the deplorable truth was far too glaring, and he was compelled at last to yield himself up to the full misery of his despair.

In this way night approached, and a dark and tempestuous looking night it was. Ponderous were the clouds that obscured the horizon, and fearfully did the wind howl across the bosom of the broad ocean at intervals. Not a star was to be seen; all was darkness and threatening horror. The waves dashed furiously against the sides of the vessel, and as our hero gazed from the small window of the cabin in which he was confined, various and torturing were the emotions which agitated his breast. Not that he was daunted; oh, no, what tempest, many as he had been in had ever yet had the power to unnerve Jack Junk?—But he thought of her he loved far dearer than his very soul, and his heart sank within him at the fate which probably awaited her. Dear as she was to him, how could he feel otherwise than distracted at the fate which probably awaited her ? Dear as she was to him, how could he feel otherwise than distracted at the fearful prospect which the present moment opened out to them both?

" Beloved Kate," he ejaculated, in a voice of the most intense emotion, " and must you— shall you indeed perish thus ?—Shall all your young hopes be annihilated—your life of innocence be thus untimely crushed? Forbid it, Heaven! I beseech You place Your fostering shield around her, and though it may be Your will that we shall never come together, I will learn, or endeavour to learn or yield to it without a murmur. Oh, how terrible, how inexpressibly terrible must be the sufferings, the terrors you are at the present moment enduring, and I am not near to afford you the least gleam of consolation. Fate seems to have conspired against us, and to whatever point we may direct our attention, no hope appears of our being extricated from the overwhelming difficulties with which we are at present surrounded."

The storm, which had only threatened so ominously, now with the speed of lightning gained strength, and burst forth in its utmost and most frightful fury. The clouds burst, and discharged torrents of rain—the thunder roared—the lightning blazed, and the wind howled in fearful gusts, raising the billows to a mountainous height, and tossing the vessel about as if she had been no more than a mere straw. Jack Junk never felt his misery greater than at that moment, when he was fettered, confined, and not able to render any assistance in the dreadful battle of the elements which was at that moment raging, and to know, too, at the same time, that poor Kate was left entirely to the bitter anguish of her own thoughts, and had no one at hand to offer to her a word of hope or consola- tion under the dreadful trial.

"By Heaven!" he exclaimed, "I shall go mad!—Jack! Jack! with all your courage this is indeed the severest trial you have ever had. To be thus embellished with the darbies at such a moment as this, and to know that there is one fair and gentle being who needs every consolation, left entirely to the mercy of a set of savages, who will exult in her misery and anguish, and endeavour to make it tenfold, surely that is far too much for one who loves her so sincerely, so ardently as I do, to endure with anything like a degree of patience. Avast, Jack! this lingo will do you no good—cannot assist her you so fondly love, and will only serve to excite you to that state of nervousness that you might dis- grace your seamanship. Oh! but it is hard to be thus placed under hatches, when your duty to your fellow-creatures demands that you should be on active service. Now, may I never crack a biscuit, or taste salt junk again, if I couldn't blubber like a child, out of nothing but pure vexation. God be with you, my poor lass, for your devoted Jack can render you no assistance but his prayers, and them most earnestly and devoutly he offers up to the Supreme giver of all good. But," he added, after a brief pause, "they will not come near me; where is Mark Stanford, or Hugh Granfield, or whatever his name may be? Why does he not come near me now to exult in what I should imagine to be the hour of his greatest triumph? Methinks it would render me some consolation even to be enabled to lend my humble aid towards the saving of this death-ship, since it contains one so young, so lovely, and so innocent. It is because his stubborn nature is unnerved, his stout heart appalled at the horrors which prevail around? Why am I left in this horrible state of suspense? Oh, God!—oh, God! help me, I beseech you!"

He pressed his hands upon his forehead, and groaned aloud in the intensity of his anguish.

Fiercer and fiercer became the storm; the sea swelled to a frightful degree, and all around threatened inevitable destruction to those who were exposed to its fury. The vessel was tossed about entirely at the mercy of the enraged waters on which she rode, and the shouts of the pirate crew, their dreadful oaths and execrations, might be heard even above the voice of the tempest. Our hero listened to all with such feelings as we will leave it to the imagination of the reader to depicture; and as well as the heavy fetters with which his limbs were encumbered would permit him, he paced the place of his confinement in the most excited state that can possibly well be conceived.

Fiercer and fiercer became the tempest; and as its violence increased, so did the oaths and execrations of the pirate crew increase in brutality of expression. The vessel was every now and then engulphed in a tremendous sea, and then the next instant it seemed as though she was about to be forced from that element, and to be hurled to the clouds. All the time the voice of the heavenly lion was perfectly terrific; the flashes of lightning that blazed across the horizon were awful; and the rain descended in a perfect deluge.

But what were the feelings of the hapless and deeply persecuted Kate Markham, during this fearful, this frightful battling of the elements?—With no one near her who could or would sympathise with her sufferings, or endeavour to impart some degree of consolation to her in a moment of such unprecedented horror, we should say that the reader will be enabled to form a pretty ready conception of them. Margaret certainly was in the cabin with her, sent thither to attend immediately upon her, in case, under the alarming circumstances, her services might be required; but the almost cruel indifference with which that female treated every- thing in which the sympathies of a better nature would have been immediately excited, rendered her presence, if possible, under such circumstances, more painful than otherwise; and at length, at the urgent request of our heroine, she retired, and left her to her own re- flections.

When Kate found herself alone, she gave free indulgence to the intense agony of her feelings, and on her knees supplicated the mercy of the Supreme. Not that she dreaded death. No! that, as she was situated, and especially with the fate that threatened her, would, in her opinion, at the moment have been a mercy; but when she reflected upon the deplorable situation of her lover, and the anguish of mind he must be enduring—only to reflect upon her helpless condition, her feelings were almost insupportabe.

From the window of her place of confinement she watched with the most painful anxiety the progress of the storm, and as the vessel heaved and throwed, like a human being in convulsions, sometimes mounting, comparatively speaking, to the sky, and then engulphed, as it were, in the wrathful bosom of the deep, she felt as if the last terrible day of judgment had arrived, and that all hope of mercy was at an end. With clasped hands the unfortunate damsel stood, and silently implored the Divine grace, and though her tears flowed fast they afforded her but little relief. The confused sounds from the ruffianly crew on deck, mingled with the most bitter oaths, added to the horrors of the scene, and increased her despair; and at length, unable any longer to support herself, she sank back upon a seat, and covering her face with her fair and delicate hands, for a few minutes gave herself up to the full horror of her feelings.

"Jack! beloved Jack!" she at last found strength to ejaculate; "and must we indeed perish thus? Shall the angry waves engulph us both, and all our hopes, without our having even the melancholy satisfaction of bidding each other farewell?—Of one parting embrace?— Great God! just as Thou art in all Thine afflictions, surely this one trial is too severe. But no, presumptuous mortal as I am, I will not dare to arraign Thine all-wise decree, but rather implore, in the humblest spirit, Thine infinite mercy, which never yet was refused to any of Thy creatures who put their trust in Thee. Jack! dear Jack! terrible as is the present moment, I feel inspired with a sweet and animating confidence that we shall meet on earth again, and that our troubles, great and almost insupportable as they are, will terminate in happiness."

Inspired with these thoughts, she became more calm, and indeed she needed much all the confidence she could muster under the peculiar and trying circumstances in which she was placed, for never was more frightful tempest at sea witnessed than that which raged at that moment, and might have appalled the stoutest heart even amongst those that were accustomed to such scenes. It was indeed astonishing how the poor girl could maintain her fortitude at all, and no one came near her who was disposed to endeavour to soothe her feelings.

From the shouts, and different observations which reached her ears from the ruffians on deck, it was evident that they considered the vessel to be in great danger; and indeed even the most inexperienced in such fearful matters, might have formed pretty nearly as shrewd a calculation as the ablest seaman on board, as to whether she would be enabled to weather tee storm.

Again did our heroine sink upon her knees, and with clasped hands, and upraised eyes, implored the protection of Heaven.

"Grant, oh, All-Merciful God," she earnestly ejaculated; "not for myself, and he whom I so fondly love alone, but for the sake of the guilty men in whose power we are, that we may not perish thus. Oh, I most humbly beseech Thee to extend thy pity to us, and not to bring us thus suddenly before Thy terrible judgment seat with all our sins upon our head. Uncle, dear Constance, shall I never behold ye more? Alas! the thought is horrible, and almost beyond endurance. But no, I will not give way to despair. God is good, and will not visit His poor, weak, guilty creatures with such a frightful calamity as this. Save my lover, and for myself I care not, but commit myself to Thy will."

Thus saying, she became more calm, much more calm than could have been expected under such awful circumstances, and contemplated the raging tempest with the most extraordinary firmness and self-pessossion. But still it was impossible for her to subdue entirely the poignant anguish of her mind, and it would indeed have been remarkable could she have done so.

Fiercer and fiercer still raged the storm, and all hope seemed to be at an end; but still no one came near our unfortunate heroine, and she was left in a state of the most horrible doubt and suspense. She withdrew herself from the window of the cabin in which she was confined, for the sight of the wild ocean in its wrath was too much for her further contemplation and throwing herself upon a seat, she endeavoured to resign herself to her fate; which now indeed appeared to be inevitable. To attempt to describe the various and conflicting thoughts which rushed in wild tumult upon her brain, would be impossible, and it was only wonderful that she was enabled to support herself with the fortitude she did at all. But in spite of everything, notwithstanding all the horrors which prevailed around, a certain degree of hope animated her, and gave her strength sufficient to support the trial to which it had pleased Providence to subject her.

But we must now return to the deck of the Black Raven, where the scene of excitement and confusion that prevailed may be much more readily conceived than even the most graphic pen could describe it. Mark Stanford traversed the deck in a state of the most furious and delirious rage, and vented the most awful curses on the storm.

"Pierce," he said, "hell and the devil appear to conspire against us. The ship makes no way; lighten her—lighten her."

"And all that can be done in lightening her, captain, has been resorted to," replied his lieutenant; "but shall we resort to any more desperate means? Shall we take the——"

"Shall we take the," repeated the pirate chief, passionately; "d—n it, Pierce, are you all aback? Do you not see that the wind is in our teeth?"

"Yes," replied the other worthy, "I not only see that, but that we have breakers a head, and unless we rid ourselves of some of our metal, we must in a very short time go the bottom."

"Rid myself of my roarers—my sea-lions—the fellows that have done so much execution against those that have dared to oppose us?" replied Stanford; "no, I'm d—d if I do !"

"Then," replied Pierce, coolly, "we shall all be d—d before our time if you will not."

"Pierce," asked Stanford, "are you afraid?"

"Afraid!" repeated the former, scornfully, "did ever you know me to entertain such a feeling? Afraid! d—n it, captain, your upper works must be out of order to entertain such an idea for a moment. Pierce, the pirate afraid! ha! ha! ha! Pardon me, captain, but the idea is so very comical that I cannot help laughing. Pierce afraid, I repeat! why, d—n it, have I not faced the storm and the enemy, in both their most terrible shapes, and did you ever find me flinch? Did you ever see one of my nerves quiver or unstrung?"

"No—no," returned Stanford, hastily, and pacing the deck with his arms folded across his chest, while his brain was distracted with various thoughts.

"Then why challenge me with fear?" demanded Pierce.

"Nay—nay," replied Stanford, recollecting himself in some measure, "we must not quarrel, Pierce. I scarcely knew what I said. Ay! hell and furies! there's a lurch!"

"Lighten her, captain, I say again," remarked Pierce; "however it may grieve you and all of us, we must get rid of some of our roarers, as you very properly call them, or we shall never be able to weather such a storm as this."

"Over with them, then," replied the pirate chief. "A-head ho !"

Several of the pirate crew rushed forward at their captain's bidding, and two or three of the small guns having been loosed from their fittings and tossed overboard, the vessel did ride a little more easy through the dreadful sea she had to encounter with, but still she was in difficulty, and all the skill of Mark Stanford, Pierce, and the other experienced hands on board, was required to keep her from foundering. The mainmast went by the board, the spars were all gone, and that the ship could live appeared impossible.

How frightful was the aspect of the heavens at that moment, as the vessel which had caused so much consternation in all minds, skimmed its way over the broad but awfully agitated bosom of the deep. Every cloud that hung upon the horizon, appeared to carry in its dark breast death to the hapless mariner who might be exposed to its vengeance. Nature seemed to have convulsed herself, to have got out of her regular organs of action, (to make a wide stretch of the imagination) to have run mad, and to endeavour to prove the destruction she could in so short a time effect amongst unthinking mortals in her rabid fury.

All was dark as a funeral pall, save when the lightning sent its vivid flash across the sky; and the roaring of the thunder, and the howling of the wind, was perfectly terrific.

Mark Stanford, or rather Hugh Granfield, and Pierce, were excellent seamen, but even they, who had weathered so many awful tempests, were alarmed and confused at the aspect of the present storm. More guns were thrown overboard, but still it seemed to ease the troubled vessel but very little.

"By all the infernal host!" said Stanford, "fortune has turned against us, and the Black Raven will have to succumb at length to those mutinous waves over which she has for so many years rode triumphantly."

"Be calm, captain," rejoined Pierce; "for although the aspect of all around is certainly as bad as it can be, I feel confident that by exerting our utmost energies, we shall yet be able to weather the storm. Ah! did not that flash of lightning reveal anything to you?"

"No," answered the pirate captain, laconically, although his eyes were at the time fixed upon the same spot as those of his lieutenant, but his mind was abstracted.

"No!" said Pierce.

"No," repeated Stanford; "to what did you allude?"

"I thought," returned Pierce, drily and pointedly, "that you might probably have observed a vessel astern."

"And what of that?" impatiently demanded Stanford.

"No more than this," answered his companion, "that from the slight glimpse of her, I could recognise her to be a man-of-war of dangerous quality, and I thought, perhaps, it might be rather inconvenient for us to come in contact just at this moment."

"By h—l, Pierce, you are right," said Mark Stanford, bethinking himself; "we are not much in a condition for fighting just at this time. But she shares the same fate as ourselves, and I know not, but that with determination, we might not master her. Ah!—I see her now!— By the devil she is just upon us!—A heavy craft she is too; and should she come athwart our hawse, a split might be the consequence. Overboard with more mettle; give us all the chance of escape you can, though, under any other circumstances, I would have scorned to have flinched from a dozen such crafts as that."

The continuous and vivid flashes of lightning now revealed distinctly a large vessel battling with the waves, and driven immediately in the course that the Black Raven was pursuing; in fact, that they should come into collision seemed to be almost inevitable. Overboard went more of the guns; but still, although greatly lightened, it was impossible for her to make any progress through the tremendous sea against which she had to contend.

All was excitement and consternation on board the pirate vessel, and the oaths of the men as they hurried to their different duties were frightful. Fiercely Mark Stanford gave his orders, whilst Pierce employed himself more coolly and actively, in different parts of the ship. Over mountain waves the ship was tossed with more than lightning speed; louder and louder roared the thunder; more terrifically bellowed and howled the wind, and still more rapidly came on the strange vessel, threatening destruction — inevitable destruction, if she should come in contact with the pirate barque. All that imagination or skill could furnish under the circumstances, were applied, but apparently with very little or no prospect of success; and destruction seemed to be threatened with the rolling of each wave.

And what were the sufferings of our heroine during this frightful season? It would be almost impossible for any language, however powerful, to convey even the slightest idea of them. Her senses were almost bewildered, and she remained for some time in a state which might almost be termed one of torpor, while at the same time she was perfectly alive to all the horrors that were passing around her, and the dangers—the imminent dangers to which they were all exposed; but when she was aroused from that, how dreadful was her agony. She clasped her hands, and raised her eyes devoutly towards Heaven, for some minutes. being totally incapable of uttering a syllable; but at length she became a little more composed, and tried to collect her thoughts, so that she might have the more fortitude to bear up against the dangers by which she was surrounded. All her thoughts, however, were upon her lover; and when she pictured to herself the agony he must be enduring at that moment in anticipating the fate which seemed almost inevitably to await her, she nearly sank under the tumult, the conflict of feelings which crowded upon her brain.

"Great God!" she exclaimed, "look down upon us, in this our hour of extremity, and do not, I humbly beseech Thee, allow us to perish thus! Jack! my own beloved faithful Jack, may Heaven give you fortitude to support these dreadful trials, and strengthen your mind with hope. Would that we were together, that we might consult, advise, and thus derive, at least some consolation; but the Almighty's will be done."

Again, as she spoke these words, she sunk upon her knees and offered up her prayers and supplications to the Supreme Being.

More dreadful became the storm; the heavens, the ocean, were convulsed to a terrible degree, and death seemed to be forewarned in every tremendous peal of thunder that burst from the overcharged clouds. Two or three times she went to the window and gazed out upon the storm, but its horrors were too great for her to contemplate for many moments, and she hastily withdrew, and once more sank into meditation.

Solemn, indeed, were her thoughts, but still in the midst of them all a certain feeling of hope came over her which encouraged her on, and tranquillised her mind, when it might otherwise have been so distressed as to be past all human endurance.

The confused and fierce sounds that emanated from the persons on deck, alarmed her, if possible, even more than the raging of the tempest; but it was in vain that she sought to close her eyes against them; the more she endeavoured to do so, the more distinct did they seem to be, and every word that by accident met her ears seemed to convey a threat or warning of her fate.

Again she approached the window of the cabin in which she was confined, and then as the lightning blazed across the sea, for the first time she beheld the vessel to which Pierce and Mark Stanford had alluded.

"Oh, had it not been such a storm as this," she ejaculated, "this vessel might have reached us, and brought me and my lover relief. Almighty Father, I implore You to abate the fury of Your just wrath against Your offending children, and let not those who so cruelly and so desperately outrage Your laws, triumph in their iniquitous designs."

She felt even more inspired with courage as she gave utterance to these words, and could even gaze with a degree of calmness upon the awful scene that was raging around. But the violent motion of the vessel, as wave after wave rushed over her, and threatened to engulph her, while the tremendous noise which every now and then followed from the throwing overboard of the guns of the pirate ship, increased the agitation of her mind.

Still she continued at the cabin window, and by the alternate flashes of the lightning, watched with the greatest anxiety the progress of the unknown vessel, and sad as was the alternative, especially under such circumstances, she encouraged a sort of latent hope of some relief being afforded her.

The oaths and the shouts of the ruffians on board the pirate barque were truly awful, and poor Kate was even more shocked by them, for it was impossible for her to close her ears to them, than she was horrified at the storm.

The storm increased; there were many feet of water in the hold; all hands that could be spared for that occasion were called to work at the pumps; but still the apparently doomed ship was little if any relieved.

During all this time of excitement, the reader may imagine what the feelings of our hero were. He paced the narrow confines of his cabin, as well as his fetters would allow him, and many and agonizing were the expressions of grief to which he gave utterance. But it was not for himself that he felt the slightest emotion; he had faced death too often in its most terrific forms to be now appalled at its approach. No, it was for that fair and beloved being, his beauteous and beloved Kate, that all his anxieties were aroused, and when he thought of the misery of her situation, and the almost utter hopelessness of her being saved from an untimely death, he was quite unmanned, and madness almost seized upon his brain.

"This craft," he said, "good as she is, too good for the rascals who hold possession of her, can never weather such a storm as this;—my eyes! it does blow great guns!—There's a lurch! more water in the hold!—To the pumps! to the pumps!—she has sprung a leak, I imagine, and nothing I think can save her. No, we shall soon all of us be introduced to our particular friend, old Davy. But my Kate, my pretty, my innocent, my kind-hearted Kate, must you, shall you perish thus? and with no one near you who loves you, and can sympathise in your feelings? Oh, the thought is dreadful! it is insupportable! And here am I, bound hand and foot like some lubberly felon, and unable to render the least assistance. Assistance! what could I do, if even my limbs were at liberty, opposed to these villains? Nothing! I shall go mad. Damme!—who's aboard?—Skipper ahoy!——"

His brain was evidently distracted, and clasping his burning temples with both his hands, the wretched young man sunk back on his seat, and for a few moments remained entirely unconscious of all that was passing around him. But at length he was awakened with tenfold sensitiveness to the horrors of his and his adored Kate's situation, and the inevitable fate which seemed to await them; and once more starting to his feet, he paced backwards and forwards in a state of agitation which may be imagined, but which it would be almost impossible to describe. Still the storm increased, and every moment showed the extent of the danger that was before them, and the almost utter hopelessness of any escape, unless by some miraculous and merciful interposition of Providence. And now for the first time our hero, as he stood by the window of the cabin in which he was confined, by the vivid lightning's flash, saw the vessel to which we have before alluded, and as he did so, a tumult of feelings swelled upon his bosom, though there was little indeed, considering the storm that was raging, to inspire him with hope.

"It is a fair trader and a British schooner, I'll swear, by her build, even from the slight glance I have had of her," he said; "oh, that it had been other weather, then indeed there would have been some chance of relief, for she would, I am certain, with the brave and honest hearts she has on board of her, soon make this death tub cry peccavi. But now, alas! she must share the same fate, and——"

He was interrupted by hearing some one at the door of the cabin, and a moment or two afterwards the bolts were withdrawn and two of the pirates presented themselves.

"How now, you sons of the devil?" said the honest tar, as he started to his feet and confronted them; "what would you?"

"Only just relieve you from these ornaments, my young sea-lion," replied one of the fellows, with a grin.

"Well, thank you for that, at any rate," said Jack, "for I must say that these are not exactly the ornaments with which the person of a gentleman should be decorated; so lend a hand, and mind you do your work handsomely, or, damme, if I don't put you upon six water grog for a month."

"Ha! ha! ha!" laughed one of the ruffians; "well, I don't so much dislike you, because you seem so jolly and contented-like under all circumstances, and especially while such a storm as this is blowing."

JACK CONFINED IN THE CABIN OF THE BLACK RAVEN.

"A storm!" replied our hero, in a voice and with a look of scorn; "damme, do you take Jack Junk for a powder monkey, or a swab, that he—"

"We," interrupted the pirate who had before spoken, "want you to work the pumps, and we shall then have a better opportunity of judging the qualities of Jack Junk, the tar for all weathers. Ha! ha! ha!"

"Very good," returned our hero with equal nonchalance; "anything for a quiet life, my Trojan. Helm's a-lee! bear a hand, take these grapnels off me, put me to the test, and you will find that Jack knows how to do his duty, if it be only to save the lives of such a rascally set off curs as you."

"Bold words, young man," said another of the pirates, "under the cir-cum-starnces; hows'-ever, we'll just give you the chance you ask for, and if you survive it, I shall only say that you are a better man than old Tom Handsail, and he has weathered the storm for more than forty years."

Our hero looked upon the man who gave utterance to these observations, and the expression of his noble intelligent features showed at once the feelings that were excited in his mind.

"More than forty years, mate?" he at last observed; " and may I ask you, out of all that long period of time, how many years of honesty you have led?"

"Honesty be d—d!" returned the pirate; "who's honest in this world?—Who lives by honesty?—Bah!—it's all a farce, as I've heered some o' them chaps as has swallered the dic- insharry say. I'm old Tom Handsail, with gray hairs upon my upper-works, that's all I've got to say about it, and, damme, if I care."

"Would that every hair of old Tom Handsail's head was silvered with honour instead of disgrace!" replied our hero, " and then should I indeed venerate them."

"Ah!" replied the old man, " you have been brought up in a different school to me, and have been taught th' art of thinking and speaking. Hows'never, such yarns as these don't suit me, so, my young shark, we will just allow you to slip your cable from these ornaments, and then to business."

"Very good!" returned Jack, " these are not the sort of embellishments that agree with the constitution of a true British seaman, when the tempest rages, and danger threatens, he is in his element, if he can lend his aid towards rescuing the lives of his fellow creatures;

'The tar's a jolly tar that can hand, reef, and steer,
Cast off, and nimbly belay——'

But, damme! I am only wasting my breath. There! cast off these infernal darbies, which ought never to disgrace or gall the limbs of one of nature's honest sons, and then see whether Jack Junk does not fulfil his promise."

In a minute or two Jack was released from his fetters, and having his fine athletic limbs at liberty, he felt himself once more a man, and endowed with even more than his natural strength and energy.

"Ah!" he remarked, " this is something better;—my limbs are free;—would any of you like, damme, would all of you like to try the mettle of Jack? Let's have a comfortable round, it will just sharpen my appetite for the dangers I have to encounter!"

"Fool!" said Tom Handsail.

"Well, now, old gentleman," retorted the young seaman, with the utmost composure. "If I were to apply to you the more polite term of villain you might feel yourself offended. How- ever, old man, I will not get out of temper with such a shattered, crazy old hulk as you; it would ill-become me to do so. How do you like this bit of a squall, eh?"

"D—n it!" exclaimed another of the ruffians, " why do we stand to be taunted by this lubber?"

"Lubber in your teeth, you hang-gallows looking swab!" retorted Jack, at the same time taking a quid of tobacco from his mouth and tossing it in the eye of the fellow who had made the remark; " when you next attempt to address a gentleman, try to learn to make use of becom- ing language. But may I ask you, old Tom Handsail—you don't say that is the very ami- able name you was baptized by?—how do you like the appearance of the present storm?"

"Avast heaving, mate," said the old man, who felt rather confused, and astounded at the cool indifference with which the young seaman treated him and his colleagues; "we will talk over these matters on some future occasion."

"Oh," returned Jack, " there cannot be a better one than the time present. It is a pretty breeze, is'nt it? You have been obliged to throw some of your mettle overboard, though, haven't you? Now that is a pity, because, you see, it cripples you so, and supposing yon government schooner, of heavy calibre, who is so close upon you, should not have been driven to the same desperate resource; supposing this storm should abate, and she should come close athwart your hawse, how would your health feel affected then, my old figure head of the Gorgon, eh? Do you not think that one half-dozen of the true and hardy, and honest hearts that are aboard that craft, would give all you rascally piratical curs the d—est thrashing that ever you had in your lives? Do you not think that those among your infernal crew, who escaped the cutlass, the pistol, or the cannon, would be strung up to the yard arm like a rope of onions? You d—d old shark, twist that into a quid; thrust it into your toothless old jaws and enjoy its flavour, if you can!"

Old Tom Handsail and his companions stood for a minute or two completely confounded at the boldness of our hero, and were unable to make any reply, whilst Jack, on the contrary, folded his arm across his chest, and surveyed them all, with a good humoured smile upon his counte- nance. But it was no time for delay. Every moment more frightful became the tempest, and the danger that impended over them all was most imminent. And above even the voice of the storm, might be heard that of Mark Stanford, as he rushed like a madman about the deck, giving hasty and unconsidered orders to those under his command, while at the same time he every now and then demanded with the most frightful oaths, why Handsail and the others delayed so long in bringing forth his prisoner, and placing him at the pumps.

"You are a daring rascal," said old Tom, at last, addressing himself to our hero; "but I have not the least doubt that before long we shall find the way to cool your courage. But come, lads, the skipper calls us, and we must obey his summons, for it is madness for us to take any notice of what this fool says. Away with him."

"Ha! ha! ha!" laughed Jack, scornfully; "now, what a pretty specimen of a mother's son you are, you old dragon! Why, damme, if you were a parent of mine, if I wouldn't toss myself overboard, and give the fish a snack out of pure disgrace and shame, may I never taste salt junk again."

"Away with him!" shouted Handsail, once more; "we have borne with him too long. Ah, that lurch! by h—l she has sprung another leak! All hands to the pumps! Coming, captain, ye ho!"

The pirates once more tried to seize our hero, but he thrust them off indignantly, and held them at bay manfully.

"Hands off, I say again!" he exclaimed, clinching his fists and standing on the defensive "or may I never go aloft but I will scuttle some of your nobs, and pour such a broadside in upon the whole of you as you never experienced before. What! you, you lubbers, have the audacity to put your grappling irons upon a true British tar? Damme if I will allow such an insult to be passed upon the service! Clear the gang way—give us sea room, and—and—d—n you all!"

Thus saying, the hardy young sailor thrust the fellows aside, and pointing to Handsail to lead the way, he followed to the place where his services were demanded. But notwithstanding the fortitude with which he had carried out this scene, his manly heart, when he reflected upon the state of mind in which his beloved Kate must be at that moment, was almost beyond endurance, and when he encountered Mark Stanford on the deck, he felt as if (so overpowered was he by the various emotions that rushed tumultuously upon his mind) he could not give utterance to a word. And certainly the scene which at that moment prevailed, was not at all calculated to ameliorate the feelings that predominated in his breast. The storm, if possible, raged more terrifically than it had done before;—the darkness was intense, it was perfectly impenetrable, save when the vivid flashes of lightning darted their forked fury across the heavens, and then the light emitted only served to reveal more distinctly the horrors by which they were surrounded. The strange vessel was still bearing hard upon their track, and the nearer she approached, the more evident was it that she would be an awkward customer to encounter with under any circumstances, but more especially disabled as the Black Raven was at that time from the injuries she had sustained in the storm.

When our hero was brought forward by Tom Handsail and the others, the pirate captain, Mark Stanford, otherwise Hugh Granfield, was pacing the deck in a state of the utmost excitement, at intervals issuing hasty and imperative orders to his crew, and then muttering the most fearful curses to himself; but when his eyes fell upon Jack Junk he advanced hastily towards him, and grasping him by the arm, he pointed over the wild deep as he exclaimed—

"Do you not see it?—Does not this storm please you?—Oh, yes, you have reason to be pleased, because it threatens us with destruction; but remember that your Kate, your beautiful, your beloved, your innocent Kate, is also aboard, and that she must share the same fate with us all, and that, probably, may lessen in no small degree your feelings of exultation and satisfaction."

"I remember all, you cowardly ruffian," replied our hero, boldly; "and in spite of the horrors by which we are at present surrounded I still set you at defiance, and put my trust in that Supreme Power whose laws you have so often outraged, and who is too merciful to permit you to triumph in your diabolical designs. Kate Markham and myself are in your power at the present moment, it is true, but we shall not be so long. No! however much you may affect to despise what I say, I tell you again that a just and terrible retribution will quickly overtake you and all the numerous and abominable crimes you have perpetrated will recoil upon yourself. Tremble, dastard, for as sure as my name is Jack Junk, the fate I have predicted awaits you."

"Rash fool!" exclaimed the pirate captain, passionately; "and dare you, especially under the present circumstances, hold out threats to me?"

"Ay," answered our hero, in the same bold tone, "and I have facts to guarantee me in giving utterance to them. See you yonder vessel?"

"Idiot! must she not share the same fate as ourselves?"

"No: I am convinced she is a fair trader, and not such a devil's craft as this, and it will never be permitted by that Supreme Being who has the guidance of everything that she should share the same fate as you and your blood-thirsty crew. See! she battles with the waves manfully; she will be upon you in a short time; she is of noble build, is she not, Captain

Stanford? and notwithstanding the disadvantages of the tempest, you may, perchance, find your match in her. The Black Raven's wings might be clipped, eh? Ha! ha! ha!"

"D——n!" cried Stanford, furiously, "am I to be taunted thus by a poor wretch whom I could crush at the bidding of a single word? Jack Junk, are you mad?"

"I know not that I am," replied the latter, with a satirical smile, and in the same cool strain; "but I believe that I have a right to be somewhat vexed."

"Away with him!" shouted Mark Stanford to the pirates; "put him to the hardest duty, and if he murmurs, lash him! torture him as you would a dog!"

"Oh, you infernal miscreant!" said the young seaman clinching his fists, and fixing upon him a look of mingled indignation and scorn; "I only wish that I had you on equal terms; if I would not amply repay you for all your tricks, may I never have the pleasure of tossing off a glass of grog again. Why—why.—But damme! I am only wasting my breath in talking to such a cowardly swab as you are."

"Away with him, I say!" commanded the pirate chief, in still fiercer accents than before; "and by way of consolation to you, my lion-hearted youth, I wish to inform you that while you go to the pumps, and to receive a flogging if you dare to disobey orders, I go to pay my devoirs to the beauteous Kate Markham. Ha! ha! ha! whose turn is it to triumph now, eh?"

"Mark Stanford," returned our hero, solemnly; "for this alone, mark my words, independently of all your other enormous crimes, you will receive such a punishment as that the stoutest and most stubborn heart might shudder at even the contemplation of. But in spite of all your threats I still defy you. You will not dare to carry them out to their fullest extent against that innocent girl who never injured you by word or deed."

"Hum, h!" replied Stanford, coolly, "you are particularly sanguine in your ideas, I must say, but nevertheless it strikes me that you are doomed to disappointment. But bear him away and do with him as I have commanded you. I will hold no further converse with him for the present."

"May the curses of Heaven light upon your head, you black-hearted ruffian!" exclaimed Jack; "but I do not despair; no, I say again that its just retribution will most assuredly overtake you, and that at the very moment when you least expect it."

"At any rate," returned Stanford, with an ironical and triumphant grin, "you shall not have the felicity of being witness to my downfall. You will be food for sharks long ere that time arrives."

"Liar!" answered our hero, firmly, "much as you threaten me, I feel confident that both myself and Kate Markham will ultimately be enabled to escape from your power before you have the opportunity of accomplishing your fiendish designs."

"Why, what a stubborn idiot it is," said Mark Stanford; "he has nothing to gaze upon but despair, and yet he will affect to encourage hopes that can never, shall never be realised. However, e'en suit your own whims and caprices, my young spark; it matters not to me. My plans are arranged and determined upon, and even this accident, alarming though it is, shall not be suffered to disconcert them. No, I tell you again, and once for all, that the lovely Kate Markham is mine, and though all the fiends of hell were arrayed against me they could not save her. I have sworn it, and I swear it again, and no power, mortal or immortal, shall induce me to break my oath. The storm continues to rage fiercely, there are no signs of its abating at present, in a short time we may founder and all become food for fishes, but still in the moment of my destruction I will triumph, yes, in that moment, she whom you love so fondly shall become my victim, and——'

"Monster!" interrupted our hero, unable any longer to control his feelings, "for it would be a gross libel to call you man, think you that that All Righteous Power who watches over the actions of us all, and Who holds the fate of us all in His hands, will ever suffer you to succeed in your hideous designs? No; I will not, cannot believe it, and therefore do I again set you at defiance, and dare you even to carry your inhuman and revolting threats into execution."

"Be it so," replied Mark Stanford, with a sneer; "continue to indulge in that idea, if you please, it will only be the cause of more bitter disappointment to you. Why, what an arrant fool you must be, with all your assumption of sagacity and wisdom, when you reflect even for an instant on the circumstances in which yourself and Kate Markham are placed. But why, I say again do I waste words with you, when I have other and more important business to attend to? I doubt not but we shall have plenty of future opportunities of discussing this subject, though whether or not it will finally be closed to your own satisfaction, I leave to you to decide. Away with him, lads, to his duty, and mind you do not spare him."

The pirates now advanced to seize him, but the hardy mariner stood on the defensive, and so imposing was his attitude, and determined the expression of his features, that they started back, and undecided and irresolute, awaited the further orders of their captain.

" Stand by, ye devil's sons !" exclaimed Jack; " or, by Heaven, I will make mince-meat of some of you in less time than I could cry Jack Robinson. Let any of ye lay your grappling irons on me if you dare, and you shall quickly find that Jack Junk can not only threaten but perform. I am ready to attend you to the sport you have cut out for me, it is not the first time that I have worked at the pumps; but still I do not care about doing it for such a crew of infernal cut-throats as you."

Mark Stanford made no reply, although he was greatly exasperated by the observations which Jack had made use of, but motioned to the pirates to bear him away, and they obeyed his orders. He then rejoined Pierce, and pacing the deck in the most disordered manner, he gazed in the greatest disorder of mind upon the horrors of the tempest.

" What think you, Pierce?" he asked, hastily, "shall we be enabled to weather this tempest?"

" Weather it," replied Pierce, " ay, bravely ; but I do like the appearance of yonder craft that is bearing down upon us."

" Ah ! by h—l !" exclaimed the pirate chief, " she seems to ride gallantly; she is fast upon us, and should she carry any heavy mettle, in our present crippled state she would prove more than a match for us. Damme ! the Black Raven must never be beaten thus, after all the bold feats she has performed."

" And she shall not be, captain," replied Pierce, "if you will only keep yourself cool and collected. She is placed in the same awkward predicament as ourselves, and what if we have lost some of our roarers, we have still sufficient left to let them understand a spice of our quality."

" True, Pierce," observed Mark Stanford, " but still it is most unfortunate that this craft should make her appearance in such a juncture. She is a British Schooner, that is quite evident."

" Oh, there can be no doubt of that," replied Pierce, "and an ugly looking customer she is. She makes way upon us fast, driven on by the fury of the tempest, and should she come in collision with us, there can be very little doubt as to the result. Those fellows are working hard at the pumps, and Jack is about one of the most industrious amongst them ; not out of any good feeling he bears you, you may rest assured, but from his anxiety to save the life of her whom you have destined for your future mistress; but still she gains upon us. She is a fast sailer, captain."

" She is, d—n her !" returned Mark Stanford.

" We must overboard with more of our mettle," said Pierce, " or we shall never be able to escape her."

" Shall we cripple ourselves altogether ?" demanded Stanford, with an oath. " Must all of those brave guns which have done such good service be sacrificed?"

" Ay," answered his lieutenant, " better that, than to come in contact with the fair trader. I fancy from her ugly appearance, that we might stand a chance of making a mistake if we were to do that."

Again the most fearful maledictions escaped the lips of Stanford, but he could not deny the truth of the observations of Pierce, and two more of the heaviest guns were thrown overboard, which, of course, lightened and eased the distressed vessel considerably, but still she made but little progress, and her situation every instant became the more perilous.

The storm instead of abating, increased in violence, and even to any one who was accustomed to such scenes it would have appeared truly appalling and frightful. The darkness continued with the same density, save when the vivid flashes of lightning, at intervals, broke in upon it ; the thunder roared in the most terrific manner, and the rain descended in a perfect deluge. It was an awful moment. The waves indeed nearly mounted to the clouds, and it seemed as though it were utterly impossible for any thing to live in such a tempest. Still the strange schooner appeared to battle with it nobly, and to bid defiance to its utmost wrath. It approached nearer and nearer to the Black Raven; it seemed utterly impossible for the latter to escape her; and the nearer she approached her, the more evident became the danger of having any thing to do with her. Pierce quitted the captain to give some instructions to the men, and Mark Stanford wound up to a pitch of desperation from the circumstances in which he was placed, having first gratified his curiosity and deadly feelings of malice, by seeing the situation in which our hero was placed, made his way to the cabin in which the unfortunate Kate Markham was confined.

CHAPTER XIII.

THE STORM CONTINUES.—THE MEETING BETWEEN MARK STANFORD AND KATE.—THE
TERRIFIC EXPLOSION ON BOARD THE UNKNOWN VESSEL.

RETURN we now once more to the deeply afflicted and much wronged Kate Markham, whose anguish of mind while all that we have endeavoured to describe was taking place may be readily conceived. The raging of the tempest, and the blasphemous shouts of the pirate crew, were of themselves more than sufficient to appal her mind, but the horrors of the situation of him whom she loved more than her own existence, and against whom the miscreant Stanford had held out so many brutal threats, tortured her more than all.

"Great God!" she exclaimed, at the same time raising her eyes devoutly towards Heaven "and must we be allowed to perish thus? Will you not interpose to rescue us, and to render the diabolical designs of this inhuman ruffian abortive? Oh, yes, I feel convinced you will; that you will not suffer us to fall victims to one who has hourly so transgressed your righteous laws. I will not despair! I will not despair, terrible though the prospect at present is before me. Dear Jack, I will bear in mind the burthen of the old song:

> 'There's a sweet little cherub that sits up aloft,
> To keep watch for the life of Poor Jack;'

and even in the midst of all the terrors by which we are at present surrounded, endeavour to look forward with hope and cheerfulness to the future."

Her spirits somewhat revived as she gave utterance to these words, and she felt inspired with fresh confidence; but still her heart was sick, though she felt more, oh, much more for the situation of her lover than her own.

With the most terrible anxiety she watched the progress of the storm, and as the unknown vessel approached nearer and nearer, the most mingled feelings agitated her breast, through the hope that if she overtook them, and the tempest abated, she would bring them relief. How fervently too did she offer up her prayers to heaven for the safety of her uncle, Constance, and all those friends so dear to her; but had she been aware of what had happened to them, her anguish of mind would have been quite insupportable.

"Beloved uncle, dear Constance, from whom I have ever experienced such unbounded affection," she ejaculated, "may Almighty God watch over and protect you, and give you strength to support this heavy trial with fortitude. We shall yet meet again, I feel confident that we shall, and that we shall be enabled to look back upon the past without regret, and to anticipate the future with the most sanguine hopes of happiness."

Alas! poor girl, little did she imagine that her uncle was no more, and that the affectionate Constance was at that time a hapless maniac. And it was fortunate to her that she was ignorant of those terrible facts, or, in spite of all her exertions to the contrary, her fortitude must have sunk under it. As it was, it was most extraordinary the firmness with which she met the severe trials to which she was subjected, and the scene that prevailed around, and which of itself was sufficient to appal even the stoutest heart. Every moment the storm increased in violence, and it seemed as if it were utterly impossible that the pirate vessel could escape destruction, but Kate committed herself and her lover to the care of Providence, and felt that resolution and confidence which could not have been at all expected under the circumstances. She could find from the motion of the ship, and the various observations of the crew, that she was very much disabled, and the throwing overboard of the cannon at different times satisfied her that the pirates considered their situation to be most imminently perilous, but still she kept up her courage in the most remarkable way, and entertained no doubt that they would ultimately escape.

In this manner about an hour elapsed, and our heroine continued at the window of the cabin in which she was confined, and gazed upon the raging of the tempest with a degree of calmness that was truly surprising, especially in one so young and delicate, and so utterly inexperienced in such matters. Still heavily the ship toiled through the angry billows, and the unknown schooner gained fast upon her, and it seemed as though, in spite of the storm, she was determined to make up to her, if possible, and to ascertain her true character. Little as Kate was acquainted in such matters, as well as the faint light which at intervals was emitted by the Heavenly fire would allow her to distinguish, she was confident that it was a British ship, and such a one as the pirate would not like to encounter, and that circumstance served to encourage her hopes, and to give strength to her resolution. Nearer and nearer it came, and as it did so, the shouts and execrations from the ruffians on deck became more furious, and convinced her that they considered their position to be a most dangerous one.

"Dear Jack," she exclaimed, "we shall yet be saved, I feel satisfied that we shall, and that our remorseless enemy will meet with that terrible retribution which the numerous crimes he has committed, and the brutal wrongs he has inflicted on our heads, so justly merit. But even should we perish in this frightful storm, will it not be much better than to meet with the revolting fate with which we are threatened by this fiend in human form? Great God of Heaven look down upon us, and let not the guilty triumph altogether."

She was interrupted in the midst of this soliloquy by the entrance of Margaret, whom she had not seen for some time, and from the appearance of whose countenance she could plainly perceive she was labouring under the greatest anxiety of mind.

"It is a fearful night, Miss Markham," she observed, in different, very different accents to those which she usually assumed; "do you not feel alarmed?"

"It is impossible for any one to feel otherwise than awed under such circumstances," replied Kate, "but still I put my trust in Providence, who never fails to protect the innocent in such moments of danger."

"Ah!" said Margaret, shrugging her shoulders; "you seem to possess much more confidence than I can boast of. Providence may be very good, but I have my doubts as to the result of this night. I have been in many a desperate storm in my time, but never in such a frightful one as the present. The Black Raven is a gallant vessel, and has weathered many a tough gale, but if she escapes destruction on this occasion, it will be by a perfect miracle; that's all I have got to say about it."

"Heaven's will be done!" ejaculated our heroine, firmly; "but yonder vessel, what think you of her?"

"I like not her appearance," replied Margaret, "especially since we have been compelled to get rid of some of our heaviest mettle; but still I do not think she would venture to attack us under such circumstances."

"God grant that she may," remarked Kate, "repugnant to my feelings as such scenes of bloodshed are."

"Humph!" returned Margaret, with a frown, "I see plainly that you anticipate a rescue, but it strikes me rather forcibly that you will be doomed to disappointment. The crew of the Black Raven are not easily to be daunted or defeated, and even should they meet with more than their match, they will not suffer themselves to be taken."

"What mean you?" demanded Kate, with a look of terror.

"Why," answered Margaret, sooner than resign themselves into the hands of the enemy, and be hanged like dogs, they would blow up the vessel, and immolate themselves and all in one fell destruction."

"Horrible!" exclaimed our heroine; "they surely would not proceed to such a dreadful extremity?"

"I have said so," returned Margaret, "and you may depend upon it, I do not speak erroneously."

"Heaven will surely never permit so dreadful a calamity," said Kate.

"We shall see," returned the woman, coolly: "it all depends upon circumstances. This strange vessel, if she be saucy, will find, perhaps to her cost, that she has no children in the crew of the Black Raven to deal with."

"Alas! alas!" sighed Kate, clasping her hands together, "how perilous is my situation. Can nothing save me from the terrible and unmerited fate with which I am threatened?"

"Why, to tell the truth, Miss Markham," replied Margaret; "whatever may be your opinion to the contrary, I do not see much prospect of it, if you feel disposed to take my word, and I have no wish to flatter you with false hopes, which it is impossible can ever be realized."

"Do you not pity me?" said our heroine, fixing her eyes stedfastly and impressively upon her countenance.

"Why," replied Margaret, "I confess I am not much used to the melting mood, for I have had so many rough trials to contend with in my life-time, that it has rendered me callous. However, I wish you no harm."

"Thanks! thanks, even for that," returned Kate. "Oh, God! you know how little I deserve to be exposed to the disgrace and peril that I am."

"Well, well," said Margaret impatiently; "enough of that, I am not used to such language as that, and it always makes me feel uncomfortable. The storm increases, our vessel has twice sprung a leak, and unless a change takes place quickly, we shall all of us be food for fishes, so you may as well make up your mind to the worst."

Poor Kate sighed and wrung her hands, but she made no reply, and Margaret continued to watch the progress of the storm for some minutes with the greatest anxiety. In the meantime the confusion which prevailed on deck increased, and plainly showed the alarm and excitement under which the whole of the pirates laboured. Kate also cast her eyes across the troubled ocean, and the frightful scene which presented itself increased her despair, and seemed fully to realise the fears and predictions to which the woman Margaret had given utterance.

"But tell me," said our heroine, at last, as a sudden thought struck her; "how have they disposed of my lover?"

"Why," answered Margaret, "he is at present engaged in assisting to work the pumps; and if he be wise, he will not attempt to disobey orders."

"Alas! alas!" sighed Kate, "dear Jack, that you should ever be exposed to such a fate; but I trust that Heaven will watch over you, and that you will yet be rescued from the power of your cruel enemies."

"Well," returned Margaret, "you may continue to encourage such hopes if you think proper; but I do not think there is much chance of their being realized."

"I should go mad could I believe to the contrary," observed Kate.

"Well," remarked Margaret, "I will not attempt to alter your opinion, but of this you may be certain, that, let whatever may happen, Mark Stanford will keep a sharp eye upon you both."

"Will he not relent?"

"Why, I should say you have had a pretty good opportunity of judging of that from the interviews you have had with him," answered Margaret. "But I must leave you, for the captain requires my services on other business."

Thus saying, without waiting for any reply from Kate, she quitted the cabin and left her to her own reflectons and all the horror of her feelings, which the reader will not require to be told were almost insupportable. She saw plainly that, let whatever might be the result of the storm, there was no hope for her and her lover, and as these thoughts crowded upon her distracted brain, her misery became still more excruciating. She clasped her hands vehemently together, and raised her eyes solemnly towards Heaven; but at length tears came to her relief, and she did feel a little more composed and resigned to the fate which seemed too surely to await her.

"Oh God!" she exclaimed; "I humbly, most humbly implore Thine All-Merciful interposition, and rest satisfied that Thou at least will not turn a deaf ear to my supplications. Thou wilt not permit this heartless miscreant to triumph altogether in his iniquitous proceedings against me and my lover."

She felt re-assured as those thoughts occurred to her, and awaited the issue of the event with much greater fortitude than could have been anticipated. But there was no hope, there could be no hope in the present aspect of the Heavens, and it was almost enough to sink the mind of our hapless heroine to the most abject state of misery. She watched the tempest in a state of mind which may be very easily conceived, and also the progress of the unknown schooner, in a state of the most inexpressible anxiety. It wore bravely against the storm, but the Black Raven being so considerably lightened by the guns that had been thrown overboard, and being at any time a fast sailer, was now greatly outstripping her, and promised fairly to get out of her reach in a short time altogether. This circumstance added to the misery and despair of poor Kate considerably, and unable any longer to look out upon the terrors of the night, she walked from the window, and paced the narrow confines of the cabin in which she was a prisoner, in a state of mind which we will not attempt to describe. Margaret had not left her more than a quarter of an hour, when she again heard some one at the door of her cabin, and it being immediately opened, Mark Stanford presented himself, evidently in a state of the utmost excitement. Kate shuddered on his entrance, and averted her looks from his repulsive features, and the pirate captain advanced hastily towards her, and, in spite of all her efforts to the contrary, took her hand and pressed it vehemently to his lips.

"You shrink from me, damsel," he said, in his usual harsh and disagreeable accents; "you still view me with the same aversion that you have been wont to do; well, e'en as you like, but I suppose I need not tell you it is useless, and that nothing whatever can save you from my power! This is a rough tempest, and it is doubtful how it will terminate; we may all of us shortly go to the bottom; however, I am determined that, let whatever may be our fate, that on which I have fixed my mind shall be accomplished."

"Cruel man," said our heroine; "have you no dread of the wrath of the Almighty when He speaks through such a terrible night as this?"

"Bah!" returned the ruffian;—"have I not repeatedly told you that I hold all such idle cant in utter contempt? Why then waste your breath in such observations?"

"What brings you here now?" demanded Kate, in a tremulous voice.

"To repeat to you," replied Stanford, "in this hour of horror the sentiments I bear towards you, and to tell you that should the storm continue much longer, and I see that our destruction is inevitable, you may prepare yourself for the consummation of that I have threatened, though perdition be my fate immediately afterwards."

"Monster!" ejaculated the blushing and distracted damsel, whilst her fair bosom swelled with indignation, and she fixed upon him such a look as might have penetrated even the most obdurate heart, and reduced it to a feeling of shame and remorse; "are you entirely insensible to every feeling of humanity? Have you no care for that Eternity upon the verge of which we are at the present moment tottering?"

"Pshaw!" returned Stanford, with a coarse laugh; "I have, methinks, told you enough to convince you that such matters as those to which you have alluded never for a moment trouble my mind. Eternity! ha! ha! ha!—a mockery!—a farce! Let fools believe in it, I do not will not. But how lovely you look, my sweet Kate, even in the midst of your scorn; what a lucky fellow I am to have obtained possession of such a prize. By all my hopes, I would not think even death too heavy a cost at which to purchase it. Rage on thou tempest, I heed you

MARGARET CONVINCES KATE OF THE HOPELESSNESS OF HER SITUATION.

not ; the pirate chief will yet triumph in the gratification of all his wishes. So fair !—so young !
—so innocent ! Such dazzling charms, that might create a sensation in the breast of even the
veriest stoic ! By all the powers, Mark Stanford, you are a lucky fellow, and you must not fail to
take advantage of the opportunity which kind fortune has thrust into your hands. You blush, maiden ;
oh, how well do those crimson blushes become those lovely cheeks. My soul is thirsty with love and
transport ; I must sip the honey from those ruby lips."

As the villain made use of these observations, he threw his arms around the slender waist of Kate,
and endeavoured to press his odious kisses upon the fair damsel's cheeks, but she resented and resisted
him with more energy than could at all have been expected.

"Miscreant !" she exclaimed, at the same time she succeeded in escaping from his hold and retreating to the farther end of the cabin ; "forbear ! You will not dare to proceed with this abominable outrage? Are you destitute of every manly feeling?"

" These heroics affect me not," replied the reckless ruffian; " only to serve me to laugh at. Kate Markham, it is time we understood each other, and I thought we did ere now.   The whole of it is, I have marked you for mine; it is folly, it is madness, as I have frequently told you, to oppose me; and why then, if you possess the sentiments that you profess to do towards Jack, do you still remain obdurate, when it is in my power to toss him overboard this instant, and make his body food for the sharks ?"

" Mark Stanford, or Hugh Granfield, whichever is your name," returned our heroine, fixing her eyes upon him in the most solemn and impressive manner : " brutal, callous and hardened as I believe you to be, I cannot yet bring my mind to the conclusion that you will fulfil all the dreadful and revolting threats to which you have given utterance."

" Indeed !" said Stanford, with a sneer, and a most sardonic grin upon his repulsive countenance, " really my fair Kate, my future mistress, you give me much more credit than I can lay claim to for mercy and forbearance.   The pirate chief of the Black Raven was never yet known to be particularly gracious to those who had not only insulted but assaulted him, and why then, should you assume that I will extend that indulgence to your lover ?   He, the reptile, the daring wretch, who not only presumed to rival me in my affections (ay, affections, girl) but to call me dog ; to endeavour to degrade me in the eyes of those by whom I was surrounded; who dared to strike me when it would not answer my purpose to retaliate because I should have betrayed myself; mercy and forbearance to him ?   Ha! ha! ha!   Mercy to a mongrel cur !   mercy to the veriest thing that crawls ; but revenge !   revenge ! tortures the most excruciating, for such a fellow as that.   Kate Markham, you hear my sentiments as regard your lover, and rest assured they will be carried out to the fullest extent.   There is no torture I can inflict upon him, that I will fail to do.   He shall be made most bitterley to rue the day when he offered insult to the humble, unpretending *Farmer* Stanford.   Ha, ha, ha !   My sweet Kate," he continued, after a brief pause, " do you remember the never to be forgotten first of May, when you, in all your pride of beauty, figured as the Queen of the Revels ?   Recollect you the scorn, the abhorrence with which you then repulsed my advances ?   Can you call to mind the insults I received from your lover, Jack Junk ?   Remember you what I said on that occasion ?   You do not ?   Well then, I will remind you, and probably it may afford you some gratification.   I told you, did I not, that the time would come when you and your lover would have reason to repent of the observations you then thought proper to make use of, and that you might discover Farmer Stanford not to be exactly the insignificant being he at that moment seemed to be ?   Do you remember that, Kate Markham ; and have I not kept my promise?   Oh, Hugh Granfield is a man of his word, depend upon it, and so you will find ere long, if you will entertain any doubts upon the subject."

" Great God," cried Kate, clasping her hands in despair; " assist me, protect me, I implore Thee, and He to whom my whole soul is devoted, for I see that it is useless to appeal to this monster in human form.   All-Merciful Supreme, I feel convinced that You, at any rate, will not desert me, but will frustrate all the cruel designs of the villain who at present holds me in his power."

" Ha, ha, ha !" again laughed Mark Stanford, scornfully ; " how it pleases me to hear you talk; knowing the power I hold over you.   You may say that death stares me in the face; that it is almost impossible the Black Raven can weather such a tempest as this; be it so, I admit it is the fact ; but still I am undaunted, and fully determined to carry out my designs to their utmost limit, though death be my portion the next instant.   Girl," he continued, grasping her arm, and dragging her to the window; " you see that vessel, which appears to be bearing down so fast upon us ?   She is a well built craft, and calculated to do us some mischief should we come in contact.   Probably you may rest your hopes upon her ; but mark me, and be sure I talk not idly or erroneously ; before ever she can come athwart our hawse, you shall be my victim, and every soul on board this craft shall be blown into that Eternity of which you have been speaking. What think you of that, my dainty lass ?"

" Oh, horrible !" replied Kate, shuddering in every limb, and especially when she noticed the determined and ferocious aspect of the wretch who addressed her.

" Yes, Kate Markham," resumed Stanford, exulting in the effect which his observations had upon our unfortunate and deeply persecuted heroine; " all that I have promised you I will most assuredly perform, so now you know perfectly well what you have to expect from the *miscreant*, Mark Stanford.   But why do I trifle thus?   One sweet embrace my adored, but scornful beauty, and then for a short time I leave you, and——"

As he spoke he threw his arms around the slender waist of Kate, and attempted to pollute her chaste lips with his odious kisses, but Providence endued her with more than her natural strength, and she resisted him successfully ; at the same time she drew with the quickness of thought, a long knife from his belt, and retreating from him a yard or two, she stood in a most determined attitude, while she exclaimed :—

"Stand back, ruffian! fiend!—dare to approach me an inch, and by the just God that rules above us, I will bury this in your heart!"

Mark Stanford staggered back, and gazed at her perfectly astounded. His first idea was to make a rush upon her and to wrest the deadly weapon from her hand, but he saw that she was resolute, and he therefore thought it would be much better to adopt a more conciliatory course.

"What, Kate, girl," he observed; "are you mad?—Ha! ha! ha!—A good joke truly. Come, come, put away that weapon; it ill becomes such taper and delicate fingers as yours. I was only jesting with you, my dainty one. Now, now—"

"Retire, miscreant!" interrupted our heroine, still wielding the knife, and evincing by her manner that she was fully prepared to carry all her threats into execution; "retire, I say, or by the just God whom I revere, I swear that either yours or my heart shall receive this knife. You have worked me up to a pitch of frenzy, and I am perfectly reckless of the consequences."

The ruffian muttered a bitter malediction between his teeth, but he did not venture to approach her, and at the moment a confused sound upon deck arrested his attention.

"Hell and furies!" he cried; "what's in the wind now? Is fortune deserting me altogether?—Kate Markham," he added, "much as you may for the present time seem to triumph, you shall have bitter cause to repent this. Oh, curses light upon this tempest! But I leave you now, with the assurance that under all circumstances I will return to you again, and that all the threats I have held out to you shall be put into execution."

"Villain!" cried Kate, with increasing courage, "I set you at defiance."

"Be it so, young lady," returned the pirate captain, with the most biting sarcasm, "we shall see whose fate it is to triumph, though, for my own part I do not despair. I go to add fresh tortures to your beloved Jack Junk. Ere long you may expect to see me again."

"Inhuman monster!" returned our heroine; "I will not condescend to speak to you again. Do your best and your worst; I will put my trust in the Supreme Being, and I feel confident that He will not desert me in the midst of this, my heavy trial."

Mark Stanford again laughed scornfully, and without attempting to make any reply, he walked from the cabin, and left our heroine to her own thoughts. Well as she had maintained her fortitude, as the reader may expect after all the dreadful threats which Mark Stanford had held out to her, and which she was so perfectly well satisfied he had the will and the determination to carry into effect, almost entirely forsook her, and the agitation of her mind was nearly more than she could find strength to endure. But it was not so much for herself as her lover that her feelings were excited; and she paced backwards and forwards, and listened to the voice of the tempest, imagining all sorts of horrors, in a state of perturbation of mind that may readily be conceived but cannot be so easily described.

"Dear Jack!" she exclaimed; "I fear, alas! that it is too certain our fate is sealed, and unless by some miraculous and merciful interposition of Providence, we shall both be doomed to destruction. But shall this heartless miscreant be allowed to succeed in all his diabolical designs? No, no, I cannot believe that he will be permitted to do so. It would indeed be monstrous to entertain such an idea. Sooner than meet with such a revolting fate as that, if it be Thy will, oh, God! let us perish in this tempest. But shall we not be permitted to meet again? Will we not be allowed to bid each other a last adieu, and——"

She was interrupted by a most violent and confused noise upon deck; the ship was agitated in a most fearful manner, and it seemed as if the moment of destruction had arrived. The shouts and oaths of the pirate crew were perfectly appalling to hear, and it was some moments ere our heroine could sufficiently recover herself to collect her thoughts; but at length she rushed to the cabin window, and terrific was the scene which then presented itself to her view. Such a fearful sea as at that moment raged, had, perhaps, seldom been witnessed before;—the waves washed over the deck of the Black Raven with tremendous fury, and it seemed utterly impossible that she could live many minutes, for her masts, her rigging, all were gone; she had sprang a leak in several places, and in fact she was little more than a hull. Still the voice of Mark Stanford might be heard above the roaring of the tempest, giving his orders to the men under his command, and at intervals giving utterance also to the most frightful maledictions, which sounded particularly awful in such a season as that. How the lightning ever and anon blazed across the Heavens, and how terrific was the voice of the thunder! But amidst all the horrors that prevailed, and much as her thoughts were occupied other ways, the eyes of our heroine were never for an instant removed from the unknown vessel, which was driven in the same track, and was nearer and nearer approaching the pirate craft. Her hopes were somehow rested upon that strange barque, and yet how little probability was there of their being realized.

"Would to Heaven!" she ejaculated, at the same time that she clasped her hands vehemently together; and raised her eyes, humid with tears, towards that Almighty fountain of grace to which she appealed; "would to Heaven that this storm did not prevail, then, indeed, might hope that this vessel would form a source of relief to us. But as it is, fate seems to frown upon us."

Most anxiously she continued to gaze upon the troubled ocean and the unknown ship, but nothing whatever as might be expected, could relieve the anguish of her mind, and every moment her fears became the more powerful. But no one now came near her, and she was left to her own dismal reflections, expecting every instant to be precipitated into eternity. The storm increased in violence, and the confusion which prevailed on deck, and the dreadful curses that escaped the lips of the pirates as they hurried about their arduous duties, rendered the horrors of the moment more intense and impressive. Poor Kate continued to pace backwards and forwards in a state of the most painful and insupportable excitement, at the same time offering up her supplications to the Supreme Being for His merciful interposition to rescue them from the fate which seemed to inevitably await them.

The strange vessel still came on faster, and faster still, and weathered the storm nobly; and it seemed as though it was almost impossible that the Black Raven could escape her, although whilst such a tempest raged as did at that time, notwithstanding the weakened and crippled state of the pirate ship, it was extremely doubtful whether she would be enabled to make any successful attack upon it. The suspence and agitation of our heroine may be readily imagined, but cannot so easily be described, even by the most eloquent pen. At length, however, she threw herself upon a seat, and covering her face with her hands, endeavoured to shut out from her thoughts the horrors that reigned around. It was useless, every instant they came more vividly and impressively to her mind, and all hope of escape from certain destruction seemed to be at an end, though certain death to her was far more preferable than the revolting fate with which she was threatened by the villain, Mark Stanford.

The almost incessant peals of thunder that rattled across the heavens were perfectly terrific, and the awful flashes of lightning that blazed across the surface of the angry deep were equally appalling. Kate saw at once that unless by a perfect miracle or some merciful interposition of Providence, nothing could save them from destruction, and she endeavoured to make up her mind to the worst. But it was a hard struggle with her feelings, and more terrible was her anxiety for her lover, whom she knew to be exposed to such danger and degradation, than for herself.

We will now leave our heroine for a short time, and return to what was passing on the deck of the pirate vessel, where a scene of excitement was prevailing which it would be a difficult task to endeavour to pourtray, especially in the colours which it merited. Mark Stanford paced the deck backwards and forwards in a hurried manner, giving his orders in a voice of passion, and mingling them with the most frightful maledictions; and it was in vain that Pierce endeavoured to pacify him, indeed he entertain the same apprehensions as himself, though he did not wish to betray them,

"By the infernal host, Pierce!" he exclaimed, furiously, "all the fates seem to have conspired against us. We shall never be able to weather this storm, for the water increases in the hold, and the pumps appear to have but little effect. Our vessel is little better than a hull and unless a sudden and miraculous change takes place, she must inevitably go to pieces. D——n! and shall the gallant Black Raven that has stood the battle and the breeze for so many years, meet with such a fate as this at last?"

"Courage, captain, courage!" replied Pierce; "it is no use giving way to despair; we shall yet be able to weather the storm, take my word for it."

"Pshaw, Pierce!" returned Stanford, impatiently, "what is the use of holding out false hopes, which I am too old and experienced a seaman to expect can ever be realized?"

"And may I ask you, captain," said his lieutenant, in reply, of what use is it to hoist those signals of distress? Will that better our condition?"

"No, but think you, man, that I can be altogether indifferent to the danger that is impending over us? At the moment too, when I imagined that my triumph was all but complete? The girl Kate, will even now escape the fate I intended for her; and see, the schooner nears us rapidly, and should she prove to be an enemy, we are in no position to defend ourselves."

"She will never venture to attack us in such a storm as this," said Pierce: "and if she should we may yet find the means to give her a warmer reception than those on board of her perhaps anticipate. The Black Raven is not going to yield so easily, I expect. Jack Junk is still at the pumps, is he not?"

"Yes," replied the Pirate captain; "and there he shall remain as long as his services are required; I will go to him and at least gratify my feelings of revenge by witnessing his degradation and sufferings."

Pierce offered not to make any reply, but busied himself in giving the necessary instructions to the men under his control; and Mark Stanford hastened to that part of the vessel where our hero and several of the pirates were occupied in working the pumps, and in a state of mind which it would be no easy matter to find adequate language to describe. Mark Stanford folded his arms across his chest, and for a few moments he gazed at him with looks of the most savage exultation ; but Jack turned upon him a glance of the utmost scorn, though his manly heart at the same time was glowing with indignation, while the anguish of his feelings when he thought of the deplorable situation of his beloved Kate was almost insupportable.

"So, my gallant rival," at length said the villain, Stanford; "you are busily and innocently employed ; it affords me much pleasure and gratification to see you so industrious."

"Villain !" replied our hero indignantly, "you may affect to triumph for awhile, but I can see plainly that you quake with fear at the danger by which we are surrounded, and the almost inevitable fate that awaits us. The elements have conspired against you, and ere long you and the wretches under your command will be summoned to your just account."

"At any rate," retorted Stanford, making an ineffectual attempt to laugh, though his looks sufficiently revealed the fears that occupied his mind ; "at any rate," he repeated, "I have one great satisfaction in knowing that you and your beloved Kate, as you call her, must share the same fate as the one you have hinted at."

"Better," replied Jack Junk, with all the calmness he could muster, "that she whom I love as never yet man loved woman, should perish thus than meet with such a fate as the one to which you had condemned her. I shall at least have the melancholy satisfaction to know that she will die innocent and undegraded."

"Indeed," sneered the brutal ruffian, and the expression of his features became more repulsive than before ; "but you will find yourself mistaken, for though we all may be plunged into eternity immediately afterwards, I swear, by all the infernal host, that the threats which I have given utterance to, shall be carried out to the very letter. Kate Markham shall become my victim, I tell you again, and nothing can save her. Hugh Granfield the pirate chief, is not the man to break his word under any circumstances, however threatening and appalling they may be, and so you shall find to your cost."

"Monster !" cried our hero, unable any longer to control his rage, and fixing upon him a look which was enough to make an impression upon even the most insensible and obdurate heart ; "you will never dare to go to the disgusting and brutal lengths which you have threatened to do."

"And are you idiot enough," returned Stanford, scornfully and triumphantly, "to imagine that I will not do as I say? Can you thus endeavour to flatter yourself with such erroneous hopes? Ha! ha! ha! But you will find that even though death should stare me in the face the next instant, I *will* complete my purpose, and laugh and exult in the tortures that I shall thus inflict upon your beauteous Kate. Even now I go to visit her, and to accomplish my designs."

"Forbear !" exclaimed the young seaman, worked up to a pitch almost bordering upon madness, "or the most terrific vengeance of Heaven will assuredly descend upon your head."

"Bah !" retorted Stanford, scornfully, "think you that I am to be intimidated or moved from my purpose by any such threats as that? What care I for the power you invoke? I scorn it, defy it, and am fully prepared to take all the consequences that may follow my proceedings. You see the storm promises not to subside, the vessel is almost a wreck, I have no time to lose. Kate Markham, even in the midst of death you shall become my victim."

"God of Heaven !" cried the excited young man, his fine eyes flashing with disgust and indignation ; "can this be permitted? Will You not interpose to prevent it? I cannot believe otherwise, and therefore, villain, I set you at defiance."

"Fool !" exclaimed Mark Stanford ; "think you, you have a weak boy to deal with, who will fail to keep his word, even at any cost, however dear to himself? But I waste time with you. I go at once to execute my purpose."

"May the curses of the Most High overtake you, miscreant !" said our hero, unable to bear himself ; "dare but to injure a hair of that poor innocent girl's head, and I again tell you that you will meet with such a punishment both here and hereafter as you now can form but a slight conception of."

Again the hardened scoundrel laughed scornfully, and viewed with the most fiendish satisfaction the mental agony which his unfortunate prisoner was enduring.

"Talk on, poor wretch," he observed ; "it does but serve to amuse me. I am totally regardless of the present and the future, and though I perish with my daring crew that which I have promised I will perform."

"Mark Stanford," said our hero, in a more subdued tone ; "I never yet humbled myself to any man, but I now earnestly implore you to relent, and to spare that innocent girl who never offended you by word or deed, and on whom you have already inflicted such unmerited sufferings. Surely you cannot entirely have become insensible to every manly feeling? Cannot the horrors that are at present raging around us, and which threaten us with destruction, make any impression upon you?"

"None!" replied the pirate, in a stern and determined tone; "I am reckless to everything Oh, this is indeed a moment of triumph to me, to witness your anguish and despair, and one. which I told you I was sure to experience."

"I will work no more," said our hero, folding his arms, and fixing upon Mark Stanford a look of hatred and defiance; "let the vessel be d—d, since matters have come to this, and our fate seems to be inevitable."

"Well!" returned the pirate captain, coolly, "you can please yourself, but I must just take the liberty of intimating to you that you must either continue to labour at the work I have set you to, or receive a sound flogging. Which do you prefer, young man?"

"Oh, this is past endurance," said our hero, his face burning with shame and indignation; "may every punishment overtake you for this. Poor Kate, may Heaven watch over you in this dreadful hour of trial, and rescue you from the revolting fate with which this fiend in human shape has threatened you."

"Well, which do you prefer?" demanded Stanford, in the same cool and deliberate manner.

"Miscreant!" replied the young seaman, "you have got me in your power, I am not in a position to defend myself, and you take a cowardly advantage of it. But oh, if I were placed in different circumstances, I would speedily make you rue the villanous conduct you are pursuing towards me and her so dear to me."

"Ha, ha, ha!" again laughed Stanford, scornfully; "you do well to talk thus boldly; but I waste time in listening to your mad ravings. Away with you to toil, dog, and I will to the charming and beloved Kate."

Poor Jack clasped his forehead in despair, and could not help groaning aloud in the agony of his feelings, but it was useless for him to offer any resistance, for he well knew that, if he did so, the villain would not fail to degrade him in the manner he had intimated, and with a heavy heart once more resuming his work at the pumps, the pirate captain leaving him to his own reflections and making his way, in a state of excitement that may well be imagined when the peril of the situation in which he was placed is taken into consideration, to the cabin in which the hapless and cruelly persecuted Kate Markham was confined, fully bent on completing his diabolical purpose, notwithstanding the almost certain prospect of death which was before him.

When he was gone the anguish of our hero's mind was almost beyond endurance, and bitterly, though mentally, because he would not subject himself to the derision of his companions, did he lament the cruel fate of himself and his adored Kate. What would become of her in the power of such a miscreant as Stanford? Was not her destruction certain? And even death would in his opinion, have been a mercy to her rather than that she should be subjected to the disgusting and brutal fate with which she was now threatened. These thoughts completely unmanned and overpowered the young seaman, and his brain was distracted almost to madness. But still he could scarcely bring his mind to believe that Providence would permit the monster Stanford to triumph in his inhuman and guilty designs, and critical even as the moment was he did not entirely despair, but trusted that something would yet occur to rescue them from the dangers by which they were surrounded.

The storm continued with unabated violence, and the only surprising thing was that the vessel was still enabled to bear against its fury in the shattered condition she was, but it was quite evident that she would not be enabled to do so much longer. The strange schooner had now got so close to her that they could in the flashes of lightning which every now and then shot across the sky, clearly distinguish her build, and there could be no longer any doubt that she was a British vessel, and that, comparatively speaking, she had received little or no damages in the storm. But the time that would elapse ere she could possibly reach them, and the probability that it might then be too late to save the unfortunate Kate from the brutal outrage which Mark Stanford contemplated, crushed all the hopes which might otherwise have been raised in the breast of our hero, and he continued to toil at the pumps in an agony of mind such as he had never before experienced. But we must now follow Mark Stanford to the cabin where Kate was confined, and describe the painful and exciting scene which took place.

The anguish of mind which Kate had been enduring, was, if possible, even greater than that which her lover was suffering, and as the time rotted dismally away, and there was not the least prospect of the storm abating, or of any assistance arriving, she gave herself up to complete despair. But her thoughts were almost entirely fixed upon her lover and those dear relations and friends from whom she was so cruelly torn, and fast her tears flowed, though that even aff orded but little relief to her overcharged bosom.

"What have I ever done," she ejaculated, "that I should be thus persecuted? Surely my fate is a cruel and unjust one, and therefore what means can I find to endure it with any degree of patience and fortitude? Poor Jack," she continued, wringing her hands, "how keenly do I feel for you, knowing full well, that even should it not be our fate to perish in this tempest, the sufferings and the degradations to which you will be subjected, and the state of anxiety in which your mind must be placed in regard to me, especially after all the threats which the heartless ruffian, Stanford, has given utterance to, and which he will not fail to put into execution, should not Providence interpose to prevent him."

She wept more bitterly than before, as these thoughts arose to her mind, and walked backwards and forwards across the cabin with distracted steps. But in vain she exerted herself to obtain the least composure. She now again watched the progress of the storm, and it was perfectly in unison with the state of her feelings at that moment. Could she have seen her lover, and been allowed to be in his company without the intrusion of Mark Stanford, or any of the other pirates, she thought she could have been somewhat more content, and that she could derive some consolation from the arguments he would make use of towards her; but of that there was, of course, not the slightest chance, and she was therefore compelled to make up her mind to the worst result. The raging of the storm as we have before said, continued to increase in fury, and the scene which prevailed around was absolutely frightful to behold; but poor Kate bore it with far greater fortitude than could have been expected under all the circumstances, and indeed she endeavoured to look upon the fate which seemed inevitably to await her with comparative calmness and resignation to that with which she was threatened by the ruffian, Stanfrod. But in the midst of it all, as we have said before, her whole anxiety was for the probable fate of him whom she loved better, far better than her own existence, and many were the prayers she offered up to the Supreme Being for mercy to be extended to him, and not to allow the monstrous designs of the miscreant who held them both in his power to prevail. Whilst she was thus occupied, she heard some one at the door of the cabin in which she was confined, and shortly afterwards it was opened and Mark Stanford, in the state of excitement in which we have described him, presented himself. Our heroine received him with much more fortitude than might have been anticipated, but still she could not help shuddering with an instinctive feeling of horror when she reflected upon the desperate and determined purpose on which he had probably come. Stanford gazed at her for a few minutes without giving utterance to a single word, but it was quite evident the thoughts that were passing in his mind, and the fearful determination at which he had arrived, notwithstanding the imminent dangers by which they were at that moment surrounded, and the little prospect there was of their being enabled to escape from them.

"The storm still rages with unbated fury," he said at length, in a tone of voice which could scarcely have been expected under such circumstances; "in a short time, nay, probably in a few minutes we may go to the bottom, but still, Kate Markham, my determination is unchanged. You shall not escape me. No, though all the powers of Heaven and earth were to oppose me, I would still complete my purpose. You hear me, girl, and I now come to put my designs into execution."

"Monster!" cried the blushing and indignant damsel, retreating from him, and fixing upon him a look that was sufficient to abash and confound the most stubborn and insensible heart, though it made not the least impression upon that of Stanford; "you will not dare thus to violate the laws of God and man? Have you no thought of the future? Can nothing daunt or make any impression upon your guilty mind? Are you completely dead to every sense of proper feeling?"

"Even so, fair Kate," replied the hardened wretch: "you have properly estimated my character in making use of those observations. Mark Stanford is not the sort of man to be intimidated at anything, depend on it; and rest well assured that he will not abandon his present designs. The cant you have just made use of makes not the least impression on me. Yes, the storm rages in all its fury, death stares us in the face, all around is fearful and hideous, but still you see me unmoved; I have sworn to possess you at any cost, and by all the powers I swear again that I will not break my oath. Frown not or turn away from me in scorn, for such idle heroics will not now avail you. You are mine, irrevocably mine, and thus by this one sweet kiss do I ratify the compact."

As the villain thus spoke he advanced nearer towards her and endeavoured to embrace her, but Kate retreated from him, and her determined demeanour, and the looks of scorn and defiance which she fixed upon him, notwithstanding the observations he had made use of, and the determination he had expressed, somewhat awed him, and he desisted for a few moments from the design he had contemplated.

"Miscreant!" she exclaimed, her lovely countenance crimsoned with the feelings of shame and indignation which naturally took possession of her breast, and the attitude in which she stood being sufficient to strike awe into the mind of even the most reckless and insensible; stand back, dare not to approach me another inch, or depend upon it, much as you may affect to despise the warning I hold out to you the most terrible vengeance of Heaven will descend upon your head. Beware—beware! Retire, and reflect upon that Eternity into which it appears we shall all of us be so shortly precipitated."

"Ha, ha ha!" laughed Stanford, scornfully, "and think you that such trash as that to which you have just now given utterance will have the smallest effect upon me? It only serves to excite in my breast scorn and derision. Retire ; you forget yourself damsel; know you not that you are in my power, that here I am supreme master, and that no one dare dispute or disobey my will? But I waste words with you; you have heard my determination, there is not a moment to be lost, and you must prepare yourself to submit to your fate. Though all the fiends of h—l were present to oppose me, they should not prevent me from the execution of my purpose."

As he thus spoke, he again approached her, and in spite of all her efforts to prevent him, he threw his arms around her slender waist, and polluted her with his odious kisses. She screamed aloud, and endeavoured to extricate herself from his hold, but it was all in vain : and again and again did the heartless and cowardly ruffian imprint rude kisses on her lips.

"Resistance is useless," he said; " the moment I have so long panted for has at last arrived, and now do I claim you for mine."

"Oh, God !" shrieked the terrified damsel, still struggling violently to release herself, though it was all to no purpose, "help me—save me from this fiend in human shape, I most humbly beseech You. Miscreant, have you no fear, and at this moment of peril especially, of the consequences that will most assuredly await the crime you contemplate?"

"I fear nothing," replied the ruffian, determinedly, and his eyes flashing with the power of the feelings which at that moment struggled in his breast, "my mind is made up, and nothing whatever can move it. Kate Markham, I have long loved you, but you scorned, rejected me, insulted me; and now I will at once gratify my wishes and revenge. Here is no one at hand that can come forward in your defence or rescue you from my power, and though we all perish the next moment, the bold rover of the seas will at least have the satisfaction to have triumphed over that proud beauty he was always ready to make any sacrifice to obtain possession of."

Again the heartless miscreant embraced her, and smothered her face with his odious kisses, and Kate struggled in vain to release herself from his brutal hold, and in the phrenzy of her feelings screamed louder than ever for help, though she knew well at the time that there was no one near who had the will or the power to rescue her from the terrible situation in which she was placed. Every moment her strength was becoming more and more exhausted, and it seemed as though it was impossible she could escape destruction, but suddenly there was a confused sound from the persons on deck, and then a broad light illumined the heavens and reflected luridly upon the angry bosom of the deep. Mark Stanford released his hold of our heroine, and staggered back aghast, thinking that something serious had happened. In an instant, however, he recovered himself, and muttering an oath, he rushed precipitately from the cabin, taking the precaution, notwithstanding the confusion of mind under which he laboured, to lock the door after him. Kate rushed to the cabin window, and she then beheld the full extent of the cause of the alarm which had been created. The strange vessel was enveloped in flames from stem to stern, and it was quite evident that her destruction was inevitable. It was an awful sight, and so close was the burning ship to the pirate vessel that Kate could distinctly see the unfortunate crew and passengers rushing about the deck, and some of them precipitating themselves into the deep to escape from the flames, only to meet with instant death. Her feelings at that moment may be very well conceived, but it would only be a waste of time for us to seek to describe them; while the confusion which prevailed on board the pirate barque, the loud shouts and fearful execrations of the daring and inhuman crew, increased, if possible the dismay and horror of the scene. It was almost more than our heroine could find strength of mind to endure. She had previously entertained some slight hopes that, if the unfortunate ship should overtake the pirates, herself and her lover might be rescued; but now, of course, these hopes were annihilated, and she saw at once that there was no chance of their escaping from the cruel fate with which they were threatened. She clasped her hands vehemently together in the intensity of her agony, and called upon Heaven for mercy and support, while at the same time she earnestly supplicated for mercy for the unfortunate individuals who were on board the burning ship. But we must leave her, and follow Mark Stanford on deck. The excitement which prevailed among the pirates was most intense, and they almost forgot the dangers by which they were themselves surrounded in the contemplation of the destruction of that ship which they had so much cause to dread.

"By all the infernal host," exclaimed Stanford, "this is fortunate; the flames have got such ascendancy that it is impossible, quite impossible that anything can stay their progress, and she must soon be burnt to the water's edge. The storm too, is abating, and we shall yet

THE STORM.—KATE ON HER KNEES IN THE CABIN.

escape the fate which for so many hours has threatened us. Our ship has stood it nobly, although she is greatly disabled."

"Ay," answered Pierce, "but will you not offer to render any assistance to the unfortunate devils who are placed in such a fearful position?"

"Assistance be d—d!" returned the brutal ruffian; "why should we sympathise with them? It is quite enough for us to look after our own safety, for we are not out of danger yet."

He had scarcely made use of these observations, when a terrible explosion was heard, which greatly agitated the deep, and shook the Black Raven convulsively.

"Ah!" cried Stanford, "the flames have reached the powder magazine, and it is all up with her, and the poor devils that were on board of her. It is not possible that one of them can be saved. So much for the unknown schooner, her fate is settled."

The shattered timbers of the ill-fated ship were seen flying in the air in all directions ; for a minute or two there was a crimson reflection on the troubled waters, and then all was the same as if no such fearful calamity had taken place. The storm too, now rapidly abated, the thunder ceased to roar, the lightning no longer flashed its forked fury, and the waves became comparatively calm ; in fact, the change that had so suddenly come over the scene was almost miraculous, and Mark Stanford was in a high state of exultation, and gave full expression to his feelings.

"Fortune favours us after all, Pierce," he said ; "and notwithstanding the disabled state of our ship, the leaks once stopped, if no second storm arises, we shall yet reach the place of our destination in safety. Kate Markham shall be mine at my leisure, though had not the storm subsided, I was fully determined that I would complete my designs in spite of the fate which might attend me immediately afterwards."

"Well," said Pierce, "I commend you for your resolution, but had you not better defer the completion of your designs until we reach the place of our destination ?"

"Yes," replied Stanford, "I think your advice is good so far as that goes ; but should we have any more stormy weather I will take good care not to delay the gratification of my revenge any longer. Though death be my portion the next moment she shall not escape me."

"And Jack Junk," asked Pierce, "what are your intentions as regards him ?"

"Why, have I not told you already," answered the pirate captain ; "to treat him with all the severity that the feelings of hatred and revenge I bear towards him can suggest, and to heap upon him every possible degradation. Oh, I will tame his proud spirit, never fear, and make him have bitter cause to repent the insults he formerly offered me. But see ! the storm has almost entirely ceased, we shall yet gain the place to which we are bound in triumph, in spite of our crippled state, and the damage done to our gallant vessel can speedily be repaired."

"Ay, ay, captain," coincided Pierce, "though this storm has certainly shaken her commission considerably."

The storm now entirely subsided, and as daylight approached, the weather became quite calm and favourable, the and leaks in the vessel having been stopped, she proceeded on her passage much better than under all the circumstances could have been anticipated. Danger over Mark Stanford and his ruffianly crew regaled themselves in the most extravagant manner, and the vessel resounded again with their boisterous mirth.

When our hero had done working at the pumps, worn out with the many hours exertion he had undergone, but more so with the anguish of his feelings, he was re-conveyed to the cabin where he had been before confined, and left to the poignant misery of his own reflections.

We need not attempt to describe the nature of what they were, for we presume that the reader will be able to form a pretty correct idea of them ; but all his anxiety was for Kate, and most agonizing were the doubts and apprehensions which took possession of his mind as to the fate which had in all probability befallen her, especially after the threats which the determined and brutal ruffian Stanford had thrown out.

"She may even now have been degraded, brought to shame and misery," he ejaculated ; 'and if so far better would it have been for both her and me had we perished in the storm that lately raged with such terrific violence. But no, I can never believe that Providence would suffer such a scoundrel as Stanford to triumph in his diabolical designs. Dear Kate, I will still try to think that we shall be rescued from the fate which seems to be impending over us, and restored to happiness. Could I think otherwise I should go mad."

By degrees he became more tranquil, and endeavoured to look forward to the future with hope and confidence, but that was a task not easy of accomplishment, and he paced the narrow limits of the cabin in which he was confined, in a state of considerable excitement.

Poor Kate too was in a most torturing state of mind, and as the rude voices of the pirates reached her ears her agitation and alarm increased, and she dreaded every moment the re-appearance of Stanford, especially as the storm had subsided, and he had no further danger at present at least, to apprehend. Her recent interview with him had fitted her mind with disgust and horror, and she dreaded the extent to which he might be urged by the violence of his passions and the determination of his purpose.

"Alas !" she sighed, "there is, I fear, no hope for us, now that the vessel which might have probably rescued us from the power of our cruel enemies is destroyed. But must I indeed become the victim of such a heartless miscreant as Mark Stanford ? Oh, I can never believe it, I can never imagine that the Almighty will desert me in such a moment of danger. And my love too, oh, what will become of him ? When I think of the dreadful threats the villain Mark Stanford has held out respecting him, and which if Providence does not interfere to save him he will not fail to put into execution, I can scarcely keep my mind within the bounds of reason Oh, Jack, dear Jack, how little did you deserve the fate which has befallen you. Kind heaven I implore you to look down with pity upon us both, and to frustrate the nefarious designs of our remorseless enemy. Any fate but that with which we are at present threatened would be preferable, and methinks I could meet it with some degree of fortitude and resignation."

Thus she continued to soliloquise for some time, and she found it impossible to tranquillise her feelings in the least degree. It was now bread daylight, and the fineness and the serenity of the weather presented a remarkable contrast to that which had recently prevailed; but notwithstanding Kate was completely worn out with fatigue and the anguish of her mind, she had hitherto been unable to obtain the least repose, and in fact, she was afraid to venture to do so, not knowing what might be the designs of her brutal persecutor. In another hour or two of anxiety and suspense, she again heard some one at the cabin door, and she trembled with alarm, thinking it was Stanford; but that was considerably abated when the door was opened and Margaret entered, bringing in her morning repast.

"No doubt you stand in need of some refreshment, Miss Markham," said Margaret, "for such a storm as that which fortunately for us is now over, does sharpen one's appetite; at least I have always found it so."

"Alas!" sighed our heroine, "I have other subjects to occupy my mind besides eating. Tell me, Margaret, is there any hope for me?"

"What, of escaping from the power of Mark Stanford?" demanded Margaret; "oh, no, if you have suffered such a notion to enter your head, all that I can say is, you must be very silly, Mark Stanford is not the man to go from his word, as I think you ought to have been convinced of ere this."

"Oh, God—oh, God!" exclaimed the unfortunate Kate wringing her hands; "what will become of me? Do you not pity me, Margaret?"

"And if I should do so," answered the latter, "of what use would that be? for I could render you no assistance."

"Alas, then," ejaculated Kate, "I see that my fate and that of my lover is sealed, unless the Supreme Being in His infinite mercy should interpose to save us. But think you that Mark Stanford will again obtrude himself upon my presence to day?"

"I don't know," answered Margaret, "but I should say that it is not at all unlikely."

"Heaven forbid!" said our heroine, "for I can never find fortitude to meet him."

"It is nonsense to give way to this weakness," said Margaret; "you are completely in the power of the pirate captain, and any resistance you may offer to his will would be worse than madness."

"But my lover?" eagerly demanded Kate; "oh, tell me, I implore you, what has become of him?"

"Why," replied Margaret, "now he has done working at the pumps he is removed to the cabin in which he was before confined."

"And what think you are the designs of the villain Stanford against him?" asked Kate.

"Why, I'm sure I can't say," returned Margaret, "but you may be very sure he will not treat him with any particular leniency."

"The monster! But I will not yet despair; something will occur to rescue us both from the dangers by which we are at present surrounded, and to bring down upon the head of our base persecutor that punishment which his numerous crimes deserve."

"Well you can encourage such ideas, of course, if you think proper," observed Margaret, "but I strongly suspect that you will find yourself mistaken. However, I wish you no harm for it cannot do me any good let it turn out as it may. But I have no time to discourse with you longer, as I have some business to attend to; I wish you good morning, and would advise you to make up your mind to the worst, and then the shock will not come so severely upon you, for you may depend upon it that all which Mark Stanford has promised he will perform."

But we might possibly become tedious were we to attempt to describe minutely all the feelings which at that time, and under such fearful circumstances, agitated the bosoms of the lovers, and it was only wonderful that they supported them with the fortitude and patience that they did. But all prospect of their escaping from the fate which threatened them, now appeared to be at an end, and there was absolutely nothing left them but to make up their minds for the worst; for disabled as the vessel was, should another storm arise that at all approached the one that had recently raged with such frightful violence, it would indeed be a miracle if it could brave it for any length of time; and even if that should not take place, and they should be able to reach the place of their destination in safety, their situation would be still more hopeless, as the miscreant Stanford would then have them both more completely at his mercy, and would stand in no fear of any attack being made upon him, which in the present crippled state of his ship, he had every reason to dread upon the sea. Thus hour after hour wore away in the most tedious and dismal manner, and our hero and heroine could find but little or no relief to the feelings which agitated their minds to an almost insupportable degree. The pirate craft bore on its way much better than could be expected under all the circumstances, and fortune in one of her capricious moods, seemed indeed to smile upon the villains, and to have completely abandoned the unfortunate victims of their infamous designs. The patience of Jack Junk was nearly exhausted and he continued to give vent to his feelings in the most bitter lamentations at the cruel destiny to which himself and his beloved and innocent Kate were exposed, and to invoke the curses and retribution of Heaven on the heads of their brutal persecutors. But of what avail was that? It only served to excite him the more, whilst hope of rescue seemed to be still farther from him than ever.

"But to be thus cast adrift, and left to the mercy of these abominable blood-thirsty sharks," said the noble hearted and brave young mariner, striking his fine open forehead with his clenched fist, and taking a few hasty strides to and fro across the place in which he was confined; " to be thus placed in the bilboes, and rendered unable to offer the least assistance or protection to that sweet lass, whom I so fondly love; to be subjected to the insults of such a squab as Mark Stanford and his rascally cowardly crew, and to have no more power to resist or resent it than the veriest powder monkey that ever smelt salt water for the first time in his life, it is too much to bear. But—but still, my own adored Kate, I will try to endure it all, for your sake, with the resolution and fortitude that becomes Jack Junk, whom his messmates have honoured with the title of the tar for all weathers; damme, if ever I disgrace the character! No, I will remain confident that, in spite of the clouds which at present are impending over our heads, and frown so darkly upon us, we shall yet be enabled to weather the storm, and to witness the wreck and destruction of those remorseless enemies who have inflicted so many and such unmerited injuries upon us."

As our hero thus spoke, his manly and handsome countenance became more animated, and his expressive black eyes sparkled with courage and determination. He felt that he and the fair and innocent girl to whom his heart was devoted, had justice on their side, and that, however unfavourable circumstances might at the present moment appear against them, they would ultimately triumph, and have the satisfaction of seeing their enemies brought to that account which their numerous blood-thirsty crimes so richly deserved. His feelings became more composed, and he endeavoured calmly to await the issue, certain that the Supreme Power would not desert either himself or his beloved Kate in the hour of their need.

The Black Raven still pursued her course, propelled by a favouring breeze, and it seemed at present as if there was every prospect of her reaching the place to which she was bound in perfect safety. Evening approached, and our hero had been for some time seated in one corner of the small cabin in which he was a prisoner, his elbows placed upon his knees and his chin resting on his hands, wrapped in meditation, when a sudden thought occurred to him, and he acted upon it at the moment. Starting to his feet, he went hastily to the door of the cabin, and tried it! By Heaven! the presentiment that had come across the young seaman's mind in so extraordinary a manner was realised, the door was open, but how it had been left so incautiously unsecured he could not imagine, and did not take much time to inquire.

" By all my hopes!" he ejaculated to himself; " this may turn out to be most fortunate. If I can but find the means of concealing myself in some part of this infernal craft, and securing the means of defence, I may yet, notwithstanding I am but single-handed, have an opportunity of rendering good service and defending my beauteous Kate. Now Heaven hear an honest seaman's prayer, and aid him in his efforts in the cause of humanity and justice."

He partially opened the cabin door, and listened. All was comparatively silent, save the low murmuring and plashing of the waves as they beat against the sides of the ship. Jack felt inspired with fresh courage, and stepped forth from the cabin, crawling cautiously on his hands and knees, the better to avoid immediate detection. He had not proceeded very far, when his hands came in contact with something, and, to his infinite gratification, it turned out to be a sword.

" This is most fortunate," he muttered to himself; " Providence at last seems to favour me in my designs. Now, if I have but the opportunity afforded me, let whatever may be the consequences, I will, at least rid the world of such a blood-thirsty miscreant as this fellow, Mark Stanford, or Hugh Granfield, as he calls himself."

He proceeded on his way without the least obstruction, and soon found a place where he could conceal himself, and overhear and observe most of what was passing among the pirates, without being under any apprehension of being detected himself. And there for a short time we will leave him.

CHAPTER XIV.

THE INTEREST THICKENS.—THE CRITICAL SITUATION OF KATE MARKHAM.—THE SUDDEN AND UNEXPECTED APPEARANCE OF JACK JUNK.—THE DESPERATE COMBAT BETWEEN HIM AND MARK STANFORD.—THE ALARM, THE INTERRUPTION, AND THE UNFORTUNATE SEIZURE OF OUR HERO.

IN the meantime, while what we have been recording in the preceding pages was taking place, Mark Stanford and his lieutenant, Pierce, were seated in one of the principal cabins of the pirate vessel, and indulging freely in the intoxicating beverage; the former particularly exulting in the cessation of the storm which had so long threatened them with destruction, and at the almost certain prospect of the success of his diabolical designs against the hapless and innocent maiden who had so unfortunately fallen into his remorseless hands.

"The triumph is mine, Pierce," said Stanford; "Kate Markham, and her lover, Jack Junk, are completely at my mercy, and I can seal their fate at any moment."

"Very true!" replied Pierce, "but there is plenty of time for the completion of your wishes; and, as we are now so near the place of our destination, I would advise you not to be in too much of a hurry."

"By the infernal host I swear, Pierce," returned the heartless and reckless miscreant, "the resistance and scorn of Kate Markham has so aroused my passions, and excited my feelings of resentment, that I cannot feel satisfied until I have fully subdued her proud spirit and gratified my revenge. And why should I delay? No; might not some other accident like the one from which we have just escaped occur to retard me in the consummation of my desires, if not to crush my hopes and frustrate my plans altogether?"

"I do not see any likelihood of it," returned his lieutenant.

"Well, well," observed Stanford, "at any rate I will not chance it. I will have another interview with her in a short time, and it will then much depend upon her own conduct whether or not I defer the completion of my wishes any longer. In the meantime, let us regale ourselves, Pierce; I feel in excellent, in more than usual spirits this evening. Spare not the grog—fill your glass—there is plenty more where that came from. Here's Kate Markham my future beauteous mistress, and may success crown all the daring designs I have in contemplation."

Pierce most cordially responded to this toast, and the ruffians continued for some time longer to carouse and to bandy the most ribald and disgusting jests one to the other. But at length the worst and most violent passions of Mark Stanford were aroused by the deep potation he had taken, and staggering to his feet, his face flushed, and his eyes flashing with an unnatural and alarming expression, he observed—

"This is the time, Pierce, this hour, this very hour shall witness my triumph over the scornful and obdurate beauty, Kate Markham."

"Hold, captain!" returned Pierce, who was somewhat more sober than his brutal companion, "had you not better reflect before you proceed to extremities? Kate has no means of escaping from you, and surely you had better postpone the gratification of your revenge to some more favourable opportunity."

"Favourable opportunity!" reiterated the pirate captain, impatiently, "when can one more favourable than the present occur? Why should I longer delay? Methinks I have already granted her more, much more than indulgence enough, and even put up too long with her contempt and reproaches. No, Pierce, my mind is fixed on it, and nothing whatever, I swear, shall move me from it."

"Pardon me, captain," Pierce ventured to interpose, "but you have drank deeply these last few hours, and your judgment is not, if I may so call it, in its proper state of health. If you would take my advice, you will at least defer this business till to-morrow, when you will be in a far better condition to combat the arguments and expostulations of Kate Markham."

"D—n!" exclaimed the drunken ruffian, furiously, "you exhaust my patience by your silly observations. What care I for the arguments and expostulations of the girl? is she not entirely at my mercy? Has she any one here to stand up in her defence? Has she not set my power at defiance? And why, then, should I spare her? No, I will not; my mind, I say once more, is fixed on it, and this hour shall the consummation of my wishes take place, though all h—l stood forth to oppose me."

"Well, captain," replied Pierce, coolly, "you know best, of course; you are your own master, and it is not my business to offer any opposition to your will. I merely ventured to throw out a few suggestions."

"Bah!" returned Mark Stanford, passionately: "I am not in the humour to receive them. Begone to your duty, and see that no one dare to interrupt me."

Pierce bit his lips, and felt his indignation rising, at the authoritative tone in which the pirate captain spoke, but he restrained his passion as well as he was able, and returned no answer and Mark Stanford quitted the cabin, and left him to his own reflections,

"The rash fool," said Pierce, when he was gone; "he seems as though he had been mad of late, and is so changed that any one who knew him well could scarcely believe he is the same desperate rover of the seas who has spread such universal terror around. Bah! I have scarcely any patience to think of it!"

As he thus spoke he walked slowly away, muttering curses at intervals between his teeth. In the meantime, Mark Stanford made his way to the cabin in which he had secured our unfortunate heroine, strongly excited by the drink he had so extravagantly indulged in, and his guilty mind bent upon the most brutal purposes. He unlocked the door, and entered the cabin, and found our heroine seated in a melancholy attitude and apparently immersed in deep and painful meditation; indeed so busily were her thoughts occupied that for a moment or two she was not aware of his presence, but when she did become so, she started hastily to her feet, and gazed upon him with a mingled expression of terror and disgust, while Stanford marked the emotions that were evidently passing in her breast with the utmost indifference and exultation.

"Villain!" at length said our heroine, in a voice of the greatest agitation; "why do you again thus intrude upon the wretched and unoffending victim of your cruelty? What is your brutal purpose with me now?"

"Kate Markham," replied the ruffian, in stern and determined accents, which made the hapless maiden shudder with horror and despair as she listened to them; "this is not the time to waste in words, and you may spare your scorn and reproaches, for they are both alike useless to you, and will, I assure you, if you think proper to believe me, have not the least effect upon me. You are mine, girl! I have purchased you at every risk, and I am ready to keep possession of you at the same cost. No foolish resistance, for it will avail you not. This hour I have set apart for love and enjoyment—this hour I have resolved shall crown the summit of my wishes, and nothing whatever shall move me from my purpose."

"Oh, mercy! mercy!" cried the horror-struck and blushing damsel, sinking on her knees before him, and clasping her hands fervently together, whilst the tears streamed rapidly down her cheeks; "oh, think, I beseech you, of my youth and unprotected state, and if you have one spark of manly feeling remaining in your breast you will abandon your monstrous designs, and if you still think proper to detain me a prisoner, far away from those kind friends and relations so dear to me, do not consign me to the fate which you threaten, and which is far too horrible and revolting even to think upon."

"Kate Markham," replied the hardened scoundrel, not the least moved by her impressive and pathetic appeal; "you should know me well by this time, and should therefore be fully aware that I never threaten that which I have not full determination to carry into execution. Why, I should be worse than the veriest idiot in existence were I not to take advantage of the opportunity which kind fortune has placed in my hands, after all the scorn and insults which have been so abundantly lavished upon me by you and he on whom your affections are placed. You ask for mercy, but I tell you, girl, again that I have none to bestow. I hail this hour as one of the greatest triumphs of my life, for it gratifies my revenge, and at the same time gives to me a mistress of whom the mightiest monarch on earth might justly be proud."

Kate Markham arose from her knees, her bosom swelling with indignation, and assuming a proud attitude of offended modesty and defiance she said :—

"Base, cowardly ruffian, whom nothing can move to a sense of shame or humanity, whom it would be a monstrous libel upon the sex to call a man, I will no longer degrade myself by suing to you for mercy or forbearance, but, putting my trust in that Almighty Power, whose most terrible vengeance will sooner or later descend upon your guilty head, I will even now, unprotected as I am, still hold you at defiance. Approach me not, for the curses of Heaven will follow the deed and bring immediate destruction upon you. Away, I say, and in your calmer moments reflect upon the hideous crime your guilty passions would urge you to commit."

"Ha! ha! ha!" laughed Mark Stanford, scornfully and ironically; "very pretty and heroic I must admit, but think you, girl, that it can have any other effect upon me than to urge me on to the completion of my purpose? You have no foolish boy to tamper with, or to frighten into obedience to your imperious will. By all the powers, Kate Markham, I never saw you look more lovely than you do at the present moment, though your eyes flash the fire of scorn, and your cheeks are crimsoned with the blushes of what you are pleased to call offended modesty. Well, e'en be it so, we shall be better acquainted by and by. But enough of this, I have been repulsed too long; but this moment decides your fate; the pirate chief claims the fair mistress on whom his soul has been so long rivetted; there is no one here to interrupt us, and thus—"

As the inhuman wretch thus spoke, he hastily advanced towards his intended victim and seized her in his arms, whilst poor Kate was so completely terrified that she was only enabled to offer the most weak resistance.

"Mercy! Mercy! God of Heaven interpose to save me!" she shrieked frantically; "monster! forbear! release your hold! Oh, spare me! spare me!"

"Your cries are useless!" replied Stanford; "there is no one here to save you!"

"Liar! hell dog!" exclaimed a stern and manly voice; "here is one who will defend that innocent girl while the least drop of blood remains in his veins!"

The pirate captain released his hold of our heroine, at this unexpected salute, and starting round aghast and with the most indescribable astonishment, beheld standing with his back against the cabin door, and sword in hand, Jack Junk!

He was so completely taken by surprise that he could scarcely believe the evidence of his senses, but Kate Markham no sooner beheld her lover, than with a loud cry of joy she flew towards him, and was immediately pressed to his bosom.

"My Kate, my adored Kate," said our hero, "look up and fear not; Providence has sent me in the moment of imminent peril to your rescue, and therefore it shows plainly that He has not deserted us. As for you, you rascally black-livered scoundrel, I—I—but damme, I will not waste words on you; you must either be a better man than Jack Junk, or before many minutes have elapsed he will cut that ugly carcase of yours into mince meat."

"D—n!" exclaimed the infuriated Stanford, who had now partially recovered himself, and drew his sword; "am I betrayed? Jack Junk here? What ho, there!"

"Avast, avast!" returned our hero, with the utmost coolness, "you may pipe all hands if you think proper; but you see I have secured the door, which you were so kind as to leave open for my admission, and before any of your lubberly crew can come to your assistance, I will at least settle my little accounts with you. Stand back, dear Kate, and see how soon I will polish this black whiskered gentleman off."

"Alas, Jack!" said the terrified maiden, "of what use is this resistance unless you have friends on board?"

"At any rate, my sweet lass," replied her lover, "if I can only manage to settle the business of this fellow, which I have no doubt I can, there will be one devil the less in the world. Come on, you swab, I am ready."

"Fool!" replied Stanford, fiercely, and rushing desperately and determinedly towards him; "then take your choice."

Their swords met and so violently that both blades sent forth a column of sparks, and the combat commenced with the most determined bravery on both sides, Stanford all the time giving utterance to the most dreadful oaths, and shouting aloud for assistance, for it seemed not at all unlikely that the gallant young seamen would prove more than a match for him. But how great was the terror of poor Kate. She could scarcely keep herself from fainting, and awaited the result of the combat in a state of the most painful anxiety, though it was quite evident that let it terminate whichever way it might, unassisted as her lover was, he must be defeated, and that it was only by some miraculous interposition they could hope to be rescued from the fate which was impending o'er their heads.

Still the combat continued with unabated courage and determination on both sides for several minutes, and it was hard to imagine which was likely to obtain the mastery over his opponent.

"Madman!" exclaimed the infuriated Mark Stanford; "of what use is this desperate resistance, circumstanced as you are? It can but serve to bring down my most terrible vengeance upon your head."

"Villain!" replied our hero, boldly, "I scorn your threats and set you at defiance. At least, if Providence desert me not, I will rid the world of such a miscreant as you."

He now renewed the combat with increased vigour, and terrific were the strokes that were dealt on both sides, but at length the sword of our hero was broke short off at the hilt, and he was then left at the mercy of his fierce adversary.

On beholding his perilous situation, Kate Markham shrieked aloud with terror, and sank breathless and exhausted upon a seat; but her lover immediately closed with Stanford, and a desperate struggle ensued, which lasted for several minutes. The pirate, however, ultimately proved to be the strongest man, and hurling the young seaman to the floor stood over him with his sword pointed at his breast, and his repulsive features distorted with mingled expressions of rage and triumph.

"Dog!" he cried, "I have you now; your life is in my hands, and this moment could I wreak my most deadly vengeance in your heart's blood!"

"Oh, mercy! mercy, Mark Stanford," shrieked the terrified damsel, rushing towards him; "spare him, I implore you, as you hope for mercy. Do not thus deliberately take the life of one who never wilfully injured you."

"Appeal not to him, my poor Kate," replied her lover; "for he is insensible to every proper feeling. Alas! fate is against us, and—and—but no I will not unman myself. Kate, beloved innocent Kate, farewell for ever: God, I trust, will protect you when I am no more."

"Jack, beloved Jack!" ejaculated our heroine in a frenzy of grief and despair, and sinking on her knees by the side of her prostrate lover; "we must not part thus! Mark Stanford, you will spare his life; you cannot surely be monster enough to be guilty of such a deed of blood."

Stanford was about to make some reply, when the cabin-door was burst suddenly open, and Pierce, and two or three of the other pirates entered, and gazed with no little astonishment at the scene which presented itself.

"How now," said Pierce, "what is the meaning of all this!"

"Why, the meaning is simply this," replied Stanford, "that this lubber has dared to make an attack on my life, and that I have succeeded in defeating him."

"Ah!" exclaimed Pierce, "has the fool been so bold? Must he not have been aware that death is almost the certain portion of those who offend in such a manner?"

"Oh, for the love of God!" again ejaculated the distracted damsel; "do not consign him to so horrible a fate; you have him completely in your power, and can prevent him from doing any harm, but, on my knees I implore you not to take his life; but if you are so determined, we will, at least both die together."

"Cease, dear Kate," said her lover, "for you talk to those who have hearts of stone, and who make robbery, rapine, and murder their trade. I had hoped that I should have lived to become your husband, and to experience the greatest bliss that could fall to the lot of man; but since fate has ordained it otherwise, we must submit with patience and fortitude. Bless you, bless you, my poor lass, it is a hard, a cruel trial for you, and—and—I shall choke! Farewell, farewell, beloved Kate, we shall meet in Heaven. But," he added, regaining his firmness, and fixing upon Mark Stanford a look of impressive solemnity; "mark my words: dare but attempt to carry your brutal designs against this innocent maiden into execution, and my dying curse shall rest upon your head and pursue you to destruction."

"Ha! ha! ha!" laughed Stanford, scornfully and triumphantly; "it does but serve to amuse me to hear the fellow rave. However, for the present I will spare him, for I have more lingering tortures in store for him to gratify my revenge. Bear him away, load him with the heaviest fetters, and see that he has no further opportunity of playing the pranks he has just now done. I will consider what punishment I will inflict upon him for the daring attack he has made upon me."

"Jack, dear unfortunate Jack," exclaimed our heroine rushing towards him, as he was suffered to rise to his feet, and trying to throw herself into his arms; "and must we indeed part thus! God of Heaven I beseech Thee to look down with compassion upon us, and not to suffer these cruel men to triumph altogether in their diabolical designs."

"My own Kate," replied her lover, "be firm, be firm; do not give way to despair, and fear not but something will yet occur to rescue us from the power of our savage enemies, and to restore us to happiness."

"Tear them asunder, and away with him!" commanded Stanford in a stern voice; "it shall soon be seen whose prognostications are correct."

Our hero was immediately seized by the ruffians and forced from the cabin, and poor Kate having given utterance to one piercing shriek, her feelings overpowered her, and she sank on the floor insensible, and she and the pirate captain were left alone. Stanford raised her in his arms, and gazed upon her pale and beauteous features with mingled feelings of satisfaction, triumph, and admiration.

"Scornful beauty," he said, "this time you again escape me, but your fate is only prolonged; you must, you shall be mine, and then indeed will my triumph be complete, and I shall be amply rewarded for the trouble I have been at to obtain possession of you."

He pressed warm kisses of rapture upon the lips of the insensible and unfortunate girl, and then placing her on a bench, he quitted the cabin and sent Margaret to attend upon her and see to her recovery. Pierce directly afterwards rejoined him.

"Well," he demanded, "have you obeyed my orders?"

Pierce answered in the affirmative, and he then requested Stanford to relate to him all that had taken place between himself and our hero. The pirate did so, and his companion listened to him with the deepest attention and astonishment.

"He is a daring fellow to a certainty," remarked Pierce, when he had concluded, "and he would be a valuable acquisition to our crew if we could only persuade him."

"Oh, there is no chance of that," replied Stanford; "force could only make him; besides that would not exactly suit my purpose. I have other designs in contemplation respecting him. Have you placed the fellow in irons?"

"Yes," answered Pierce, "the heaviest we have got."

KATE MARKHAM DEFENDING HERSELF AGAINST THE PIRATE.

"That is right," observed the pirate captain, "and how did his temper seem when you left him?"

"Why, you may pretty well guess that he is by no means satisfied with his treatment."

"Ha! ha! ha!" laughed the ruffian, "that is no more than I expected, of course; but he will have reason to be more dissatisfied with his treatment yet."

"No doubt of it," returned Pierce, with a disagreeable grin, "he has fallen into the right hands for that. But do you intend to inflict any further punishment upon him at present?"

"Why," answered Stanford, "he richly deserves it, for the daring attack he made upon me; however, I do not think that it would be prudent to do so at present, considering the effect it might have on Kate Markham."

"Exactly so," coincided Pierce, "that is what I have been thinking."

"His own reflections, I should think, and the suspense of mind he will be in at the fate which is hanging over the head of Kate, will be a sufficient punishment to him."

"No doubt of it," said his companions; "but you will not attempt to put your designs against the girl into execution until we reach the end of our voyage, after what has occurred, will you?"

"Why," replied Stanford, "my patience is almost exhausted; but perhaps it would be advisable to defer the gratification of my wishes until we reach the place of our destination."

"Certainly it would," remarked Pierce.

"If all goes on as favourably as it does at present," said Stanford, "it will not be long before we reach the end of our voyage."

"Before many hours are over, I fancy, captain," said Pierce in reply.

"Then will I no longer delay the completion of my designs," remarked the pirate captain, "I am all impatience till the moment of my triumph arrives, and I would not abandon my hopes for the richest booty that ever floated upon the broad bosom of the deep."

He was interrupted by the appearance of Margaret.

"Well, how fares the prisoner?" he demanded.

"No better than could be expected," replied Margaret.

"Has she recovered her senses?" asked Stanford.

"She has," returned Margaret, "or I should not have left her. I have, however, persuaded her to retire to rest on the promise that you would not again intrude upon her."

"'Tis well," observed the pirate; "you will keep a strict watch over her, Margaret, in case your services should be required."

"I will do so," answered Margaret; and after receiving some further instructions from Stanford, she retired, and once more left him and Pierce to themselves. But we will now once more return to our hero, who, placed in heavy irons which he could with difficulty support, was enduring a state of mind which was almost sufficient to drive him to madness, and from which he in vain endeavoured to obtain some relief. But it was not the thought of the fate which probably awaited himself that tortured him; but the dreadful and revolting one with which his beloved Kate was hourly threatened, nay, to which she had perhaps already fallen a victim; for after the scene he had witnessed in the cabin, and the observations he had heard escape the desperate villain's lips, he could not for a moment believe that Stanford would much longer delay the execution of his brutal wishes, and unless Providence interfered her fate seemed to be sealed; it appeared impossible that anything could save her. These thoughts were insupportable, and racked his brain to distraction. He recalled to his memory all the many hours of happiness they had passed together in their earlier days; the bright hopes they had formed, and which had every prospect of being realised; and a thousand times he cursed the fatal moment when the arch-fiend Stanford had made his appearance in the neighbourhood where they had resided and had cast his guilty eyes upon poor Kate. What a strange and cruel fatality seemed to attend them both, and from which it appeared that they had no means of escaping.

"Would that I had succeeded in ridding the world of such a miscreant," he said, "for though my own life would perhaps have been sacrificed to the vengeance of the pirate crew, they surely would not have been monsters enough to injure poor Kate. Alas! that idea reason tells me is preposterous and fallacious. The wretches are insensible to every feeling of pity. They are inured to scenes of bloodshed, and delight in the sufferings of their fellow creatures. Neither myself nor Kate can expect any mercy from them, and it will only be by a perfect miracle if we escape from them. But to be kept in this terrible state of dread and suspense, to be thus tortured, degraded like a common felon, it is almost too much for human nature to endure with any degree of patience. My hopes did somewhat revive when I beheld the British schooner so close upon the pirate vessel. But it seems as if the fates had conspired against us altogether, and every circumstance that occurs serves to add to our disappointment and to bid us despair."

He struck his forehead with the power of his emotions as he thus spoke and sinking on a seat, the hardy young seaman who had faced so many dangers on the ocean was quite overcome, and in the agony of his feelings could almost have wept like a woman. By degrees, however, the violence of his anguish somewhat abated, and he endeavoured to reflect upon the situation of himself and Kate calmly and dispassionately. This was a difficult task to accomplish, and he succeeded but indifferently. In fact, where could he look for hope, seeing that they were in the power of such wretches, and that there was not the least chance of any assistance arriving to their rescue? It would have been worse than folly to have entertained such an idea, and he had nothing left but to trust to the goodness of the Supreme, and to commit himself and Kate to His care.

Worn out with fatigue notwithstanding he was, so torturing were the thoughts that continued to harass his brain, that he found it utterly impossible to compose himself to rest, and he continued wrapped in deep meditation, and totally indifferent to everything that was passing around him, and in this manner hour after hour passed drearily away.

It was some minutes after the departure of the villain Stanford from the cabin, ere our heroine was restored to sensibility; and after she was, for a few moments she had but a wandering recollection of what had taken place. At length the whole truth rushed upon her brain, and in a voice of the greatest agony she exclaimed :—

"Ah, it was no dream, then; I am still a wretched prisoner on board the pirate vessel, and in the power of that monster Stanford, who has threatened my destruction, and that of him to whom my soul is so fondly devoted. Good God! how horrible is that thought! Would to Heaven that I had never more awoke to sense or feeling!"

"It is not of any use to give way to this violent state of agitation," said Margaret, "for what will it avail you? If you will take my advice you will endeavour to submit to your fate with patience, since there is not the least chance of your being able to escape from it."

"Submit to such a fate as that which I am threatened!" ejaculated Kate, wringing her hands, "Oh, never! nature revolts at the bare idea. Are you a woman that you can thus coolly talk to one of your own sex? Shame, shame, Margaret, I blush for you."

"You are at perfect liberty to entertain whatever opinion of me you may think proper, Miss Markham," replied Margaret; "but I have only told you the truth, and what is the use of your deceiving yourself with false hopes?"

"Alas!" sobbed the poor girl, "I shall go mad. Is there no hope of any assistance arriving to rescue me from this terrible situation?"

"None whatever," answered Margaret; "I have told you so frequently, and you ought to have been convinced of it long ere this."

"But my lover," said Kate, "what have they done with him? They threatened to murder him. Tell me, I beseech you, does he still live?"

"He does," answered Margaret, "though he could scarcely have expected that his life would have been spared a single instant, after the daring attack he made upon the pirate captain."

"He did it in my defence," said the damsel; "but I shudder with horror when I reflect upon the dreadful sufferings to which he will doubtless be subjected."

"It was the act of a madman, situated as he is, and he must expect to be punished for it," replied Margaret. "Many a one has had to walk the plank for a far less offence than that."

"But they will not murder him, oh, say they will not?" said our heroine, in distracted accents.

"Why I cannot say anything about that," replied Margaret; "if it is the captain's wish, they will not long hesitate about it, of that you may rest assured."

"Horrible!" exclaimed the poor girl; "how can I reflect upon that without my brain going distracted? But where is he now?"

"Loaded with irons and strictly confined till the captain's pleasure is known," answered Margaret; "he will not have a chance of committing a similar outrage, I'll warrant."

Kate looked at the woman for a moment or two reproachfully, and then burst into a violent flood of tears and sobbed bitterly. Margaret, in spite of the insensibility of her temper, could not help feeling somewhat moved at the grief and despair of the poor girl, and she said in more gentle accents than she had hitherto assumed,

"Come, come, Miss Markham, it is no use to give way to this violent grief which will not serve to alter your situation, but on the contrary, will only tend to increase its misery; much depends upon your conduct as to the treatment which your lover will receive from Stanford; and if you really entertain the sentiments you profess towards him, you will bear that in mind."

"Oh, how can I act?" sighed Kate; "what can I do that would save him? Think you that I can ever consent to the brutal and disgusting wishes of Mark Stanford?"

"And of what use is it for you to remain obstinate?" demanded Margaret; "for if you do not consent he will be sure to resort to force to obtain the gratification of his will, and how can you help yourself? Mark Stanford is not the sort of man, I can assure you, to be intimidated from his purpose. You should reflect seriously upon all this, and make up your mind at once as to how you will act."

"I have made up my mind already," returned the blushing and indignant damsel; "my determination is fixed, and that is that I will sooner perish than become the degraded being that the villain Stanford would make me."

"Well," said Margaret, in her usual careless way, "you know best, and you may make up your mind as to that which is sure to follow. But it is no use for us to talk further upon this subject, since we do not seem likely to agree. I would advise you to seek some repose after the excitement you have undergone."

"Oh, no," answered our heroine, "I cannot rest; my mind is too violently agitated and distracted to suffer me to do so."

"It will do you good," remarked Margaret, "and you have nothing to fear; Stanford will not venture to intrude upon you again without giving you previous notice."

"May I believe you?" asked Kate, eagerly, and fixing upon her a look of suspicion.

"You may," replied Margaret; "I have no interest in telling you a falsehood."

"Well then," said our heroine, after a moment or two's hesitation, "I will endeavour to comply with your request; but leave me, for I would fain commune for a few minutes alone with my own thoughts."

"Be it so," returned Margaret, "you may rest yourself perfectly satisfied that no one will enter this place unless it is myself, and that will merely be to see whether there is anything that you may require."

Kate made no answer to this, and Margaret retired from the cabin. But no thoughts of sleep ever entered the mind of our heroine. Was it all likely that they would, agitated and heartbroken as she was? No sooner had Margaret departed than she knelt down, and in the most fervent accents implored the mercy and protection of Heaven for herself and her lover; and while she gave utterance to this prayer her tears flowed fast, and her voice was almost stifled by sobs. Having ceased, she again rose, and paced to and fro in a state of the most painful and unconquerable excitement, which increased every moment the more vividly the horrors of the situation of herself and her lover, and the almost certain fate that awaited them, were presented to her mind's eye. The observations that Margaret had made use of, although they were harsh and unfeeling, had made a powerful impression on her, for she felt convinced they were substantially correct, and that, if possible, added to her terrors. What feelings of disgust and indignation swelled her bosom when she thought of the bold and brutal advances which the ruffian Stanford had made at the recent interview, and how she shuddered at the idea of her and our hero being entirely at the mercy of such a miscreant, without their having the least power to help themselves. Her brain became bewildered, and sinking on a seat she for a time became almost unconscious of what was passing around her. She was soon, however, aroused to recollection, only to experience still greater anguish of mind; and and thus she continued for more than an hour, and tried, but in vain, to obtain some degree of tranquillity. At length, however, being completely exhausted with fatigue of body and anguish of mind, she did retire to rest, hoping that a few hours sleep might serve to revive her and to inspire her with fresh fortitude to meet the dangers by which she was beset on every side. It was some time ere the drowsy god descended upon her eyelids, and then her rest was feverish and broken, and her imagination was disturbed by frightful visions, which arose to it in rapid succession, and made her frequently start with terror and look around her, in the confusion of her thoughts not knowing where she was. At length she awoke for good, and how long she had slept she could not form the least conjecture, but the rays of the sun were streaming full in at the cabin window, and Margaret was sitting by the door and was watching her attentively.

"How long have you been here, Margaret?" asked our heroine.

"About two hours," answered Margaret.

"What is the time?"

"It is now mid-day," returned her attendant; "you have slept a long time, but your sleep seemed much disturbed."

"Alas! yes," answered Kate; "how could it be otherwise, agitated as my mind is with such painful thoughts? But have you seen Stanford this morning?"

Margaret replied in the affirmative.

"And did he make any observations respecting me?" asked our heroine, anxiously.

"Merely to inquire after your health," answered Margaret.

"And think you that he will visit me again shortly?"

"No," replied Margaret. "From the observations which I accidentally heard him make to Pierce, I do not think you will see much of him again until we have reached the place of our destination, which, if the wind continues favourable, will be in the course of a few hours."

"Heaven be thanked for that," said our heroine, fervently; "and grant that in the interim something may transpire to rescue myself and my lover from his power."

"If you encourage any such hopes as those," remarked Margaret, "I am afraid you are doomed to be disappointed."

"You do not sympathise with me, Margaret," said our heroine; "and you seem to exult over my misfortunes."

"No, I do not," replied Margaret, "for what interest can it possibly be to me? Moreover, bad as the opinion may be that you have imbibed against me, I would, did it lay in my power, render you any assistance to escape from the fate to which Stanford has doomed you."

"You would?" said our heroine, eagerly. "Do you indeed speak seriously, Margaret?"

"I do," answered the latter; "but, as I have frequently before told you, I have no power.

I am bound like a slave to this vessel, and it would be a warrant for my death, my immediate death, should it be discovered that I had given utterance to the observations I have just made use of to you."

"Oh, horrible!" ejaculated Kate; "have you never had any means of extricating yourself from such a degrading and dangerous position?"

"None whatever," returned Margaret, and some expression of feeling did pass over her features, and a feeling of emotion and extreme remorse evidently took possession of her mind as she gave utterance to the words, though she struggled hard to subdue it. "What hope, what means were there for me, girl?" she continued, and her countenance at the same time became still more violently agitated. "I will briefly relate my history to you, though to few it has been told, and a few words will suffice to tell it; then, perhaps, you will not judge so harshly of me as you do at present."

"I judge not harshly of you, Margaret," said our heroine, who was greatly moved by her manner; "but I cannot do less than regret to find any one of my sex placed in the deplorable and disgraceful situation in which you are now. Pray proceed."

"My history of misfortunes," observed Margaret, after a slight pause, "as I before told you, will be very brief. Girl, you are young and innocent; I was once the same. I lived at home with my parents—they were in humble circumstances—my father was a fisherman; may the just God pardon me for what I am about to say, but I have reason to curse his memory, for he was a villain!"

"Dreadful! dreadful!" ejaculated Kate, with a look of horror; "forbear, Margaret; surely you can have no just cause to speak thus unnaturally of the author of your being."

"Will you hear me out, girl?" demanded the woman Margaret, with an expression of countenance which was quite painful to look upon; "or do you decline to listen to my plain and simple statement of facts?"

"Proceed," replied our heroine in a faint voice, and whose interest was, at the same time, greatly excited, "I will not again interrupt you."

"My father," resumed Margaret, "was, I repeat, a villain of the blackest dye, and I have every reason to curse his memory, for it was by his base artifices and his cupidity, that I was plunged into the misery and degradation of which you have been pleased to remind me. I have told you before that he was a fisherman; but he was a man of the most wild and reckless, the most brutal habits. He became connected with the worst of characters, smugglers, pirates, desperadoes who were ready to do anything for the sake of lucre. My mother—oh, a kind gentle mother she was; pity that fate should ever have united her to such a wretch—tried all in her power to withdraw him from his dangerous and guilty course, and what was the reward she received?—Treatment the most brutal, the most monstrous, the most savage, that the human mind can possibly form a conception of. But I am becoming tedious, and my mind is never in any condition to dwell upon these awful and revolting reminiscences. There was one, a youth about my own age, good, honourable, industrious and manly, whom I loved with all the fervour that maiden could ever feel towards one whom she considerd to be worthy of her heart's best affections, and who returned my passion with equal ardour and sincerity. We had been brought up together from the earliest period of childhood, and we had been led to flatter ourselves with the blissful hope that the day would arrive when we should become united together in the indissoluble bonds of matrimony. But Edgar Trevanion (such was his name) was only a humble fisherman's son, and the man I am compelled to designate by the name of father thought to *sell* me (mark the term, girl) sell me to better advantage, and he watched his opportunity to do so, though at the same time he assumed the most plausible demeanour towards us, and pretended to favour our suit; nay more, the time was even appointed for our nuptials to take place, and we were happy in the anticipation of the bliss that was in store for us, or at least, which seemed to be in store for us; and my gentle and beloved, but unfortunate mother was happy too, for much as she had experienced from the cruelty of her husband, she deemed not that such hypocracy and consummate villany could exist in his breast. It wanted but a month to the time appointed for the nuptials of myself and Edgar Trevanion to be solemnized, when all at once a change came over the manners of my father, and he assumed an air of independence that was greatly at variance with his humble circumstances. He was constantly inebriated; neglected his usual avocations, and at different times displayed large sums of money, for the possession of which he refused to render any account. In vain my poor mother remonstrated and expostulated with him; the only return she had was the most brutal abuse and sometimes blows. But some explanation of his conduct was given when he peremptorily commanded my lover never more to venture near his dwelling, and candidly told him that he had only been deceiving him all along, and had always resolved that I should never become his wife."

Margaret paused for a minute or two, and an expression of the most violent emotion passed over her features. Kate was also much moved and deeply interested in her narrative, and awaited its resumption with some degree of impatience.

. "There are many years elapsed since that time," at length continued Margaret, "and my heart has become stone; but I can still remember how poignant, how insupportable was my anguish when that cruel decree was made known to me. It was a wonder that madness did not seize upon my brain; but no, I was reserved for a still more dreadful fate. Myself and Edgar were not even allowed the melancholy consolation of a parting interview; and for a few days I was insensible to all that was passing around me. My youth and naturally strong constitution, however, at last prevailed, and I was enabled to leave my chamber. The same day a stranger was introduced to our cottage, of tall and commanding appearance, but whose general deportment immediately inspired me with a feeling of disgust and dread. My father termed him his benefactor and treated him with the most marked respect and deference, which the stranger seemed to receive with an air of indifference, and as a matter of right.

"He was a man about forty years of age, tall and robust, with features of the most repulsive and determined description. He assumed an air of freedom towards me which shocked myself and my poor mother, but in which he was encouraged in every possible way by my other unnatural parent, who frowned sternly and threateningly whenever I repulsed his bold advances or seemed in the least way to recoil from him. He took great pains to display a large quantity of valuable jewellery; and frequently his purse, which appeared to contain a vast sum in gold, was drawn as if by accident from his pocket. He tried hard to engage me in conversation, but I shuddered in his presence, and returned him scarcely any, or if at all the most evasive answers to any of the questions he thought proper to put to me. The looks which he at times fixed upon me filled me with a feeling of horror and indignation, and I would have given the world had I been permitted to retire; but my father had so contrived, designedly, no doubt, to place me between him and himself, and therefore, I had not the least chance of escaping. There was a great supply of drink, which had been brought to our cottage a day or two previously, and of which the stranger and my father partook freely, and endeavoured to persuade my mother and myself to do the same; but I suppose I need not tell you, Miss Markham, without success. The stranger possessed great fluency of speech; he was evidently a man who had seen much of the world in all its various phases, and he could converse upon any subject with the greatest eloquence; but still there was nothing that could do away with the prejudice with which he had inspired me. But I am afraid I am becoming prolix."

"Oh, no," answered Kate Markham, the narrative having for a time diverted her thoughts from her own sufferings; "I pray you proceed, Margaret, for indeed you deeply interest me. In what character was he introduced to you?"

"As a Mr. Arundel, an East India merchant, who was anxious to promote the welfare of my father and his family," answered Margaret. "He remained with us till a late hour, and I thought he was never about to depart, and my agitation and suspense increased every moment. Never in my whole life had I experienced such moments of misery as I did at that time. But at length he arose to retire, and you may guess my feelings when he intimated that it was his intention to call the following day, at which my father expressed the most unbounded pleasure, and frowned angrily upon myself and my poor mother because we did not respond to him. When he was gone, my father, turning to my mother and myself, said: 'Well, what think you of our new friend?'—We neither of us returned any answer, for we were fearful that the only one we could conscientiously give would only serve to exasperate him, and we consequently remained silent.

"'Why do you not reply?' he demanded, sternly; 'but I will put the question more immediately to you, Alice,' he added, addressing himself to my mother. 'What think you of the future husband of our daughter?'

"I uttered a cry of terror and clung to my mother, whilst her countenance was blanched with astonishment and disgust at this unexpected announcement, which she found it impossible to conceal.

"'Her future husband, Walter?' she said at length; 'are you mad, or labouring under the influence of drink?'

"'Neither,' replied my father passionately. 'I repeat that Mr. Arundel has made proposals to me for the hand of Margaret; it is an act of great condescension on his part, and I should indeed have been mad had I rejected him.'

"'Oh, God, father!' I at length found strength and courage to ejaculate, 'you surely cannot be serious; you will not be so cruel and unjust as to think for a moment of sacrificing me to such a repulsive looking being as the man you have this day introduced. Have you forgotten that my heart is devoted to Edgar Trevanion and that nothing whatever can alter the sentiments I entertain towards him? Have you forgotten all the solemn promises you have so frequently made to him? Have you——'

"'I have forgotten nothing girl,' interrupted my brutal parent, sternly; 'but I will not suffer my will to be disputed. Edgar Trevanion is a poor spiritless beggar without a penny in the world; Mr. Arundel is rich, and that makes all the difference. So, to cut the matter short, the former must endeavour to console himself without you, and the latter will have the pleasure, since he seems to consider it one of calling you his own. No nonsense, girl, for I will not listen to it. I have made up my mind; fortune is offered to me and us all, and I should be an arrant fool to reject it, and to continue the life of toil and poverty I have for so many years led!'

"'Then,' said I, with a look of disgust which I could not repress, 'for the sake of gold you care not to whom you sacrifice me; how much misery and shame you reduce me to? By heaven, I will not tamely submit to any such monstrous outrage and injustice, though your most bitter curse should descend upon my head!'

"The most indescribable rage distorted the features of my father as I gave utterance to these words, still clinging with feelings of the most powerful emotion to my poor mother, and it was some seconds ere he could articulate a syllable.

"'Girl!' he at length exclaimed, furiously, 'dare you offer anything in opposition to my will? Beware! beware, I say, for although I am your own father, you know me not yet. A few days only shall decide your fate. Mr. Arundel loves you, at least he covets the possession of you, and that is all the same to me, and by all my hopes I swear——'

"'Hold, Walter—husband; if I dare still call you by that name,' interrupted my horror-struck mother; 'to what rash vow would you give utterance? Have you entirely stifled all the feelings of nature and humanity in your breast?—'

"'Be cautious what you say, Alice,' said my father in a hoarse voice, and his face inflamed with the excitement of the feelings that were raging in his breast; 'beware what you say, I repeat, for I am in no humour to bear with contradiction.'

"'I have been more than twenty years your wife, Walter,' replied my mother calmly, 'and in all that long period I defy you to say, if you speak the truth, that I have ever in the least swerved in my duty towards you; why then should I fear to expostulate with you when you would perform an act of gross injustice and inhumanity? This is our only child; she has ever been kind, affectionate, and dutiful towards us;—you know that her affections are indissolubly fixed upon Edgar Trevanion; you know at the same time that he is worthy of her; you have solemnly pledged yourself that she should become his bride, and no other's; and why then for the love of lucre would you seek to blight her young hopes and prospects, and render her miserable for ever? Bethink yourself, Walter, and pause ere you sacrifice our child to——'

"'To what?' passionately demanded my father.

"'To one,' returned my unfortunate mother in the same tone of calmness, "to one, who, judging from his manners, (though may Heaven pardon me if I suspect him wrongfully) I believe to be a villain and a hypocrite!'

"'A villain and a hypocrite!' repeated my father, bursting with rage, 'dare you apply such epithets to one who has proved himself to be my friend? You little know the secret power he possesses or you would not venture to give utterance to such words. But I will not be opposed; you have heard my decision, and you will find that I will not fail to adhere to it. I will no longer toil like a slave when I can so easily purchase my emancipation from it. To-morrow we depart hence.'

"'To-morrow?' said my mother, with a look of the most inexpressible astonishment and alarm.

"'Ay, to-morrow,' was his reply, 'and never again, I hope to return to it.'

"'Where, where would you take us?' ejaculated my mother and myself in a breath.

"'That you will find out anon,' he replied.

"'You are mad with drink, Walter,' said my mother, 'you know not what you say.'

"'Do not seek to exasperate me, Alice,' returned my wretched guilty parent.

"'Ah, exclaimed my mother, as a sudden thought seemed to flash upon her brain, 'I read the full extent of your villany now, and shudder at you. You would place this poor child entirely at the will of the miscreant whom you introduced here to day, and care not if even her ruin be accomplished so that he supplies you well with gold. Monster! unnatural monster! for I will no longer call you husband, I—'

"'By all the powers of darkness!' interrupted my unnatural parent, in a voice that was sufficient to strike terror into the breast of all who heard it, 'you try my patience beyond all bounds. I can endure no more! Away to your chamber, and leave this obstinate girl to me.'

"'Never!' exclaimed my mother, in determined accents, and folding her arms around me: 'you would consign her to misery and degradation, and sooner, by Heaven, would I sacrifice my life than that you should separate us.'

" 'Idiot!' cried my father, clenching his fists and advancing towards us, 'know you what you would do?'

" 'Yes,' replied his unfortunate wife with calm dignity, 'I would save her from the power of a miscreant and that of a wretch who is unworthy to be called her father!'

He uttered a sort of wild yell; his features were frightfully distorted; his eyes were perfectly bloodshot with rage. I saw the glittering blade of a knife in his hand; I was paralyzed with horror—it was all the work of an instant—he flew like a wild beast upon my mother—I heard one appalling shriek, which has wrung in my ears ever since—I saw a stream of blood flowing down my dress—I felt the affectionate arms that had held me relax in their hold—my brain swam round—a sea of liquid fire seemed to float before mine eyes, and—I remember no more."

Here Margaret paused in her awful recital, overcome by the power of the torturing emotions which the recollection of those appalling incidents had conjured up, and gasped for breath.

"Oh, dreadful!" said our heroine at length. "And did your wretched, guilty father indeed murder the unfortunate author of your being?"

"Alas! he did," answered Margaret; "that fatal blow plunged her prematurely into eternity, and I never saw her more."

"Never saw her more?" repeated Kate, with a look of astonishment.

"No," returned her companion, "I was not even permitted to gaze upon her lifeless corse. Now, think you, damsel, that you are the only person in the world who has experienced the most terrible of misfortunes?"

"Alas, no," replied Kate, "after the dreadful narrative you have been relating to me."

"But listen," said Margaret, somewhat recovering herself, "for the awful facts are not yet half told."

"Oh," said our heroine, "is it possible that anything more horrible is to be related?"

"Yes," returned Margaret, "if you will only listen patiently to me. When I recovered my senses I discovered myself in a place which was strange to me altogether, and persons were engaged in restoring me. For the moment I could not recollect where I was, or who were around me; but at length I beheld my father, and then all the horrors of what had taken place flashed upon my memory, and I ejaculated,

" 'You here, father?—no, no, not father—I dare not, cannot call you by such a name after the horrible scene I witnessed. Where is that gentle, that kind and unoffending being who ever proved so faithful and affectionate a wife to you?'

"He seemed agitated, and could not return any immediate answer; at length recovering himself and reassuming his wonted sternness, he said—

" 'Question me not, girl, for I am in no humour to be interrogated, especially by you; suffice it to know that she who brought you into the world you will never behold again.'

"I uttered a cry of horror, and fixed upon him a look which should have penetrated to his guilty soul, but it made no impression upon him.

" 'Oh God!' I cried, 'my worst, my most horrible fears are confirmed then; you have murdered, savagely murdered one of the best of women, and for that depend upon it the curse of offended Heaven will pursue you to the end of existence.'

" 'Hold! rash girl!' he cried passionately, and fixing upon me a fierce and threatening look; 'the deed is done, and nothing whatever can recall it; this is not the time for reproaches, and I am insensible to them.'

"The agony of my feelings for a few moments choked my further utterance, and covering my face with my hands I wept bitterly, while he paced backwards and forwards, and seemed to view my sufferings with little or no emotion.

" 'But where am I?' I at length demanded, as a sudden and fearful thought flashed upon my brain; 'what place is this? and why am I brought hither?'

" 'I can answer your questions in that respect promptly and without any hesitation,' he said cooly; 'you are in the power of him who was introduced to you as Mr. Arundel, and you are on board the pirate vessel, the Black Raven.'"

"Ah!" ejaculated our heroine, with a look of astonishment, "this very vessel?"

"The same," answered Margaret.

"And was Stanford and the person who had introduced himself to you on shore as Arundel one and the same individual?"

"No," replied Margaret, "Mark Stanford, or Hugh Granfield, as I believe his real name to be, succeeded my destroyer in the command of this ship at his death, which took place some years ago in a terrible conflict with a British cruiser off the Coast of Guinea. But to proceed: You may judge of the horror, the anguish, and despair of my feelings on receiving this terrible information, for I saw at once that I was lost, and that nothing could save me. In vain I implored my cruel parent to have mercy on me, and rather to stretch me a lifeless corpse at his feet than to consign me to a fate that was far too dreadful and revolting to think upon; he was

THE DESTRUCTION OF THE STRANGE VESSEL BY THE " BLACK RAVEN."

quite inexorable, and had evidently made up his mind to carry the whole of his diabolical threats into execution."

"Oh, what a stern and brutal mind he must have possessed, thus to act towards his only child," remarked Kate.

"He must, indeed," returned Margaret ; "but you have not heard the full extent of his villany yet. Overcome by the insupportable power of my emotions, I at length again became insensible, in which state I remained for some hours, and for several days afterwards I was in such a deplorable condition, both in body and mind, that they began to entertain the most serious apprehensions as to the result, and there was every possible attention paid to my recovery, though I hourly prayed that death would put a period to my sufferings, since I saw plainly that otherwise my doom was sealed. At length, however, my youthful constitution triumphed, and I was sufficiently recovered to be visited by my persecutor, accompanied by my guilty parent.

The scene which took place on that occasion I shall not attempt to describe, for no doubt you can form a pretty adequate idea of it. The villain Bransdon, for that was his right name, urged his odious suit in the most bold and brutal language, and in which he was aided by my inhuman father, who held out the most terrible threats to me if I offered any useless resistance. It was all to no purpose that in distracted accents I supplicated their mercy and forbearance; they were totally callous to my anguish, and insensible to my appeal, and when they quitted me it was with the assurance that no power on earth could shake them in their determinations. Several days elapsed, during which time I need not inform you what was the poignant anguish of mind I endured, and more especially as all escape from the fate with which I was threatend was gone. But I must hurry to the conclusion of my dismal narrative, for I have already detained you too long, and I have business to attend to. In order the better to accomplish their monstrous designs without resistance, they contrived to mix a powerful drug with my drink, which steeped my faculties in insensibility, and when I recovered myself I found to my horror and despair that the miscreant Bransdon had triumphed, and that I was a ruined and degraded being. How bitter were the curses and reproaches which I heaped upon the head of my heartless destroyer, and my guilty and unnatural parent; but they heeded them not, and I was lost for ever. How could I help myself? I was completely in their power, I had not a friend near to interpose in my behalf, and from that fatal moment I became the unfortunate victim to the brutal passions of the villain Bransdon. Can you wonder that such a fate as this should change the very nature of my feelings, and that I should become what you see me now? I hated myself and all the world, and gave myself up with a sort of heartless indifference to the cruel destiny into which I had been so remorselessly plunged. My destroyer behaved towards me with much comparative kindness, but need I say that I loathed and despised him, and that had the opportunity have presented itself, I would not have hesitated to have taken his life? But as to my father, the feelings of horror and disgust I entertained towards him, I cannot find language to give expression to."

"But did you never find an opportunity to escape from a life which you say was so abhorrent to your feelings?" asked Kate.

"No," replied Margaret; "and if I had, whither could I have gone? What was to become of me, friendless and degraded as I was? No, horrible and revolting even as the idea was, there was nothing left for me to do but to submit to my cruel fate with all the patience and resignation I could, and in time I succeeded much better than under all the circumstances could have been expected."

"But what became of your father?" inquired our heroine.

"Why," replied Margaret, "we had not been very little more than a twelvemonth on board the pirate vessel, when he lost his life in a quarrel which took place between himself and one of the crew, and thus a terrible but just retribution speedily overtook him for the diabolical crimes he had committed."

"The pirate captain, you say, also perished same years since?" said Kate.

"He did," answered Margaret.

"And could you not then have escaped?"

"Probably I might have done so, but I had no inclination. I had been too long inured to the life to wish to abandon it, and enter once more upon the world, in which I could not expect to find anything else but insult, misery, and shame. This vessel had become my home; I had none other to fly to, and therefore how could I act otherwise than I have done?"

"But did you never hear what became of your lover, Edgar Trevanion?" interrogated Kate.

"No," replied Margaret, "but such was the intensity of the love he bore towards me, that I have no doubt he died of grief and despair. But my story is done; now you will be fain to acknowledge, Miss Markham, I should think, that you are not the only one in the world who has experienced misfortunes of the most poignant and cruel description."

"True," coincided our heroine, "and believe me I sincerely and deeply symphathise with you, Margaret."

"Oh," remarked the latter, re-assuming her usual air of indifferance, "sympathy is of no use to me, and I seek it not; my doom has been sealed many years, and I have made up my mind to it. But I must be going. You may rest your mind contented, for I tell you again that you need not fear any further intrusion from Mark Stanford, for the present, at any rate."

"Oh, but that he would abandon his guilty designs altogether," sighed Kate; "methinks I could then forgive him even all the misery he has already caused me."

"It is no use to encourage any such hopes," said Margaret in reply, "for they can never be realised. Mark Stanford has fixed his mind on you, and as I have repeatedly assured you nothing whatever will induce him to abandon his purpose. It is not likely that he will do so, after all the trouble he has been at to obtain possession of you; and the recent bold attack of your lover will but serve to strengthen his determination, depend on it. It was a rash and mad act, for what good could he expect would result from it? Even if he had succeeded in taking the life of Mark Stanford, do you not feel convinced that you would both have been sacrificed immediately to the vengeance of the crew?"

"Alas, 'tis too true," sighed our heroine: "Heaven only knows what will become of us both, surrounded as we at present are by such unparalleled dangers. Oh, what must be the sufferings of my beloved friends and relations, if they be indeed still alive, though at times my heart forebodes that some terrible calamity has befallen them. Tell me, Margaret, I implore you, have you heard anything from Stanford or any of the other pirates to justify those suspicions?"

"No," replied Margaret, "I have not, and you may be sure that they would take good care not to reveal anything of the kind to me. But I must bid you good day, and I would again advise you to compose your feelings, for giving way to this violent state of grief cannot serve to better or ameliorate your situation, but, on the contrary, will only tend to aggravate it."

"Alas, Margaret!" returned our heroine, in melancholy accents; "how vainly do you advise me; what consolation can I find with all these melancholy, these terrible prospects before me?"

"Well, Miss Markham, I have nothing more to urge upon the subject," "observed Margaret; "but Stanford will begin to grow surprised and impatient at the length of my absence."

Kate returned no answer, and Margaret retired from the cabin and left her to her own reflections, What the nature of those were we need not take the trouble to seek to describe, and for some time she was completely absorbed in the misery of her feelings. It was quite clear to her, that unless something miraculous occured to prevent it her fate and that of her lover was sealed, and the longer she ruminated upon it, the more certain it seemed to her. She wrung her hands in despair and wept bitterly.

The brief narrative of Margaret had deeply interested her, and it seemed but too probable at present that a similar fate awaited her. But we should become tedious were we to particularize all the thoughts that occurred to her, and which all bore the same complexion. It may be enough to say that the day wore tediously away; the vessel dashed rapidly on its way; and Kate was suffered to remain without any interruption, which was some relief to her mind.

CHAPTER XV.

THE PIRATES' RETREAT ON THE ISLAND.—THE TREATMENT OF THE LOVERS.—THEIR DESPAIR.—A STORM AT SEA, AND A SHIPWRECK.—THE UNEXPECTED REAPPERANCE OF THE MANIAC, HERBERT.

THE sufferings of Jack Junk, as may be expected, were unmitigated, and no one visited him except the ruffian who brought him his coarse and scanty meals, and from him he could not elicit any information that was at all calculated to alleviate the anguish of his feelings, or to give him the least idea as to the fate which was intended him, though from the brutality of the miscreant in whose power he was, he could not but anticipate one of the most brutal and inhuman description. But he did not at all regret the attack he had made upon Stanford; how could he do so, when he by that means, at any rate, rescued poor Kate for the present from the savage designs of her infamous and diabelical persecutor? But that the wretch would ultimately succeed, there seemed too much reason to fear, and that thought drove the noble-hearted young seaman almost to a pitch of frenzy. His limbs ached with the weight of the fetters with which the ruffians had loaded him, and what added to his bodily anguish, he was unable to lie down, or to rest himself in the least degree.

"Oh, Jack Junk," he cried, in the bitterness of his feelings, "to think that you should ever be placed in such a degrading situation, and by a crew of such cowardly ruffians. But I could bear my own misfortunes manfully, I know, were it not for the deplorable situation of that poor girl whom I love so fondly, and for the disgusting fate with which she is so cruelly threatened. By Heavens! it almost drives me mad to think of it. But no, it cannot be; if there is a just Providence above, which I never yet doubted, such heartless miscreants will not be petmitted to triumph, and their villany will recoil upon themselves. God give her strength and fortitude to endure the severe trials to which she is unfortunately subjected, and to resist successfully the designs of her remorseless enemy until something may occur to rescue her from his power, and to restore us both again to happiness."

He became considerably more composed as these thoughts flashed upon his mind, and for some time remained without giving utterance to another word. He, however, imagined to himself the dreadful state of mind which Kate must now be in, more especially when she thought of the dreadful fate which Mark Stanford would in all probability inflict upon him, in revenge for the attack he had made upon him; but he could not believe that the pirate would venture to persist in his designs for the present, after the terrible shock her feelings had sustained, and the alarming condition to which she must in consequence be reduced, and every delay brought with it some small degree of hope.

Hour after hour passed away without any change taking place in the situation or feelings of our hero, and his eyes, from the window of the cabin in which he was confined, wandered with the utmost anxiety across the deep. At length, towards the approach of evening, he was aroused from his meditations by a loud and confused noise upon deck, and he felt certain that something particular had happened. Looking more intently across the ocean, however, he soon discovered the cause, for he perceived land at a distance, towards which the vessel was rapidly making her way, and he had not the least doubt that that was the place of her destination. This idea filled him with various thoughts, and he awaited the result with considerable impatience and suspense. The nearer the vessel approached, the more distinct view, of course, our hero had of the land, and from what he could perceive, it appeared to be a small rocky island, but easy of access. In what part it was situated, he could not form the least conjecture; but that was almost a matter of indifference to him, for whereaver it was, he felt confident that the pirates had some place of security, from which there was no chance of their escaping, or any probability of their receiving any assistance from the persons who might inhabit the island.

He was interrupted in the midst of those reflections by hearing some one at the door, and the next moment it was thrown open, and Mark Stanford again stood before him. He remained for a minute or too gazing earnestly upon him, and with a mingled expression of hatred and revenge; and when he did speak it was in accents of the most disagreeable description.

"So, my daring Jack Junk," he said at length, with a bitter sneer; "I have you again secure, and quite safe from doing any mischief. It was a bold trick for you to venture to raise your hand against me; but I rather suspect that your courage is a little cooled down by this time. You do not seem to enjoy those irons much."

"Villain!" replied our hero; "I heed not your ironical remarks; the day of reckoning will yet come, I feel assured, and a terrible day it will be for you. I only regret that I did not succeed in ridding the world of such a heartless, cowardly, and bloody-minded monster."

"Indeed!" said the pirate, biting his lips, and frowning; "you do well to affect to despise my threats, though I know very well that you entertain very different thoughts to those which you have just now expressed. But you had better be a little more cautious in the choice of your language when you are addressing yourself to me, or you may probably repent it when it is too late."

"What other language can I address to such a fiend in human shape?" replied our hero boldly. "But I wish not to waste words with you; your sight is odious and disgusting to me. What brings you here on this occasion? To triumph over the contemplation of my misery, I have no doubt. Be gone! and leave me to my own thoughts."

"Fool!" exclaimed Stanford, "it is I who alone command here, and who shall dare to question or disobey my will? One word from me and you would instantly be swinging a ghastly corpse in the air, in the sight of her you love, or walking the death plank; but no, I have another and more exquisitely torturing fate in store for you, and from which it would be as useless for any one to attempt to rescue you, as to compel the vast waters of the mighty deep to stand still. See you yon island to which we are approaching? It is the place of our destination. Oh, it is a rare place for the execution of my purpose. It has but few inhabitants, and they are all in my service, and sworn to obey my will. On that island is a building, strong and impregnable as one of the castles of old—it belongs to me; and a noble retreat it is. There the pirate chief at intervals rests from his numerous toils and perils on the deep, and sets discovery at defiance. That is destined to be your future prison. It has numerous dungeons buried deep in the bowels of the earth, and well adapted for your accommodation, and I have no doubt that you will be satisfied I have taken every precaution for your safe custody."

"You may taunt me as much as you think proper," returned our hero, coolly, and recovering his usual firmness, "for I heed you not; I know well the heartless villain I have to deal with, and have consequently made up my mind for the worst."

"It is well for you that you have," said Stanford; "though I question much if you can form any adequate idea of that which is in store for you. But your beloved Kate, what think you of the situation in which she will be placed?"

"God help her!" said our hero, fervently, and with much emotion, "for without His merciful interposition, I fear that she is, indeed, lost! But, Mark Stanford, cruel and remorseless as I know you to be, I cannot, dare not believe that you will proceed to the guilty extremities you have threatened."

"Indeed," said Stanford, "and what makes you entertain any doubts upon the subject?"

"Because," replied our hero, "I cannot think you entirely insensible to the claims of female innocence, unless you are a demon instead of a man."

"Well," returned Mark Stanford, with a half-laugh; "such is the estimate, young man, that you have hitherto presumed to form of my character, and you therefore cannot feel greatly astonished if I were to prove to you by my conduct that you have not been much mistaken. When you knew me only as the simple Farmer Stanford you treated me with scorn, opprobrium, and insult; now you know me for Hugh Granfield, the commander of the Black Raven, the rover of the seas, and at the same time that yourself and her whom you love are in my power, it behoves me, I think, to retaliate, and consequently, I tell you again, that from me you can expect no mercy. Did I not tell you, when we were on land, and you little suspected the power I possessed, that the time would come when I would repay you and the fair Kate most amply, for all the treatment I had received from you, and when you should have reason to tremble at my name? And have I not kept my word? Think you any longer that I am the contemptible individual you once took me to be? Suppose you, for an instant, that I will fail to carry my threats into execution to the very letter? If you do, you must be even a greater idiot than I take you for. No, no, Hugh Granfield will teach the rash fools who have dared to despise his power, how much they have cause to dread him, and how perfectly weak and helpless they are when opposed to him. You behold the place we are so rapidly approaching, I say again? There is the pirate's castle, and there the scene of his triumph. There the proud and scornful beauty, Kate Markham, shall become the mistress of Hugh Granfield, the terror of the seas, and the *gallant*, the *daring* Jack Junk, the tar for all weathers, his helpless slave, the mere toy in his hands for the gratification of the deadly revenge he bears towards him."

As the atrocious wretch gave utterance to those words, an expression passed over his features that was perfectly hideous, and stout even as was the heart of the young seaman, he could not gaze upon it without an inward and unconquerable feeling of horror and disgust. Mark Stanford noticed his emotion with the most malignant feelings of exultation, and a savage grin overspread his repulsive features. But at length our hero sufficiently recovered himself to give utterance to the following words, which he spoke in a tone of determination, and which could not fail to have some little effect upon the pirate captain—

"Cowardly, dastardly ruffian, (for what else can you be, thus to exult over and taunt those whom evil fate has placed within the exercise of your cruelty?) think you that the Almighty power you affect to despise will suffer you to carry forth those brutal designs into execution? Have you no fear of the consequences that may follow any such attempt? Yes, I am satisfied from your blanched cheeks and quivering lips, that, in spite of your nonchalance and empty bravado, you have, and that, powerless as you have now rendered me, you still quiver under my observations, and know that—you feel I speak the truth—apparent though your triumph seems to be at present, a terrible retribution will overtake you, and save, at least, that innocent damsel whom you have doomed to destruction from your power, and at the same time plunge you into that abyss of shame and misery which your crimes so richly merit. I dare you to do the worst that your savage nature can suggest to torture me, but at the same time I now invoke the heaviest curses that the Almighty can inflict upon you head, and I know that my prayers will not be unheard, if you attempt to carry out your demonical threats into execution against that helpless maiden, to whom my whole soul is devoted. You may torture me, tear me limb from limb, but you shall yet be stayed in your demon work against that fair being whose immaculate virtues must be a protection against all such scoundrels as yourself."

"Have you done?" demanded the ruffian, at length recovering himself, and laughing ironically; "well, I must say, it is rather a bold speech for a person placed in your position, but it only serves to amuse me much; seeing the utter helplessness in which yourself and Kate Markham are placed. You affect to be confident, so am I; and upon those terms we will separate; but, at the same time, I again assure you that all I have promised I will fulfil, let whatever may be the consequences to myself. I heed them not; Hugh Granfield has hitherto been triumphant, and he does not despair of being so still. I comply with your wish, and leave you to your own reflections."

Thus saying, the pirate captain once more fixed a malignant look of triumph upon his unfortunate prisoner, who was too much overpowered by his feelings of emotion and indignation to make any reply at the moment, and retired from the cabin in which he was confined. After he was gone our hero remained for a few moments in a state of excitement which we need not take the pains to endeavour to describe, and as well as the heavy irons that encumbered his limbs would permit him, he paced backwards and forwards, and gave vent to his feelings in the most melancholy language.

"To be thus placed under hatches," he ejaculated, "when all my energies are required, and all the consolation I could offer to support and console my beloved and innocent Kate, is surely too much for the patience and fortitude of man to endure. How have we either of us deserved this? But I will not arraign the will of the great Commander aloft, or despair that He will yet interpose to rescue us from the fate which at present seems to be impending over us. No, my sweet lass, but a little while, and, notwithstanding the darkness of the present prospects that surround us, I feel satisfied that we shall triumph over our bitter and deadly enemies, and be restored to that happiness we have both endeavoured to deserve. You fall a victim to such an atrocious miscreant as this Mark Stanford, or Hugh Granfield, or whatever is his name? Pshaw! he very idea is monstrous! I will not encourage it—I will never believe that the God of truth and justice, will permit such an act of iniquity to take place."

These thoughts made him feel more calm, and he resumed his place at the window of the cabin, and watched the progress of the vessel as it rapidly made its way towards the island; and as it did so, he saw everything to corroborate the assertions of Stanford, in the appearance the island presented, and therefore was there the greater reason for his confidence in the escape of himself and Kate from the fate which at present seemed to be impending over them, to give way, as he more narrowly watched the place of their destination. Turning round a sweep in the ocean, he caught a distinct view of a powerful building, apparently surmounting a lofty rock, and which he had no doubt was the one to which the pirate chief had so triumphantly alluded. It seemed to be built of stone, and possessed four towers, which, as Stanford had remarked, as far as our hero could perceive appeared to be almost impregnable. From the loftiest of these towers could be commanded an uninterrupted view of the ocean for many miles extent, and there was evidently every facility afforded for men of the desperate character of Hugh Granfield and his daring crew. But still it seemed most remarkable to Jack that a place so prominently situated, should hitherto have escaped the suspicion of such vessels as happened to pass near the island; and he awaited with some anxiety to know by what means they had escaped detection. The mystery was, however, to be solved to him in time.

Nearer and nearer the pirate ship approached the destined place, and at length veering round a certain point, they entered a creek, which afforded them a ready means of casting anchor, and of being hidden from immediate observation by surrounding rocks, also of effecting an easy landing. They passed to a certain point, and the anchor was then cast; and our hero awaited the result on the termination of their voyage in a state of the greatest anxiety.

In the meantime, as may be imagined, the feelings of our heroine, as they neared the place of their destination, were in as great a state of excitement as those of her lover, the more especially as she feared the consummation of her fate to be so near at hand. She had her notice directed to the island as soon as Jack, from the shouts which proceeded from the pirate crew; and anxiously she watched it, while her heart sank within her, and she gave herself up almost entirely to despair.

"Alas! alas!" she sighed, "how terrible and hopeless does my fate appear to be. How wild and cheerless seems to be the place to which we are being borne, and what prospect is there of any escape? These barren rocks seem to frown despair upon me, and to bring the certainty of my fearful and revolting destiny still more vividly to my mind's eye. Oh, Jack, dear, faithful partner of my misfortunes, what must be your feelings at the present moment!"

She paused, for at that moment the door of the cabin in which she was confined was opened, and Margaret, whom she had not seen for several hours, again entered.

"Oh, Margaret," ejaculated the damsel, "I feel glad that your are come, for probably you can and will ease my doubts and suspense, and inform me whether the land which now appears in sight of us, and towards which we seem so rapidly bearing, is the place of our destination?"

"It is, Miss Markham," answered Margaret, "and observe you not that tower above one of the rocks, which seems to be almost suspended in mid air?"

"I do," replied Kate.

"That is the place to which we are bound," observed Margaret, "and which is destined to be your future prison, at least until you have yielded to his wishes. It is a strong building, well adapted to his purpose, and many are the extraordinary scenes I have witnessed in it. All who are on the island (which is only a small one,) are in his pay, and therefore he has nothing to fear."

"You speak recklessly, Margaret," said Kate, with a look of reproach; "after what you have recounted to me of your own misfortunes, have you no pity for me?"

"Yes," replied Margaret, "and although you may think differently, I would assist you if I could, but I have not the power. I would advise you to muster all the firmness you can, for that is the only thing on which you have to depend in your present situation."

"Alas!" sighed Kate, "how can I be firm under all the painful circumstances by which I am surrounded at present? Oh, God!—what hope is there left for me and my lover, consigned as we are completely to the mercy of such a heartless miscreant as he, who hold us in his power? Whilst his vessel was still prowling upon the broad bosom of the deep, accident might have sent us some chance of rescue, but now——"

"Nay," interrupted Margaret, "if you have ever entertained any such thoughts, I can assure you they were quite erroneous. Who ever yet encountered the Black Raven that did not suffer defeat? Besides, if Stanford should see the tide of fortune flowing against him, depend upon it that he would not fail to secure his partial triumph in the destruction of yourself and he on whom you seem to have placed your affections."

"Oh, horrible!" exclaimed our heroine; "is it possible that there can be such a demon in human form in existence?"

"It is not only possible but true; of that I can assure you, and I only do so for the purpose of banishing from your mind any false hopes you may hitherto have encouraged," answered Margaret. "But think not that I am harsh, unfeeling, or insensible in the observations I have made to you; a different, a far different feeling has come over me towards you within the last few hours only; and if I could assist you, and extricate you from your present difficulties, I would."

"Oh, thanks, thanks for that assurance," said Kate, fervently; "for it does impart something like a gleam of hope and consolation to my afflicted and lacerated heart. But what brings you to me at the present moment?"

"Merely to prepare you for our landing," replied Margaret, "which will take place in a few minutes. You see that we are rapidly nearing the island."

"Yes, yes," said our heroine, hastily; "what is it called?"

"I know not the original name of it, if it ever had one," said Margaret; "but my destroyer, in whose possession it formerly was, and who first discovered it, gave it the name of 'The Black Raven's Home.'"

"And where is it situated?" eagerly asked the fair prisoner.

"Somewhere on the coast of Africa," answered her companion.

"And what is the origin of that building, and how did it come into the possession of the pirates?"

"That I know not; it was there that Bransden conveyed me, soon after he had effected my destruction; and during the time we remained there, he greatly added to its strength. In fact, it is a complete fortress; and the pirates hold the entire dominion of the island, and have never in my recollection been molested. Indeed, the place appears to be so remote from any other part of the world, that no one seems to be aware of its existence, or if they have by accident touched near it, they certainly appear not to have taken any notice of it."

"Most extraordinary!" ejaculated our heroine. "I am completely lost in amazement. I shudder at the idea of entering it."

"And well you may, Miss Markham," rejoined Margaret, "for though it has its spacious apartments, fitted up in the first style of elegance and luxury, it has also its most frightful dungeons for the refractory, or for those who may oppose the pirates' will. Many, no doubt, have been immured in those dungeons, never to return from them again alive."

"Oh, dreadful!" ejaculated Kate, clasping her hands, "can an All-just Providence suffer such horrors and atrocities to exist without His special retribution?"

"You will probably find that what I have stated to you is not at all exaggerated," returned Margaret; "and I mention them to you not to torture your feelings, but merely to caution you as to your future conduct towards the man in whose power Fate has placed you, and whom it would be worse than madness to attempt to resist."

"Would you, then, have me tamely yield to his diabolical wishes?" demanded the blushing damsel, and her fine eyes flashing with the feelings of indignation that filled her virtuous and gentle bosom.

"I would merely advise you to be cautious in your conduct," replied Margaret.

"By the just God!" exclaimed our heroine, emphatically, "I would sooner suffer a thousand of the most lingering deaths than I would passively yield to the base desires of that monster in human form."

"Those words are bold, Miss Markham," said Margaret; "but what power have you, unprotected as you are, of carrying them into effect?"

"I will trust in the goodness and mercy of Heaven to bear me out," answered our heroine; "and I feel confident that it will not forsake me in such an hour of need."

"Well, I hope it may not," remarked Margaret, with some degree of sincerity in her tone; "though, under all the circumstances as they at present exist, I much fear that you are doomed to be disappointed. You will likewise remember that the fate of your lover depends entirely upon you."

"Alas! alas!" sighed Kate, wringing her hands, and tears gushing to her eyes, "it is that which tortures me more than all. Oh, tell me, what is now his situation?"

"The same as I have before described it to you precisely," answered Margaret.

"And he will be confined in yonder fearful building to which we are so rapidly approaching?" said the unfortunate damsel, in a tone of anguish the most indescribable.

"Undoubtedly so," returned her companion, "and in one of those dungeons I have given you a description of. He cannot expect otherwise, after the rash attempt he made upon Stanford's life. His ultimate fate, I repeat, entirely depends upon you."

"Oh, God!—oh, God!" ejaculated Kate, in accents of despair, "instruct me how to act. I shall go mad!"

"Firmness and prompt decision will alone avail you in this emergency," said Margaret. "You may think me harsh and unfeeling; but knowing the desperate situation in which you are placed, I do but advise you for the best."

"Oh, horrible!" replied the poor girl, fixing upon her a look in the expression of which were blended terror and despair; "how frightful, how revolting are the alternatives you point out to me!"

"They may appear to be so, Miss Markham," replied Margaret; "but they are the only ones I have to offer you, and it is no fault of mine if they are repugnant to your feelings. But see, we have entered the creek, and are preparing to cast anchor. I must rejoin Mark Stanford, for he will probably require to see me—I shall probably return to you again in a few minutes."

Having given utterance to these words, without giving Kate time to reply, Margaret left her; and for a few minutes her mind was so bewildered that she was almost unconscious of what was passing around her. But at length the noise that prevailed on deck from their casting anchor, and making preparations to land, aroused her, and she approached the window of her cabin and watched the proceedings as well as she was enabled to do so. The building, which she had been informed was to be her future prison, now stood out in bold relief before her eyes, and inspired her bosom with a feeling of dread which she found it impossible to conquer; and various were the painful thoughts which passed in rapid succession before her mind. Something, however, of far more importance, shortly diverted her attention, and absorbed her every feeling. Suddenly she saw a boat lowered over the ship's side, into which two of the pirates leapt, and were quickly followed by two others, leading between them her unfortunate lover, heavily ironed, and whose countenance, as she caught a faint glimpse of it in the bright moonlight which now streamed across the ocean, appeared ghastly pale and distorted by a variety of the most torturing and indescribable emotions.

How shall we seek to describe the feelings of the poor girl at that moment? Her heart turned deadly sick;—she clasped her hands vehemently together, and could not repress a scream, though there was no one to hear her or likely to take the least heed of her anguish.

Having been placed in the boat, our hero turned one look of anguish towards the vessel, as if doubtful whether it was intended that her whom he so fondly loved was to follow, and Kate had then a more distinct view of his countenance, and the anguish of her mind was increased when she saw the deep expression of despair that was stamped upon it. But it was only for a very brief period that she was permitted to gaze upon it; another moment and the boat put off from the vessel, and dashed on its way towards the island. The moon shone so brightly that she was enabled distinctly to watch its progress, and she did so with the deepest intensity and anxiety of feeling. It was not long in reaching the shore, and having landed, her unfortunate lover and the pirates were quickly hidden from her view; but still she remained with her eyes steadily fixed upon the spot, and in about ten minutes she observed the pirates return to the boat, and plying themselves to the oars, once more made their way towards the vessel, which they reached in a short time, and two of them came on board, while the others remained in the boat, apparently waiting for further orders. Kate guessed full well what they would be, and she was not long kept in suspense. She heard the tread of hasty footsteps outside her cabin, and directly afterwards the door was thrown open, and Pierce and another of the crew appeared. Our heroine shrunk back on beholding them, and could not conceal the terror she experienced, but her emotion was too great to suffer her to speak, and Pierce advancing towards her, said in abrupt tones—

"We have arrived at last at the place of our destination, young lady, and Jack Junk is already safely housed; we must trouble you to follow him, for such are our captain's orders."

"Heaven have mercy upon me, and protect me!" ejaculated the poor girl, in a voice of anguish.

"Well, well," returned the ruffian Pierce; "it is not our place to listen to any such jargon as that; all that we have to do is to obey our instructions, and those are to convey you as quickly as possible, after your lover, to our *rather* formidable retreat yonder."

PIERCE ENDEAVOURS TO ROUSE THE PIRATE FROM HIS SUPERSTITIOUS FEARS.

"Well," said our heroine, mustering all the fortitude she could for the desperate occasion, "I submit, for well I know that it is useless to remonstrate with men so entirely destitute of every proper feeling as yourselves. I place myself in the hands of that Almighty Power, whose laws I have never yet wilfully broken, and sincerely trust that He will see both myself and the much-wronged man who has fallen into your hands through the difficulties which at present surround us."

As the beautiful Kate thus spoke, she clasped her hands, and raised her eyes devoutly towards Heaven, and she then calmly resigned herself to the guidance of the ruffian Pierce and his companions. She was far more composed and firm than could have been expected from a person placed in her fearful and peculiar situation, and even Pierce and the other ruffians were astonished and abashed, and could not help treating her with some little degree of respect. All that she feared, was, that she would encounter the miscreant, Mark Stanford, when they arrived upon deck, for the bare sight of him she felt confident would fill her breast with horror, and quite unnerve her for the task she was so anxious to perform. However, she was spared that pain and annoyance, for, whatever might have been the intentions of the pirate captain previously, he had abandoned them, and did not make his appearance at the time of poor Kate's departure.

On arriving on deck, our heroine cast her eyes mournfully towards the black and formidable prison to which she was about to be consigned, as its dark wall frowned like a monstrous libel upon the bright moonlight which streamed with such effulgence upon all around,—and she could not repress a deep and heartfelt sigh; but it was not so much on her own account as that of her lover, whose sufferings she well knew at that moment, must be most excruciating, and almost insupportable. She had not, however, many moments given her for reflection, for at that moment Pierce slightly but significantly nudged her arm, and pointed to the boat, and glancing her eyes towards it, she had the satisfaction to perceive that Margaret was already in it, and she, therefore, prepared to enter it with more alacrity than she could otherwise have done. Pierce handed her into the boat himself, and two more of the pirates following; and then Kate, almost overpowered by her feelings, sank into the arms of Margaret, and became nearly insensible. Margaret uttered a few words of encouragement and consolation to her, and they revived her, and the boat moved rapidly on its way towards the place of their destination, which they were not long in arriving at. Having landed at the same spot where she had seen them land her lover, they turned round an abrupt angle of the rock, and Kate had then a clear view of the island, in the broad and mellow light of the moon, and also of the gloomy building to which the ruffians were conveying her, and whose dark walls seemed to frown despair upon her.

The building, as we have before stated, was situated on the summit of a lofty and apparently almost inaccessible rock, and our heroine wondered by what means they could reach it; but she was not long kept in suspense upon that subject, for on arriving at the foot of the rock, she beheld a small cavity just sufficiently wide for one person to pass through at a time, and on passing through it, and one of the pirates having opened a lantern which he had brought with him for the purpose, she perceived that they were in a pretty spacious cavern evidently formed by the hands of nature, and at the further end of it was a rude and lofty flight of steps hewn out of the solid rock, and which must have been a work of considerable time and labour, and it was indeed wonderful how it could ever have been accomplished. Pierce and the other pirates, led her towards these steps, followed by Margaret, and they immediately began to ascend them. They were winding, and seemed to conduct to the very summit of the rock; but the task of ascending them was one of great fatigue, and Kate was frequently compelled to halt on the way, in order to rest herself, and regain her breathe. At length, however, they emerged from the rock, and stood immediately before the gloomy building.

Our heroine cast her eyes around her in despair, and the view she had of the island, and the surrounding ocean, was of the most extensive description, and inspired her with a feeling of awe which she found it impossible to control. But very little time was allowed her to indulge in this contemplation, for Pierce having took a key from his pocket, applied it to the lock of a ponderous door, which, after much exertion, yielded, and they entered a dark passage of not very considerable extent; which having quickly traversed, they came to the top of a narrow staircase, which seemed to lead to some of the places under the building. Kate shuddered as they began to descend them, and clung to Margaret, who tried to inspire her with firmness, and not altogether without success, for she partly recovered herself, and descended the stairs with a steadier and more resolute step than could have been expected. On reaching the bottom, they found themselves in a subterranean passage, and on each side of which were heavy doors, at different distances, and which seemed to open upon a series of vaults or dungeons, and which fully corroborated the statement of Margaret. Kate shuddered and trembled as she passed them, and wondered to herself whether her unfortunate lover was confined in one of them; but she did not venture to question her ruffianly conductors, and she heard no sounds proceed from any of them which would have convinced her that any hapless being was at that time incarcerated in them.

Having traversed the full extent of this dismal passage, they arrived at another door, the bolts of which Pierce withdrew, and they then found themselves at the foot of a wide and lofty staircase, which evidently led to the upper part of the building, and on gaining the top, and passing along a gallery, on either side of which were several doors, which seemed to open upon different apartments, they turned round an angle to the left, and immediately afterwards stopped at a door, between the chinks of which a light glimmered, and led our heroine to suppose that it was inhabited. Pierce unlocked it, and they entered a spacious and rather well furnished apartment, in which a cheerful fire was blazing. There were two windows in the room, but they were heavily barred, and gave it all the aspect of a prison. Kate sank exhausted on a seat, and Pierce having gazed at her for a moment or two in silence, said—

"This and the apartment beyond it, are those which are allotted to the present use of yourself, Kate Markham, and Margaret. I wish you good-night, and pleasant dreams and reflections to you."

"Alas! alas!" sighed our heroine, "and is there no hope for me?—But tell me where is my lover confined?"

"In the other tower," answered Pierce; "but I dare say you will hear more of him when our captain pays you a visit, which no doubt he will shortly do, in order to congratulate you on your save arrival at the place of your destination."

Kate made no reply, but wrung her hands in the anguish of her feelings.

"You will attend to your instructions, Margaret?" said Pierce; "you will find refreshments in the adjoining room."

Having given utterance to these words, he and his companions quitted the room, and Kate and Margaret were left to themselves. For some time after they had departed, our heroine was too much overpowered by her feelings to speak, but she gave vent to her emotions in a copious flood of tears, and the bitter sobs that escaped her bosom were quite piteous to hear. Margaret evidently felt for her, but she did not attempt to interrupt her, for she thought that the free indulgence in her grief might serve to alleviate, in some degree, the anguish of her feelings.

"Oh, God!" poor Kate at length exclaimed, "how terrible is my situation!—how fearful is the fate which so mercilessly pursues me and he to whom my heart is so fondly devoted! Confined in this gloomy building, and entirely at the mercy of our ferocious and remorseless persecutor, we are shut out entirely from all hope; and what can we expect but that inevitable destruction will overtake us? Better, far better would it have been for us had we both perished in the storm, rather than be consigned to such a fate as that which is at present impending over us. Oh, Margaret, do you not pity me?"

"You may believe me that I do," replied Margaret; "but of what avail is that? I have no power to assist you, as you must be aware, situated as I am, or I would willingly do so, prejudiced even as you may be against my character."

"If I have wronged you, Margaret," said our heroine, "I sincerely regret it, and beseech your forgiveness—but surely you will be ready to make every allowance for a person placed in my deplorable and hopeless situation?"

"I do so, Miss Markham," returned her companion, "and would advise you not unnecessarily to distress yourself."

"Alas!" ejaculated Kate, "how can I do otherwise? Has not the miscreant Stanford got me completely in his power?—and can I expect that he will fail to put his diabolical threats into execution?"

"Endeavour to remain firm," observed Margaret, "and to hope that something will yet occur to rescue you and your lover from his power."

"Alas!" sighed our heroine, "I feel that it would be little short of madness for me to do so. Confined in this dreadful place, far away from our native land, and without a friend who has the means, if they even had the will, to interfere in our behalf, what hope is there for us? Oh, God! as these thoughts flash upon my brain, I feel as if I am about to go distracted! Dear Jack! how terrible must be the anguish, the insupportable agony of mind you are now enduring! Would to Heaven that I were permitted to be near you, that I might endeavour to impart to you some consolation. The hardened villain, Stanford, has threatened to heap his vengeance upon your head—and too well do I know his character to imagine that anything will move him from his sanguinary and deadly purpose!"

"Your lover acted rashly in making so daring and hopeless an attack upon the pirate captain," remarked Margaret.

"True," coincided Kate; "but was there not every excuse to be offered for him, when he saw me placed in so terrible a situation? Dear Jack! Providence will surely not allow you to suffer for that noble and manly act. Will the wretch, in whose power we both are, remain deaf to my supplications?"

"Experience," replied Margaret "should convince you that he will. It is only by a compliance with his wishes that you can hope to save your lover."

"For Heaven's sake do not mention such a thing," said out heroine; "for the bare thought of it makes me shudder with disgust and horror. Death by the most lingering tortures would not be half so dreadful as the revolting fate to which you have alluded."

"And yet, Miss Markham," observed her companion; "it would be cruel and unjust to lead you to suppose that any resistance on your part would be of the least avail. While you were on board the Black Raven, there was some slight degree of chance for you, but here there is none."

"Too well I feel the force of what you say," ejaculated our heroine; "and I tremble with horror and apprehension. I shall go mad."

"Be calm," said Margaret; "for these bursts of agony will only serve to increase the evils by which you are surrounded."

"Be calm?" returned the damsel, shaking her head mournfully; "Oh, how utterly useless it is for you to talk to me thus! And those beloved friends I have left behind me; oh! what has become of them? Dear uncle! beloved Constance! what fate has befallen you? Tell me, Margaret, I beseech you, do you know anything concerning them?"

"I do not," answered Margaret; "or I would communicate it to you."

"Alas!" sighed Kate; "the more I think of them my heart misgives me; I fear that something dreadful has happened to them, the more especially when I recall to my memory the confusion and agitation which Mark Standford evinced on each occasion when I alluded to them."

"Do not encourage any such apprehensions," said Margaret, "for I trust that they will prove to be unfounded. But come, you had better partake of some refreshment; for you must much need it now."

"Oh, no," returned the poor girl; "my heart is too full to suffer me to eat."

"Nay," said Margaret, "try to take a little; it will serve to revive you."

Kate returned no answer, but sinking back in her chair, she covered her face with her hands, and again burst into a paroxysm of sobs and tears. Margaret opened the door of the room, which was fitted up as a chamber, and contained a couple of beds, and brought forward the refreshment which she found upon a table, and placing it before her, once more endeavoured to prevail upon her to partake of it. Our heroine, however, could only be induced to taste a small portion of wine, and then turned away from the table with the same sickly and trembling feeling.

All was profoundly still in the building, and they might almost have been led to suppose that they were the only persons in the place.

"And has Mark Stanford left the ship?" interrogated Kate.

"Doubtless he has by this time," replied Margaret, "and is at present in the house."

"What a shuddering sensation of fear comes over me at that thought," remarked our heroine. "Should he venture to intrude upon me by his hated presence, in my present state of mind, alas! what will become of me?"

"Nay, Miss Markham," returned her companion; "do not entertain any such apprehensions, for I can confidently assure you that they are unfounded. Stanford will not venture to visit you to-night, and you may perceive we have the means of preventing intrusion by fastening ourselves in."

"But I shall see him to-morrow, no doubt," said the damsel, "and be again compelled to listen to his odious and sinful vows. Oh, how I tremble at the thought. God of Heaven, I humbly, but earnestly implore Thee to look down with mercy upon myself and my unfortunate lover, and not to suffer the brutal wretch who holds us in his power, to triumph altogether in his diabolical designs."

"Courage, Kate Markham," observed Margaret, "and depend upon it that your supplications will not remain altogether unheard. But it is late, and as you must be worn out with fatigue and anxiety of mind, had you not better retire to rest?"

"Rest!" repeated our heroine, in the most melancholy accents; "alas! I fear there will be none for me. How can I hope to obtain rest, with all these dreadful thoughts upon my mind? Oh, my unfortunate lover, and how are you situated? How frightful, I have too much reason to fear, are the sufferings to which you are subjected by our cruel enemy."

"And of what use is it to give way to those dismal thoughts and feelings?" demanded Margaret; "be firm, and, after all, things may not turn out so bad as you anticipate."

"Comparatively happy, indeed, should I be," replied Kate, "could I encourage the feelings you have just now expressed; but when I take into consideration all the fearful circumstances of the situation of myself and he who is by far more dear to me than my very existence, I find that it is utterly impossible. Of what use is it for me to encourage delusive hopes which I fear can never be realised?"

"And if you thus give way entirely to despair," returned Margaret, "are you not the more likely to fall an easy victim to Mark Stanford?"

"By Heaven, it cannot be!" exclaimed our heroine, with fresh energy, and struggling against her feelings, "the Almighty will not permit the guilty wretch Stanford to triumph altogether in his nefarious and disgusting wishes. It would be to arraign the justice and mercy of the Supreme to imagine such a thing!"

"There you spoke as you ought to do," remarked Margaret, the alteration in whose behaviour was most extraordinary; "and I would advise you to continue to indulge in such feelings. But come, it is useless to remain longer in conversation, so let us hasten to bed, and live in hopeful expectation of what to-morrow will produce."

"Margaret," said our heroine, "I do now believe that you sympathise with me in my misfortunes, and I feel sincerely grateful to you for it."

"I require no thanks, Miss Markham," replied her companion; "but I must be allowed to repeat that I would serve you if I could, though I see no probability at present, at any rate, of my being able to do so. Should the opportunity ever occur, you may depend upon me."

Our heroine again returned her acknowledgments, and Margaret having secured the door on the inside, they entered the chamber, which, as we have before stated, was fitted up with every degree of comfort. Here Kate once more sank on her knees, and supplicated in the most devout and earnest tones, the protection of Heaven; and then, at the urgent request of Margaret, she suffered her to assist her to undress, and retired to bed; but it was some time ere the painful and conflicting thoughts which harassed her mind would permit her to sleep; but at last worn out with the unusual fatigue and exertion she had undergone, the drowsy God descended upon her eyelids, and she obtained a short respite from her cares and anxieties.

The place in which Jack Junk was confined, was situated at the top of one of the towers, and was a small stone room, destitute of every other furniture than an old mattress, and which received light from a small sky-light only. The walls were black and damp, and the atmosphere was most nauseous and suffocating. They did not remove his irons on placing him there, and his limbs were tortured with the pain they caused. But what were all his bodily, compared with his mental sufferings? For some time after the ruffians had left him, he was in a state of mind bordering upon frenzy, and gave utterance to the most wild and rambling observations, railing against the cruel fate which pursued him, and invoking the heaviest curses upon the head of his remorseless and diabolical persecutor. But far still greater was the agony which the fearful situation in which his beloved and faithful Kate was placed, created in his breast than his own sufferings, and for some time he was unable to find the least degree of hope or comfort.

"Oh, Kate! unfortunate Kate! how unmerited is the cruel destiny it is your hard lot to endure," he cried; "it would seem that Providence had forsaken you altogether, and left you at the mercy of one of the greatest miscreants that ever disgraced society. And what have you ever done to deserve this? Your whole life has been one of virtue and innocence, and in endeavouring to do all the good in your power for your fellow-creatures, and surely this is not the reward you should receive for it. Confined in this fearful building, so far away from the land of your birth, and without any one at hand to render you the least assistance, what will become of you?—What can save you from the awful and revolting fate with which Mark Stanford has threatened you?—I shall go mad!—And here must I remain, knowing your inevitable fate, and without having it in my power to render you the least assistance. Oh, Jack, Jack, this is the severest storm you have ever encountered, and quite unmans you. Great God, I earnestly implore you to look down with mercy upon us, and to interpose to rescue us from the power of this fiend in human shape."

He clasped his hands together, and for some time the extreme anguish of his feelings deprived him of the power of utterance. He fancied to himself the scene which would take place when Mark Stanford and Kate should meet again. How would she be able to repulse his bold and disgusting advances? and of what use would be all the resistance which she could offer, when opposed to such a hardened and determined villain? Her fate was sealed, and there seemed to be no possibility of her escaping from it; and that thought again drove him to a point verging upon distraction.

"And must one so fair and innocent as my poor Kate, become the helpless victim of such a monster as this pirate captain?" he cried, after a pause; "must all her bright hopes be annihilated; her sunny prospects become for ever shrouded by the black clouds of shame and sorrow, and despair? Forbid it, Heaven! for the thought is too dreadful, too revolting to dwell upon. Oh, would that my sword had been buried in the miscreant's black heart, when we lately encountered each other; for although my own life would probably have paid the penalty of the deed, she would at least have been saved from shame and degradation. Oh, that I had him now at my mercy, I would have ample revenge for all the cruelty of which he has been guilty. My poor Kate, surely such manifold sufferings as those to which you are subjected, are sufficient to break your heart; and it is not possible that you can much longer bear up against them."

Again he was compelled to pause, in consequence of the overwhelming power of his emotions, and he groaned aloud in the bitterness of his despair. Worn out with the anguish of his mind and body, he threw himself, as well as his irons would permit, on the stone bench, by which the gloomy and wretched place in which he was confined, was surrounded, and for some time gave himself up to those racking thoughts which it would be a fruitless task for us to attempt to describe.   All the scenes of his past life moved in rapid succession before his imagination, and the awful contrast which the present suggested, tended, if possible, to increase his emotion, and to mock at every attempt he made to encourage hope.   Alas! what an unfortunate day it was that introduced the villain Mark Stanford to them, and how deeply he regretted that he had not sooner become acquainted with his real character, when all the evils which had since taken place might have been prevented.

In this dismal and painful manner the time wore on, and our hero must have been several hours in his present place of confinement; but no one came near him, and though he frequently listened attentively, his ears could not catch the least sound that was stirring in the building; but he imagined that the pirates had placed him in too remote a part of the house from that occupied by themselves for him to hear them.   To sleep was impossible, and the most frightful ideas continued to haunt and harass his disordered imagination.   It was not without the greatest difficulty that he could restrain his feelings within the bounds of reason, and again and again he cursed his hard fate, and lamented the hour that ever he was born.

At length the light from the window, or skylight, above his head, showed him that it was morning, and a short time afterwards he heard heavy footsteps ascending the stairs which led to the place where he was confined; the bolts were withdrawn, and the door being opened, one of the pirates entered, bringing with him a pitcher of water, and a coarse black loaf, which having placed by his side, he was about to retire without saying a word, when our hero eagerly exclaimed—

" Stay one moment, I request of you, and answer me a question or two."

"I have no right to answer questions," returned the man; " but what is it you wish to know ? —Be quick, for I have no time to waste."

" Tell me," said Jack Junk, " is the unfortunate Kate Markham brought to this building?"

" She is," answered the man; " and no doubt our captain will soon be able to satisfy her of his power, if she be not convinced already."

" The cowardly miscreant !" observed our hero, swelling with indignation.

" Well," said the pirate, " that may be your opinion, my young sea-lion, the tar for all weathers, as you are called, I believe; but it strikes me rater forcibly that Hugh Granfield, the rover of the seas, has proved sufficient to the lubbers that have come in contact with him, that he does not want for bravery.   And let me give you a bit of wholesome advice, young man, and it may not be altogether lost upon you, that bravery does not alway exist in wearing his Majesty's uniform, and in swallowing the plums so plentifully supplied by the Admiralty lords to such innocents as you, whilst they swallow all the pudding and get fat on it; I say that bravery is the best which boldly resists all such impostures, and makes an independence of its own."

" Why—why," said our hero, somewhat diverted from his melancholy thought, by the novelty of the pirate's ideas; " damme, if you aint quite a philosopher.   Where might you happen to have gone to school?"

' Lor' bless you, my hearty," returned the man, with the same coolness, " I never went to school at all: I was born so.   But let me offer you one more word of simple advice, and that is not to be quite so plentiful of your abuse, to be rather more choice in your language when addressing such gentlemen as us, or you might, perchance, find yourself slung up at the yard-arm, some fine morning, Mr. Jack Junk, before you could as much as cry 'Jack Robinson.' Good morning to you."

The fellow was again going to leave the miserable room in which our hero was confined, when the later once more detained him, and, in an impressive manner observed :—

" Be not so hasty, mate ; I see you are not altogether a bad sort of a fellow, and I dare say you will be able to make some allowances for a brother tar placed in the situation that I am. Kate Markham, my darling Kate, will not be sacrificed to—to—Never mind, I will not give utterance to the words which my feelings would prompt me to; your captain, this Mark Stanford, as he calls himself, will not persist in carrying out his threats against that inno-cent girl?"

" Why, as for that," answered the pirate, " it is his business, and not mine ; but, as you have asked me for my opinion, I will give it you, candidly, as I entertain it, and that is this, that all our captain has promised or threatened to do, he will perform, even at the hazard of his life. Therefore, if you are wise, you will not flatter yourself with false hopes, for it is not at all likely that Hugh Granfield is going to abandon a prize which has cost him so much trouble to obtain possession of.   As surely as your name is Jack Junk, will Kate Markham become the mistress of Hugh Granfield, the commander of the Black Raven and the rover of the seas."

"No!" exclaimed our hero, energetically, "by all my hopes, it cannot, will not be—the great Commander who sails aloft, and steers us through all difficulties, will never permit one of His fairest craft to be thus quicksanded, or driven on a lee-shore by such a rascally swab as the fellow you disgrace yourself by calling captain."

"Well, my lad," returned the pirate, cooly, "I suppose you have a right to enjoy your opinion as well as myself, and all the harm I wish you is, that you may not be disappointed in your hopes."

"But—"

"I have no more questions to answer, mate!" interrupted the pirate; "good morning." And before our hero had time to make use of another observation, the man had departed.

Jack struck his forehead in despair, and in vain endeavoured for a considerable time to regain anything like composure, or to collect his thoughts; but at last he said—

"And thus is it designed, Jack, after all the years that you have been buffetted about, cradled in the deep as you were, you are wrecked at last, cast upon a desolate island, and bereft of rudder or compass, unable to take the soundings, or to take the weather-gauge of hope. My poor girl—my poor girl. But no, I will not entirely despair; I have too firm a confidence in the mercy of Providence, to believe that she, so lovely and so good, can ever meet with the fate with which she is at the present moment threatened."

He endeavoured to console himself and to become more firm by entertaining and encouraging such thoughts as those, and he certainly succeeded much better than the painful circumstances under which she who held the sole dominion of his heart, nay, his very soul, and himself, could have led any person to suppose. Still the time passed most drearily away, and there was nothing whatever in the dismal place in which he was confined to relieve his thoughts. Had their been an accessible window, by which he could have obtained a view of the island and the surrounding ocean, it might have been the means of diverting his mind from the more painful business which occupied it, but as he was situated, he was left entirely to despair. But we will leave him, for the present, and return to the pirate captain, Hugh Granfield, who having left the vessel after the debarkation of our hero and heroine, was seated in one of the apartments of the Raven's nest, (as he had thought proper to call the impregnable building of which he had, for many years been the master), regaling himself over a bottle of brandy, and exulting in the success of his diabolical designs so far.

"Well accomplished, Hugh Granfield," he soliloquised to himself; "well accomplished, although it has not been without an arduous struggle, and the cost of gold. But what care I for that? I have now in my power, not only the means of vengeance, but a treasure which monarchs might envy, and trust me but I shall know how to take advantage of the opportunity which fortune has provided me with of gratifying all my wishes. Kate Markham, within those strong and gloomy walls in the midst of the wide ocean, on a spot of which I am the supreme sovereign, far away from those who might interpose in your behalf, what chance is there of your escaping the fate to which I have destined you? Of what avail will be the resistance which you are certain to offer to the gratification of my will? none whatever! it would be preposterous to do so. Scornful beauty, the hour of my triumph approaches; and yet—psha! why this qualmishness? why the singular feeling that comes over me? Is it well that the murderer should become the seducer of his victim's daughter? Who spoke? Bah! I am becoming childish, and yet I could almost have sworn that I heard some one say 'murderer!' Nay, 'twas a mere idle phantasy; and yet, can I banish from my memory the ghastly features of Horace Markham, when, clinging to the vessel's side which I then commanded, I severed his hand from his arm, and consigned him to his fate? Can I forget the corpse of that mysterious man, Reuben of the Cliff, floating upright before my eyes after his brutal assassination? Can I cease to remember the—"

"Why, how now, captain?" asked Pierce Raker, entering hastily; "you look agitated and alarmed, when you should be all joy and exultation. What is the meaning of this?"

"I have been thinking of the past, Pierce," replied the pirate captain.

"Thinking of the devil!" returned the former, abruptly; "think only of the triumph you have achieved—that you have the girl and your rival securely in your power—that you can accomplish all the designs upon which you have fixed your mind at any moment you please, and there will be no room for the sombre looks which you at present assume. But pray, of what may you have been thinking so seriously?"

"Of the deeds of the past," replied Mark Stanford;—"of the inhuman murder of the damsel's father;—of the dying observations of Reuben of the Cliff; of the more than probable assassination of Mr Markham; of——"

"Ha! ha! ha!" interrupted the hardened villain, Pierce, ironically; "you need not proceed with your summary of all those horrible affairs, for what you have already stated are quite sufficient for me. Qualmish again, I see you are. Bah!—I have no patience with such absurdities, and surprised I am that the captain of the Black Raven, the terror of the ocean, should yield himself to such weakness. Horace Markham you sacrificed to gratify your revenge, it was gratified, and there was an end to that business;—the old maniac, Reuben of the Cliff, knew too many of your secrets, and therefore, if you had any value for your own safety, it was fit he should be got rid of; the uncle of Kate Markham, if he be dead, which I have no doubt he is, lost his life entirely through his own mad precipitation, and should not trouble your mind for an instant. Every other consideration ought to yield to the satisfaction that you have achieved the point you wished, namely, to get the lovely Kate in your power, and that all your wishes can be gratified at any moment you please."

"Well," observed Stanford, still hesitating, but endeavouring to conquer the reproaches of conscience before the banterings of Pierce;—"I must acknowledge that there is some truth in the observations you have made; but still, I cannot exactly conquer certain forebodings which have lately taken possession of my mind, that the time is fast approaching when my career will be at an end, and—"

"Forebodings!" again interrupted Pierce, impatiently; "oh, what sickening nonsense is this;—fit conversation for a child, but totally unworthy of one who has been accustomed to brave all perils and difficulties like yourself, and who is supposed to be invulnerable to fear."

"Invulnerable to fear, Pierce?" said the pirate captain, proudly, and in a moment assuming his accustomed demeanour; "and so I am;—but who is invulnerable to the voice of conscience? Pierce Raker, we may possess hearts of adamant, we may brave horror in its most ghastly shape: we may laugh to scorn that which would make ordinary individuals quake and tremble; but the small still voice of conscience must be heard, however callous we may attempt to be, and however we may seek to close our ears against it."

"Well, I declare, captain," remarked Pierce, with another ironical laugh, "you would make a most excellent parson."

"No jeers, Pierce," returned Stanford, frowning, "for I am not in the humour to brook them. You know not all the particulars of my strange and eventful life, or I doubt much if you would treat so idly the observations I have made use of; but some other time, probably, I may make you better acquainted with them, and then you will be in a better condition to judge of the reason of my present conduct."

"Very true, captain," said Pierce, "I hope I have not offended by what I have said, and, perhaps, as it does not seem to be agreeable to you, we may as well drop the present subject."

"Yes, yes," replied Stanford hastily quaffing off a bumper of brandy; "perhaps I have been weak and foolish in giving way to the impressions which for the moment came over me, but I will endeavour to think no more of them. Drink, drink! We are here, in our rock-based castle; fortune smiles upon me, as it has ever hitherto done, and why should I give way to gloomy thoughts?"

"Why, that was my impression, captain," said Pierce, "and that made me make use of the observations I did. Who can boast a prouder palace than the rover of the seas? Who can pride themselves upon possessing a fairer mistress than Kate Markham, his future partner?"

"True, true, Pierce," replied the pirate captain, regaining his wonted spirits; "but my prize, my lovely prize, the beauteous Kate—you have secured her in the apartments that were prepared for her reception, have you not?"

"Certainly," answered Pierce.

"'Tis well," observed Stanford; "and how did she appear in spirits?"

"She assumed much more fortitude than I had expected."

"That is also fortunate," said Stanford;—"to-morrow I will see her, and once more make those advances towards her which it will be madness in her to attempt to resist. May I never again float upon salt water, if she shall not be wholly mine before a week has elapsed."

"Well spoken, captain," said Pierce,—"and what is there to prevent you from gratifying your wishes to their fullest extent?"

"Nothing whatever, that I can perceive at present."

"It is impossible that you can be foiled in your designs, if you are determined."

"And of that you may rest assured I am. Jack Junk is also secure enough, now."

"Perfectly so."

"Ha! ha! ha!" laughed the villain, Mark Stanford, triumphantly, "I dare say his reflections at the present moment are very pleasant."

"No doubt they are," returned Pierce. "But what are your future intentions as regards him?"

"Oh, that entirely depends upon Kate," replied Stanford.

"You do not intend to sacrifice his life?"

"No, perhaps it would not be policy for me to do so."

"I do not think it would."

THE COMBAT BETWEEN JACK JUNK AND THE PIRATE.

"That would have too serious an effect upon Kate," remarked Stanford; "and perhaps deprive me at once of her whom it has cost me so much trouble and expense to obtain possession of."

"True," coincided Pierce.

"Oh, Pierce!" said Stanford, "I have marked out such a career of bliss with that scornful beauty, that I feel myself totally inadequate to describe. Do you not summon to your recollection that memorable first of May, when she not only rejected, repulsed my advances as Farmer Stanford, but also insulted me?"

"Perfectly well, captain."

"Do you not remember the treatment I received from her lover; the scorn with which I was treated? The blow I received from him who is now my prisoner?"

"Is it likely that I can forget it, captain?" demanded Pierce.

"And that proud upstart is now my prisoner, and at my mercy," said Mark Stanford, with looks of savage exultation.

"He is,' said Pierce, "and I presume that he has little mercy to expect from you?"

"Such mercy as the wolf bestows upon the lamb," returned the pirate captain. "Oh, it will be my delight to torture him, and what can more tend to do so than the degradation of her to whom he is so fondly, so ardently devoted? Even now the thoughts of the agony he must be enduring at the situation of himself and his beloved Kate, and the certainty that there is no chance of their being released from my power, is bliss to my imagination. But what will be his feelings when he knows that all which I have threatened is accomplished, and his Kate, his innocent Kate, is lost to him for ever? Ha! ha! ha!—there is triumph in the thought, and—Hark!"

"What now?" demanded Pierce, hastily, seeing his villanous companion start and turn pale.

"Did you not hear a sound?"

"A sound! what sound?"

"A groan."

"Pshaw!" returned Pierce, contemptuously, "you must have been dreaming."

"Dreaming! what, with my eyes and ears wide open?" said the pirate captain, in a hollow voice, and gazing earnestly towards the window of the room in which they were seated, and through which the moonbeams streamed proudly;—"I tell you, Pierce, again, that I heard a groan, solemn as from the precincts of the tomb, and as distinctly as sound ever smote my ears."

"Are you mad?"

"No, but I must be so if I could disbelieve the evidence of my senses."

"Those senses are evidently wandering," remarked Pierce, with a half laugh. "Why, captain, I really am surprised at you, and can scarcely believe that it is the daring Hugh Granfield to whom I am speaking."

"You may treat my observations lightly," returned the pirate captain with his eyes still fixed upon the window, "but I speak the truth."

"Nonsense! it must have been the wind that deceived you," said Pierce. "Take some more brandy, and endeavour to drown these strange fancies."

"No—no," said Stanford, in a faint voice, "I—I cannot drink just now. What can be the meaning of this strange and unconquerable feeling that has come over me?"

"Drink—drink, I say again," replied Pierce, "and that will doubtless dissipate it."

"No, no, I—I cannot!"

"Why do you fix your eyes so steadfastly upon that window?"

"Do you not see anything?"

"See anything? certainly not, except the moonbeams," answered his companion; "your senses have evidently for the moment left you. Come, come, do not give way to such absurdities as these; arouse yourself."

"There, again!" faintly ejaculated Stanford, and grasping the arm of Pierce; "you must have heard that."

"I heard nothing," was the reply; "what are you now dreaming about?"

"Pierce," said the pirate captain, in a hollow voice, and which bespoke the extreme emotion and excitement under which he laboured, "you mock me."

"I have no wish to do so," replied the former; "but I would fain banish from your mind the ridiculous and erroneous ideas that have taken possession of it."

"I again distinctly heard that solemn groan," said Stanford.

"What an absurdity is this."

"It is none, Pierce; and now, oh, horror, it glares upon me! look—look! 'tis there still! Oh, this can be no mockery, it is no delusion!"

Pierce did indeed gaze in the same direction as that towards which the eyes of his trembling companion were fixed so steadfastly, but he could behold nothing, and he endeavoured to divert his attention—but in vain.

"Oh how awful!" gasped forth the guilty man: "and yet so like him when in life. Shade of my murdered victim, avaunt! I dare not gaze upon you! Your ghastly looks freeze my soul with horror! Pierce—Pierce, shield me—save me!"

Thus wildly ejaculating, Mark Stanford, overpowered with feelings of terror, sunk in the arms of his astonished companion, and hid his face on his shoulder.

"Well," observed Pierce, after a pause; "this is most unaccountable. There is nothing here to alarm you, captain Arouse yourself, I say again."

"Are you blind? would you seek to deceive me?" said Stanford. "I saw it plainly—it could be no delusion of the brain."

"It could be nothing else," returned Pierce; "I have watched earnestly in the direction you indicated, and could not perceive anything."

Mark Stanford now ventured to raise his head, and gazed once more in the direction of the window.

"Ah!" he said, "it is not there now—but a moment since, and its filmy eyes were fixed upon me."

"What was it you imagined you beheld?" asked Pierce.

"It was no imagination," replied Stanford, hastily; "it was the ghastly countenance of Horace Markham I saw, at the very moment when I mentioned the name of his daughter."

"Psha!" observed Pierce, with a look of incredulity, "I could not have believed you capable of such weakness, captain. Come, take some more brandy, and that will revive you."

"Well," said Stanford, after a pause, and having recovered himself in some measure; "I must have been deceived."

"It is certain that you were," answered Pierce; "you have suffered your imagination to lead you astray, captain."

"And yet I could have sworn that I saw the death face peering in at the window in the moonlight," said the pirate captain.

"Banish such an idea from your mind," returned his companion, "for it is unworthy of you. Drink—drink!"

Mark Stanford did indeed drink copiously, and in a short time he recovered himself altogether and even ventured to laugh at his previous terrors.

"I will no more give way to such weakness as that which I have just now displayed," he said; "let the past be forgotten—it is enough for me to know that I triumph in my present designs, and I will not fail to find the resolution to pursue them. Kate Markham is mine, and no earthly power can release her from me."

"Well said, captain," replied Pierce, "and now you talk like yourself again."

"To-morrow, I will visit her," said Stanford; "no longer will I delay, and then shall she find that I am determined to carry out all the threats I have made to their fullest extent."

"Well, captain," observed Pierce, "now you certainly do speak a little more reasonable, than, I must be permitted to say, you have spoken upon the same subject for some time past. Of course, it is no use wavering, or giving way to the heroics (don't they call them so?) of these young girls; the main thing in this—you know that you have a certain object to obtain, and that must be obtained, and consequently, it is useless to stand upon the nicety, capriciousness, or would-be delicacy of the individual who opposes you, but at once achieve your object at all risks."

"You speak well, Pierce," said Stanford, "you speak reasonably, and I perfectly agree with you in all that you have stated respecting my fair prisoner and her lover. I shall act on your advice. I will see my friend, Jack Junk, presently, and no doubt the meeting, and the observations I shall have to make to him, will afford his mind some rational relaxation under his present solitary circumstances."

"Ha! ha! ha!" laughed the villain, Pierce, exultingly; "not a bad idea that, of yours captain. Yes, I fancy that the pride of the ocean, the tar for all weathers, will begin to think that he has run-aground this time. But I must again congratulate you, Stanford, upon having been able to bring your mind to form the resolution in spite of all misgivings of conscience (if you will so term it), to persist in your designs against Kate Markham. She is a lovely girl, Captain, and one that the pirate chief should be proud of as a mistress; and, although she may at first affect to despise and hate you, you have it in your power, at any rate, to make her succumb to your wishes, and to become all that you can wish her."

"Right, Pierce," remarked the pirate chief, "and it shall indeed be my fault if I do not avail myself of the opportunity which is thus afforded me."

"A wise determination," said Pierce, "and allow me, at the same time that I make use of there observations to say, that it would be the veriest of folly for you to again entertain those idle fears and superstitions which so lately agitated you mind."

"Idle fears and superstitions you may call them, if you will, Pierce," replied Mark Stanford; "but still I cannot divest my mind of the impression that I both saw the ghastly face of my murdered victim, Horace Markham, peering at the window yonder, and likewise heard his hollow and unearthly voice denounce me as a murderer,"

"Nonsense, man," said Pierce; "you are labouring under a delusion."

"Well, probably I may; but——"

"Do away with such thoughts," interrupted Pierce, "for they are totally unworthy of you. It was all imagination, I say again, depend on it. The dead never rise again. But this is a dismal subject: you do not drink, captain."

"Ay, ay—drink, drink!" said ——, quaffing off, at the same time, a bumper of brandy.

"It is the antidote for all cares and anxieties, the determined enemy of gloomy thought and weak misgiving. I approve of your observations, Pierce, and will try to follow the advice they convey. A truce with all those dull and sombre thoughts. Hugh Granfield, the proud Rover of the Seas, feels his power, and will laugh all danger to scorn, as he has hitherto done."

"Again well said," remarked his companion. "And now it does me good, and pleases me right well to talk with you. But the hour waxes late. I must bid you adieu. Should you require my services, of course you know I am at any moment ready at your commands."

"Very good," rejoined Stanford. "Farewell for the present. I would indeed wish to be alone."

Pierce Raker nodded his head assentively to the latter observation, and withdrew without making use of any further remark. When he was gone, however, Stanford exhibited anything but the composure he had assumed during the latter part of his presence, and for some minutes he traversed the room in which he was with hasty and disordered footsteps, whilst any one who had seen the workings of his countenance at that might have observed the extraordinary excitement of mind under which he at that time laboured.

"I could have sworn," he said; "that I saw the ghastly features of my murdered victim, glaring upon me, and heard the solemn tones of his voice as if they had proceeded from the inmost recesses of the tomb. Can this have been caused alone by the workings of my troubled conscience? I can scarcely believe that it was; I can with difficulty imagine that I could have been so glaringly deceived. But, pshaw! I am surprised at myself, and if I continue to give way to this weakness, I shall bring myself into contempt with that daring crew who have been hitherto accustomed to look upon me with awe. I will no more of it; Hugh Granfield the pirate captain will continue to merit the desperate and determined character he has hitherto obtained. All goes as well as I could possibly wish it; the girl and her lover are both secure in my sea-girt retreat, and what have I to fear? Why should I any longer delay the gratification of my wishes? Why should I heed her reproaches? No, Kate Markham, your resistance is useless; I will no longer retard the fulfilment of my threats, let the future consequences to myself be whatever they may."

Thus the villain continued to soliloquise for some time longer, but, at length, having in a great measure regained his composure, he retired to rest, and the gloomy building became wrapped in the most profound stillness.

We will now return once more to our hero, whose anguish and anxiety of mind suffered but little or no relief; indeed it could not be expected that it would under all the painful and alarming circumstances in which his beloved Kate and himself were placed. He pictured to himself, in the most vivid characters, the sufferings the poor girl must be enduring; the insults to which she would be exposed by the brutal ruffian, Mark Stanford; and as he did so, his fortitude nearly forsook him; and he clasped his aching forehead in despair.

It was about the middle of the day that he was pacing the place of his confinement, as well as the heavy irons with which his limbs were loaded would permit him, and giving way to these sad and overwhelming reflections, when the belts of the door were suddenly withdrawn, and Stanford the next instant stood before him. An expression of the most deadly malice and fiendish exultation overspread his forbidden features; but the young sailor met him with a bold look of defiance, and an undaunted demeanour; and after a brief pause, he said—

"Brutal villain! think not that I am unprepared for this meeting, or that I will flinch from it. You come here to taunt and endeavour to torture me by your threats; but you will find that I am firm. 'Tis true, that the triumph at present appears to be yours, but there is One above whose power is supreme, and who will not permit the good and innocent to fall victims to your diabolical designs. Beware! for as sure as you stand there, a terrible retribution will ere long overtake you."

"And dare you threaten, dog?" demanded the pirate, fiercely; "dare you, who are entirely at my mercy, and whom I could this moment consign to a death of the most excruciating torture, venture thus to speak to me? By the infernal host, this is almost trying my patience too far; but, no—why should I heed what the poor idiot in the frenzy of his despair gives utterance to? You flatter yourself with the idea, or at least, pretend to do so, that I shall not be allowed to triumph altogether in the designs upon which I have fixed my mind; but what is to prevent me? Have I not both yourself and the fair, but scornful, Kate Markham securely in my power? And think you that I will neglect to avail myself, and that immediately, of the opportunity which is thus afforded me of gratifying the passion with which she has inspired me? You must be a greater fool than even I took you for, if you can sincerely think so. All opposition to my will is useless—'tis madness! Hugh Granfield claims that lovely mistress it has cost him so much trouble to obtain possession, and but a few short hours, my gallant Jack Junk, and depend upon it, her fate shall be decided. Let that assurance impart consolation to your soul, if it can. I now go to greet my future victim."

"Mark Stanford," said our horror-struck and disgusted hero, "can you possess a mind so black and savage, as not to be moved with one feeling of pity towards that innocent and helpless girl?"

"What can you expect from the monster, the miscreant, Stanford?" said the latter, with an ironical laugh. "Think you that I will be that weak fool to hesitate now that I have proceeded thus far? Already have I delayed the accomplishment of my designs too long, but my mind is now fully made up, and nothing whatever can move me from the execution of my purpose."

"Then may the curses of offended Heaven pursue you, and blast you in the very moment of your expected triumph," exclaimed Jack, worked up to a pitch of distraction. "Oh, Kate, Kate, must you indeed fall a sacrifice to the brutal passions of such a wretch as this? But, no, it cannot be! Nature and humanity revolt at the bare idea! She will yet be saved—she will yet be saved!"

"Indeed?" sneered the pirate, "it is well for you that you can flatter yourself with such hopes; what a pity it is for you that they should be destined to be disappointed. Ha! ha! ha! Saved! Bah! who is to save her? Here, far away from her native land, what hope is there for her? Who can form the least idea where she is? and even if they did, of what use would the knowledge be to them? Who would venture to attack me in my impregnable hold? They must be madmen, bent on rushing on their own destruction, if they did. But why do I thus waste words with you, when my time could be so much more agreeably occupied in the society of my fair prisoner? I leave you to your reflections, my gallant Jack Junk; probably when next we meet, I shall have to inform you of the accomplishment of my wishes, which, no doubt, will prove rather agreeable intelligence to you."

"Oh, God!—oh, God!" groaned our unfortunate hero, completely unmanned by the overwhelming power of his emotions, "this indeed is torture, most exquisite, it is insupportable! Mark Stanford, hear me!"

"No more!" said the pirate, sternly, as he stalked abruptly from the room, and left the young seaman in a state of mind which it would be impossible to do adequate justice to by any attempted at description, but which the reader will probably find no difficulty in forming a just conception of. He sank on the bench which surrounded the room in which he was confined, and covering his face with his hands, for some time gave himself up altogether to the agony and despair of his feelings.

In the meantime, Mark Stanford made his way to the apartment in which the beauteous Kate was incarcerated, and her terror and disgust on his entrance were so excessive, that it was not without the greatest difficulty she could prevent herself from fainting. Her agitation, however, made not the least favourable impression upon her brutal persecutor, and he surveyed her for a few minutes with his usual looks of exultation.

"Leave the room, Margaret," he said at length; "we must be alone."

"Oh, no—no—no!" ejaculated the terrified Kate, and clinging to her companion; "do not leave me, I implore you, for the love of Heaven!"

"Obey my orders!" commanded Stanford, peremptorily, and again addressing himself to Margaret; "I will summon you when I again require your attendance."

Poor Kate could not repress a groan of agony, and sunk despairingly, and almost unconscious in a chair, whilst Margaret, without venturing to make any reply to the pirate captain, retired from the room.

Mark Stanford continued to contemplate the innocent victim of his brutal persecution for a short time with mingled feelings of triumph and admiration; but at length he ventured to advance towards her, and to take her hand. She started with horror at his loathed touch, and hastily disengaging her hand from his hold, retreated to the farther end of the room, and fixed upon him a look which was sufficient to awe any man who had not become entirely callous to every sense of feeling.

"Fair Kate Markham," said the ruffian, "this is no time for trifling, and I am perfectly invulnerable to all the reproaches you may think proper to heap upon me. You know the sentiments I entertain towards you, and I now come to tell you that you must prepare yourself to yield to them without delay. I have waited patiently long enough, but since I see that you are determined to continue to treat me with scorn and abhorrence, I am resolved no longer to neglect availing myself of the opportunity which kind fortune has afforded me. Arguments or expostulations would only be thrown away upon me, and therefore you may as well spare yourself the trouble of making use of them. But why should you object to me? Because I am a pirate, forsooth! Nay, girl, I am wealthy as a prince; I am prepared to love you with all the fervour of the most ardent heart; you shall reign the mistress of my soul, and have numerous willing slaves to do homage to you; you——"

"Forbear, forbear, cruel man!" hastily interrupted the trembling damsel, "for my blood freezes with horror in my veins while I listen to you."

"Kate Markham," said Standford, "I tell you again that it is complete folly for you to attempt to offer any resistance to my will, and that I am totally indifferent to your reproaches. It is sufficient for me to know that I have you entirely in my power, and that there is no mortal power that can frustrate or obstruct me in my designs. I am determined, and not all the tears or supplications you may make can have the effect of changing me from my purpose."

"Heaven look down with pity on me!" exclaimed our distracted heroine, "for otherwise I am lost!"

"No longer than to-morrow will I delay the accomplishment of my wishes," said Stanford, with a look of determination, and not the least moved by the extraordinary emotion which the poor girl evinced, ; "so you may as well prepare yourself, and no longer encourage hopes which, at any time, you might have been convinced were entirely fallacious."

"To-morrow!—only till to-morrow!" gasped forth Kate, in a voice half-choked with sobs, and shuddering with the most uncontrollable dread; "oh, recall your words, abandon your monstrous and unholy purpose, if you would not see me stretched a corpse at your feet."

"Nay, nay, Kate Markham," said Sandford, "what is the use of giving yourself up to this violent state of agitation? It cannot avail you anything, and certainly will not have the effect of inducing me to abandon my determination. No! by this one fond kiss, I swear"—

"Help! help! oh, Heaven!" shrieked the frantic girl, and struggling violently, as the hardened miscreant tried to embrace her, and to polute her lips with his odious kisses.

"Nay, nay, my proud beauty!" said Mark Stanford, "you struggle in vain."

And as he thus spoke, he encircled her slender waist with his arms, and again and again he pressed warm kisses upon her lips. Overpowered, exhausted, terrified, poor Kate uttered a faint scream, and instantly became insensible.

The pirate captain having placed her inanimate form upon a sofa, summoned Margaret into the room, left our unfortunate heroine in her charge, and retired.

It was a considerable time before Margaret could succeed in restoring Kate to a state of consciousness; and when she did, she looked wildly round the apartment for a few seconds, and then ejaculated—

"Oh, God! where am I?—Where is that brutal miscreant who lately horrified and insulted me by his presence?"

"Compose yourself, Miss Markham," replied Margaret; "Stanford has left you in my care, and doubtless will not again venture to intrude upon you for the present."

"Alas, Margaret!" sobbed the poor girl," what will become of me?—To-morrow he has threatened that my fate shall be decided, and in what manner can I hope to escape from it, situated as I am?"

"Short as the time is," returned Margaret. "something may yet occur between this and then to frustrate his designs; or he may be prevailed upon to grant you a little more delay."

"Ah, no! Margaret," ejaculated our heroine, " I have too much reason to fear, from all he said, and his general conduct towards me since I have been in his power, that he is determined. I shall go distracted at the thought. And my poor lover, too, what will be his fate?"

"That depends, as I have frequently said, in a great measure upon you," replied Margaret.

"Alas! if that be the fact," sighed Kate, "and I have too much reason to fear that it is, his case is indeed hopeless. What can I do to save him, to which the feelings of honour and virtue are not opposed?—Nothing!—nothing!—And it is that conviction which makes me feel tenfold more wretched. Dear Jack, in what terrible dangers have you been involved for my sake! May Heaven, in its infinite mercy watch over you, and thwart the monstrous designs of our mutual appressor. But is he still confined in the same place, as that in which he was when we were first brought to this building?"

"He is," answered Margaret; "it is not likely they would remove him; but that is all I know of him at present, Kate."

Our heroine remained silent for a few minutes, and struggled violently to conquer the feelings of emotion which agitated her breast, and in which she partially succeeded, and became much more composed than could have been very well expected, after what had taken place between herself and Mark Stanford.

That night a terrible tempest arose after the whole of the inmates of the pirate's retreat had retired to rest, and Mark Stanford was aroused from a deep sleep into which he had fallen by the fury of its voice, and started from the bed in a state of excitement and confusion. He rushed to the window, and the sight which he encountered was of the most terrific description, and made even he, who had for so many years been exposed to such numerous perils on sea and land, shudder. He hastily dressed himself, and had scarcely done so, when he heard the voice of Pierce outside his chamber, asking for admittance.

"By the infernal host, Pierce," said Mark Stanford, when Pierce had entered the room, "this is a storm, with a vengeance;—there will many a gallant vessel founder ere the morning."

"True, captain," replied Pierce, "I have seldom seen such a storm as this, and I have witnessed a few in my time too. I wonder how our vessel, the Black Raven, fares?"

"Ah!" said Stanford, "I would that I were on board of her, for should any accident occur to her—Come, Pierce, we must hasten to her without delay."

"It will be impossible to reach her in such a storm as this; it would be certain death to those who should make the attempt."

"Nonsense, Pierce," returned the pirate captain, impatiently: "have you turned coward? Think you I can rest calmly here, and knowing at the same time that our noble craft is exposed to all the horrors and dangers of this frightful tempest? We must reach her at all hazards."

"Very well, captain," said Pierce, "I am ready to obey you, and I wish that fortune may not desert us in this desperate undertaking."

"No more," said Stanford; "you suffer your fears to get the better of your reason. Let sufficient of the crew follows us, to man all the boats we have at hand."

"Very well," coincided Pierce; "will you wait here while I go to execute your orders?"

"Yes," answered the pirate captain, "but do not be longer than you can help, for we have not a moment to lose; much, if not everything, depends upon our promptitude."

Pierce then quitted the room, and for a few minutes Mark Stanford was left to himself. He again walked to the window, and gazed upon the furious battling of the elements in a state of the greatest uneasiness; but he was quickly interrupted in his meditations by the return of Pierce.

"All's ready, captain," remarked the former; "I have obeyed your instructions; the men are on their way towards the cliffs."

"'Tis well," returned Stanford, enveloping himself in a huge cloak; "then we will follow them, and at once remove all doubts as to the real situation of the Black Raven. Come, Pierce."

Pierce followed the pirate captain, though it was evident it was with no very satisfactory feelings that he did so, and they made their way from the building, and entered upon the open air, and the fierce battering of the tempest; the men having gone before them, as Raker had stated, towards the cliffs.

Certainly it was a most fearful night: it was a frightful convulsion of nature. It appeared as if the final destruction of the world had arrived, and all hope for the miserable sinners who inhabited it was at an end. How the wind bellowed—the thunder roared—the ocean howled, as if in exultation over the numerous victims it was every moment engulphing. How tenfold awful did the repeated flashes of lightning make the frightful scene appear. It was with difficulty indeed that any person could stand up against the fury of such a storm—but the anxiety of the pirate chief for the fate of his vessel, supported his energies, and made him feel as though he could face and brave any danger; he folded his mantle closer around his form, and he and Pierce hurried on towards the cliffs, exchanging no words by the way. They had not proceeded any considerable distance, however, when they met two of the men who had been sent on before them, hurrying towards the Black Raven's nest (which, we have before stated, the pirates thought proper, to designate the formidable building in which they had formed one of their haunts), apparently in a state of considerable excitement, and out of breath.

"How now?" demanded Stanford, hastily, at the same time that a fearful presentiment passed across his mind; "who are you hastening from the duty you were sent upon."

"Captain," replied one of the men, in a breathless state of agitation, "I am sorry that we have such bad news for you."

"Bad news, you swab!" said Stanford, impatiently and passionately, "what do you mean?"

"Our gallant vessel, the Black Raven, which has braved so many dangers——"

"Ah!" interrupted Stanford and Pierce, in a breath, "what of her?—speak! quick, as you value your life!"

"She has broken from her anchor," replied the pirate, "and is nowhere to be seen."

"Liar!" exclaimed Mark Stanford, furiously, and his eyes flashing fire, "you try to mock me—to jest with me—but beware, for I will inflict such a punishment upon you for your daring as I warrant will daunt all future attempts of the kind. My noble vessel—my Black Raven, the terror of the ocean—the cradle of so many manly and daring spirits, run adrift—lost!—'tis a monstrous lie!"

"It is as Will Danston states, unfortunately, too true, captain," observed the companion of the man who had communicated the fatal intelligence; "you have but to go to the cliffs to convince yourself."

"My vessel gone, with all the treasure and the bold hearts she contained?" cried the pirate chief, at the same time his whole frame was convulsed, and the distortion of his repulsive features, as the lightning glared upon them, was quite frightful to behold; "by the infernal host, it must be false! Follow me, Pierce, and if I find that those rascals have deceived me, I will invent such a punishment for them as never yet was conceived by human being."

"Be calm, Stanford," remonstrated Pierce Raker, "for these bursts of passion cannot possibly be productive of any good. There is too much reason to apprehend, from the appearance of the night, that the statement of Will Danston and his companion is too true."

"D—n!" cried Stanford, in the same furious tones;—"if it be so, the power of the pirate chief is lessened indeed. Follow me, thou birds of ill-omen;—follow me, you Will Danston, Dog, do you hear what I say?—"

"Dog in your teeth, bullying cur!" retorted Will Danston, boldly;—"I will not follow you any longer, for I know if I do that my pathway will be to the gallows from which you deserved to dangle years since!"

"Ah! a mutineer!" exclaimed Stanford, drawing a pistol hastily from his belt;—"by hell! I will not give you the opportunity of walking the path to which you have alluded. Die! daring knave, and——"

"Held, captain!" interrupted Pierce. "What would you do? Destroy one of the best of our crew?" But before he could arrest the villain's arm, he had discharged the contents of the pistol in the breast of the unfortunate man, and he sank immediately a corpse upon the earth. His companion looked on with a sullen expression of horror and disgust, but he offered no observation.

"It is thus that Hugh Granfield punishes all those who dare to rebel against his authority!" said the Pirate.

"'Twas a rash deed," remarked Pierce, "and may be productive of much mischief. Poor Will."

"Bah!" cried Stanford, "are you, too, going to advocate his cause, Pierce? But, why do we delay? We have everything at stake! Follow me!—and mark me, Sam Barnford; if I find that you have hoisted false signals, you shall be food for fishes in less than a quarter of an hour!"

Sam Barnford cast one look of pity at the bloody corpse of his comrade, and a feeling at that moment passed within his breast, which it was well for him his brutal captain could not read; but he made use of no observation, but followed in silence, and with a sullen, dogged step.

In a few minutes they reached the cliffs, and met the remainder of the crew who had been ment to an the boats, and all that had been stated by Will Danston and his companion was then confirmed—the pirate barque was no where to be seen.

To describe the scene which then followed would be indeed an arduous task. Mark Stanford on discovering the loss of his vessel, was perfectly frantic, and the dreadful oaths to which he gave utterance might be heard even above the hoarse voice of the tempest.

"Man the boats, cowards!" he cried;—"why do ye stand idling there, when you should go in pursuit of our floating castle? Away with ye, I say; launch the long boat, of which I will take the command, and you, Pierce—"

"Are you mad, captain?" interrupted Pierce, boldly and determinedly; "do you not see that it is impossible, as I before told you, to brave such a sea as this?—and that it would be certain and immediate death to all who should be mad enough to attempt it?—"

"You desert me then, all of you!" cried Stanford, in the same distracted state:—"away then, lubbers, I will, by myself, alone brave all the terrors which you dare not encounter!"

As he thus spoke he was madly rushing towards one of the boats, when Pierce grasped his arm firmly and detained him from his rash purpose, and, at the same moment, Mark Stanford, the so much dreaded Rover of the Seas, overpowered by the extraordinary excitement of his feelings, sank exhausted.

"Remain here a few of you," said Pierce, addressing himself to the pirates, "and watch what takes place. Should any opportunity present itself, you will go in search of our unfortunate vessel, which, I fear, disabled as she is, will never be able to weather such a storm as this. The rest follow me, and assist me in conveying the captain to our retreat."

The men nodded assent to these commands, and Mark Stanford being raised on their shoulders, was borne away, Sam Barnford following slowly behind with the same sullen aspect and demeanour.

"Bloody miscreant!" he muttered to himself; "I exult in that which has taken place, to your discomfiture. The cold blooded murder of poor Will Danston shall not go unrevenged at the earliest opportunity, depend upon it."

THE PIRATE EXULTING OVER THE MISERY OF JACK JUNK.

Mark Standford was conveyed without delay to the retreat upon the rock, and was soon restored to consciousness, but it was some time before he could regain the least composure, for the fate of the vessel, in such a storm as still continued to rage, seemed to be inevitable, and he seemed to consider the loss of that as almost tantamount to his ruin. However, at length he became more calm, and with Pierce he proceeded to the summit of one of the loftiest towers of the building, in order to watch the progress of the storm. They had not been many minutes there, when they heard the report of signals of distress above the voice of the thunder, and by the broad glare of the lightning could behold a vessel struggling with the mountainous waves at a short distance from the shore; but they could discern sufficient of her to find that it was not the Black Raven, and the hopes of Mark Stanford, which had been suddenly excited, were in a moment crushed. No assistance could possibly have been afforded the unfortunate ship, if even there had been those at hand who were willing to render it; nearer and nearer it was dashed towards the shore, and it was evident to Mark Stanford and his companion, that it must be dashed to pieces on the rocks. Presently they lost sight of it altogether, and it then seemed evident that its doom was sealed; that it had foundered.

Whilst all these events were taking place, the sufferings of our heroine may well be imagined; and after Margaret had passed some time in seeking to tranquillise her mind, she left her for a short period in order to learn all the particulars she could.

Kate, after she had quitted the room, sank on her knees, and for the moment forgetting the difficulties under which herself and her lover were placed, she devoutly offered up her prayers to Heaven for the preservation of the unfortunate beings who were exposed to the terrors of the night, whether on the land or the sea. She then walked to the window of her apartment, which commanded an extensive view of the surrounding ocean, and gazed with feelings of the most unbounded awe upon the terrors of the storm. The sight was almost too appalling for her feelings, and retiring once more to her seat, and burying her face in her hands, she was about to resign herself to her own gloomy meditations, when Margaret returned.

"Well, Margaret," she asked eagerly, "have you heard anything of importance?"

"Yes," replied Margaret, "and that which I am certain, will afford you some satisfaction."

"Oh, what is it?"

"The Black Raven has been broken away from her anchor in the tempest, and is no where to be seen; she will doubtless perish in the storm."

"Oh, Heaven be thanked for that," remarked Kate; "for it will lesson the power of my cruel and remorseless persecutor."

"It will," coincided Margaret, "and having just returned from the cliffs, he is now in a state bordering upon madness."

"And yet,—" observed our heroine, as a sudden thought flashed upon her mind.

"Yet, what, Miss Markham?—" inquired Margaret.

"How many unfortunate beings will meet with an untimely death, should the pirate vessel perish?" replied Kate.

"I should think, miss," returned her attendant, "that you can feel but little sympathy with them, considering the crimes they have committed."

"And yet it is awful that they should be summoned before that awful tribunal which they are so ill prepared to face," remarked Kate. "But this, at any rate, I should suppose, will retard the accomplishment of the dreadful and revolting threats which Stanford held out to me only to-day."

"No doubt of it," replied Margaret, "and should inspire you with new hopes. Did I not tell you that something would occur to prevent the accomplishment of Mark Stanford's designs at the time he threatened?"

"Oh, yes, you did, Margaret."

"Take courage then," observed the latter "and I should not at all wonder but something will happen to rescue you from his power altogether."

"Oh, do you indeed think so?" said Kate eagerly.

"I do," answered Margaret, "and although at first, I know, you were prejudiced against me, you have my best and most sincere wishes that what I prognosticate may be realised."

"Oh, thanks, thanks," said our heroine, fervently. "Pardon me, if I wronged you by one ungenerous or unjust thought; but I know you will be able to make due allowances for the agitation and despair of my mind, and that you will also be ready to admit, that your conduct towards me at first was very different to what it is now, and that I had a right to suppose you were my enemy?"

"Very true," returned Margaret, "but I was compelled to assume the character I did towards you, or I might have worked my own destruction, and could not possibly have effected you any good."

"I see perfectly well the prudence of your conduct now," remarked our heroine, "and I owe you a debt of gratitude for the interest you have taken in my fate. But would that my lover and I could be made acquainted with what has taken place, it might then inspire him with hope."

"I dare say it will soon reach his ears, by some means or other," said Margret.

Kate Markham made no answer, but she once more walked to the window, whither Margaret followed her, and they both watched the progress of the storm with the deepest interest. They heard the signals of distress, and saw the unfortunate vessel that was being tossed about by the stormy billows; and deep was the sympathy which our heroine felt for the hapless beings that were on board of it, especially when its sudden disappearance showed too plainly the fate which had befallen it.

*   *   *   *   *   *

The cold blooded and heartless murder of Will Danston by the captain caused the greatest excitement among the majority of the pirates, with whom he was a great favourite. They were filled with indignation, which feeling Sam Barnford took good care to encourage all that he could. Whilst Stanford and Pierce were watching the storm from the tower, they held a secret consultation together; resolutions were passed, and they all swore to a man, to avenge their comrades savage death at the earliest opportunity. Thus it is that the greatest villains in a moment of passion and thoughtlessness, often do the very thing to bring about their own destruction; and little did Mark Stanford anticipate the fearful change which only a few short hours were destined to work in his fortunes.

The night passed away, the storm subsided, and Mark Stanford and Pierce, accompanied by two or three of the pirates, walked forth to the beach at an early hour with the hope of discovering some traces of the Black Raven; but they were doomed to disappointment; it was no where to be seen; they could imagine no other than that it had perished in the storm, and Mark Stanford raved and cursed like a madman.

"An infernal spell is upon me," he exclaimed, as he paced the beach backwards and forwards in a state of the utmost despair; "has fortune deserted me all at once, when I thought she was smiling most upon me? May the curses of h—l pursue——"

"Hold, captain," interrupted Pierce, "what is the use of giving way to this violence?"

"D——n!" cried Mark Stanford in the same passionate tones; "think you I can be calm under such circumstances as these? Does not my noble vessel contain the principal portion of my treasures and some of my bravest men, and yet you would have me be calm and patient under such a loss as that?"

"We know not that she is lost yet, captain," remarked Pierce; "and it will be quite time enough for us to lament when we have ascertained that fact."

CHAPTER XVI.

EXTRAORDINARY DISCOVERIES.—WHO IS JACK JUNK?—THE DOWNFALL OF THE PIRATE CHIEF.—THE RESTORATION OF THE LOVERS TO THEIR NATIVE LAND, AND HAPPY CONCLUSION OF "THIS STRANGE EVENTFUL HISTORY."

YES, it was indeed Herbert, the solitary, the maniac whom our hero had so strangely encountered, and in whose fate he felt so remarkable an interest. Being placed upon a couch, and all the available means applied for his restoration to life, (most of the pirates, at the head of whom was Sam Barnford, having assembled in the room, apparently out of curiosity) Mark Stanford folded his arms across his chest, and for a few minutes contemplated him with the most earnest looks, whilst the expression of his features showed at once the inward emotions that were working in his breast.

"Sir Herbert Haughton!" he said, at length, in a tone of voice which showed at once that he was unconscious for the moment that there was any person but himself present; "what strange fatality is this? Did I ever, after these lapse of years, expect to behold him again?"

"Sir Herbert Haughton!" repeated Pierce; "I have heard the name before; you seem to know him, then, captain?"

"Ask me no questions," replied Stanford, fiercely; "do I know him? yes, yes; but why should his unexpected re-appearance thus agitate me? I have him now in my power, and——Fools! why do you seek to restore him to life? Rather let my knife penetrate his heart, and thus I——"

As the villain thus spoke, he drew a dagger from his belt, and was rushing on the insensible and defenceless man, when Pierce arrested his arm, and drawing him aside, he said—

"Hold! what would you do? are you going mad altogether! you know this man, and seem to have reason to fear him; but he is in your power and that should suffice you. Ah! see, he revives!"

The unfortunate man did, indeed, recover, and raising himself in the bed, gazed for a few moments wildly and vacantly around him.

"Where am I?" he said; "still in the midst of the storm, and about to rejoin that wife and child, whom by the artifices of a villain, a fiend in human shape, I consigned to death? No, no!" he added, suddenly springing from the bed with much more strength than could have been expected under the circumstances, and standing erect in the room; "I am alive, and the sense of reason, so long wandering, again dawns upon me. Who are ye, that thus surround me? Ah!—do my eyes deceive me?—No, no!—Fiend! monster! murderer! I knew you, rising as you do, like some ghastly phantom before my eyes; and I will have retribution in your life's blood! Miscreant!—Where is my wife?—Where my innocent boy?—I,

Sir Herbert Haughton, whom you robbed, deceived, am here to confront you, and thus will I tear the truth from your throat !"

As he thus spoke, he sprang like a tiger upon Mark Stanford, and attempted to seize him by the throat, but the pirate was prepared for him, and hurled him violently away to the farther end of the room, at the same time he exclaimed :

" Rash fool !—I acknowledge who I am, but you are in my power, and it is nothing less than madness to offer any opposition to me. Secure him, and bear him to a dungeon !"

Pierce Raker attempted to do so, but Sir Herbert struggled with him desperately, and succeeded in wresting the sword from his hand, and at the same moment he plunged it in his body, and Pierce with a dreadful oath, fell bleeding on the floor.

" Ah !" he exclaimed, his features frightfully distorted ; " by hell, I am slain !"

For a moment or so, so great was the surprise that this sudden and unexpected event had excited in the mind of Mark Stanford, that he stood completely astounded and speechless, and Sir Herbert having left the sword in the body of Pierce, who was writhing in agony, also stood as if paralyzed to the spot, and gazed wildly around him.

" Dastards ! knaves !" at length cried Stanford, fiercely ; " will you see murder committed without resenting it ?—Seize him, I say, or by the infernal host I swear that every man of you shall swing like a dog before the lapse of an hour !"

" Indeed !" returned Sam Barnford, with an ironical laugh ; " but methinks you are mistaken, Master Hugh Granfield, or Mark Stanford. Comrades, remember the cold-blooded murder of poor Will Danston ;—now is the moment for revenge !—Seize the tyrant !

The words had scarcely escaped his lips when the pirates rushed upon Stanford, and disarming him, held him powerless and a prisoner, at the same time they raised a loud shout of triumph, which might have been heard all over the building.

" Have all the fiends of hell conspired against me ?" cried the villain, Stanford, in a hoarse voice ; " am I to be thus defeated ?"

" Yes," said Pierce Raker, in a faint voice, " our career I feel is at an end, and I admit the justice of it."

" Ah !" exclaimed Sir Herbert, advancing towards the pirate captain ; " has the moment I have so long panted for at length arrived ?—Do I triumph? But, wretch ! monster ! where is my wife and child, whom I sacrificed through your diabolical means ?"

" I triumph, even in my downfall !" returned Stanford, a fiendish expression of malice at the same time overspreading his repulsive features. "Sir Herbert Haughton, the wife and child whom you so deeply lament, both met with a frightful and untimely death."

" Oh, horrible ! horrible !" ejaculated the unfortunate baronet, clasping his forehead in despair ; " I am justly punished for my cruelty. But not one of them spared ?"

" Calm yourself, Sir Herbert," said Barnford, " and all may yet turn out better than you now anticipate. See to Pierce, comrades, and look to you prisoner—the daring and much dreaded Rover of the Seas—ha ! ha ! ha !—I will return to you anon."

" May the curse of hell attend you, dog!" said Stanford. " To be thus defeated !—Oh, that my hands were at liberty, how soon would I wreak my vengeance on your head."

" No doubt of it, most gallant captain," replied Barnford, ironically ; " but I do not intend to afford you the opportunity, depend upon it."

Thus saying, he quitted the room, and left Pierce Raker writhing in agony, Mark Stanford furious with rage and terror, and Sir Herbert Haughton lost in wonder and confusion.

Our hero, in his dismal place of confinement, had passed many hours of the most indescribable misery, in listening to the voice of the storm, and sleep had never for a moment afforded him a respite from his sufferings, though at times a ray of hope would dawn upon his mind, though why it did so he could not imagine. He was immersed in the most gloomy thoughts, when he was aroused by hearing some one ascending the stairs, and directly afterwards the bolts were withdrawn, and the door opening, Sam Barnford appeared before him.

" Ah !" said Jack, eagerly, " what brings you here ?"

" To communicate news to you that I think will afford pleasure," replied Barnford.

" Pleasure !" repeated our hero, looking at him incredulously ; " do you mock me ?"

" No, indeed I do not," replied Barnford ; " I could have no interest in doing so. The Black Raven has been cast adrift in the storm ; myself and my comrades have mutineered against Mark Stanford, who is now a prisoner, and you and Kate Markham are at liberty."

" At liberty !" exclaimed the young seaman in accents of delight and astonishment ; " is it possible ?"

" It is true," replied Barnford ; "and, moreover, I have to inform you that your companion upon the island from whence we took you, and who is now known as Sir Herbert Haughton, has been saved from shipwreck, and is below ; no doubt you will be glad to see him."

" The unfortunate Herbert also restored !" ejaculated our hero ; " I can scarcely believe the evidence of my senses; this is, indeed, most wonderful. But my beloved Kate; shall I again behold her?"

"You will," replied Barnford, "and that in a few minutes. But, come, I will release you from these fetters, and then I will get you to follow me. Methinks, Mark Stanford, I shall well have avenged the murder of Will Danston."

It was impossible for our hero to give adequate expression to the feelings of pleasure and gratitude which animated his breast, so sudden, so unexpected, and remarkable was the change; in fact, it seemed to him more like a dream than reality; but Barnford having removed the irons from his limbs, conducted him from the place in which he had been confined, and led him to the apartment of our heroine. But how shall we describe the meeting between the lovers? Language must fail entirely to do it justice, and we will therefore pass hastily over it. When they had in some measure regained their composure, and all that had taken place had been explained to our heroine, they followed Barnford to the room where he had left the defeated Mark Stanford, Pierce, and Sir Herbert. The pirate captain had been bound hand and foot, and was giving utterance to the most fearful maledictions; Pierce was still living, but in a most exhausted state, and Sir Herbert was gazing intently upon Stanford, and so deeply wrapped in meditation, that he did not notice the entrance of Barnford and the lovers; but Stanford no sooner beheld them than his countenance became distorted by rage, and he again gave utterance to a volley of the most frightful imprecations. This aroused Sir Herbert, and beholding our hero, with a cry of astonishment and delight, he rushed towards him, exclaiming—

"Ah! do my eyes deceive me? No! by Heaven 'tis the companion of my solitude; he whom I used to delight to call by the name of son! Oh, welcome!—welcome! this is, indeed, a most joyous meeting!"

Our hero returned his greeting with equal ardour and sincerity, and it was some time before either of them could speak a word; whilst Mark Stanford gazed on with all the deadly malice of a fiend.

"But those features!" at length said Sir Herbert, gazing earnestly in the countenance of our hero; "there is an expression about them which goes immediately to my heart; tell me, what are you?"

"A mere humble sailor, Sir Herbert," answered Jack; "but I trust an honest man. And this is my Kate, my beloved, innocent Kate, whom that lubber would have consiged to destruction."

"Yes, yes," said Sir Herbert, impatiently, and still keeping his eyes fixed stedfastly upon the features of our hero; "but your name? your name."

"They call me Jack Junk," answered the young seaman, "but I never knew my parents."

"No?" said Sir Herbert with a look of astonishment and anxious curiosity.

"'Tis true," said our hero, "I was found at sea, rescued from a burning vessel, supposed to be the Mary; I was clasped to the breast of her whom I have every reason to believe was my mother; I was saved by him from whom I have taken my name, and another honest seaman named Joe Trennant, but the vital spark had quitted the bosom of that unfortunate being who bore me."

"Good God!" ejaculated Sir Herbert, with the most powerful emotion; "how wonderful is the coincidence. Can it be?—My wife and infant boy were on board the Mary, through the base means of that brutal miscreant; that vessel I afterwards heard was lost, and that every soul on board of her had perished. It was then that madness seized upon my brain, and I abandoned my property both in the Indies and England, and fled to the island on which you found me. Strange hopes and emotions agitate my bosom; tell me, young man, I beseech you, and as quickly as possible, how long is it since you were found in the manner you have described?"

"From what I have been informed," answered our hero, "it is now about three and twenty years ago."

"By Heaven!" exclaimed Sir Herbert, still more agitated than before; "it is the very time. Oh, my beloved, much injured, and ill-fated wife! But this suspense is insupportable; tell me was anything found upon you by which your identity might be established?"

"Yes," answered our hero, equally agitated; "the clothes I had on at the time are still preserved, and a small silver locket was suspended from my neck."

"Have you that locket by you?" demanded Sir Herbert, breathlessly.

"I have," replied our hero, producing it; "it is here!"

"God of Heaven!" exclaimed the baronet, with a burst of the most indescribable emotion, as he gazed upon it, "it is true; this is proof sufficient; you are my son, my Everard, preserved in the most miraculous way to console me in my declining days! Son! son! Oh, God!"

"Father! dear father! may I, indeed, call you by that blessed, that revered name?" exclaimed our hero, and he rushed into the arms of that parent whom he had never expected to behold. We must leave the scene which followed to the imagination of the reader.

"D—n!" cried the infuriated Mark Stanford, "am I to be foiled every way?"

"Yes," said Pierce, in a faint voice; "our career is at an end, and now I feel the justice of the doom which has overtaken us. I—I am dying, and I will therefore make a clean breast of it. Kate Markham, your father met not with a natural death; he was doomed to walk the plank by Mark Stanford, or Hugh Granfield, as his right name is; I murdered your uncle, and old Reuben of the Cliff, who knew all Granfield's secrets, and——"

Before he could finish the sentence, Pierce Raker, with one fearful groan of agony, expired. Kate uttered a shriek of horror, and fell insensible in the arms of her lover; and here we will drop a veil over the scene which followed.

*   *   *   *   *   *

We should become tedious were we to dilate upon our story; but a few more words then, and we have done. In three days after the remarkable events we have just recorded, an English vessel put in at the island for fresh water, and received the whole inmates of the pirates' haunt on board. Mark Stanford, whose fortitude at the certainty of the fate which awaited him, entirely forsook him, being detained a close prisoner; and they were soon on their way to England, which they reached in a few weeks. The meeting which took place between them and Constance, who had but recently recovered her senses, may be well imagined; as for poor old Joe Trennant, he was in perfect ecstasies, more especially when he found that his boy— his favourite Jack Junk, had discovered his parent, and that he was the son of a wealthy baronet.

Sir Herbert Haughton had no difficulty in arranging his affairs, and he and his son, and Kate Markham and her cousin, Constance, went to reside in his splendid mansion, which was situated in the immediate neighbourhood, which, from old associations, was so dear to them.

Sam Barnford and the other pirates were pardoned, but the villain, Hugh Granfield, suffered an ignominious death upon the scaffold. Nothing more was ever heard of the Black Raven, so that there could be little doubt that she perished in the storm.

In a few months our hero led his faithful Kate to the altar, and the auspicious event was celebrated with becoming magnificence. To add to the universal joy, the lover of Constance, who had been for several years detained a prisoner abroad, suddenly returned to his native place, and their sentiments having undergone no change, they were happily united, Sir Herbert bestowing a handsome marriage portion upon the bride, as a reward for her numerous virtues.

Margaret was taken into the service of our heroine, and remained her faithful attendant till her death, which did not take place for many years.

Our hero in a short time was promoted to the command of a vessel, and remained as he had always proved himself to be "THE TAR FOR ALL WEATHERS!"